JORGE CORONA   WITH JEN HICKMAN

FEATHERS

Published by
ARCHAIA™

FEATHERS, February 2019. Published by Archaia, a division of Boom Entertainment, Inc. Feathers is ™ & © 2019 Jorge Corona. All Rights Reserved. Archaia™ and the Archaia logo are trademarks of Boom Entertainment, Inc., registered in various countries and categories. All characters, events, and institutions depicted herein are fictional. Any similarity between any of the names, characters, persons, events, and/or institutions in this publication to actual names, characters, and persons, whether living or dead, events, and/or institutions is unintended and purely coincidental.

BOOM! Studios, 5670 Wilshire Boulevard, Suite 400, Los Angeles, CA 90036-5679.

Printed in China. First Printing.

ISBN: 978-1-68415-307-7, eISBN: 978-1-641-44160-5

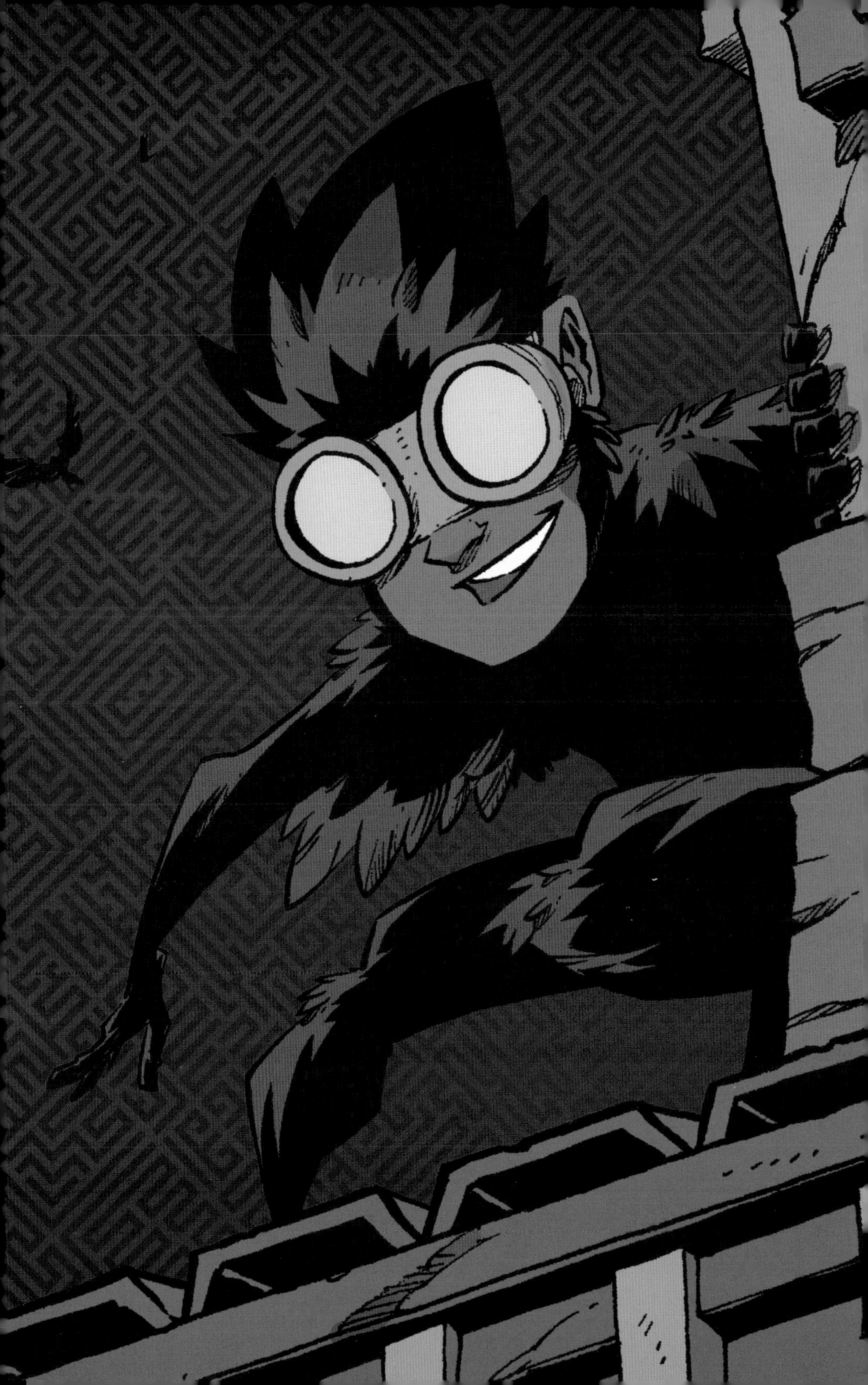

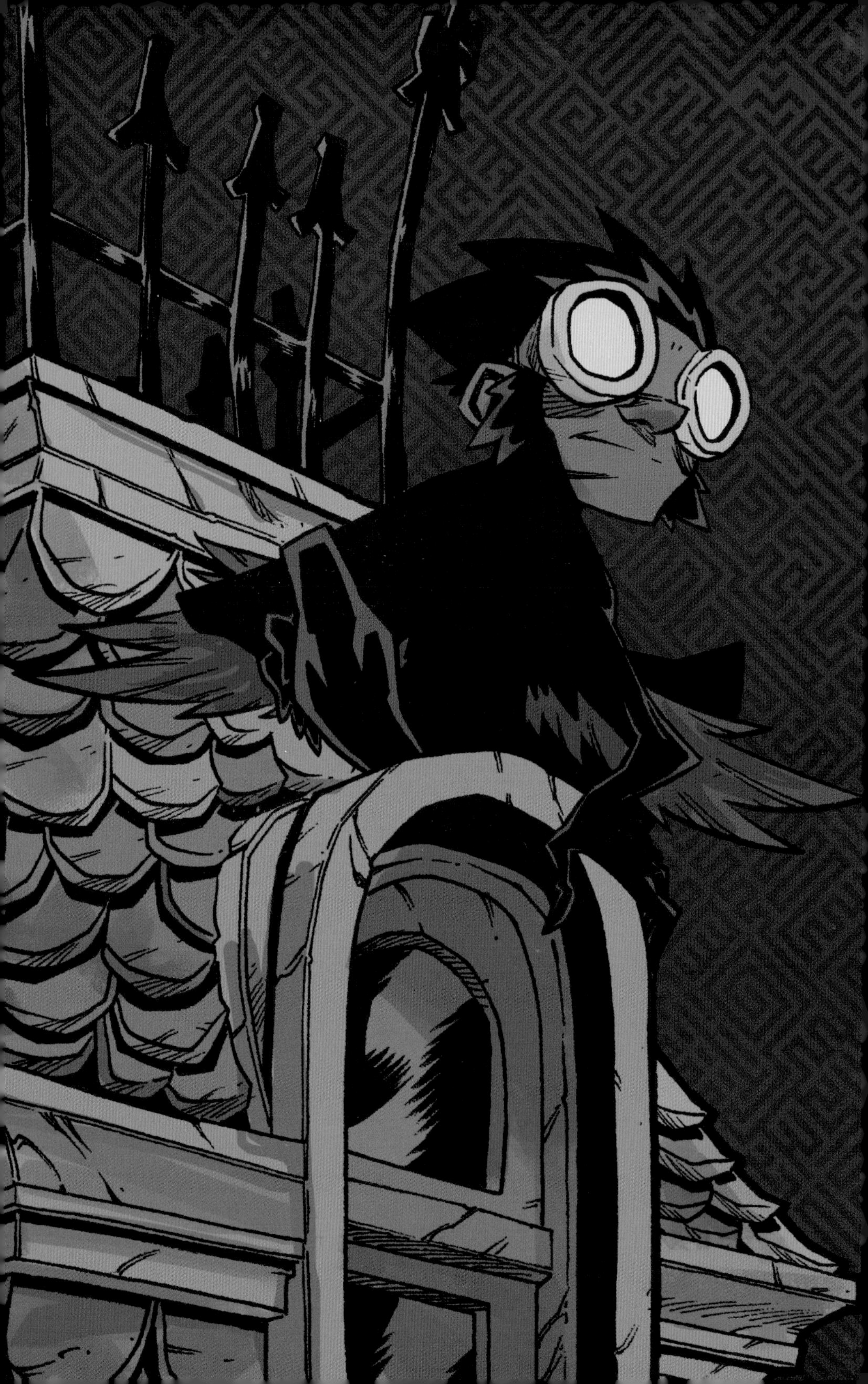

WRITTEN & ILLUSTRATED BY
JORGE CORONA

COLORS BY
JEN HICKMAN

LETTERS BY
DERON BENNETT

COVER BY
JORGE CORONA

DESIGNER **JILLIAN CRAB**
ASSISTANT EDITOR **MARY GUMPORT**
ORIGINAL SERIES EDITOR **REBECCA TAYLOR**
COLLECTION EDITOR **IAN BRILL**

CREATED BY **JORGE CORONA**

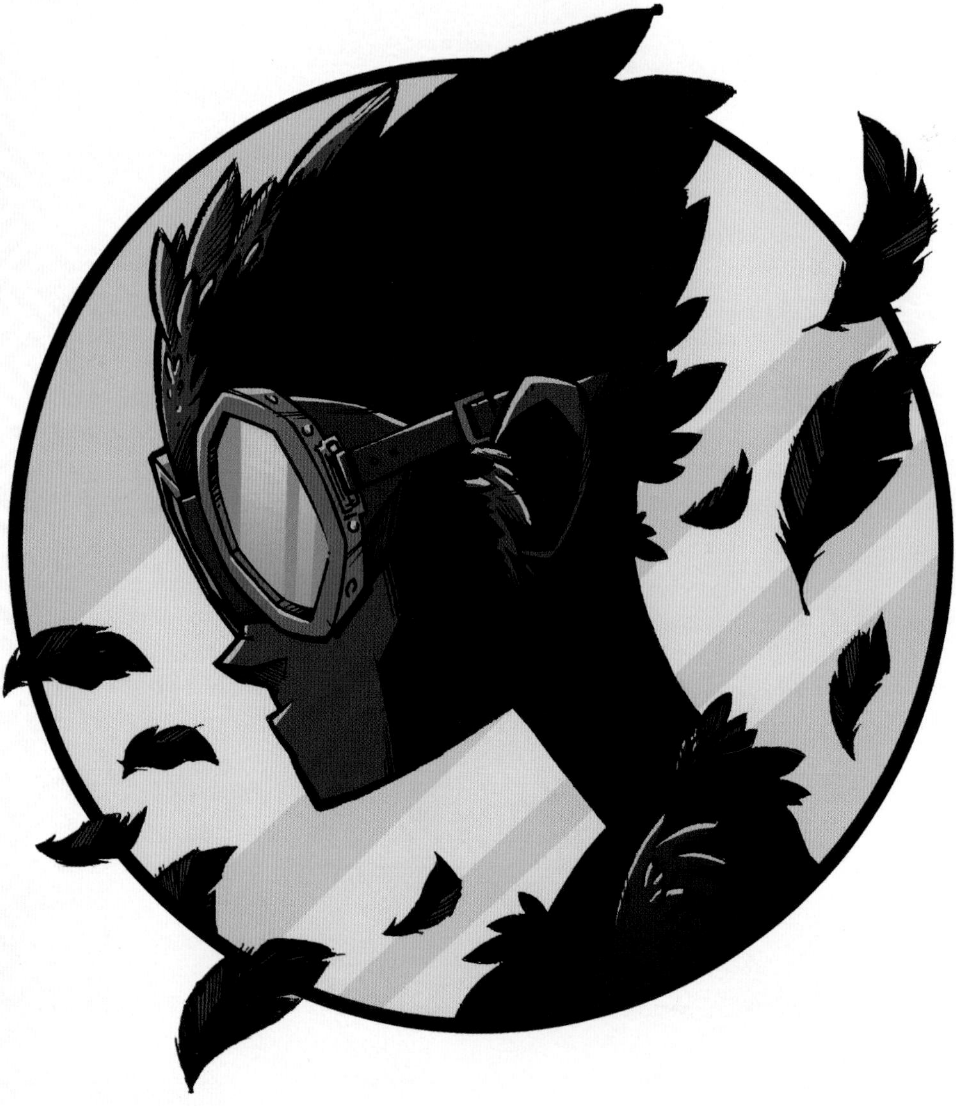

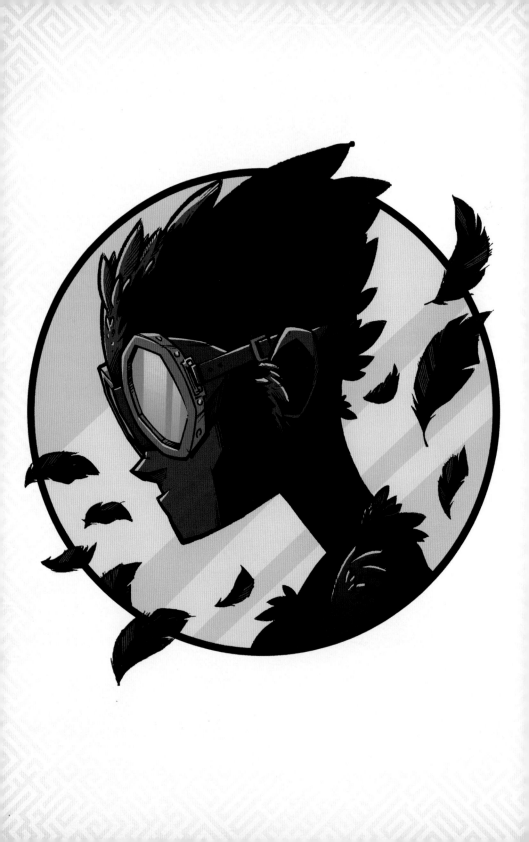

FOREWORD

The story of *Feathers* is a perfect example of an idea that took a life of its own. It started as a personal storytelling exercise of a *Beauty and the Beast* type of narrative, the tale of a boy and a girl forming a friendship against all odds in a world that would oppose it. That core idea remained, but little by little the concepts and surroundings expanded, shaping the world and the story you now hold in your hands.

The story of Poe and Bianca is one about duality, about the meeting of opposites, and about coexistence. In a world that keeps pushing for extremes, where everything is black or white, their story tries to find a middle ground.

Thank you for picking up this book, let yourself get lost in the Maze, and tag along with its ghosts, discovering a world bigger than what our characters expected, but a world that fits within each and every one of us.

Special thanks to my parents, Elisa Quijano and Heberto Corona, and to Morgan Beem, for their support, inspiration, and company while creating this world. Thanks to Rebecca Taylor and Mary Gumport for their tireless dedication and complete trust in shaping together this book. And last but not least, thanks to Jen Hickman, Deron Bennett, and Jillian Crab for helping me bring to life the story you're about to read.

Jorge Corona
Maracaibo, 2015

CHAPTER
ONE

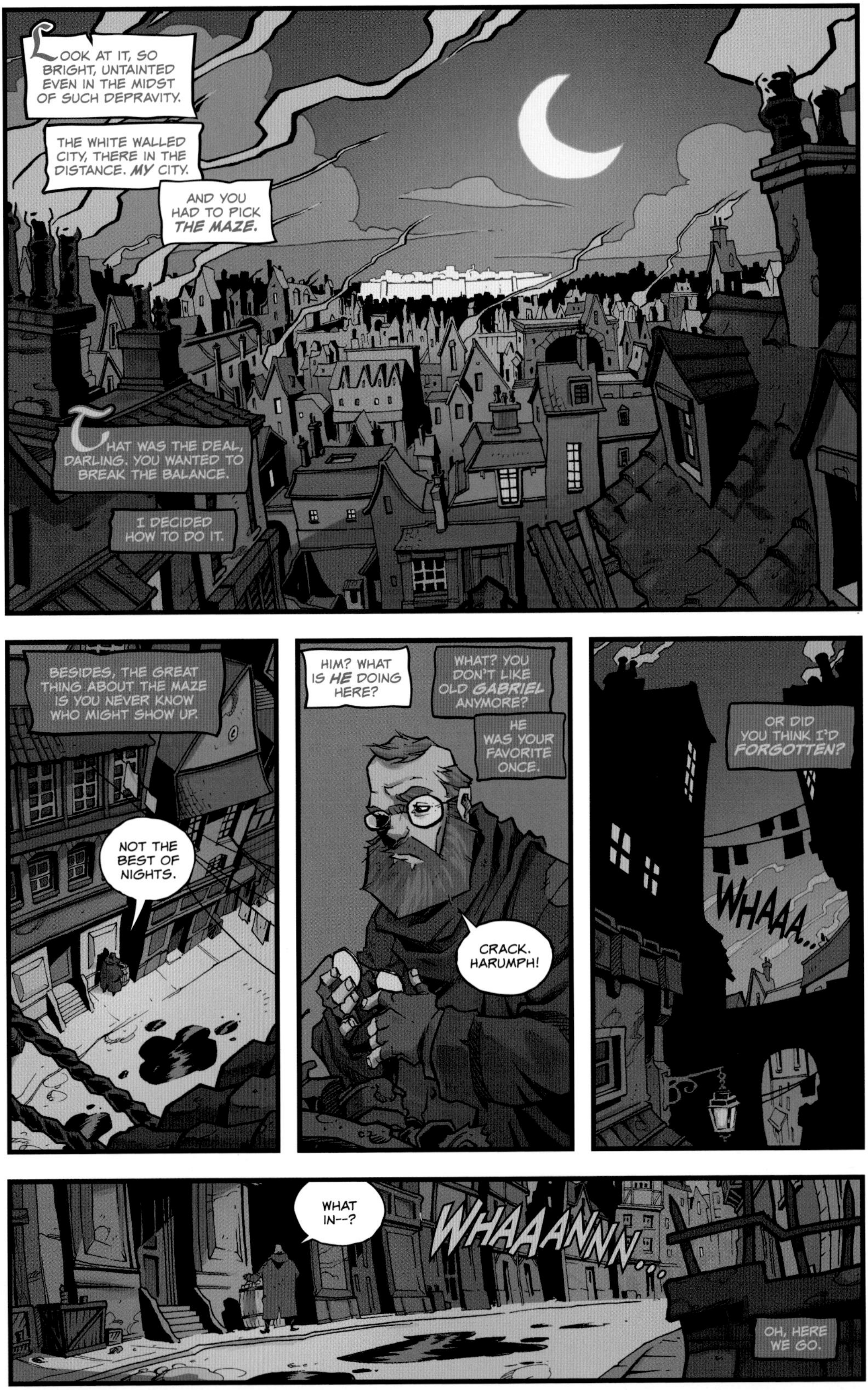
LOOK AT IT, SO BRIGHT, UNTAINTED EVEN IN THE MIDST OF SUCH DEPRAVITY.
THE WHITE WALLED CITY, THERE IN THE DISTANCE. MY CITY.
AND YOU HAD TO PICK THE MAZE.
THAT WAS THE DEAL, DARLING. YOU WANTED TO BREAK THE BALANCE.
I DECIDED HOW TO DO IT.
BESIDES, THE GREAT THING ABOUT THE MAZE IS YOU NEVER KNOW WHO MIGHT SHOW UP.
NOT THE BEST OF NIGHTS.
HIM? WHAT IS HE DOING HERE?
WHAT? YOU DON'T LIKE OLD GABRIEL ANYMORE?
HE WAS YOUR FAVORITE ONCE.
CRACK. HARUMPH!
OR DID YOU THINK I'D FORGOTTEN?
WHAAA...
WHAT IN--?
WHAAANNN...
OH, HERE WE GO.

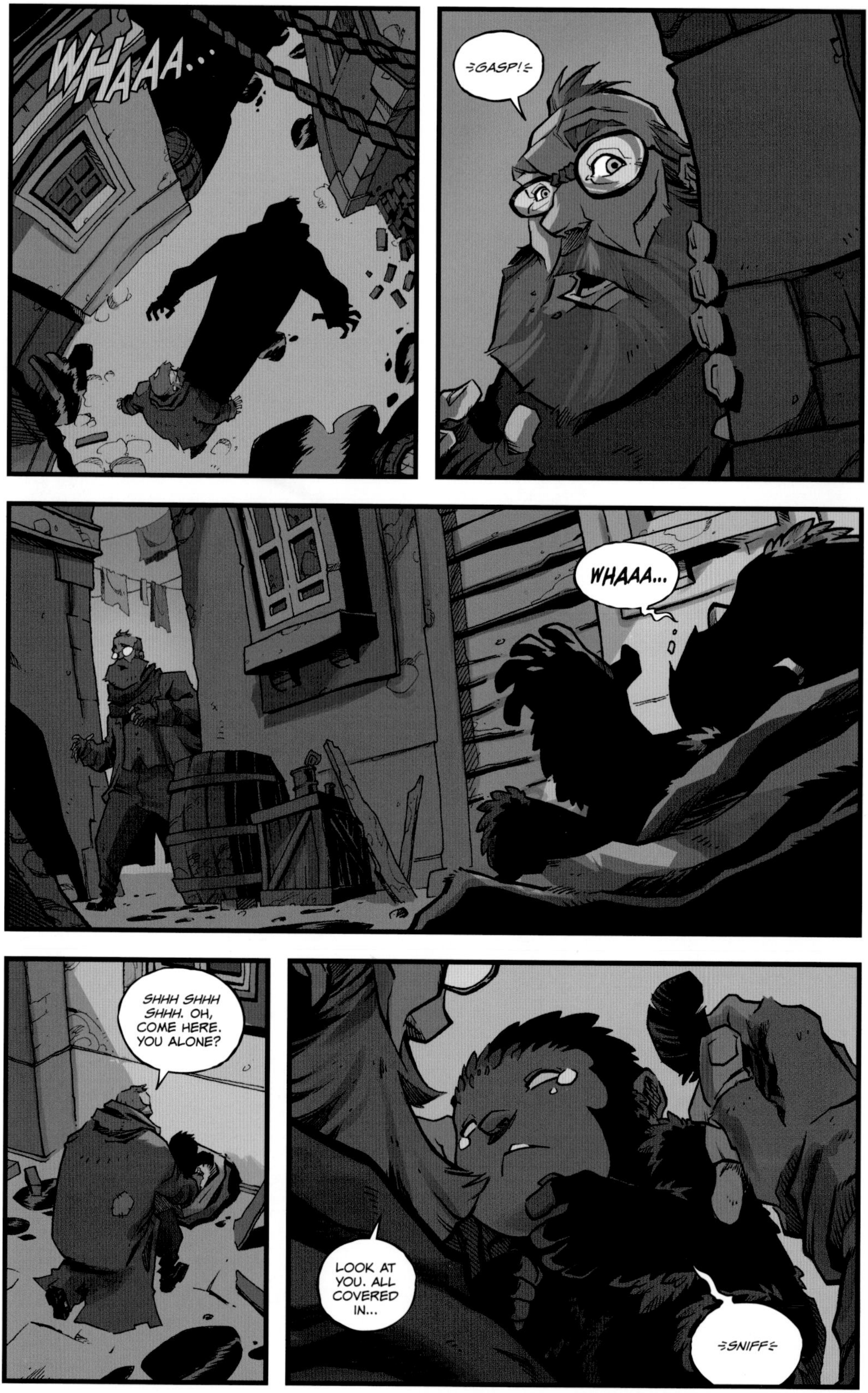
WHAAA...
≈GASP!≈
WHAAA...
SHHH SHHH SHHH. OH, COME HERE. YOU ALONE?
LOOK AT YOU. ALL COVERED IN...
≈SNIFF≈

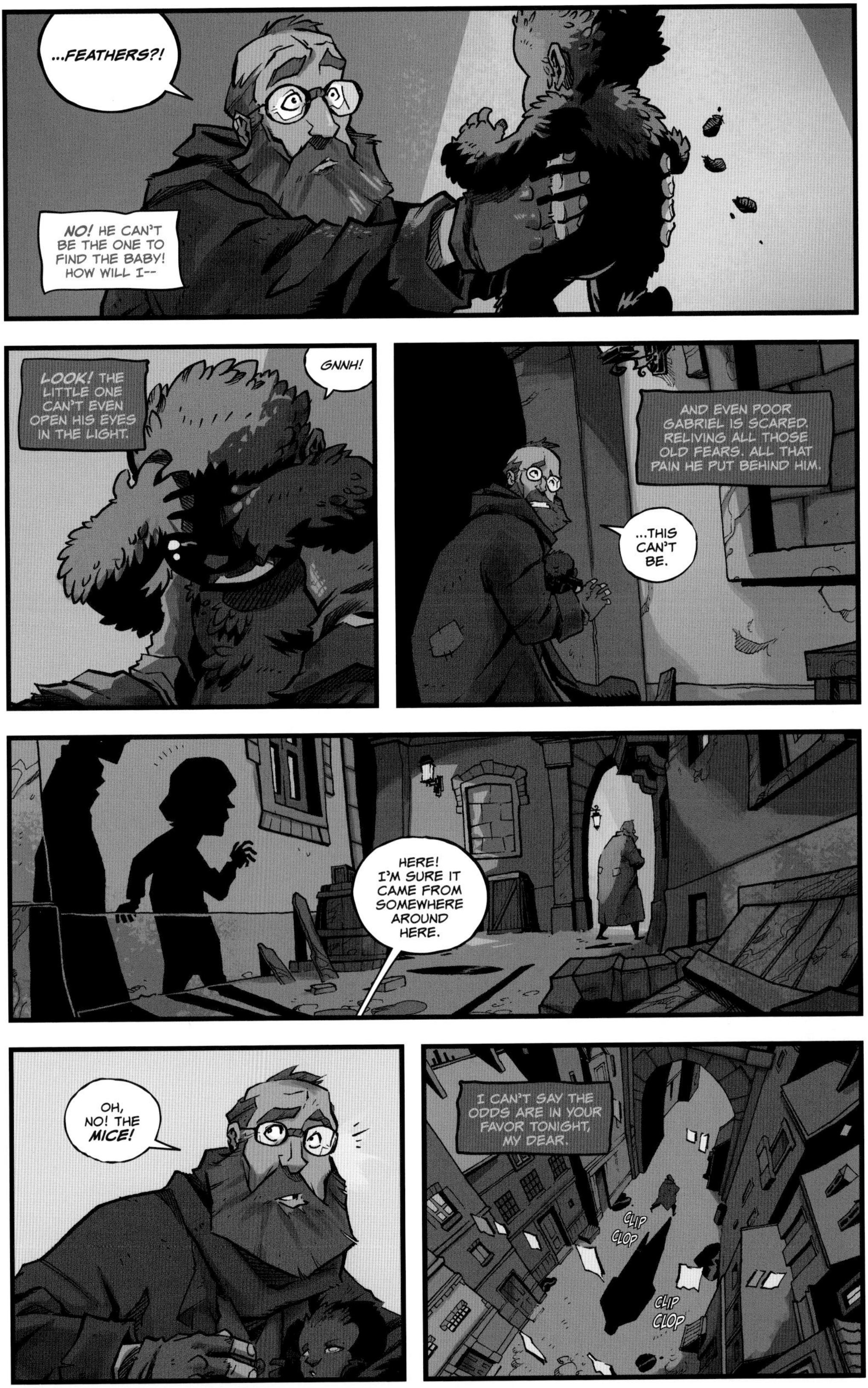
...FEATHERS?!
NO! HE CAN'T BE THE ONE TO FIND THE BABY! HOW WILL I--
LOOK! THE LITTLE ONE CAN'T EVEN OPEN HIS EYES IN THE LIGHT.
GNNH!
AND EVEN POOR GABRIEL IS SCARED. RELIVING ALL THOSE OLD FEARS. ALL THAT PAIN HE PUT BEHIND HIM.
...THIS CAN'T BE.
HERE! I'M SURE IT CAME FROM SOMEWHERE AROUND HERE.
OH, NO! THE MICE!
I CAN'T SAY THE ODDS ARE IN YOUR FAVOR TONIGHT, MY DEAR.
CLIP CLOP
CLIP CLOP

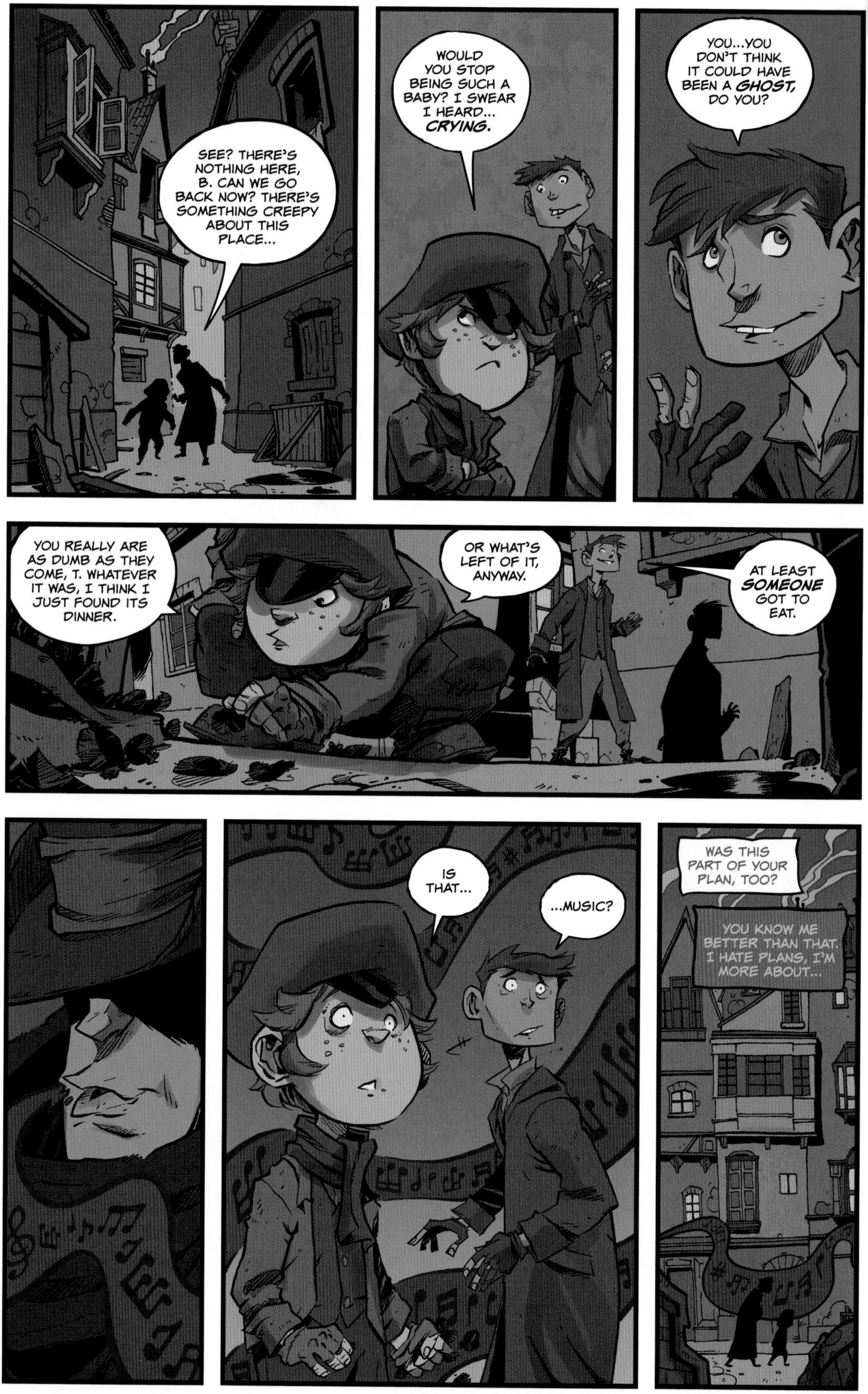
SEE? THERE'S NOTHING HERE, B. CAN WE GO BACK NOW? THERE'S SOMETHING CREEPY ABOUT THIS PLACE...
WOULD YOU STOP BEING SUCH A BABY? I SWEAR I HEARD... CRYING.
YOU...YOU DON'T THINK IT COULD HAVE BEEN A GHOST, DO YOU?
YOU REALLY ARE AS DUMB AS THEY COME, T. WHATEVER IT WAS, I THINK I JUST FOUND ITS DINNER.
OR WHAT'S LEFT OF IT, ANYWAY.
AT LEAST SOMEONE GOT TO EAT.
IS THAT...
...MUSIC?
WAS THIS PART OF YOUR PLAN, TOO?
YOU KNOW ME BETTER THAN THAT. I HATE PLANS, I'M MORE ABOUT...

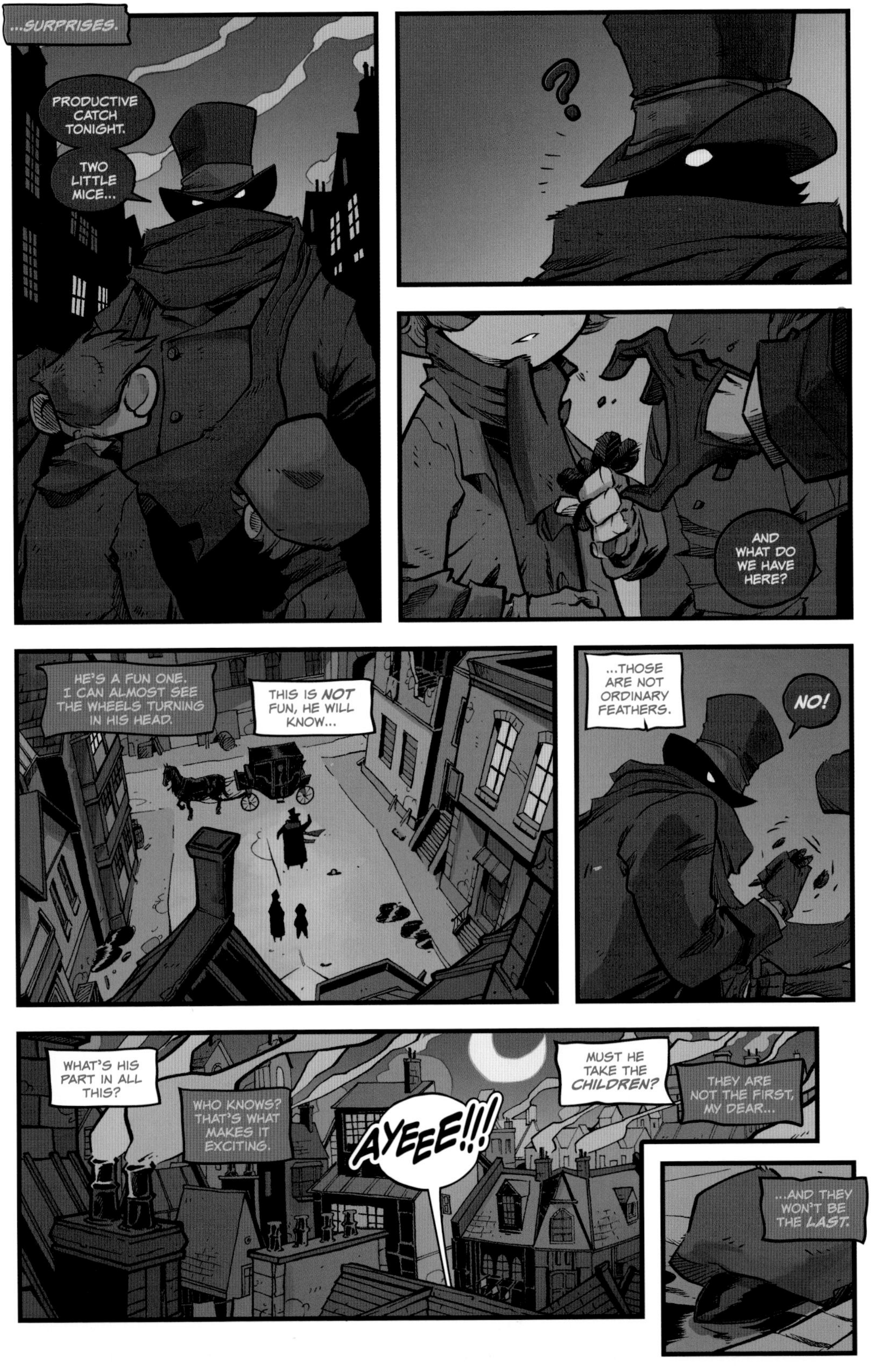
...SURPRISES.
PRODUCTIVE CATCH TONIGHT.
TWO LITTLE MICE...
?
AND WHAT DO WE HAVE HERE?
HE'S A FUN ONE. I CAN ALMOST SEE THE WHEELS TURNING IN HIS HEAD.
THIS IS NOT FUN, HE WILL KNOW...
...THOSE ARE NOT ORDINARY FEATHERS.
NO!
WHAT'S HIS PART IN ALL THIS?
WHO KNOWS? THAT'S WHAT MAKES IT EXCITING.
AYEEEE!!!
MUST HE TAKE THE CHILDREN?
THEY ARE NOT THE FIRST, MY DEAR...
...AND THEY WON'T BE THE LAST.

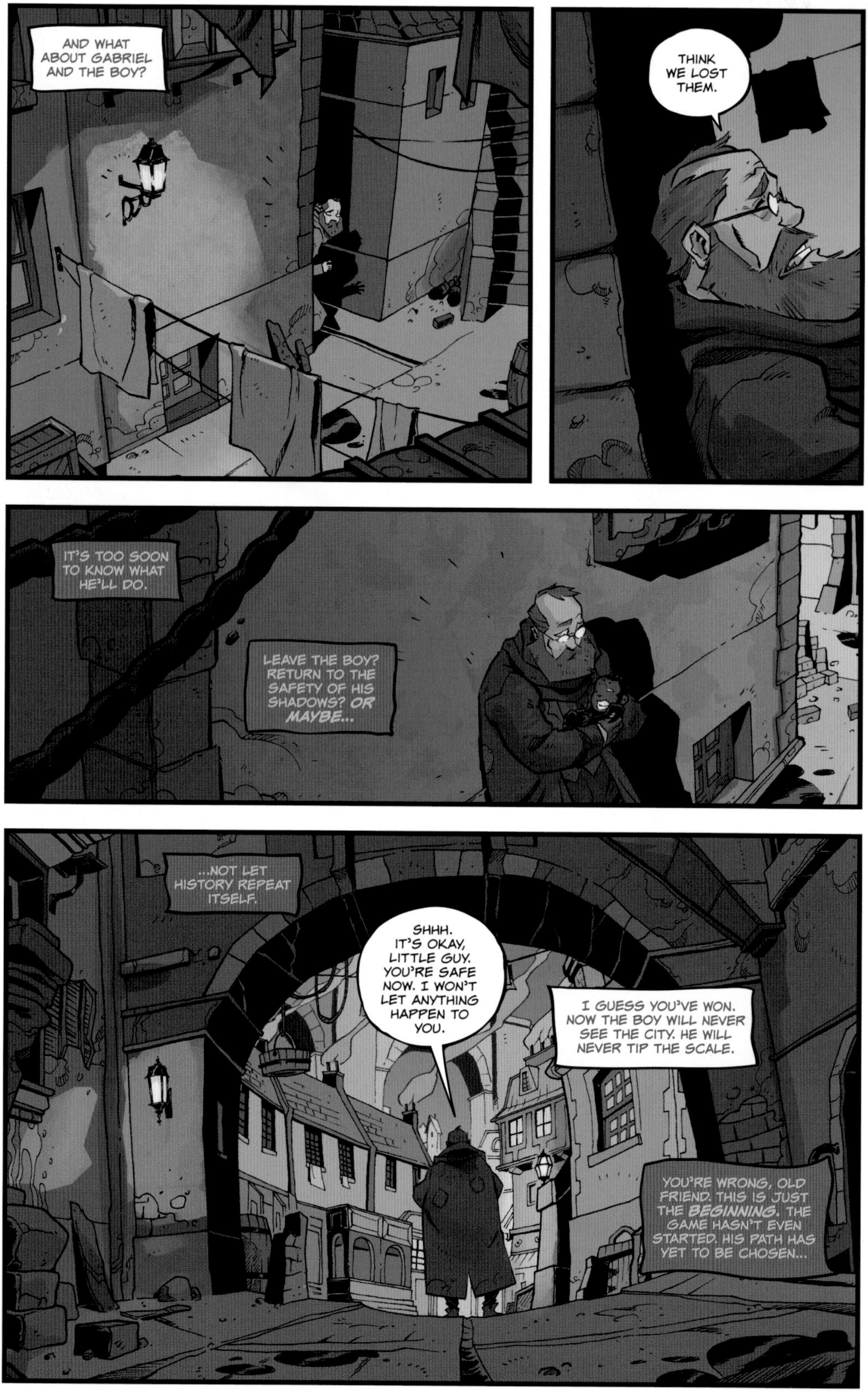
AND WHAT ABOUT GABRIEL AND THE BOY?
THINK WE LOST THEM.
IT'S TOO SOON TO KNOW WHAT HE'LL DO.
LEAVE THE BOY? RETURN TO THE SAFETY OF HIS SHADOWS? OR MAYBE...
...NOT LET HISTORY REPEAT ITSELF.
SHHH. IT'S OKAY, LITTLE GUY. YOU'RE SAFE NOW. I WON'T LET ANYTHING HAPPEN TO YOU.
I GUESS YOU'VE WON. NOW THE BOY WILL NEVER SEE THE CITY. HE WILL NEVER TIP THE SCALE.
YOU'RE WRONG, OLD FRIEND. THIS IS JUST THE BEGINNING. THE GAME HASN'T EVEN STARTED. HIS PATH HAS YET TO BE CHOSEN...

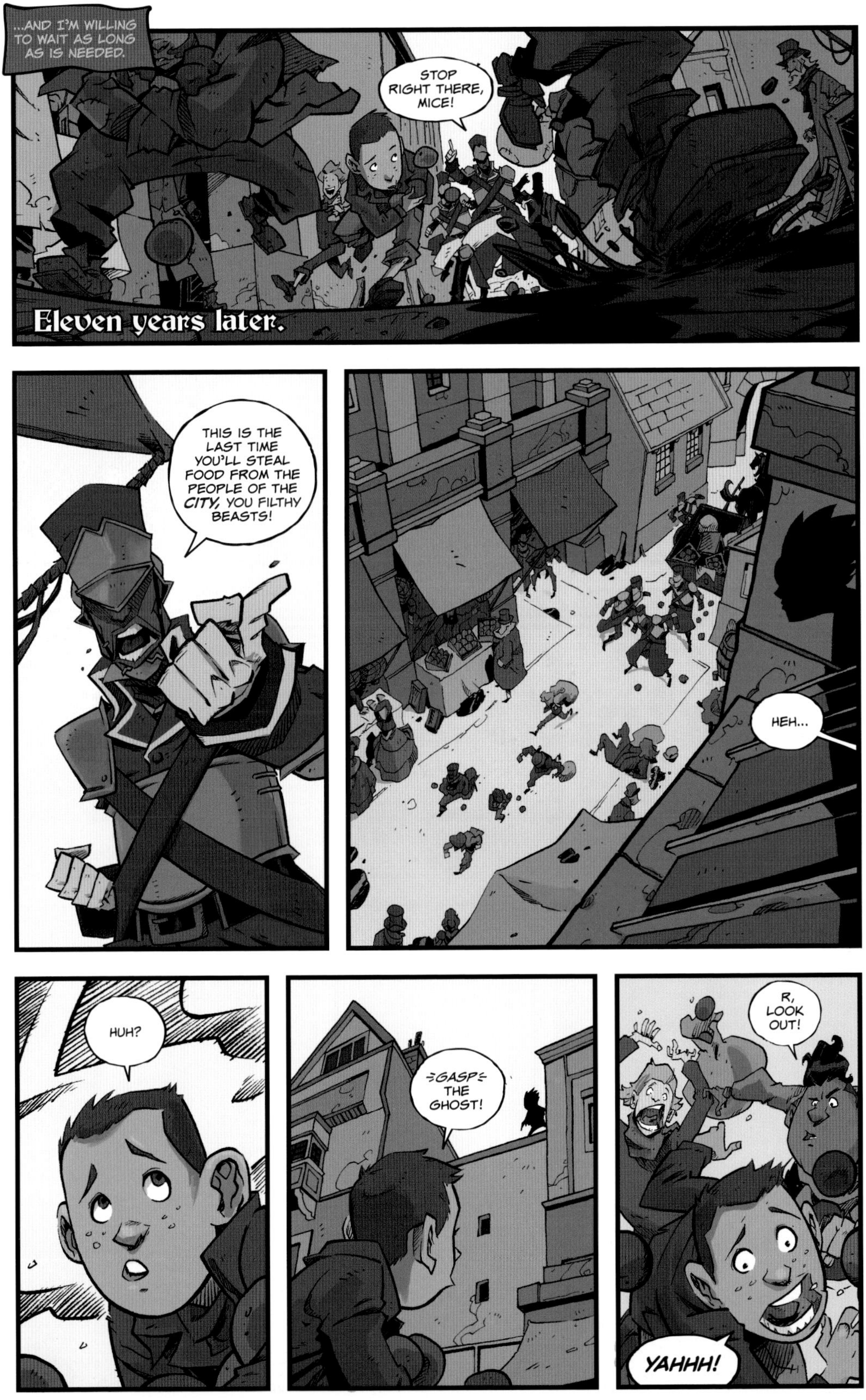
...AND I'M WILLING TO WAIT AS LONG AS IS NEEDED.
STOP RIGHT THERE, MICE!
Eleven years later.
THIS IS THE LAST TIME YOU'LL STEAL FOOD FROM THE PEOPLE OF THE CITY, YOU FILTHY BEASTS!
HEH...
HUH?
GASP THE GHOST!
R, LOOK OUT!
YAHHH!

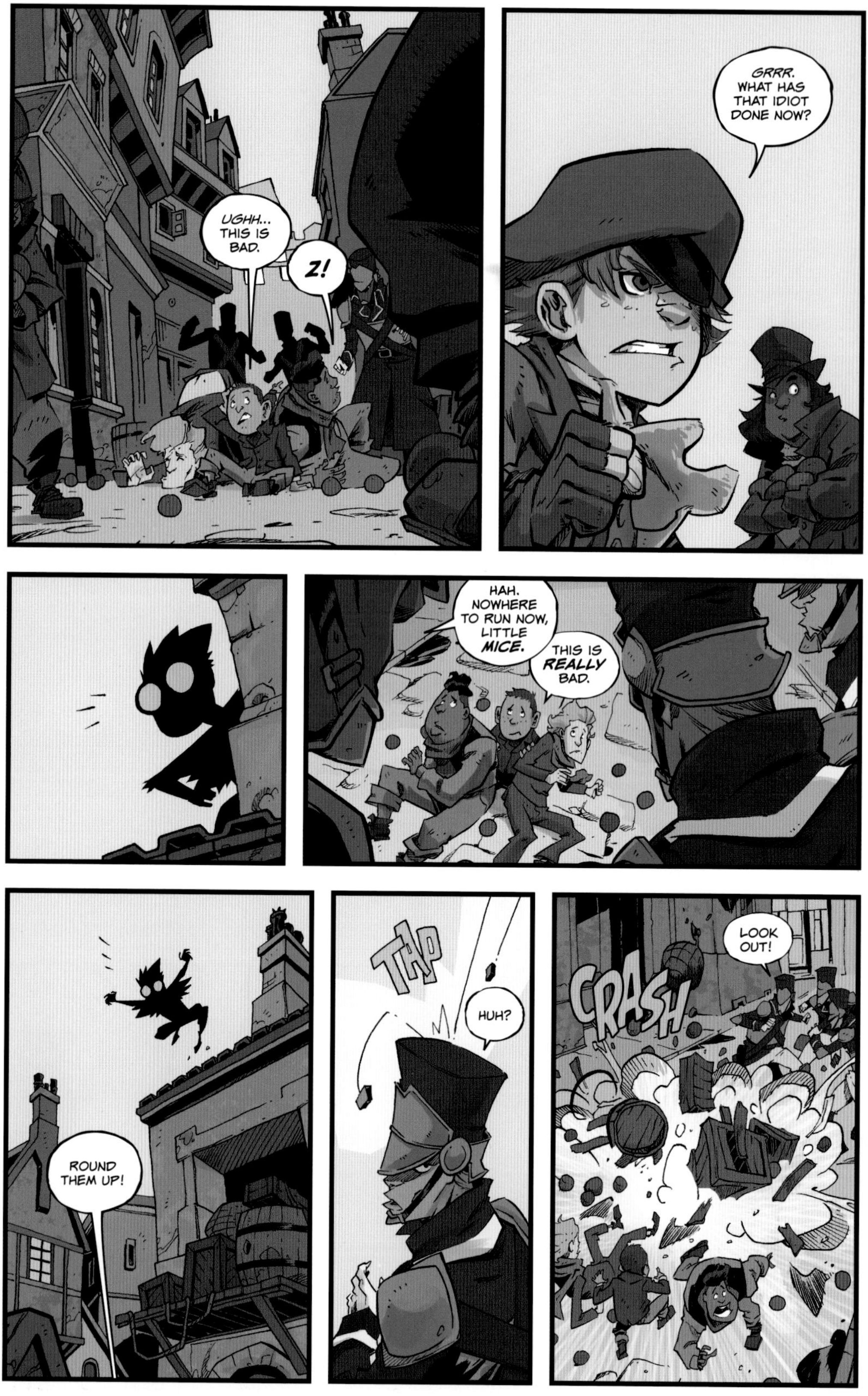
UGHH... THIS IS BAD.
Z!
GRRR. WHAT HAS THAT IDIOT DONE NOW?
HAH. NOWHERE TO RUN NOW, LITTLE MICE.
THIS IS REALLY BAD.
ROUND THEM UP!
TAP
HUH?
CRASH
LOOK OUT!

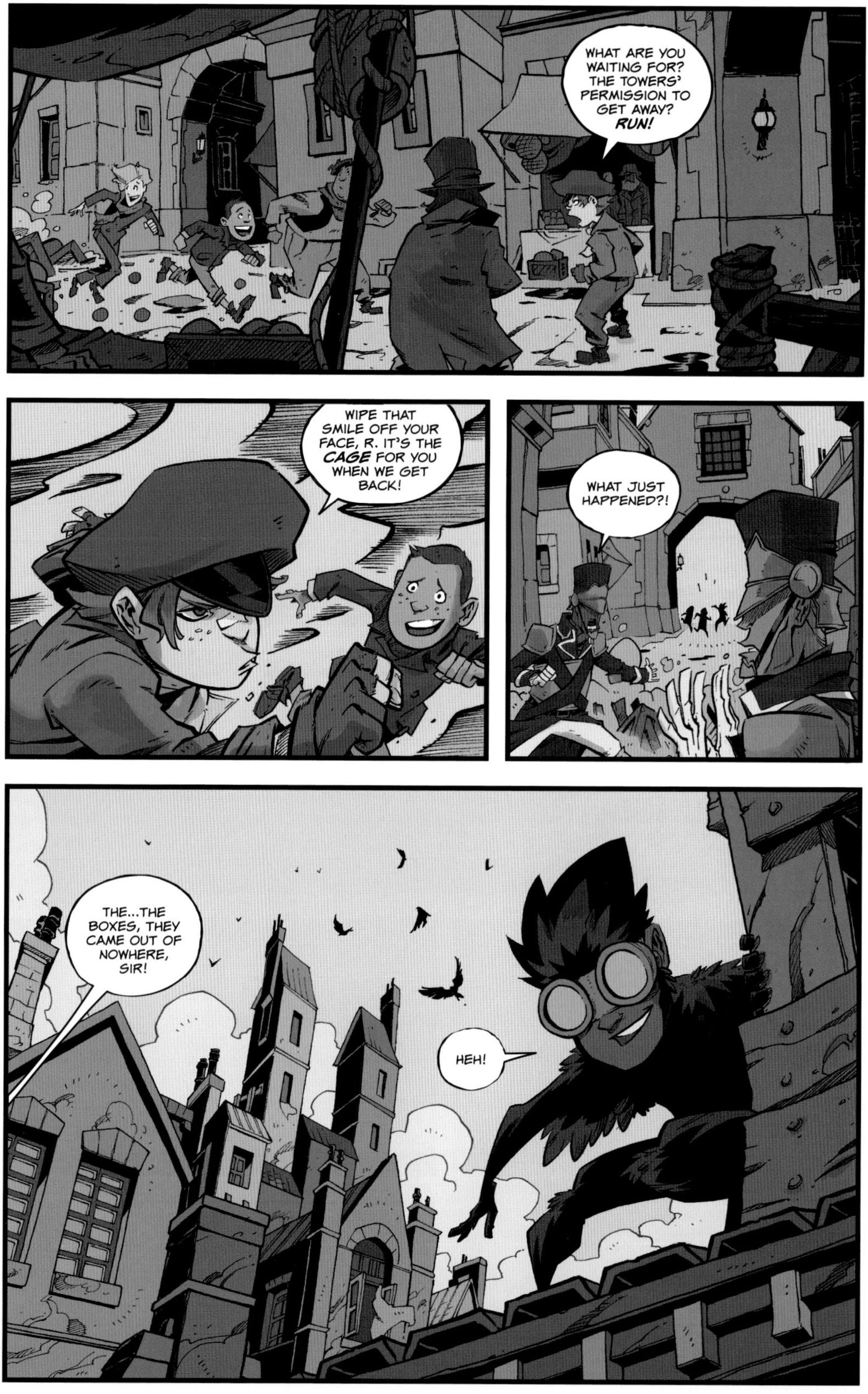
WHAT ARE YOU WAITING FOR? THE TOWERS' PERMISSION TO GET AWAY? RUN!
WIPE THAT SMILE OFF YOUR FACE, R. IT'S THE CAGE FOR YOU WHEN WE GET BACK!
WHAT JUST HAPPENED?!
THE...THE BOXES, THEY CAME OUT OF NOWHERE, SIR!
HEH!

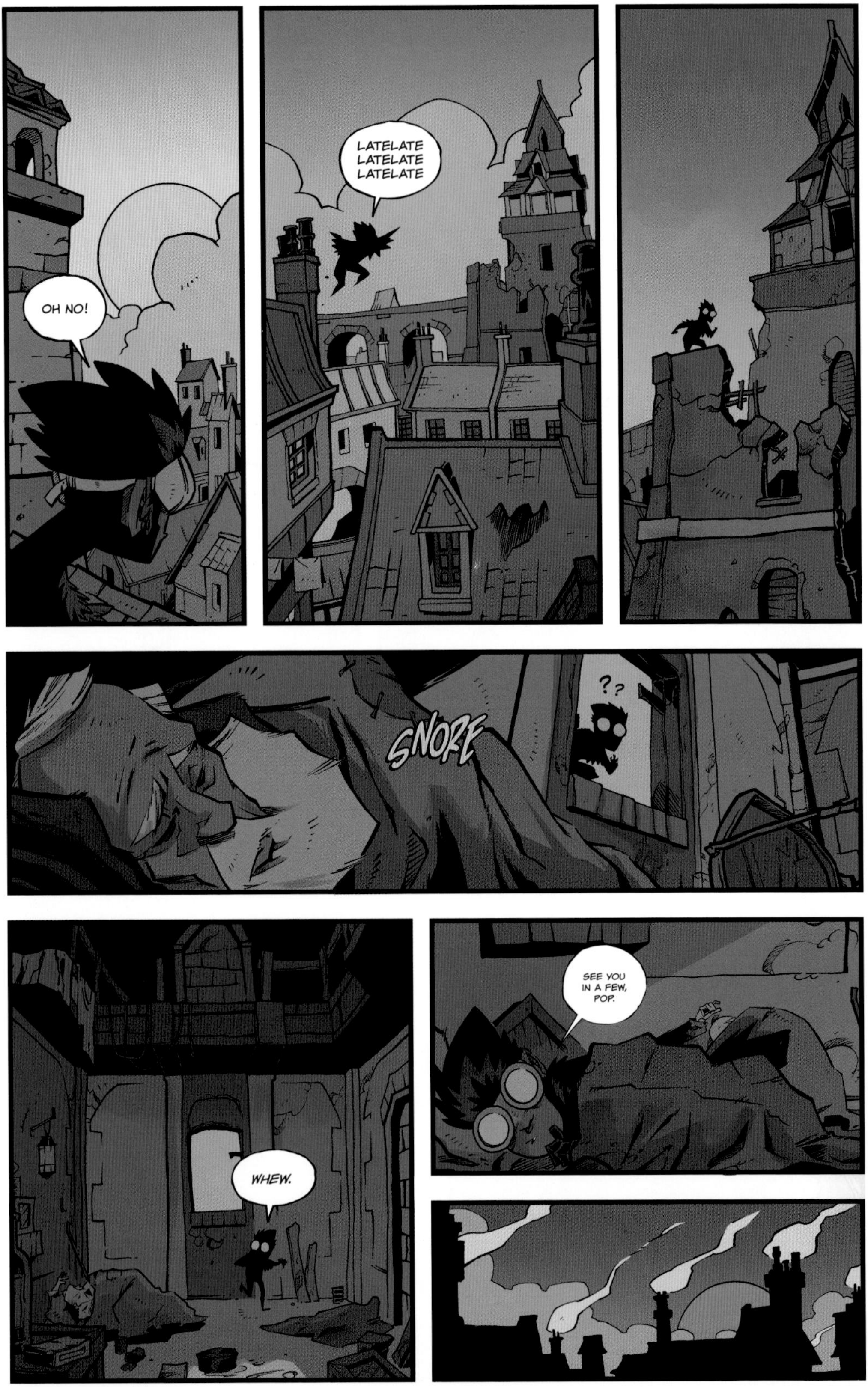
OH NO!
LATELATE LATELATE LATELATE
SNORE
??
SEE YOU IN A FEW, POP.
WHEW.

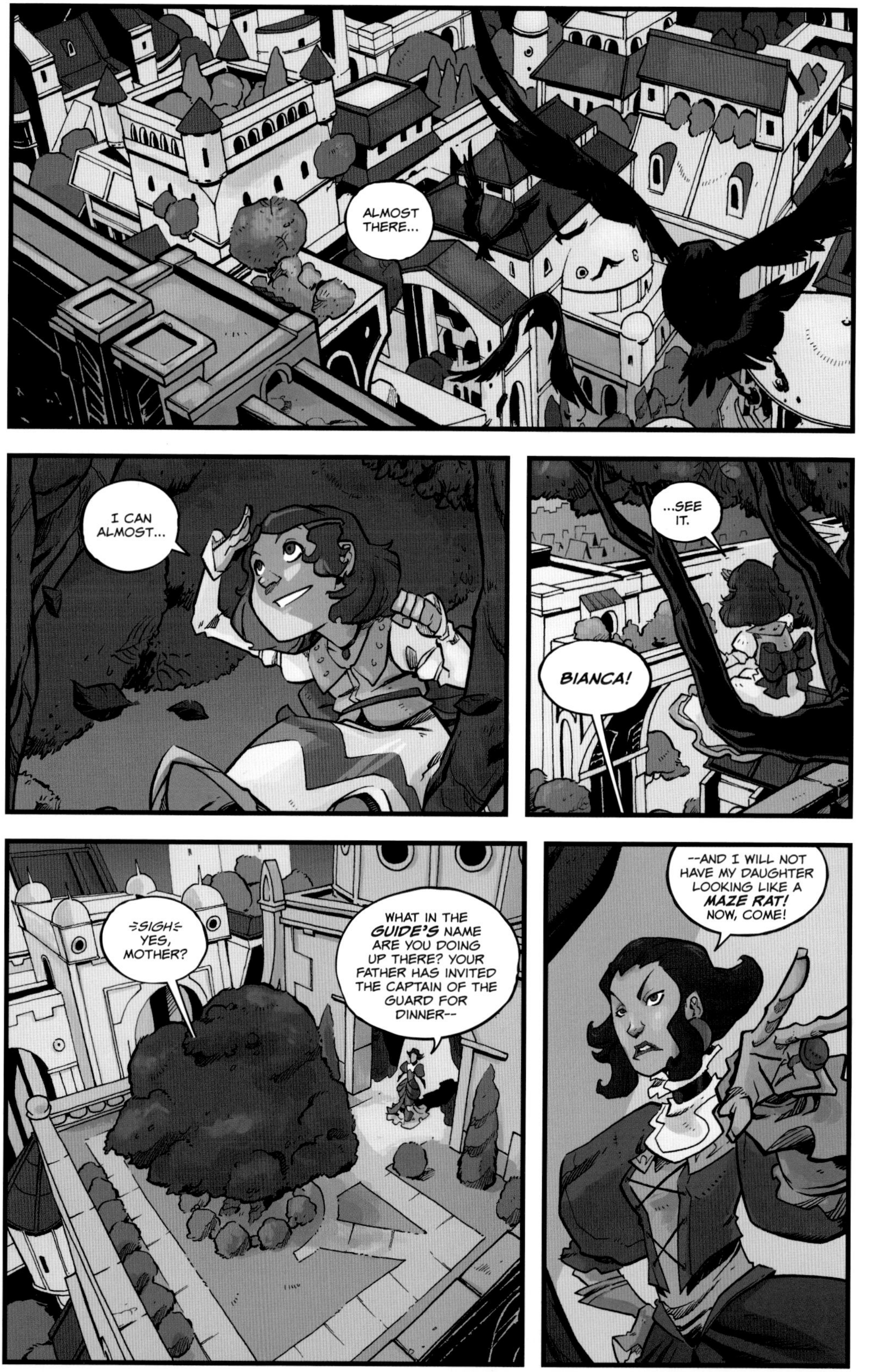
ALMOST THERE...
I CAN ALMOST...
...SEE IT.
BIANCA!
⚟SIGH⚞ YES, MOTHER?
WHAT IN THE GUIDE'S NAME ARE YOU DOING UP THERE? YOUR FATHER HAS INVITED THE CAPTAIN OF THE GUARD FOR DINNER--
--AND I WILL NOT HAVE MY DAUGHTER LOOKING LIKE A MAZE RAT! NOW, COME!

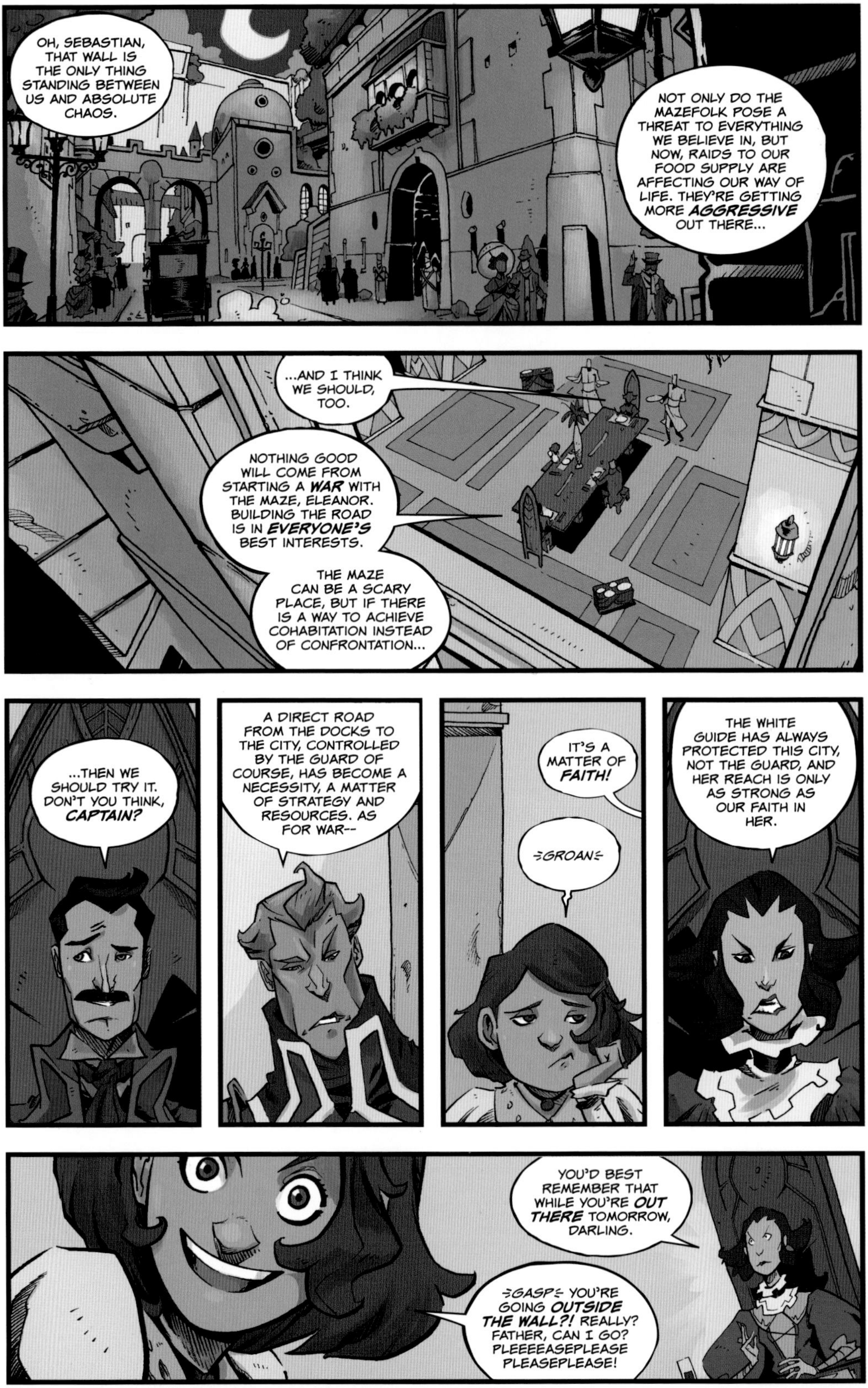
OH, SEBASTIAN, THAT WALL IS THE ONLY THING STANDING BETWEEN US AND ABSOLUTE CHAOS.
NOT ONLY DO THE MAZEFOLK POSE A THREAT TO EVERYTHING WE BELIEVE IN, BUT NOW, RAIDS TO OUR FOOD SUPPLY ARE AFFECTING OUR WAY OF LIFE. THEY'RE GETTING MORE *AGGRESSIVE* OUT THERE...
...AND I THINK WE SHOULD, TOO.
NOTHING GOOD WILL COME FROM STARTING A *WAR* WITH THE MAZE, ELEANOR. BUILDING THE ROAD IS IN *EVERYONE'S* BEST INTERESTS.
THE MAZE CAN BE A SCARY PLACE, BUT IF THERE IS A WAY TO ACHIEVE COHABITATION INSTEAD OF CONFRONTATION...
...THEN WE SHOULD TRY IT. DON'T YOU THINK, *CAPTAIN?*
A DIRECT ROAD FROM THE DOCKS TO THE CITY, CONTROLLED BY THE GUARD OF COURSE, HAS BECOME A NECESSITY, A MATTER OF STRATEGY AND RESOURCES. AS FOR WAR--
IT'S A MATTER OF *FAITH!*
GROAN
THE WHITE GUIDE HAS ALWAYS PROTECTED THIS CITY, NOT THE GUARD, AND HER REACH IS ONLY AS STRONG AS OUR FAITH IN HER.
YOU'D BEST REMEMBER THAT WHILE YOU'RE *OUT THERE* TOMORROW, DARLING.
GASP YOU'RE GOING *OUTSIDE THE WALL?!* REALLY? FATHER, CAN I GO? PLEEEEASEPLEASE PLEASEPLEASE!

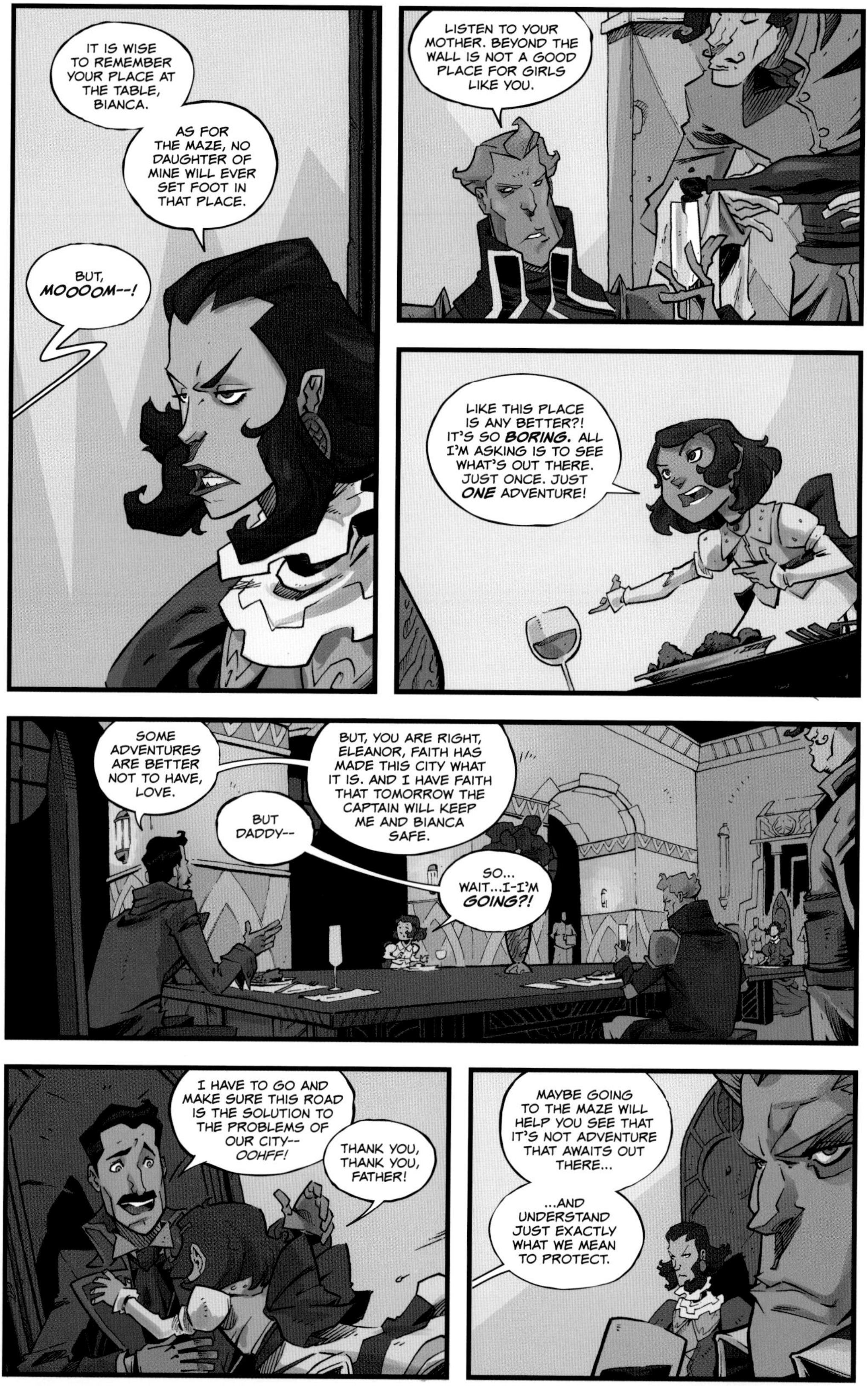
IT IS WISE TO REMEMBER YOUR PLACE AT THE TABLE, BIANCA.
AS FOR THE MAZE, NO DAUGHTER OF MINE WILL EVER SET FOOT IN THAT PLACE.
BUT, MOOOOM--!
LISTEN TO YOUR MOTHER. BEYOND THE WALL IS NOT A GOOD PLACE FOR GIRLS LIKE YOU.
LIKE THIS PLACE IS ANY BETTER?! IT'S SO BORING. ALL I'M ASKING IS TO SEE WHAT'S OUT THERE. JUST ONCE. JUST ONE ADVENTURE!
SOME ADVENTURES ARE BETTER NOT TO HAVE, LOVE.
BUT, YOU ARE RIGHT, ELEANOR, FAITH HAS MADE THIS CITY WHAT IT IS. AND I HAVE FAITH THAT TOMORROW THE CAPTAIN WILL KEEP ME AND BIANCA SAFE.
BUT DADDY--
SO... WAIT...I-I'M GOING?!
I HAVE TO GO AND MAKE SURE THIS ROAD IS THE SOLUTION TO THE PROBLEMS OF OUR CITY-- OOHFF!
THANK YOU, THANK YOU, FATHER!
MAYBE GOING TO THE MAZE WILL HELP YOU SEE THAT IT'S NOT ADVENTURE THAT AWAITS OUT THERE...
...AND UNDERSTAND JUST EXACTLY WHAT WE MEAN TO PROTECT.

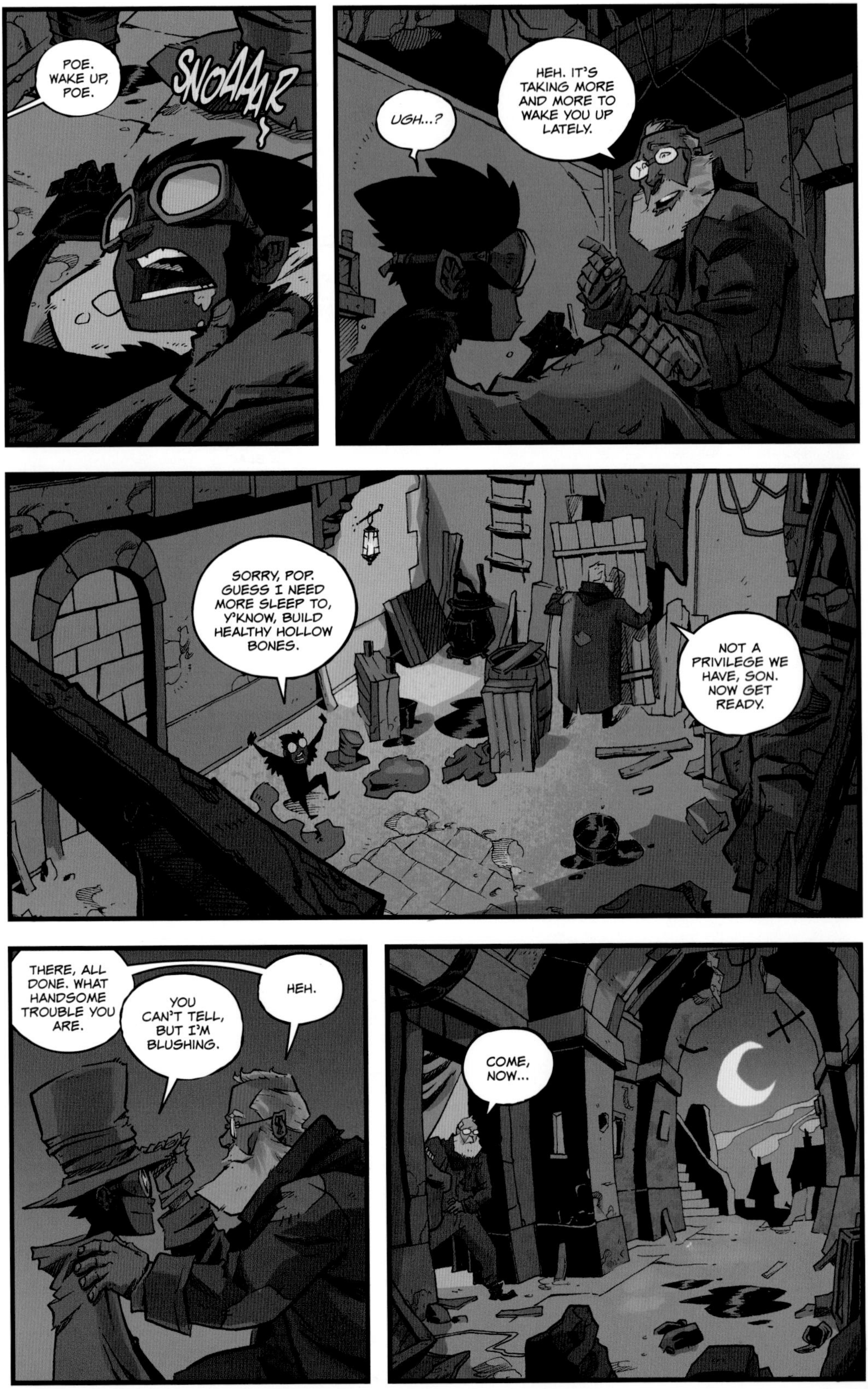
POE. WAKE UP, POE.
SNOAAAR
UGH...?
HEH. IT'S TAKING MORE AND MORE TO WAKE YOU UP LATELY.
SORRY, POP. GUESS I NEED MORE SLEEP TO, Y'KNOW, BUILD HEALTHY HOLLOW BONES.
NOT A PRIVILEGE WE HAVE, SON. NOW GET READY.
THERE, ALL DONE. WHAT HANDSOME TROUBLE YOU ARE.
YOU CAN'T TELL, BUT I'M BLUSHING.
HEH.
COME, NOW...

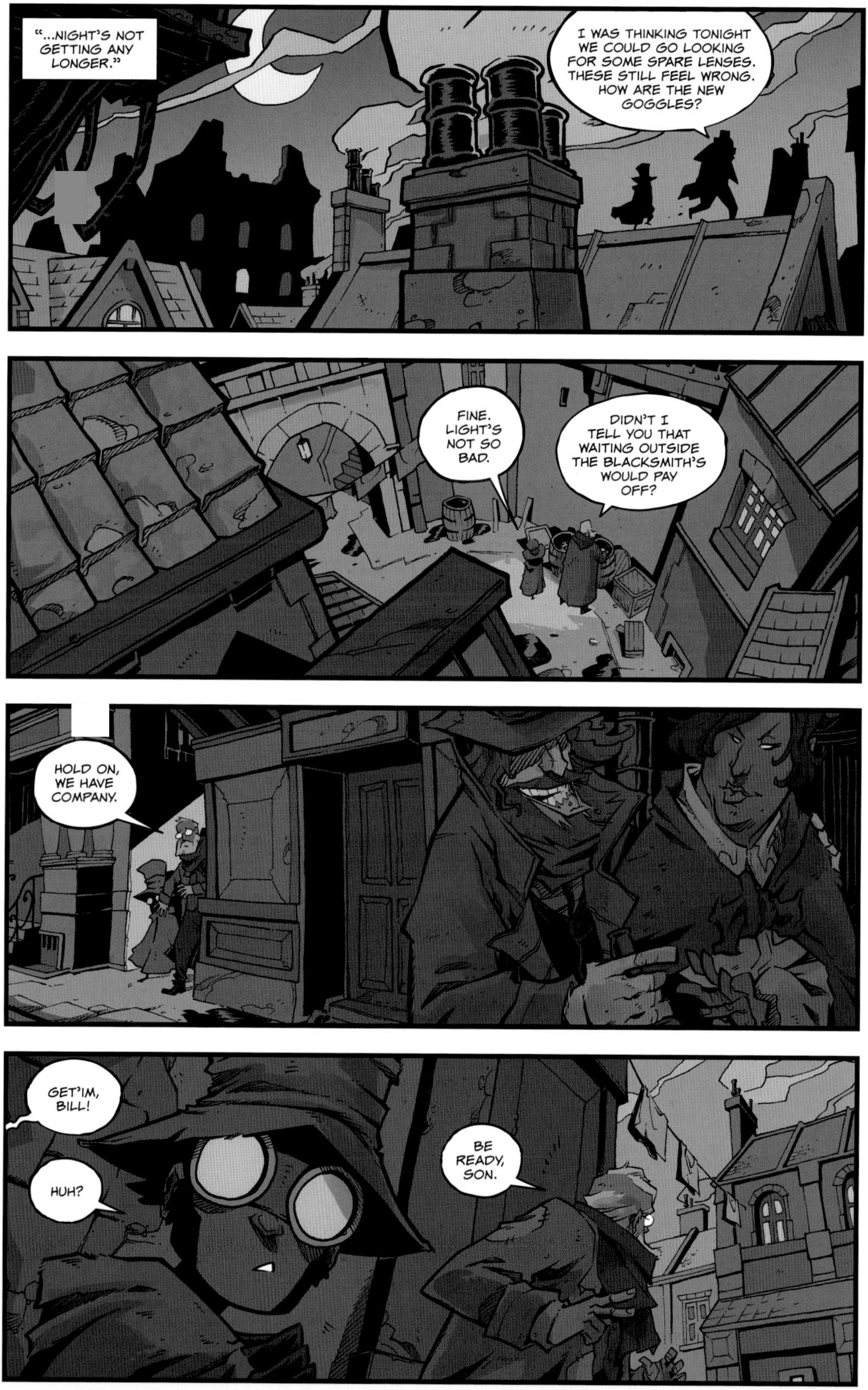
"...NIGHT'S NOT GETTING ANY LONGER."
I WAS THINKING TONIGHT WE COULD GO LOOKING FOR SOME SPARE LENSES. THESE STILL FEEL WRONG. HOW ARE THE NEW GOGGLES?
FINE. LIGHT'S NOT SO BAD.
DIDN'T I TELL YOU THAT WAITING OUTSIDE THE BLACKSMITH'S WOULD PAY OFF?
HOLD ON, WE HAVE COMPANY.
GET'IM, BILL!
HUH?
BE READY, SON.

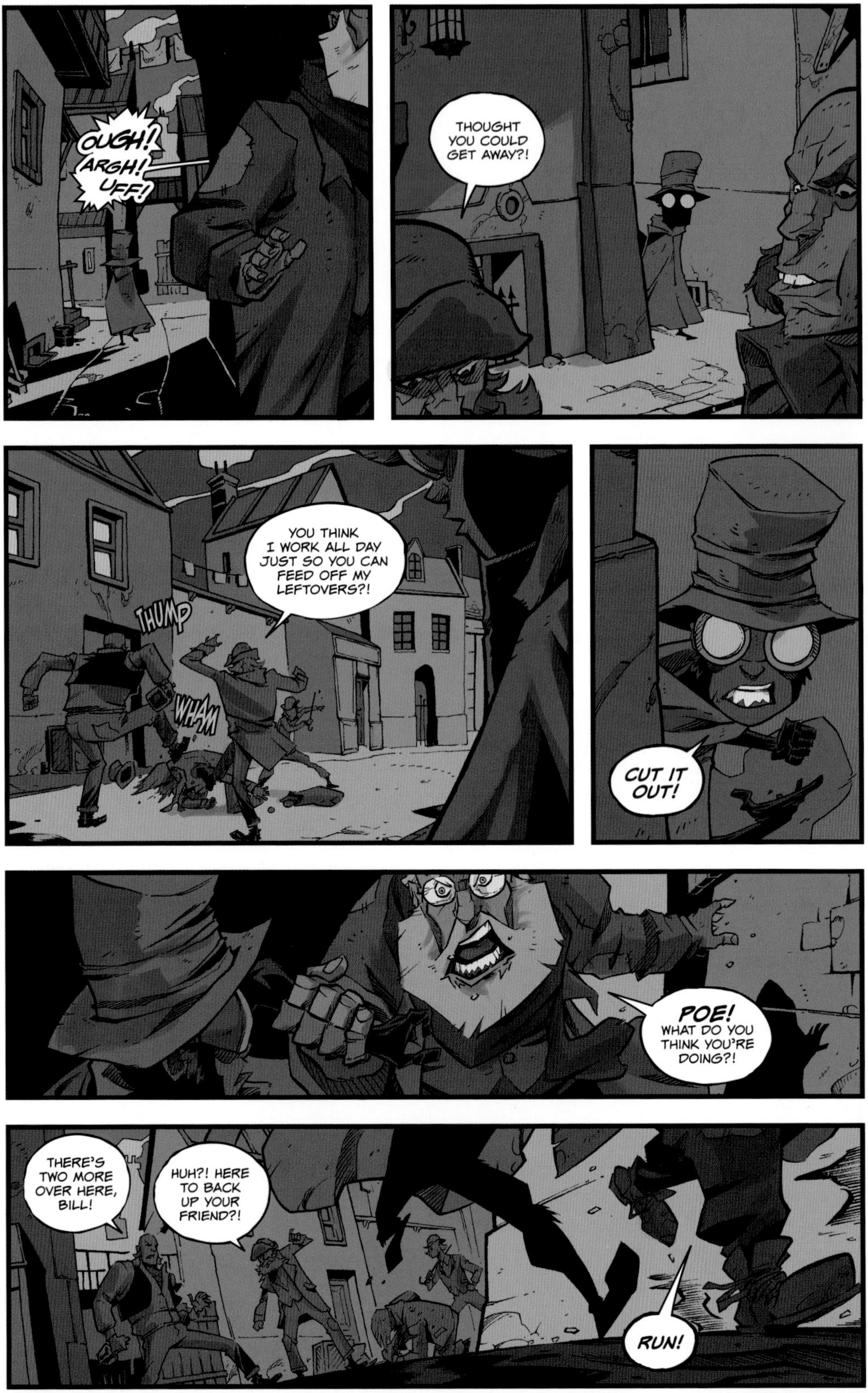
OUGH! ARGH! UFF!
THOUGHT YOU COULD GET AWAY?!
YOU THINK I WORK ALL DAY JUST SO YOU CAN FEED OFF MY LEFTOVERS?!
THUMP
WHAM
CUT IT OUT!
POE! WHAT DO YOU THINK YOU'RE DOING?!
THERE'S TWO MORE OVER HERE, BILL!
HUH?! HERE TO BACK UP YOUR FRIEND?!
RUN!

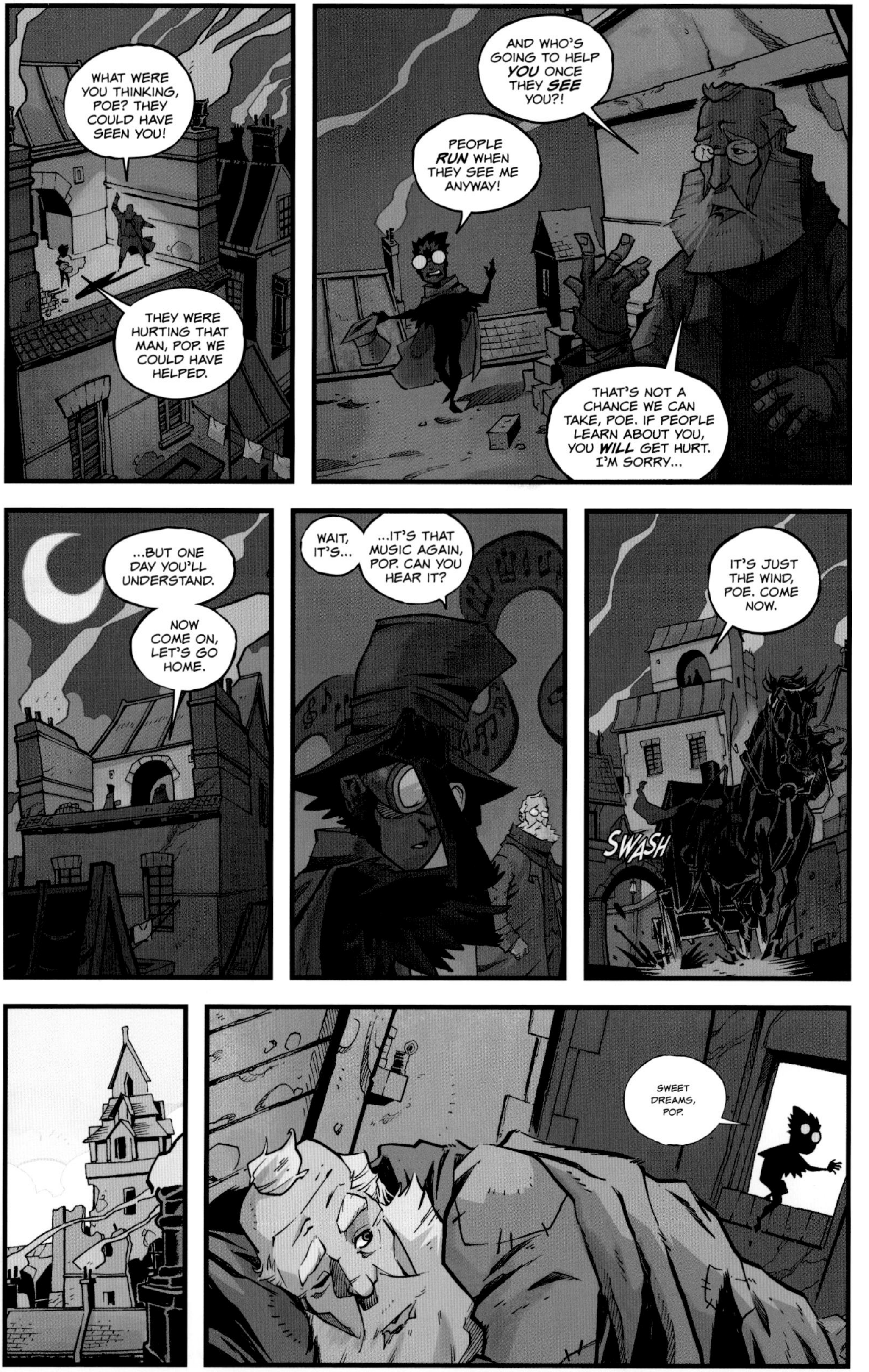
WHAT WERE YOU THINKING, POE? THEY COULD HAVE SEEN YOU!
THEY WERE HURTING THAT MAN, POP. WE COULD HAVE HELPED.
AND WHO'S GOING TO HELP YOU ONCE THEY SEE YOU?!
PEOPLE RUN WHEN THEY SEE ME ANYWAY!
THAT'S NOT A CHANCE WE CAN TAKE, POE. IF PEOPLE LEARN ABOUT YOU, YOU WILL GET HURT. I'M SORRY...
...BUT ONE DAY YOU'LL UNDERSTAND.
NOW COME ON, LET'S GO HOME.
WAIT, IT'S...
...IT'S THAT MUSIC AGAIN, POP. CAN YOU HEAR IT?
IT'S JUST THE WIND, POE. COME NOW.
SWASH
SWEET DREAMS, POP.

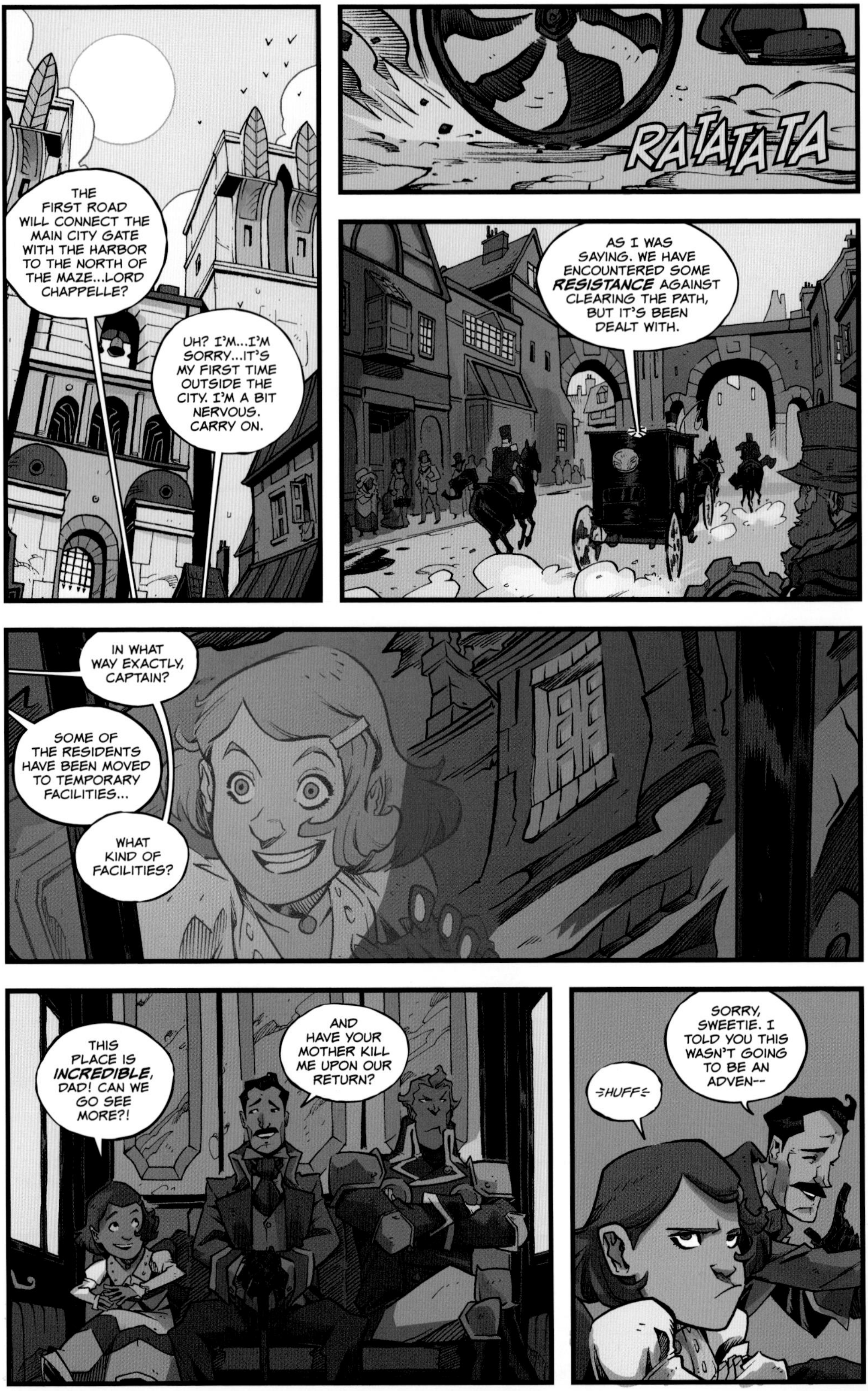
THE FIRST ROAD WILL CONNECT THE MAIN CITY GATE WITH THE HARBOR TO THE NORTH OF THE MAZE...LORD CHAPPELLE?
UH? I'M...I'M SORRY...IT'S MY FIRST TIME OUTSIDE THE CITY. I'M A BIT NERVOUS. CARRY ON.
RATATATA
AS I WAS SAYING. WE HAVE ENCOUNTERED SOME RESISTANCE AGAINST CLEARING THE PATH, BUT IT'S BEEN DEALT WITH.
IN WHAT WAY EXACTLY, CAPTAIN?
SOME OF THE RESIDENTS HAVE BEEN MOVED TO TEMPORARY FACILITIES...
WHAT KIND OF FACILITIES?
THIS PLACE IS INCREDIBLE, DAD! CAN WE GO SEE MORE?!
AND HAVE YOUR MOTHER KILL ME UPON OUR RETURN?
HUFF
SORRY, SWEETIE. I TOLD YOU THIS WASN'T GOING TO BE AN ADVEN--

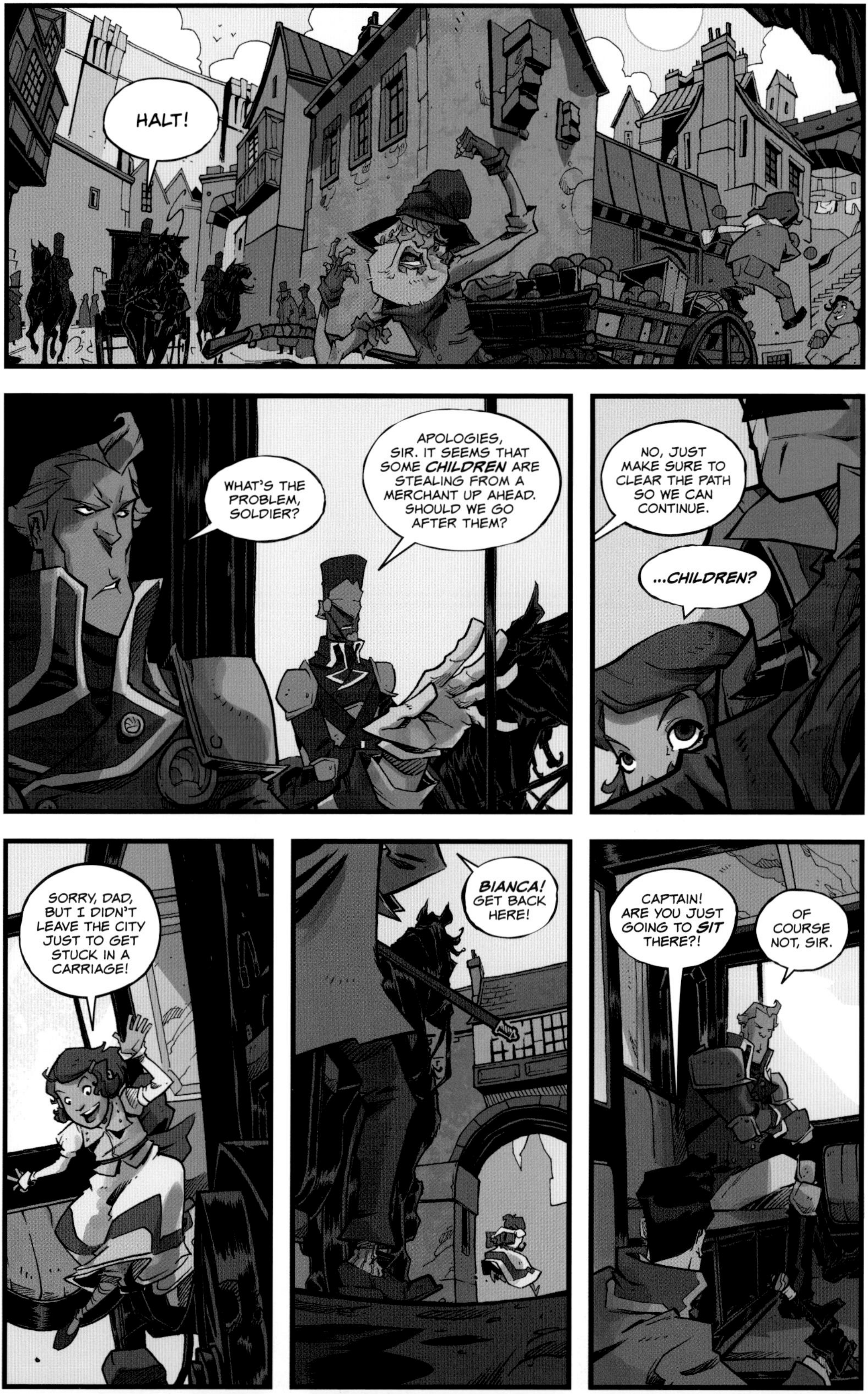
HALT!
WHAT'S THE PROBLEM, SOLDIER?
APOLOGIES, SIR. IT SEEMS THAT SOME CHILDREN ARE STEALING FROM A MERCHANT UP AHEAD. SHOULD WE GO AFTER THEM?
NO, JUST MAKE SURE TO CLEAR THE PATH SO WE CAN CONTINUE.
...CHILDREN?
SORRY, DAD, BUT I DIDN'T LEAVE THE CITY JUST TO GET STUCK IN A CARRIAGE!
BIANCA! GET BACK HERE!
CAPTAIN! ARE YOU JUST GOING TO SIT THERE?!
OF COURSE NOT, SIR.

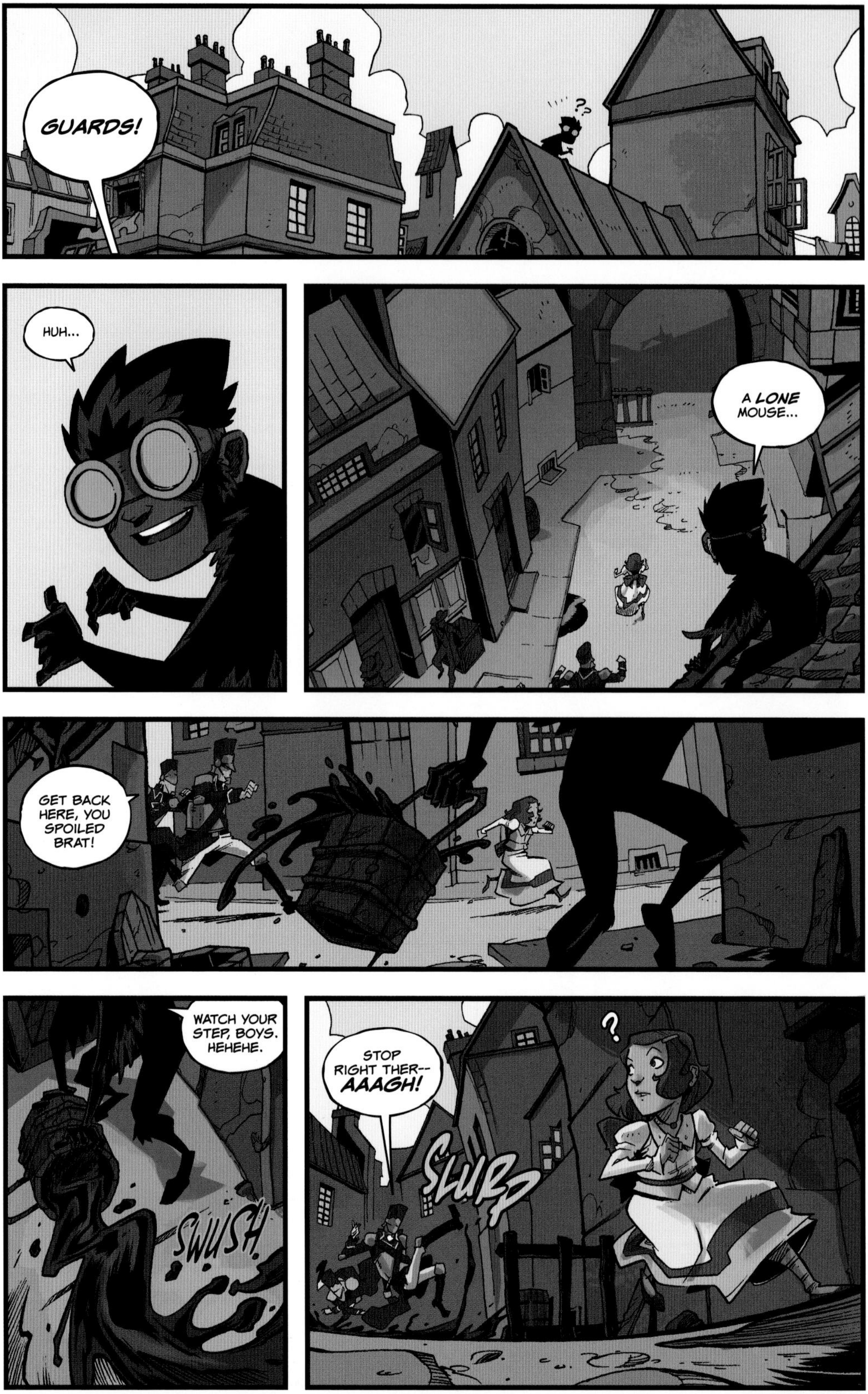
GUARDS!
HUH...
A LONE MOUSE...
GET BACK HERE, YOU SPOILED BRAT!
WATCH YOUR STEP, BOYS. HEHEHE.
SWUSH!
STOP RIGHT THER-- AAAGH!
SLURP

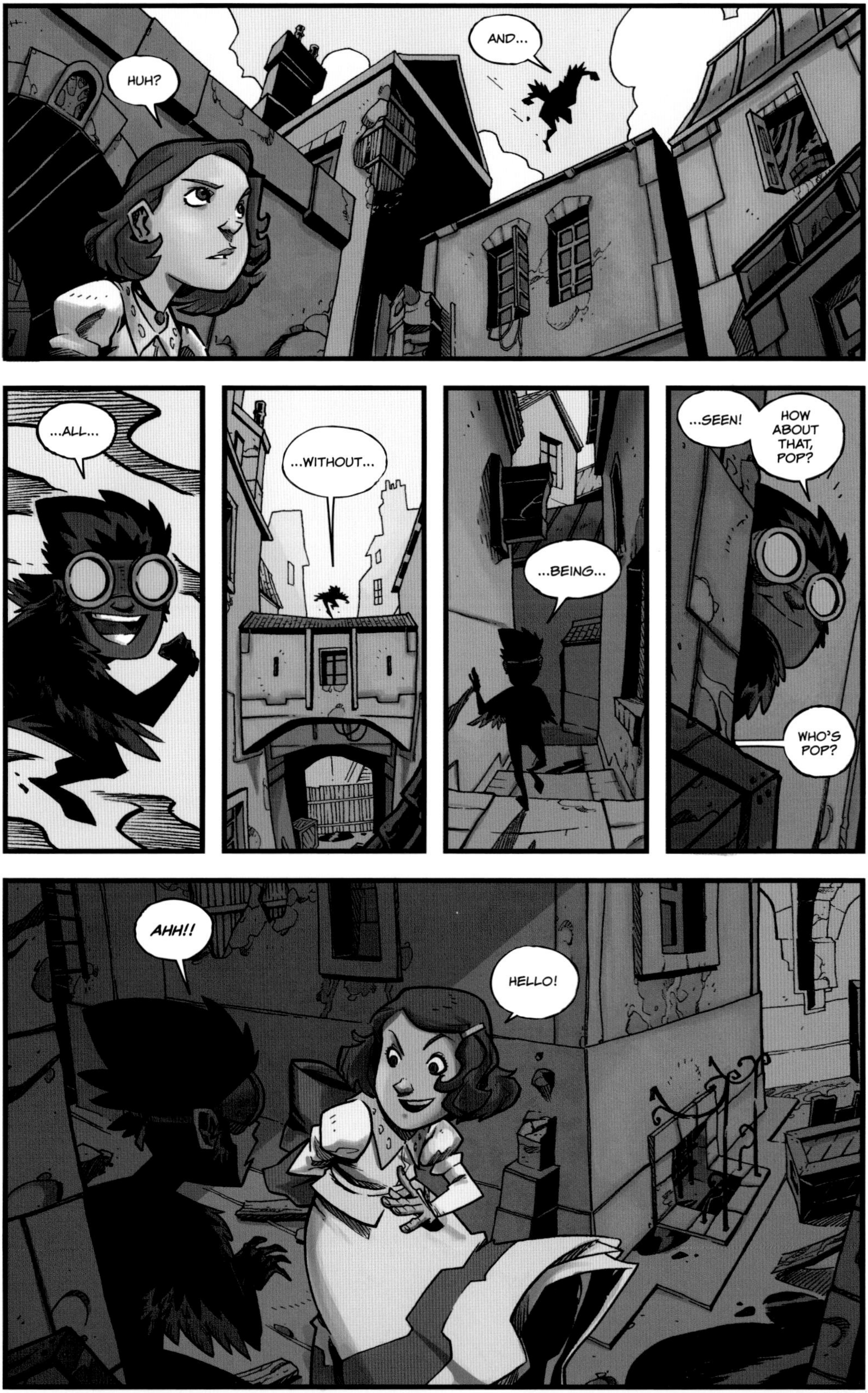
HUH?
AND...
...ALL...
...WITHOUT...
...BEING...
...SEEN!
HOW ABOUT THAT, POP?
WHO'S POP?
AHH!!
HELLO!

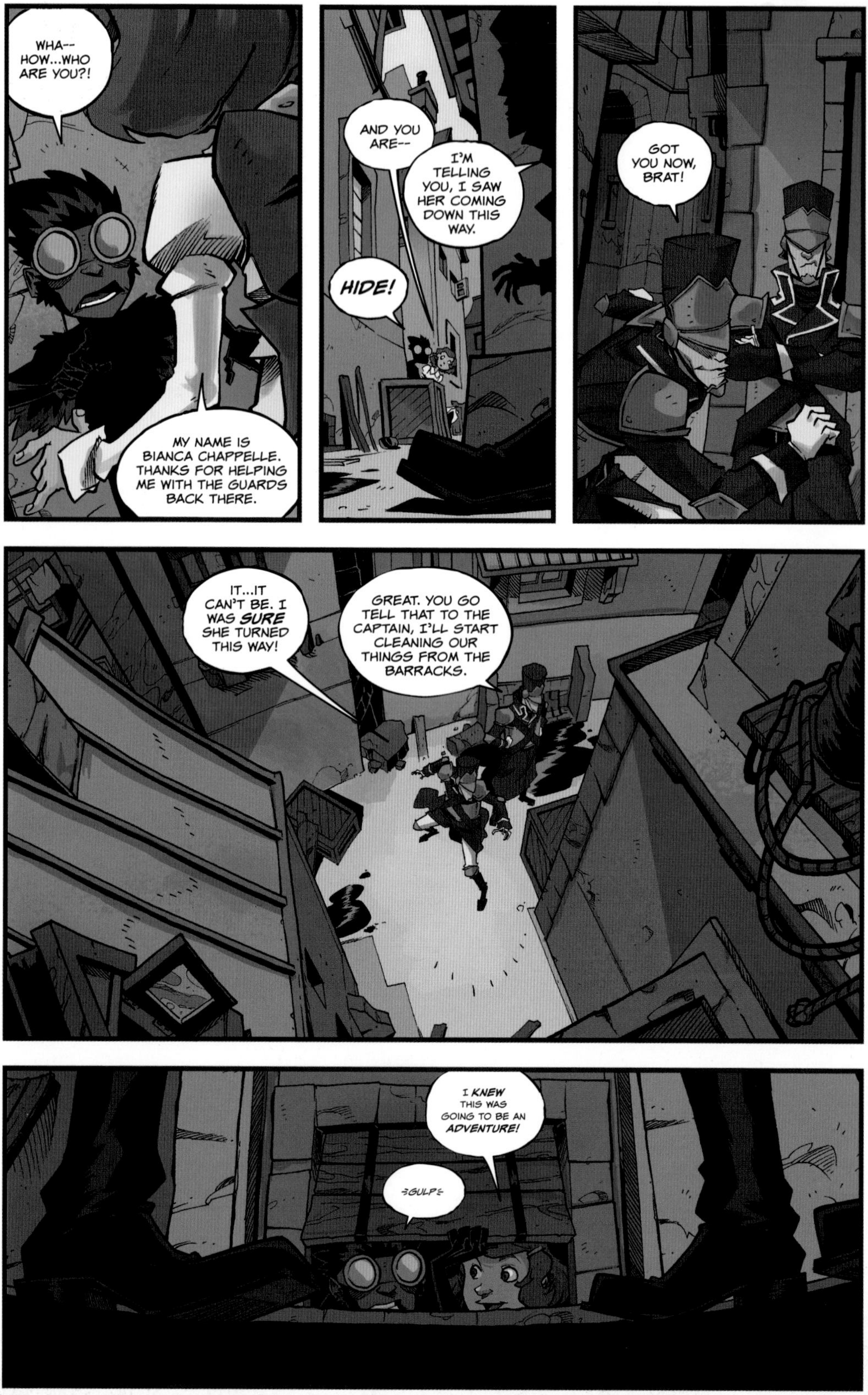
WHA-- HOW...WHO ARE YOU?!
MY NAME IS BIANCA CHAPPELLE. THANKS FOR HELPING ME WITH THE GUARDS BACK THERE.
AND YOU ARE--
I'M TELLING YOU, I SAW HER COMING DOWN THIS WAY.
HIDE!
GOT YOU NOW, BRAT!
IT...IT CAN'T BE. I WAS SURE SHE TURNED THIS WAY!
GREAT. YOU GO TELL THAT TO THE CAPTAIN, I'LL START CLEANING OUR THINGS FROM THE BARRACKS.
I KNEW THIS WAS GOING TO BE AN ADVENTURE!
GULP

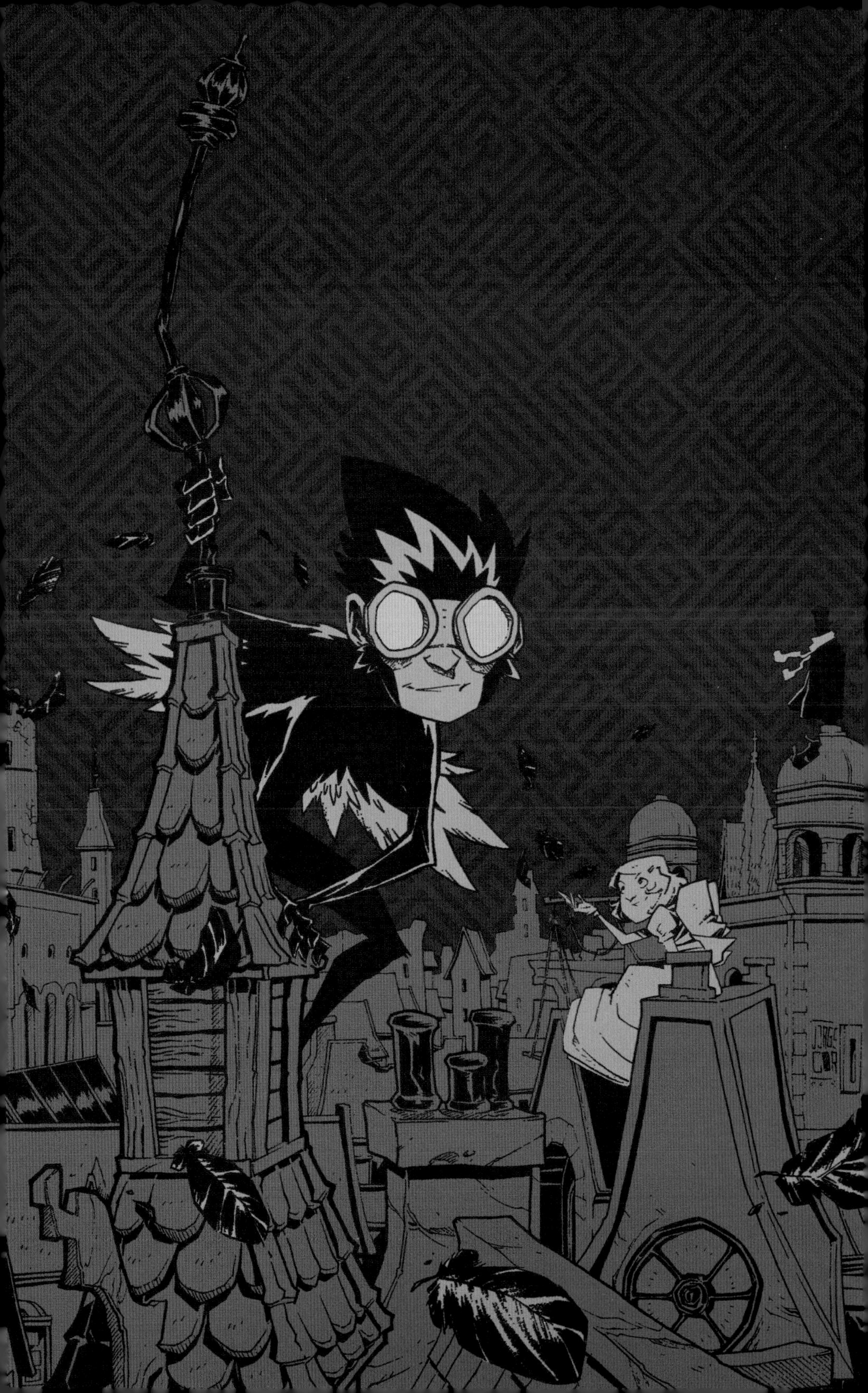

CHAPTER
TWO

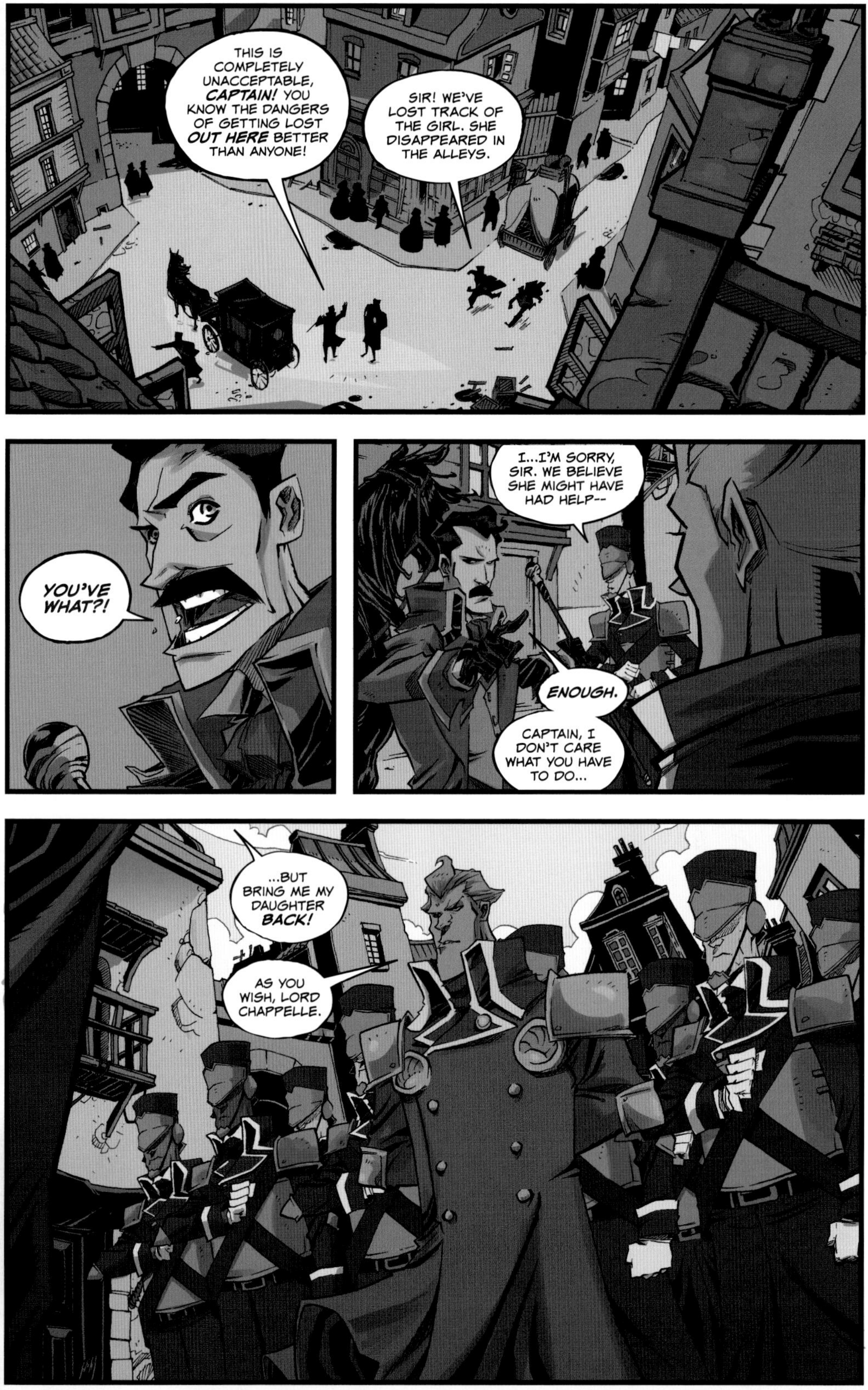
THIS IS COMPLETELY UNACCEPTABLE, CAPTAIN! YOU KNOW THE DANGERS OF GETTING LOST OUT HERE BETTER THAN ANYONE!
SIR! WE'VE LOST TRACK OF THE GIRL. SHE DISAPPEARED IN THE ALLEYS.
YOU'VE WHAT?!
I...I'M SORRY, SIR. WE BELIEVE SHE MIGHT HAVE HAD HELP--
ENOUGH.
CAPTAIN, I DON'T CARE WHAT YOU HAVE TO DO...
...BUT BRING ME MY DAUGHTER BACK!
AS YOU WISH, LORD CHAPPELLE.

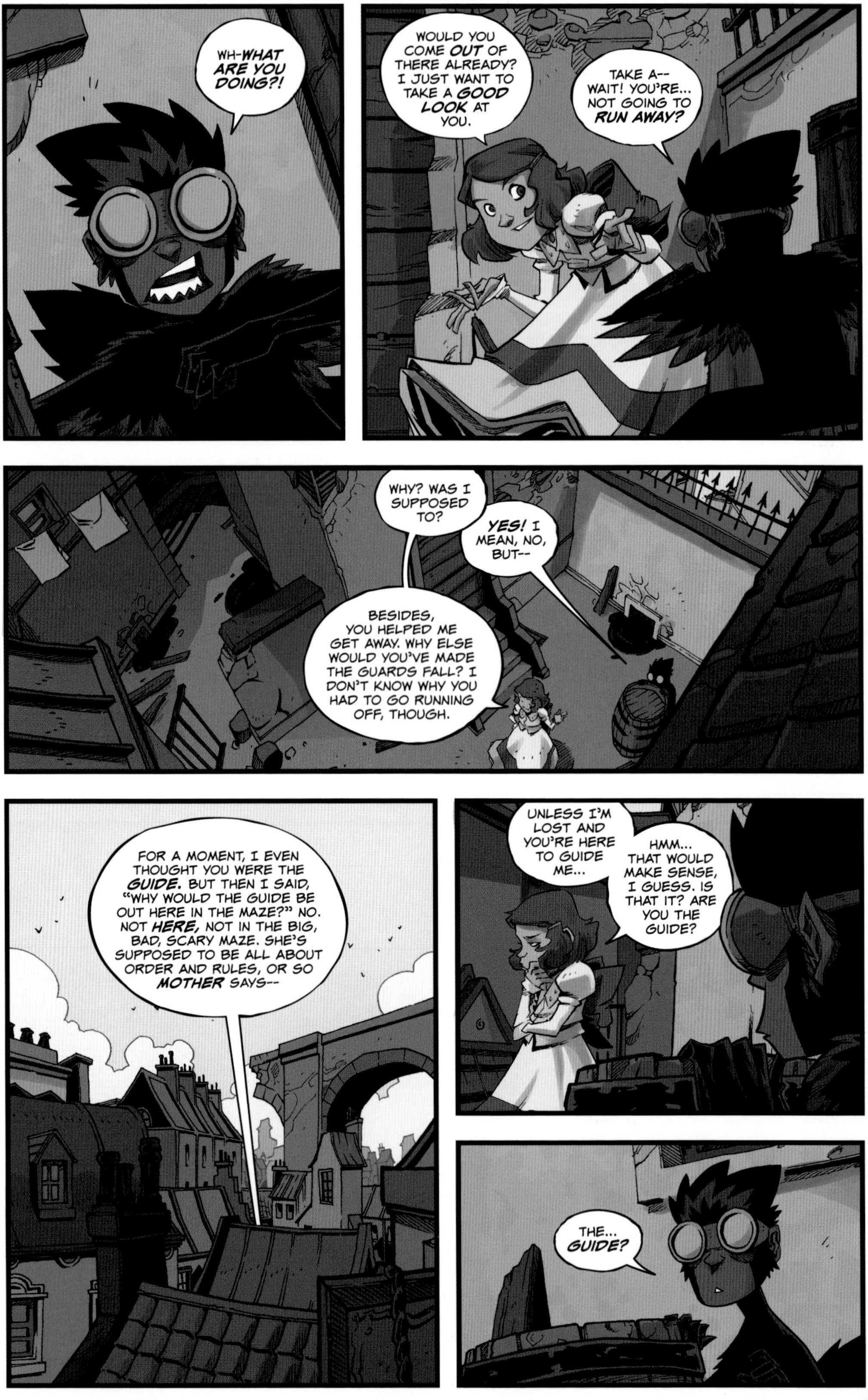
WH-WHAT ARE YOU DOING?!
WOULD YOU COME OUT OF THERE ALREADY? I JUST WANT TO TAKE A GOOD LOOK AT YOU.
TAKE A-- WAIT! YOU'RE... NOT GOING TO RUN AWAY?
WHY? WAS I SUPPOSED TO?
YES! I MEAN, NO, BUT--
BESIDES, YOU HELPED ME GET AWAY. WHY ELSE WOULD YOU'VE MADE THE GUARDS FALL? I DON'T KNOW WHY YOU HAD TO GO RUNNING OFF, THOUGH.
FOR A MOMENT, I EVEN THOUGHT YOU WERE THE GUIDE. BUT THEN I SAID, "WHY WOULD THE GUIDE BE OUT HERE IN THE MAZE?" NO. NOT HERE, NOT IN THE BIG, BAD, SCARY MAZE. SHE'S SUPPOSED TO BE ALL ABOUT ORDER AND RULES, OR SO MOTHER SAYS--
UNLESS I'M LOST AND YOU'RE HERE TO GUIDE ME...
HMM... THAT WOULD MAKE SENSE, I GUESS. IS THAT IT? ARE YOU THE GUIDE?
THE... GUIDE?

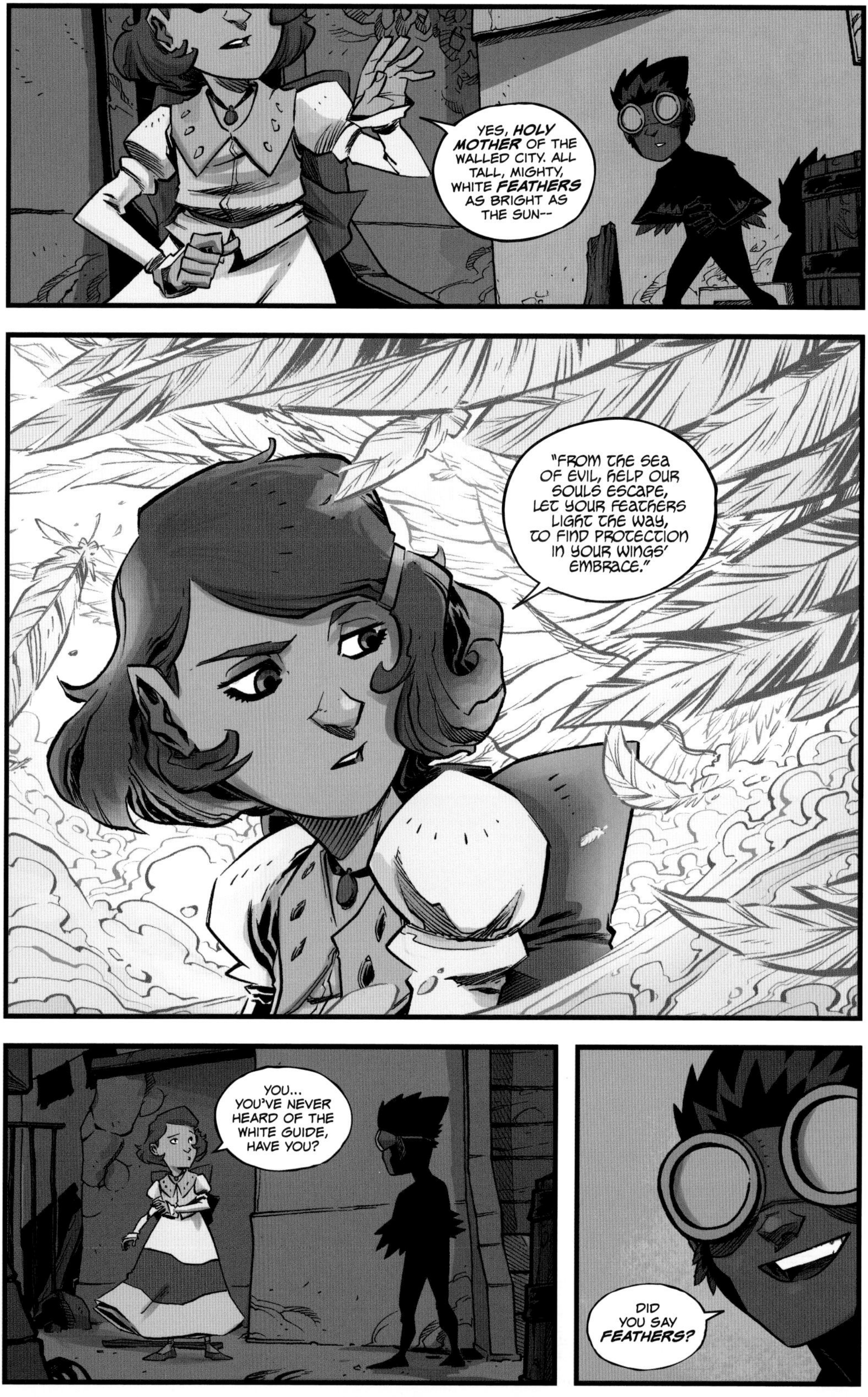
YES, HOLY MOTHER OF THE WALLED CITY. ALL TALL, MIGHTY, WHITE FEATHERS AS BRIGHT AS THE SUN--
"FROM THE SEA OF EVIL, HELP OUR SOULS ESCAPE, LET YOUR FEATHERS LIGHT THE WAY, TO FIND PROTECTION IN YOUR WINGS' EMBRACE."
YOU... YOU'VE NEVER HEARD OF THE WHITE GUIDE, HAVE YOU?
DID YOU SAY FEATHERS?

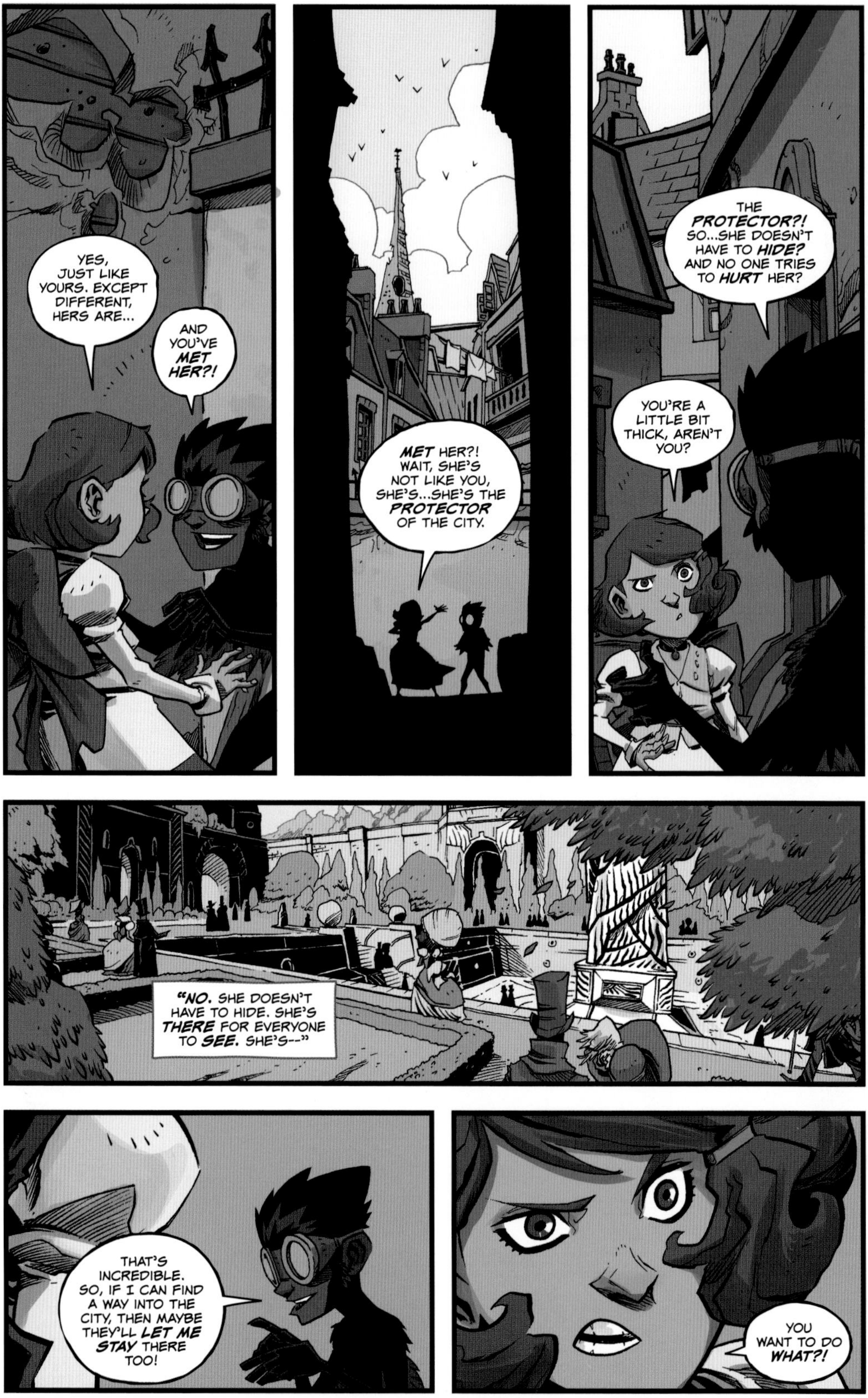
YES, JUST LIKE YOURS. EXCEPT DIFFERENT, HERS ARE...
AND YOU'VE MET HER?!
MET HER?! WAIT, SHE'S NOT LIKE YOU, SHE'S...SHE'S THE PROTECTOR OF THE CITY.
THE PROTECTOR?! SO...SHE DOESN'T HAVE TO HIDE? AND NO ONE TRIES TO HURT HER?
YOU'RE A LITTLE BIT THICK, AREN'T YOU?
"NO. SHE DOESN'T HAVE TO HIDE. SHE'S THERE FOR EVERYONE TO SEE. SHE'S--"
THAT'S INCREDIBLE. SO, IF I CAN FIND A WAY INTO THE CITY, THEN MAYBE THEY'LL LET ME STAY THERE TOO!
YOU WANT TO DO WHAT?!

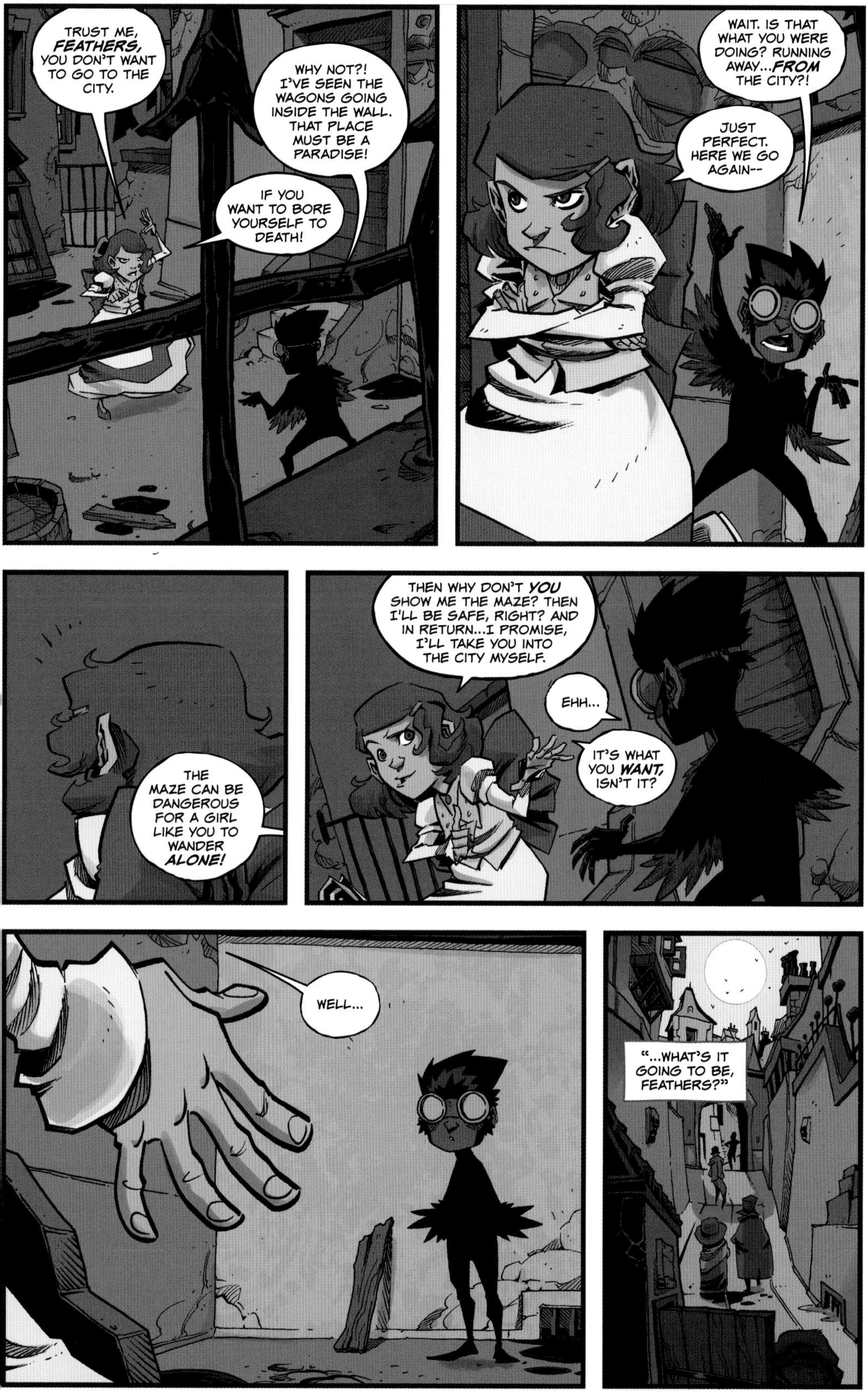
TRUST ME, FEATHERS, YOU DON'T WANT TO GO TO THE CITY.
WHY NOT?! I'VE SEEN THE WAGONS GOING INSIDE THE WALL. THAT PLACE MUST BE A PARADISE!
IF YOU WANT TO BORE YOURSELF TO DEATH!
WAIT. IS THAT WHAT YOU WERE DOING? RUNNING AWAY...FROM THE CITY?!
JUST PERFECT. HERE WE GO AGAIN--
THE MAZE CAN BE DANGEROUS FOR A GIRL LIKE YOU TO WANDER ALONE!
THEN WHY DON'T YOU SHOW ME THE MAZE? THEN I'LL BE SAFE, RIGHT? AND IN RETURN...I PROMISE, I'LL TAKE YOU INTO THE CITY MYSELF.
EHH...
IT'S WHAT YOU WANT, ISN'T IT?
WELL...
"...WHAT'S IT GOING TO BE, FEATHERS?"

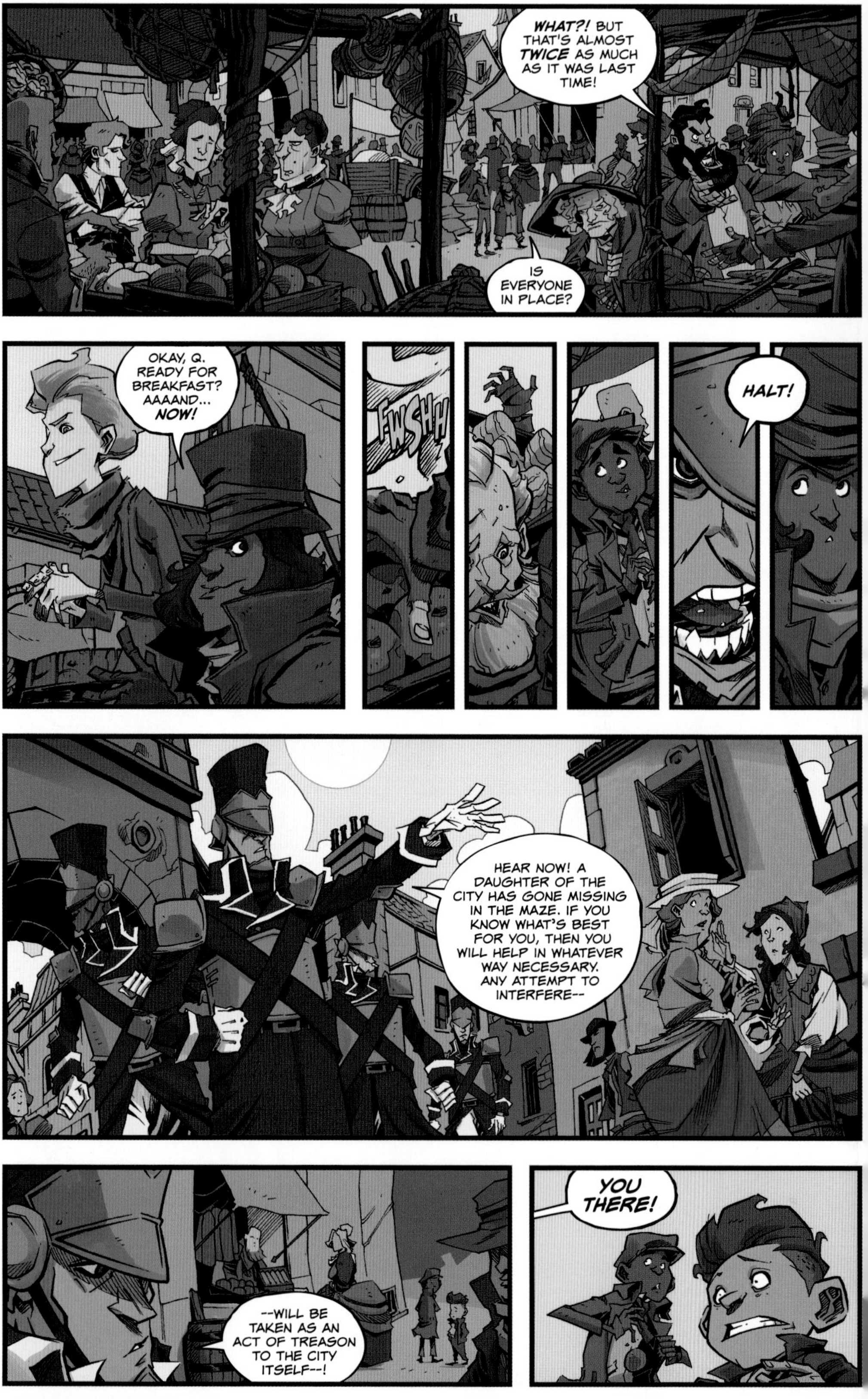
WHAT?! BUT THAT'S ALMOST TWICE AS MUCH AS IT WAS LAST TIME!
IS EVERYONE IN PLACE?
OKAY, Q. READY FOR BREAKFAST? AAAAND... NOW!
FWSHH
HALT!
HEAR NOW! A DAUGHTER OF THE CITY HAS GONE MISSING IN THE MAZE. IF YOU KNOW WHAT'S BEST FOR YOU, THEN YOU WILL HELP IN WHATEVER WAY NECESSARY. ANY ATTEMPT TO INTERFERE--
--WILL BE TAKEN AS AN ACT OF TREASON TO THE CITY ITSELF--!
YOU THERE!

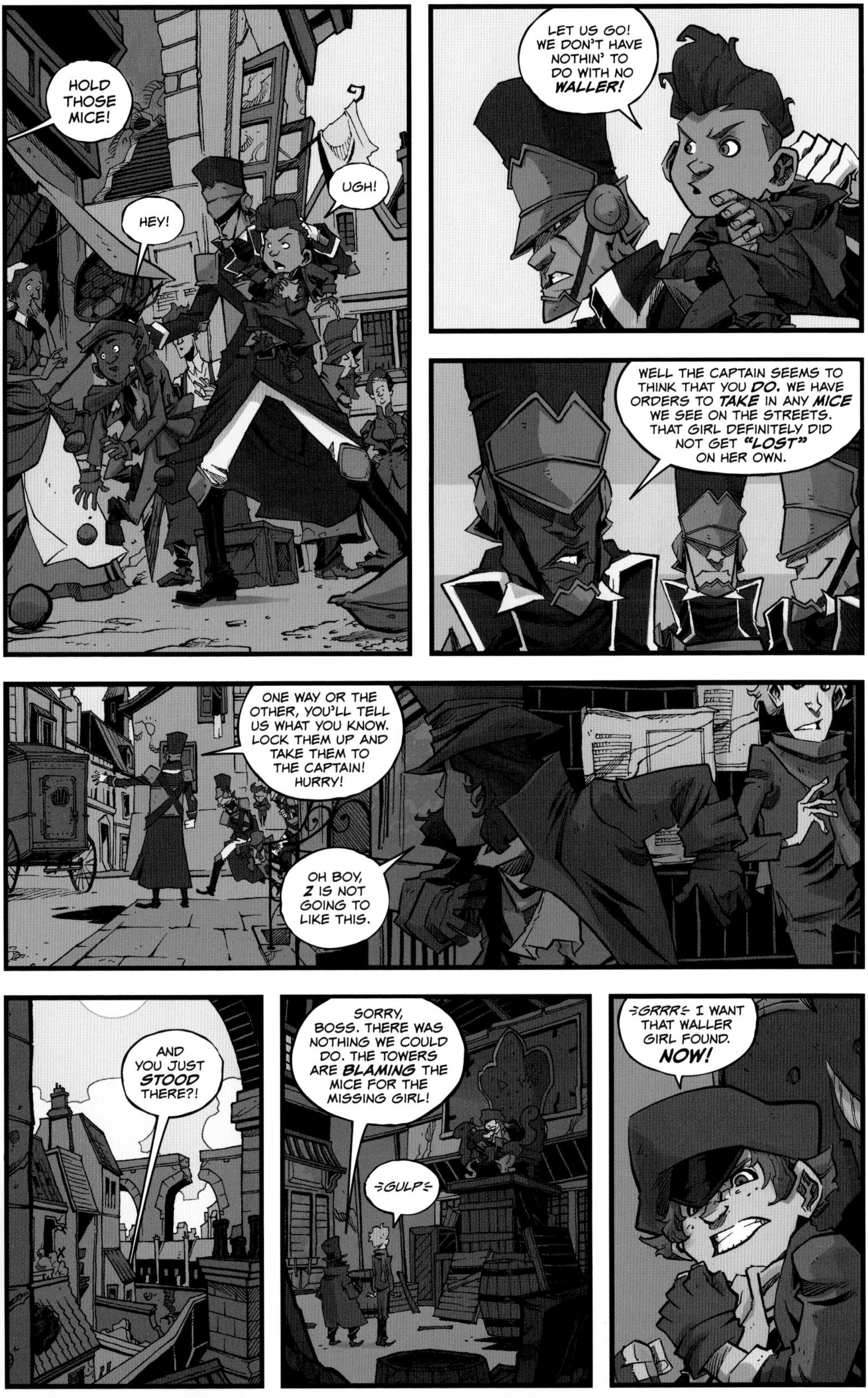
HOLD THOSE MICE!
HEY!
UGH!
LET US GO! WE DON'T HAVE NOTHIN' TO DO WITH NO WALLER!
WELL THE CAPTAIN SEEMS TO THINK THAT YOU DO. WE HAVE ORDERS TO TAKE IN ANY MICE WE SEE ON THE STREETS. THAT GIRL DEFINITELY DID NOT GET "LOST" ON HER OWN.
ONE WAY OR THE OTHER, YOU'LL TELL US WHAT YOU KNOW. LOCK THEM UP AND TAKE THEM TO THE CAPTAIN! HURRY!
OH BOY, Z IS NOT GOING TO LIKE THIS.
AND YOU JUST STOOD THERE?!
SORRY, BOSS. THERE WAS NOTHING WE COULD DO. THE TOWERS ARE BLAMING THE MICE FOR THE MISSING GIRL!
GULP
GRRR I WANT THAT WALLER GIRL FOUND. NOW!

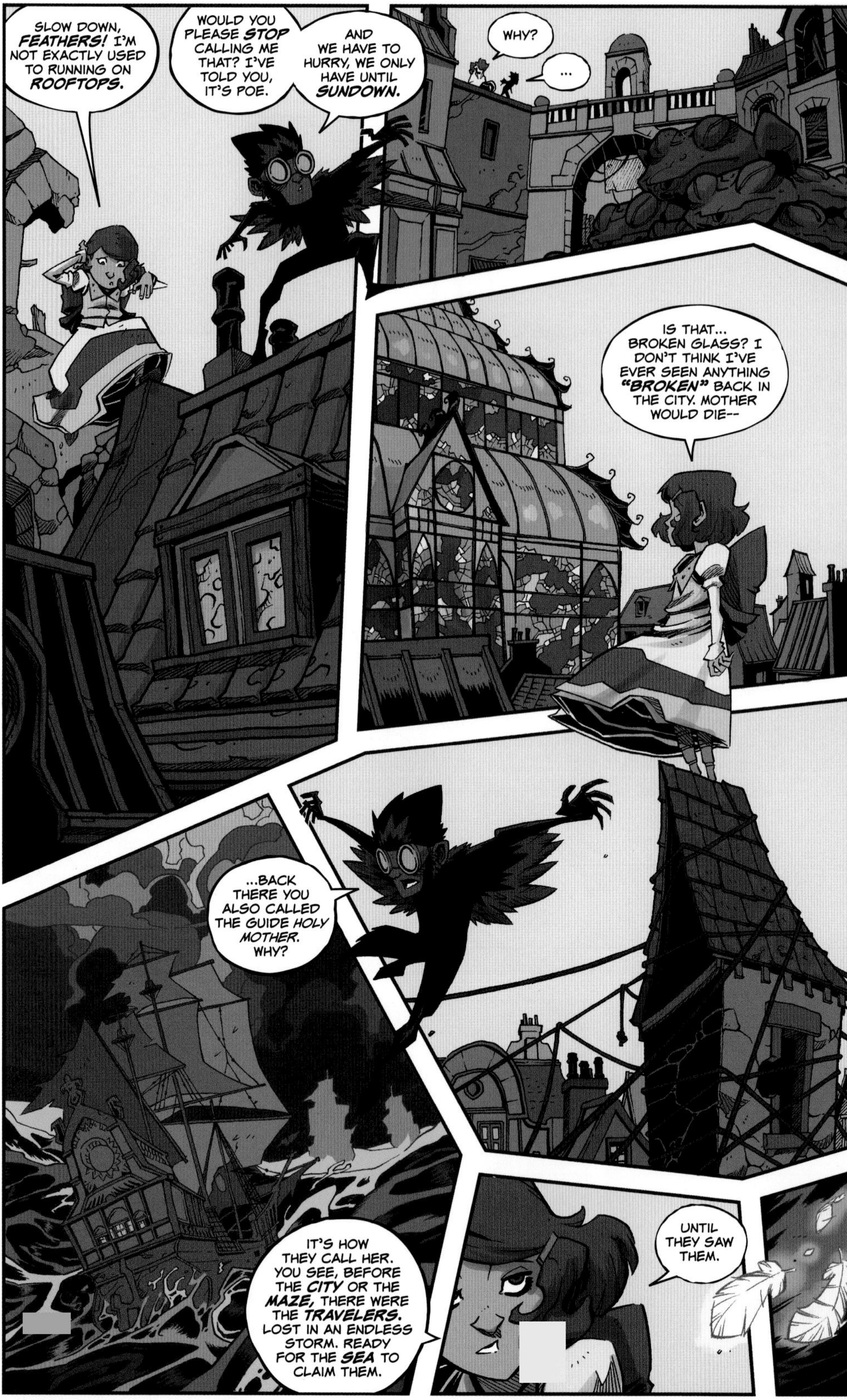
SLOW DOWN, FEATHERS! I'M NOT EXACTLY USED TO RUNNING ON ROOFTOPS.
WOULD YOU PLEASE STOP CALLING ME THAT? I'VE TOLD YOU, IT'S POE.
AND WE HAVE TO HURRY, WE ONLY HAVE UNTIL SUNDOWN.
WHY?
...
IS THAT... BROKEN GLASS? I DON'T THINK I'VE EVER SEEN ANYTHING "BROKEN" BACK IN THE CITY. MOTHER WOULD DIE--
...BACK THERE YOU ALSO CALLED THE GUIDE HOLY MOTHER. WHY?
IT'S HOW THEY CALL HER. YOU SEE, BEFORE THE CITY OR THE MAZE, THERE WERE THE TRAVELERS. LOST IN AN ENDLESS STORM. READY FOR THE SEA TO CLAIM THEM.
UNTIL THEY SAW THEM.

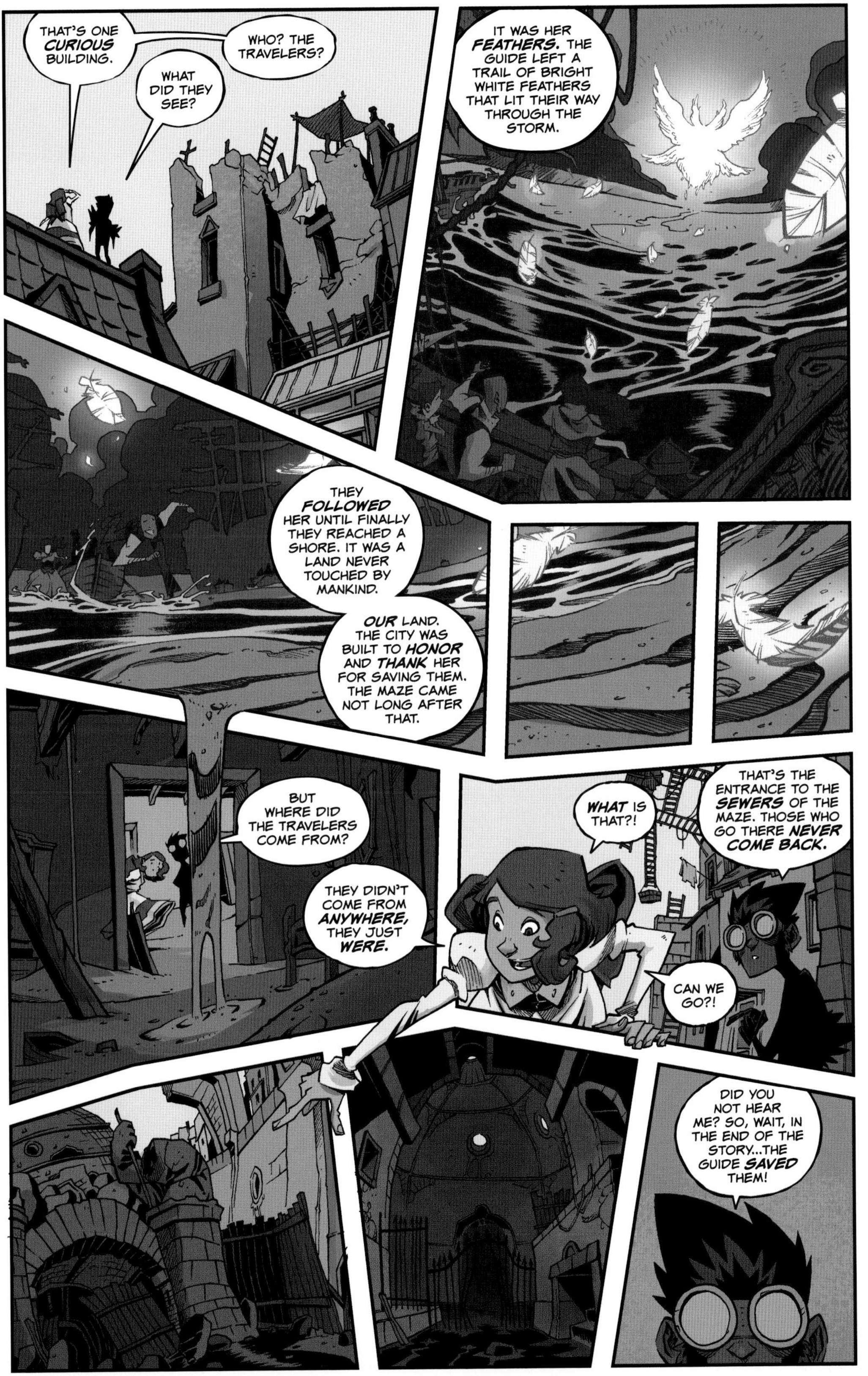
THAT'S ONE CURIOUS BUILDING.
WHO? THE TRAVELERS?
WHAT DID THEY SEE?
IT WAS HER FEATHERS. THE GUIDE LEFT A TRAIL OF BRIGHT WHITE FEATHERS THAT LIT THEIR WAY THROUGH THE STORM.
THEY FOLLOWED HER UNTIL FINALLY THEY REACHED A SHORE. IT WAS A LAND NEVER TOUCHED BY MANKIND.
OUR LAND. THE CITY WAS BUILT TO HONOR AND THANK HER FOR SAVING THEM. THE MAZE CAME NOT LONG AFTER THAT.
BUT WHERE DID THE TRAVELERS COME FROM?
THEY DIDN'T COME FROM ANYWHERE, THEY JUST WERE.
WHAT IS THAT?!
THAT'S THE ENTRANCE TO THE SEWERS OF THE MAZE. THOSE WHO GO THERE NEVER COME BACK.
CAN WE GO?!
DID YOU NOT HEAR ME? SO, WAIT, IN THE END OF THE STORY...THE GUIDE SAVED THEM!

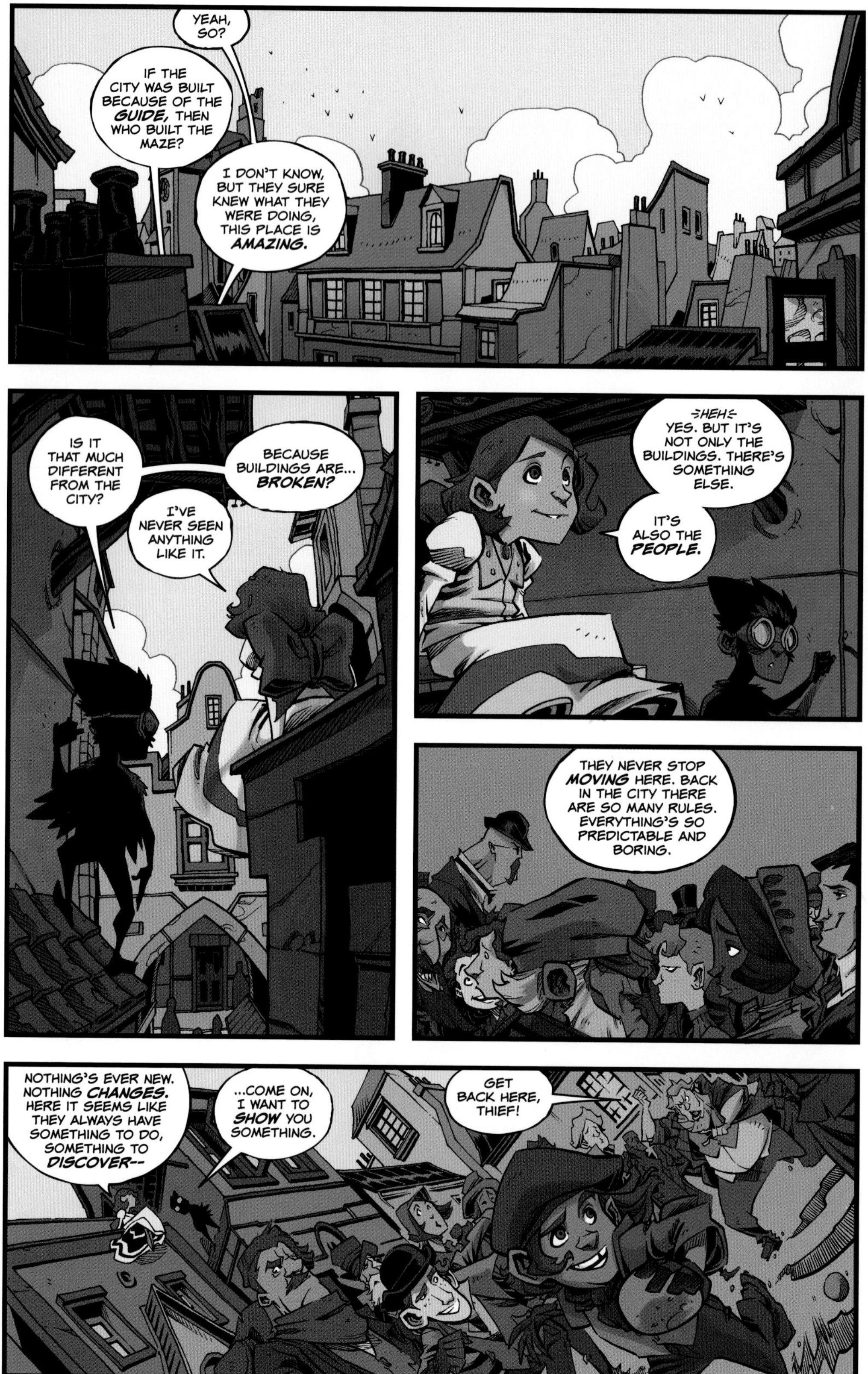
IF THE CITY WAS BUILT BECAUSE OF THE GUIDE, THEN WHO BUILT THE MAZE?
YEAH, SO?
I DON'T KNOW, BUT THEY SURE KNEW WHAT THEY WERE DOING, THIS PLACE IS AMAZING.
IS IT THAT MUCH DIFFERENT FROM THE CITY?
BECAUSE BUILDINGS ARE... BROKEN?
I'VE NEVER SEEN ANYTHING LIKE IT.
HEH
YES. BUT IT'S NOT ONLY THE BUILDINGS. THERE'S SOMETHING ELSE.
IT'S ALSO THE PEOPLE.
THEY NEVER STOP MOVING HERE. BACK IN THE CITY THERE ARE SO MANY RULES. EVERYTHING'S SO PREDICTABLE AND BORING.
NOTHING'S EVER NEW. NOTHING CHANGES. HERE IT SEEMS LIKE THEY ALWAYS HAVE SOMETHING TO DO, SOMETHING TO DISCOVER--
...COME ON, I WANT TO SHOW YOU SOMETHING.
GET BACK HERE, THIEF!

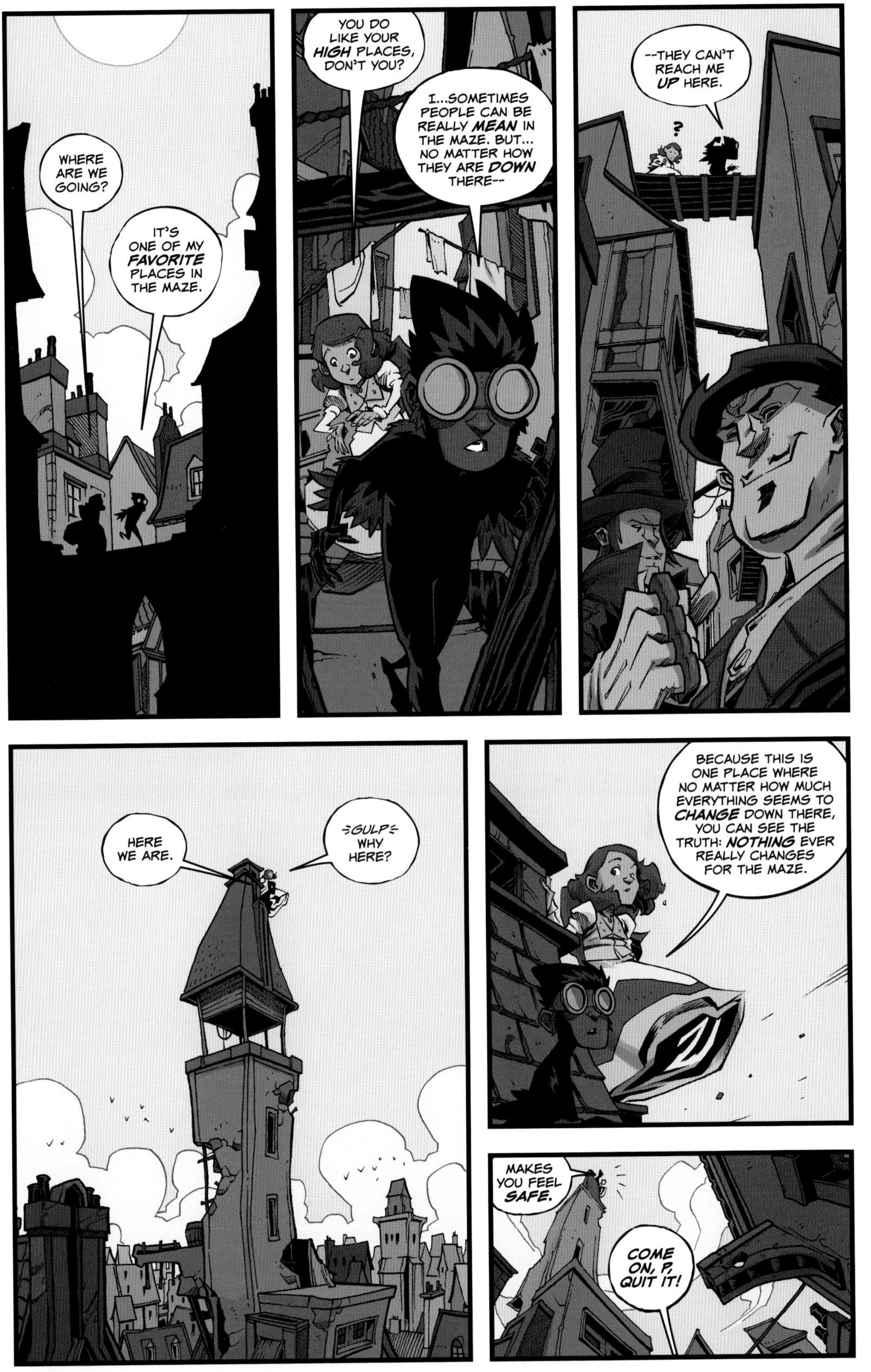
WHERE ARE WE GOING?
IT'S ONE OF MY FAVORITE PLACES IN THE MAZE.
YOU DO LIKE YOUR HIGH PLACES, DON'T YOU?
I...SOMETIMES PEOPLE CAN BE REALLY MEAN IN THE MAZE. BUT... NO MATTER HOW THEY ARE DOWN THERE--
--THEY CAN'T REACH ME UP HERE.
?
HERE WE ARE.
GULP WHY HERE?
BECAUSE THIS IS ONE PLACE WHERE NO MATTER HOW MUCH EVERYTHING SEEMS TO CHANGE DOWN THERE, YOU CAN SEE THE TRUTH: NOTHING EVER REALLY CHANGES FOR THE MAZE.
MAKES YOU FEEL SAFE.
COME ON, P, QUIT IT!

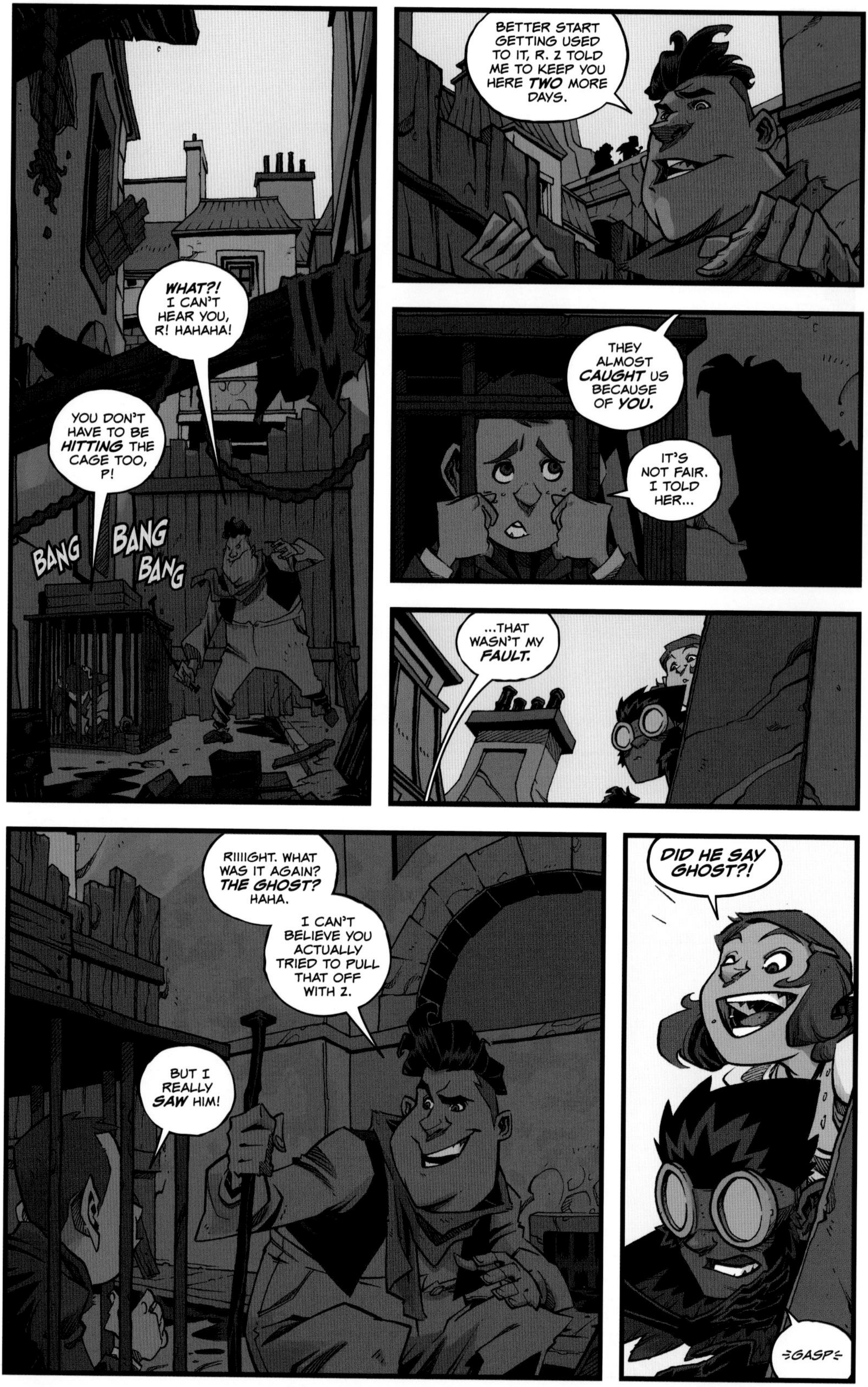
WHAT?! I CAN'T HEAR YOU, R! HAHAHA!
YOU DON'T HAVE TO BE HITTING THE CAGE TOO, P!
BANG
BANG
BANG
BETTER START GETTING USED TO IT, R. Z TOLD ME TO KEEP YOU HERE TWO MORE DAYS.
THEY ALMOST CAUGHT US BECAUSE OF YOU.
IT'S NOT FAIR. I TOLD HER...
...THAT WASN'T MY FAULT.
RIIIIGHT. WHAT WAS IT AGAIN? THE GHOST? HAHA.
I CAN'T BELIEVE YOU ACTUALLY TRIED TO PULL THAT OFF WITH Z.
BUT I REALLY SAW HIM!
DID HE SAY GHOST?!
GASP

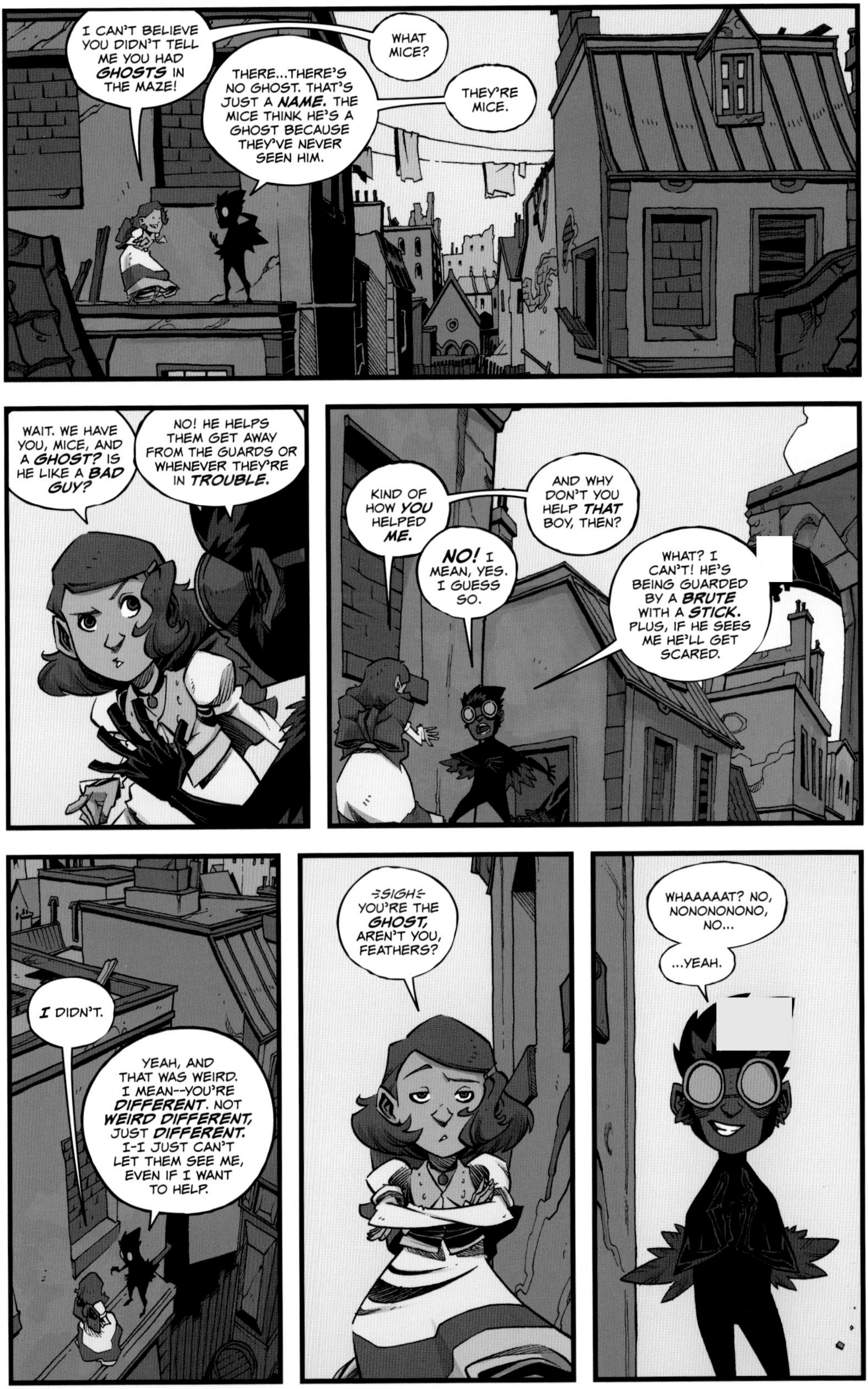

I CAN'T BELIEVE YOU DIDN'T TELL ME YOU HAD GHOSTS IN THE MAZE!
THERE...THERE'S NO GHOST. THAT'S JUST A NAME. THE MICE THINK HE'S A GHOST BECAUSE THEY'VE NEVER SEEN HIM.
WHAT MICE?
THEY'RE MICE.
WAIT. WE HAVE YOU, MICE, AND A GHOST? IS HE LIKE A BAD GUY?
NO! HE HELPS THEM GET AWAY FROM THE GUARDS OR WHENEVER THEY'RE IN TROUBLE.
KIND OF HOW YOU HELPED ME.
NO! I MEAN, YES. I GUESS SO.
AND WHY DON'T YOU HELP THAT BOY, THEN?
WHAT? I CAN'T! HE'S BEING GUARDED BY A BRUTE WITH A STICK. PLUS, IF HE SEES ME HE'LL GET SCARED.
I DIDN'T.
YEAH, AND THAT WAS WEIRD. I MEAN--YOU'RE DIFFERENT. NOT WEIRD DIFFERENT, JUST DIFFERENT. I-I JUST CAN'T LET THEM SEE ME, EVEN IF I WANT TO HELP.
=SIGH= YOU'RE THE GHOST, AREN'T YOU, FEATHERS?
WHAAAAAT? NO, NONONONONO, NO...
...YEAH.

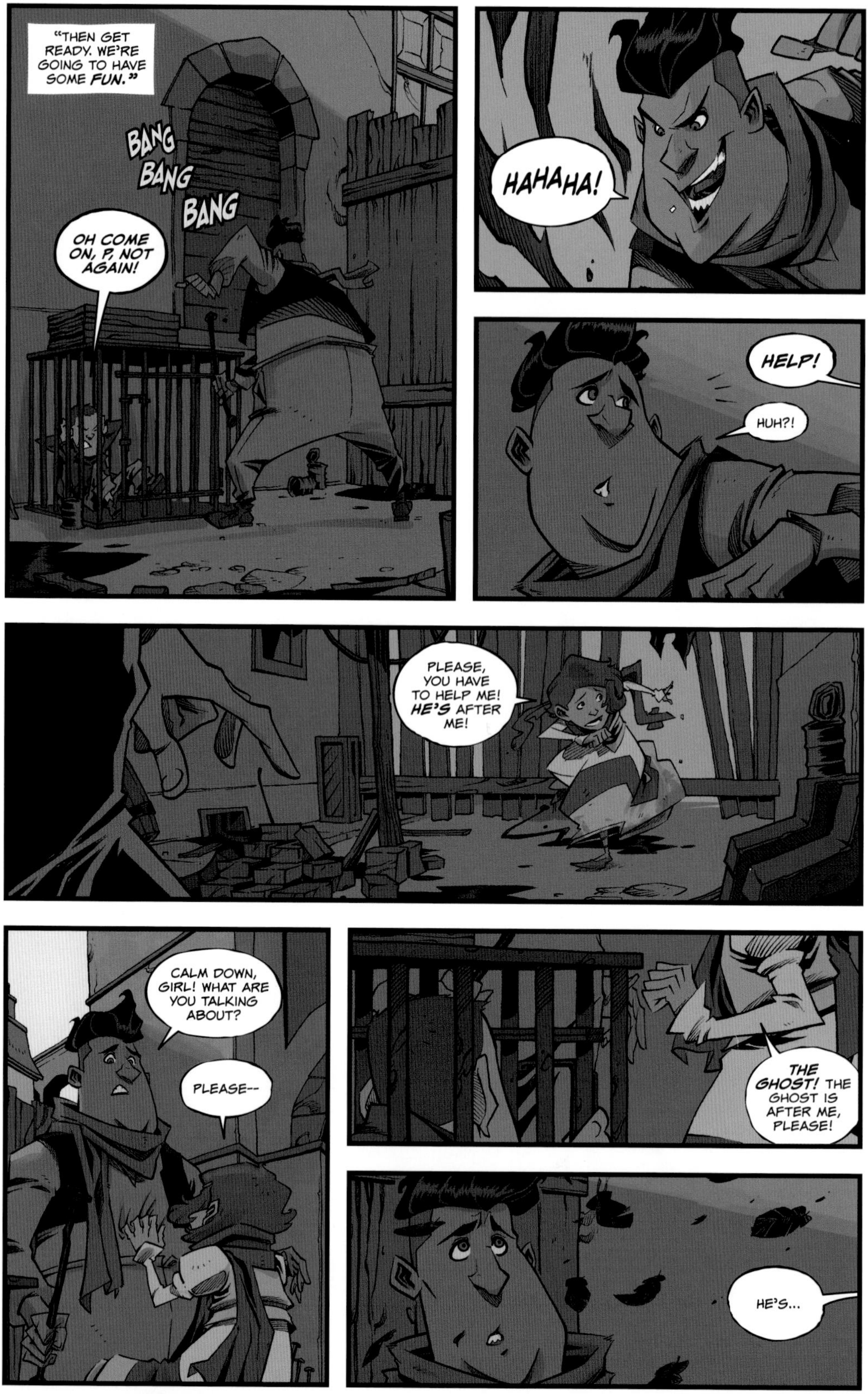
"THEN GET READY. WE'RE GOING TO HAVE SOME FUN."
BANG
BANG
BANG
OH COME ON, P, NOT AGAIN!
HAHAHA!
HELP!
HUH?!
PLEASE, YOU HAVE TO HELP ME! HE'S AFTER ME!
CALM DOWN, GIRL! WHAT ARE YOU TALKING ABOUT?
PLEASE--
THE GHOST! THE GHOST IS AFTER ME, PLEASE!
HE'S...

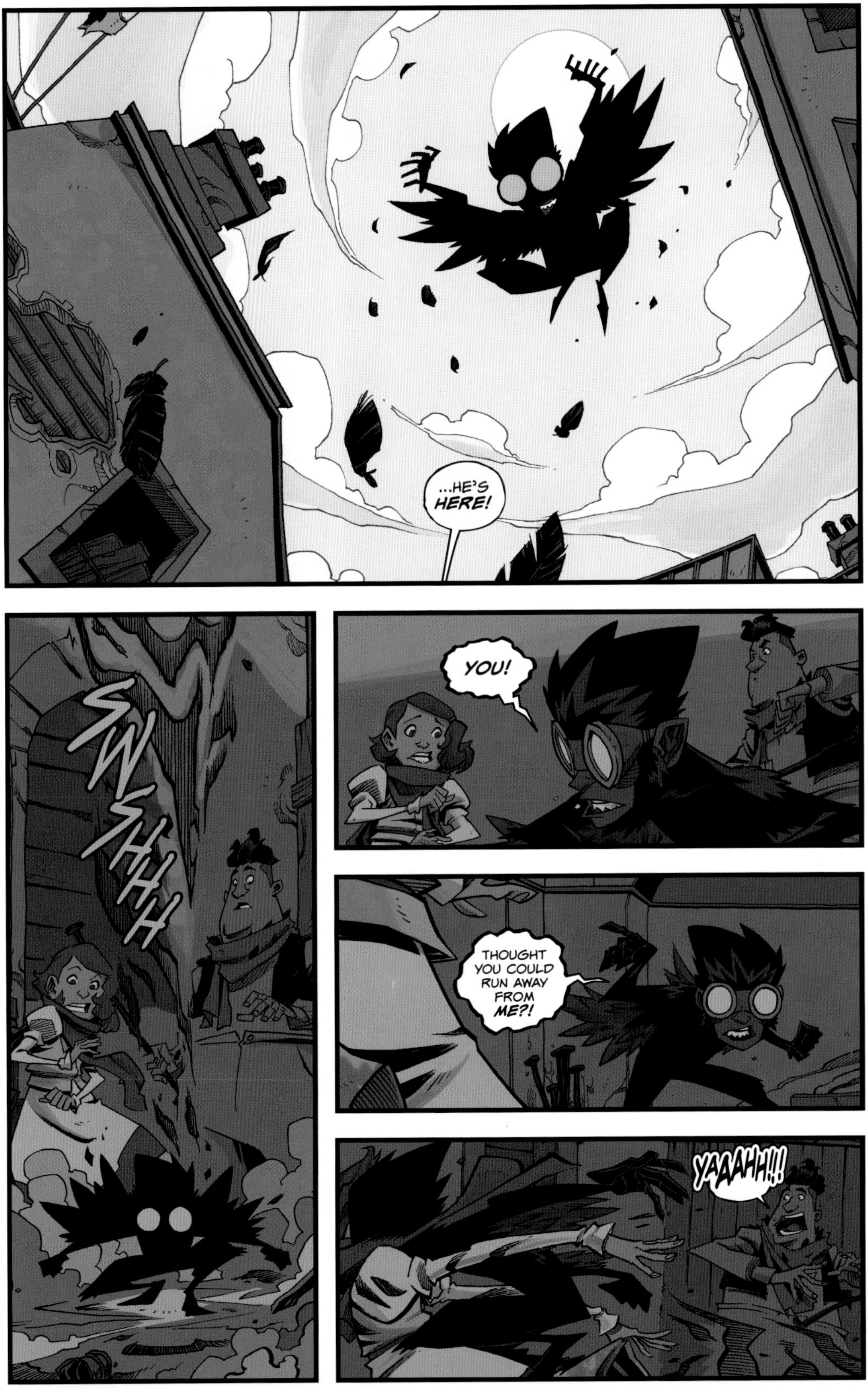
...HE'S HERE!
SWSHHH
YOU!
THOUGHT YOU COULD RUN AWAY FROM ME?!
YAAAHH!!!

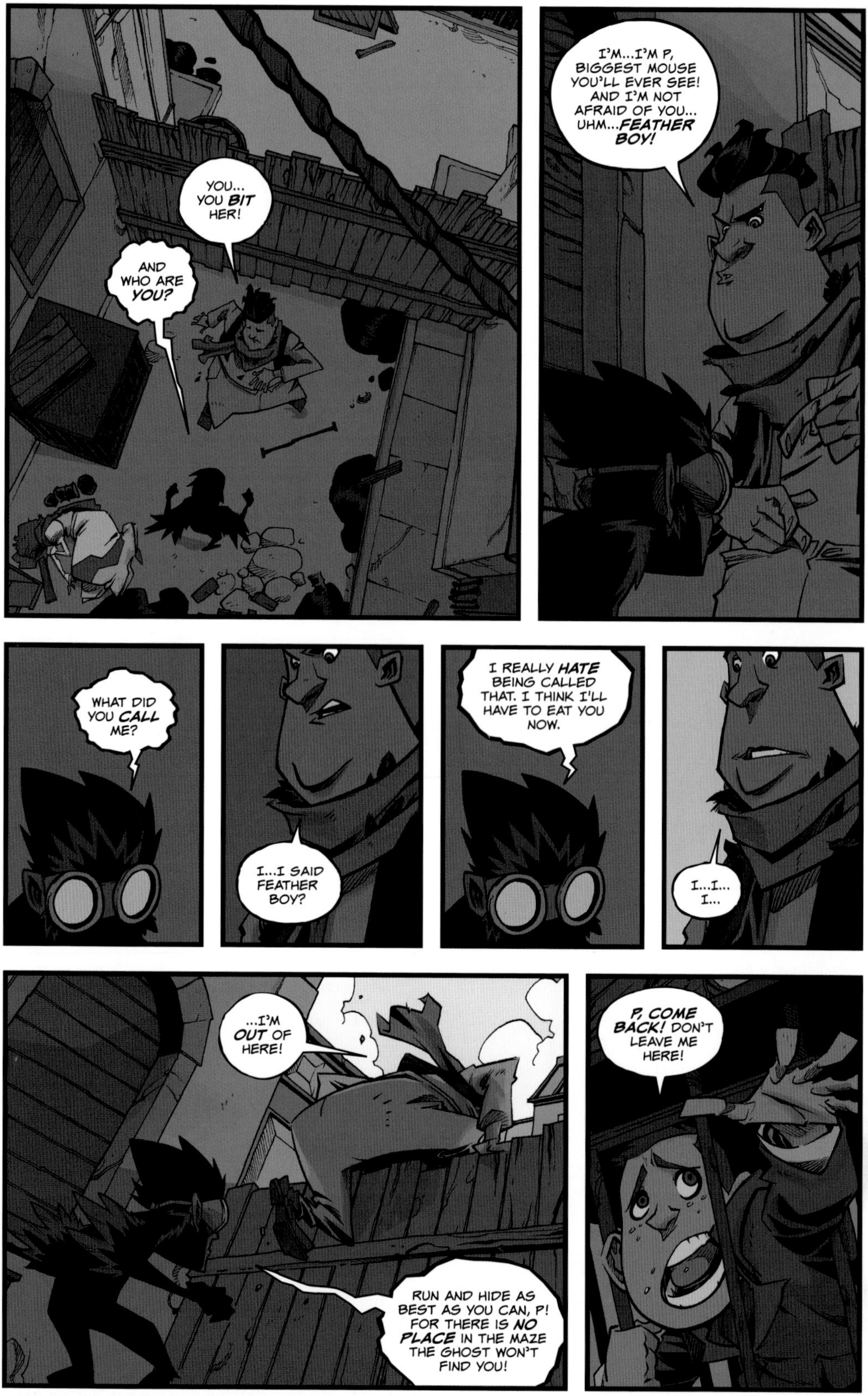
YOU... YOU BIT HER!
AND WHO ARE YOU?
I'M...I'M P, BIGGEST MOUSE YOU'LL EVER SEE! AND I'M NOT AFRAID OF YOU... UHM...FEATHER BOY!
WHAT DID YOU CALL ME?
I...I SAID FEATHER BOY?
I REALLY HATE BEING CALLED THAT. I THINK I'LL HAVE TO EAT YOU NOW.
I...I... I...
...I'M OUT OF HERE!
RUN AND HIDE AS BEST AS YOU CAN, P! FOR THERE IS NO PLACE IN THE MAZE THE GHOST WON'T FIND YOU!
P, COME BACK! DON'T LEAVE ME HERE!

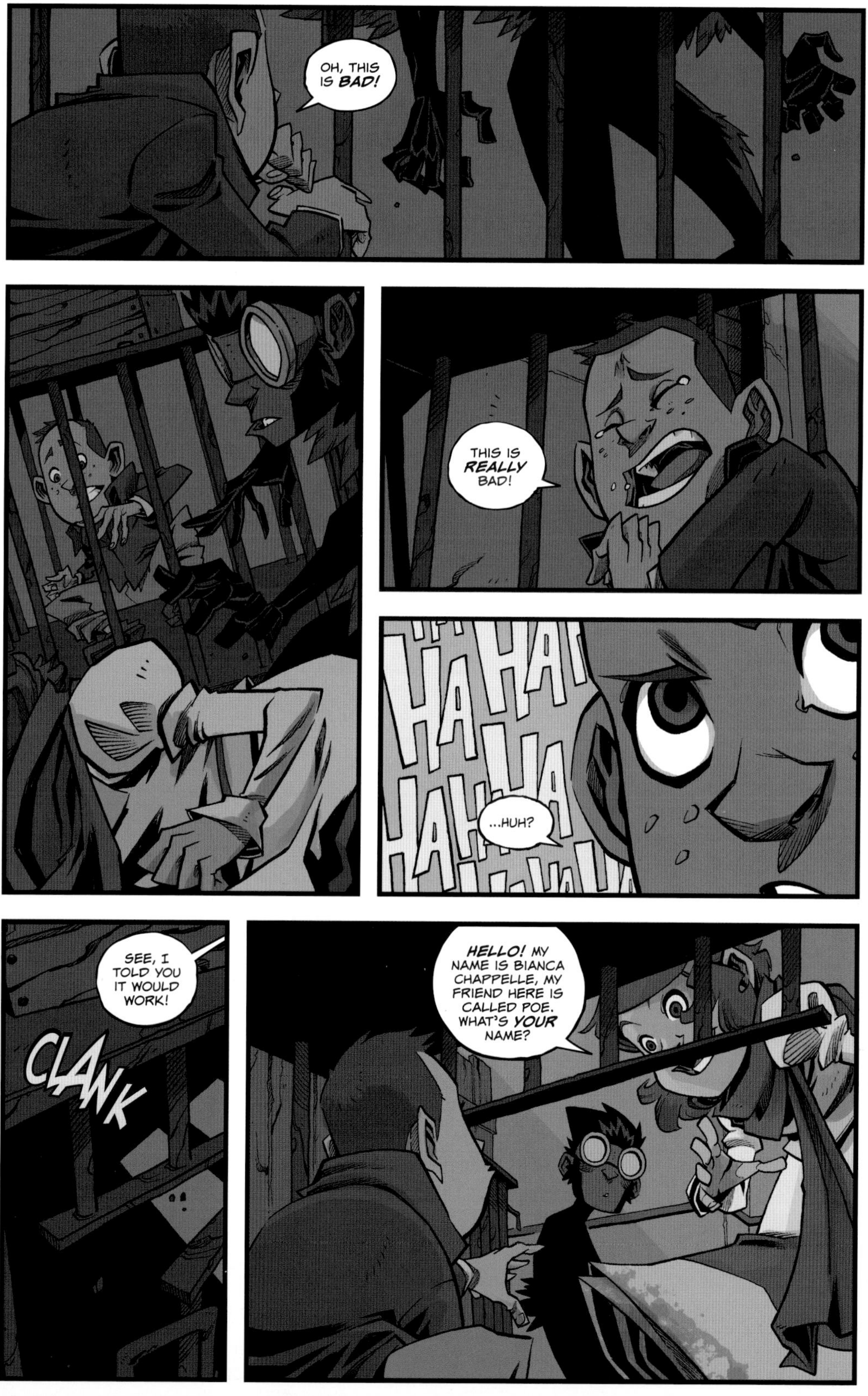
OH, THIS IS BAD!
THIS IS REALLY BAD!
HA HA HA HA HA HA HA HA HA
...HUH?
SEE, I TOLD YOU IT WOULD WORK!
CLANK
HELLO! MY NAME IS BIANCA CHAPPELLE, MY FRIEND HERE IS CALLED POE. WHAT'S YOUR NAME?

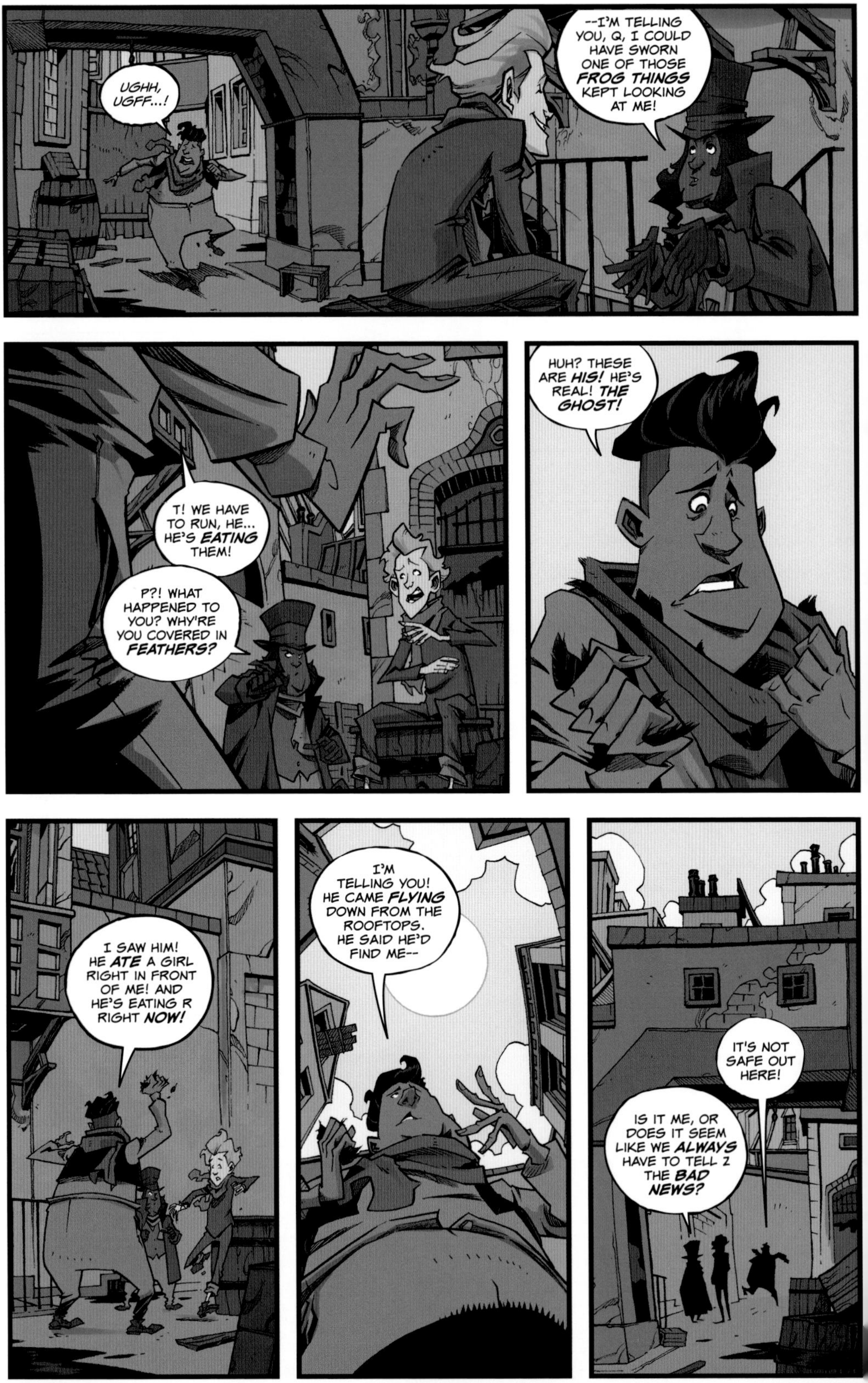
UGHH, UGFF...!
--I'M TELLING YOU, Q, I COULD HAVE SWORN ONE OF THOSE FROG THINGS KEPT LOOKING AT ME!
T! WE HAVE TO RUN, HE... HE'S EATING THEM!
P?! WHAT HAPPENED TO YOU? WHY'RE YOU COVERED IN FEATHERS?
HUH? THESE ARE HIS! HE'S REAL! THE GHOST!
I SAW HIM! HE ATE A GIRL RIGHT IN FRONT OF ME! AND HE'S EATING R RIGHT NOW!
I'M TELLING YOU! HE CAME FLYING DOWN FROM THE ROOFTOPS. HE SAID HE'D FIND ME--
IT'S NOT SAFE OUT HERE!
IS IT ME, OR DOES IT SEEM LIKE WE ALWAYS HAVE TO TELL Z THE BAD NEWS?

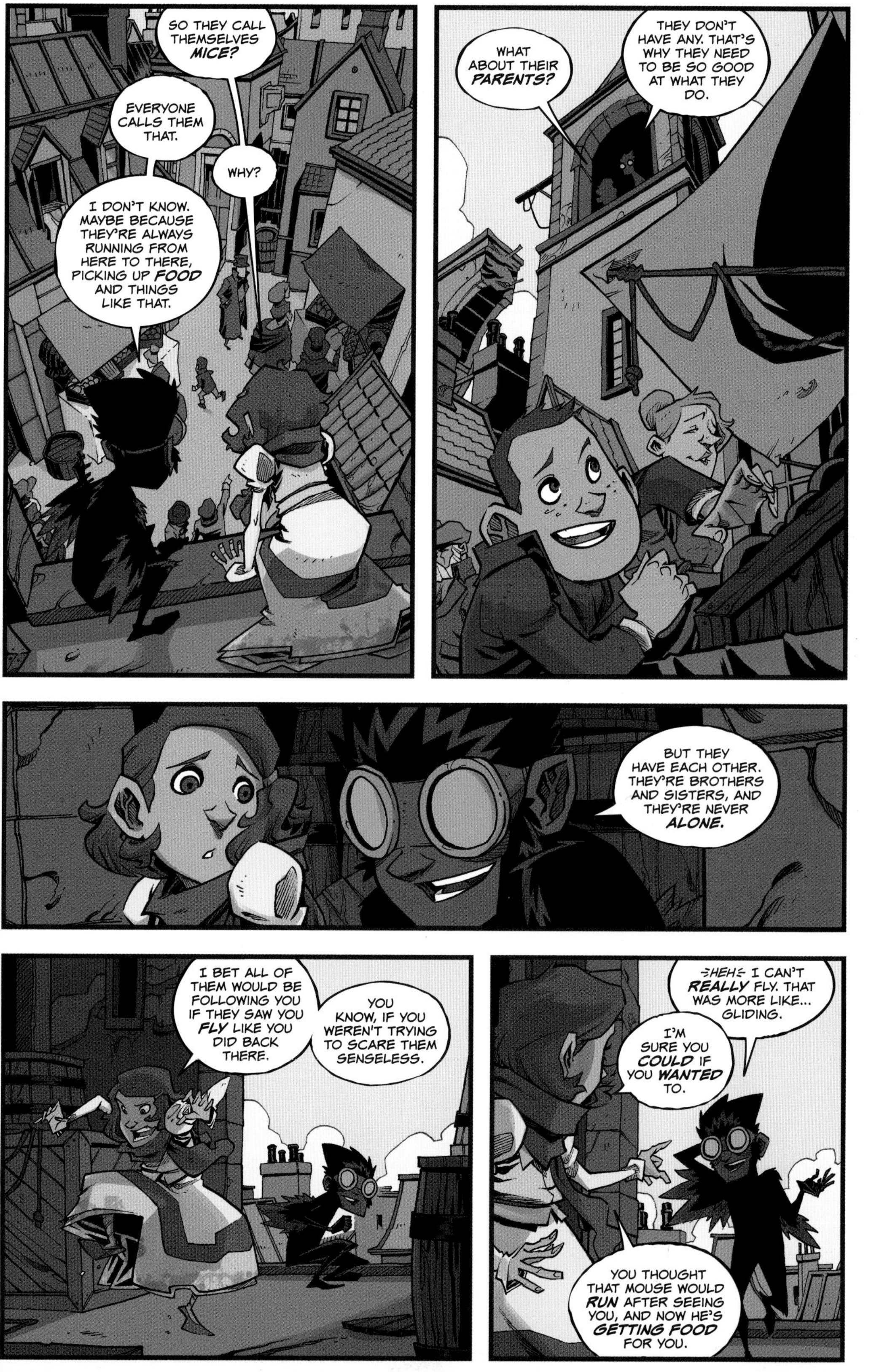

SO THEY CALL THEMSELVES MICE?
EVERYONE CALLS THEM THAT.
WHY?
I DON'T KNOW. MAYBE BECAUSE THEY'RE ALWAYS RUNNING FROM HERE TO THERE, PICKING UP FOOD AND THINGS LIKE THAT.
WHAT ABOUT THEIR PARENTS?
THEY DON'T HAVE ANY. THAT'S WHY THEY NEED TO BE SO GOOD AT WHAT THEY DO.
BUT THEY HAVE EACH OTHER. THEY'RE BROTHERS AND SISTERS, AND THEY'RE NEVER ALONE.
I BET ALL OF THEM WOULD BE FOLLOWING YOU IF THEY SAW YOU FLY LIKE YOU DID BACK THERE.
YOU KNOW, IF YOU WEREN'T TRYING TO SCARE THEM SENSELESS.
=HEH= I CAN'T REALLY FLY. THAT WAS MORE LIKE... GLIDING.
I'M SURE YOU COULD IF YOU WANTED TO.
YOU THOUGHT THAT MOUSE WOULD RUN AFTER SEEING YOU, AND NOW HE'S GETTING FOOD FOR YOU.

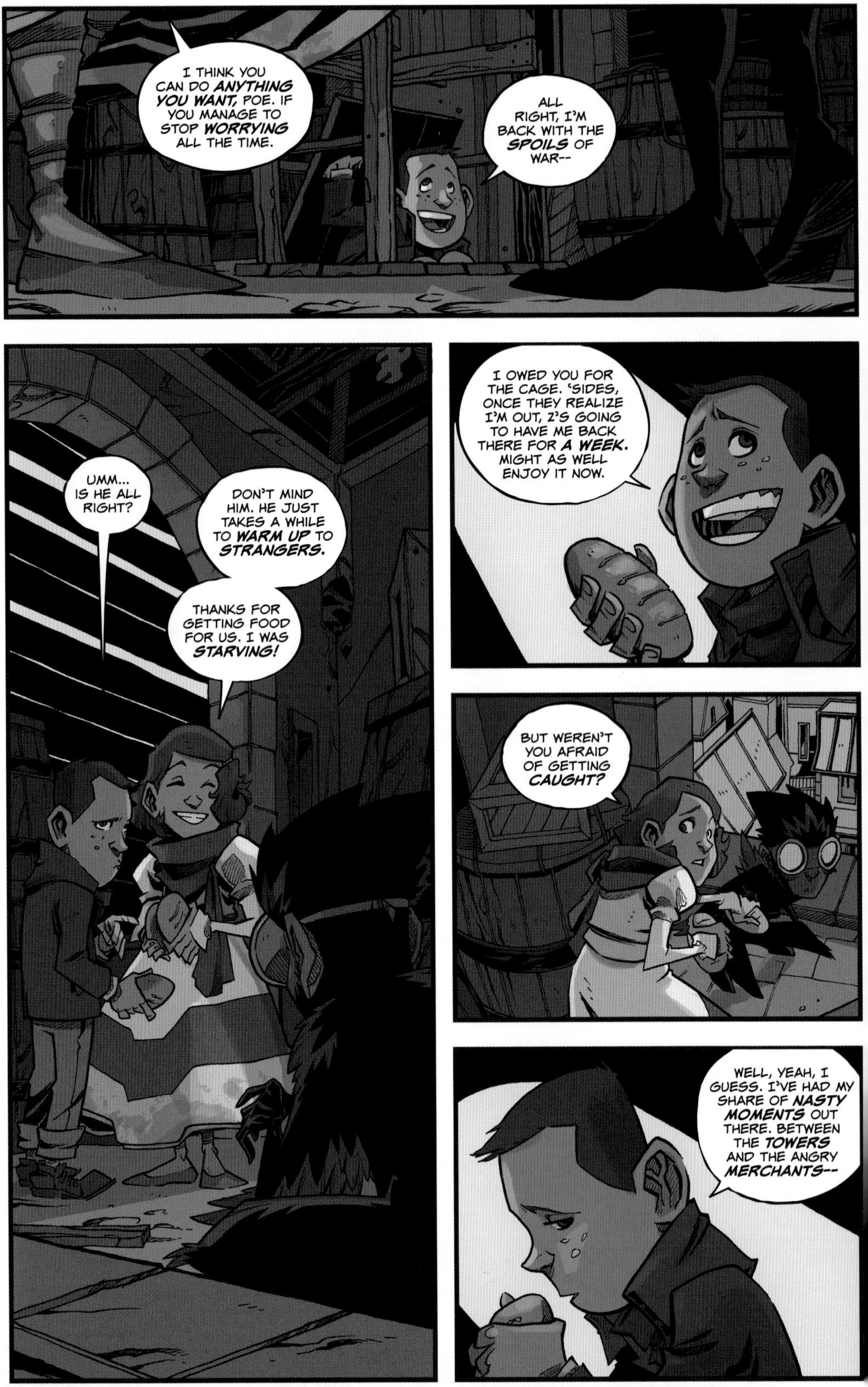
I THINK YOU CAN DO ANYTHING YOU WANT, POE. IF YOU MANAGE TO STOP WORRYING ALL THE TIME.
ALL RIGHT, I'M BACK WITH THE SPOILS OF WAR--
UMM... IS HE ALL RIGHT?
DON'T MIND HIM. HE JUST TAKES A WHILE TO WARM UP TO STRANGERS.
THANKS FOR GETTING FOOD FOR US. I WAS STARVING!
I OWED YOU FOR THE CAGE. 'SIDES, ONCE THEY REALIZE I'M OUT, Z'S GOING TO HAVE ME BACK THERE FOR A WEEK. MIGHT AS WELL ENJOY IT NOW.
BUT WEREN'T YOU AFRAID OF GETTING CAUGHT?
WELL, YEAH, I GUESS. I'VE HAD MY SHARE OF NASTY MOMENTS OUT THERE. BETWEEN THE TOWERS AND THE ANGRY MERCHANTS--

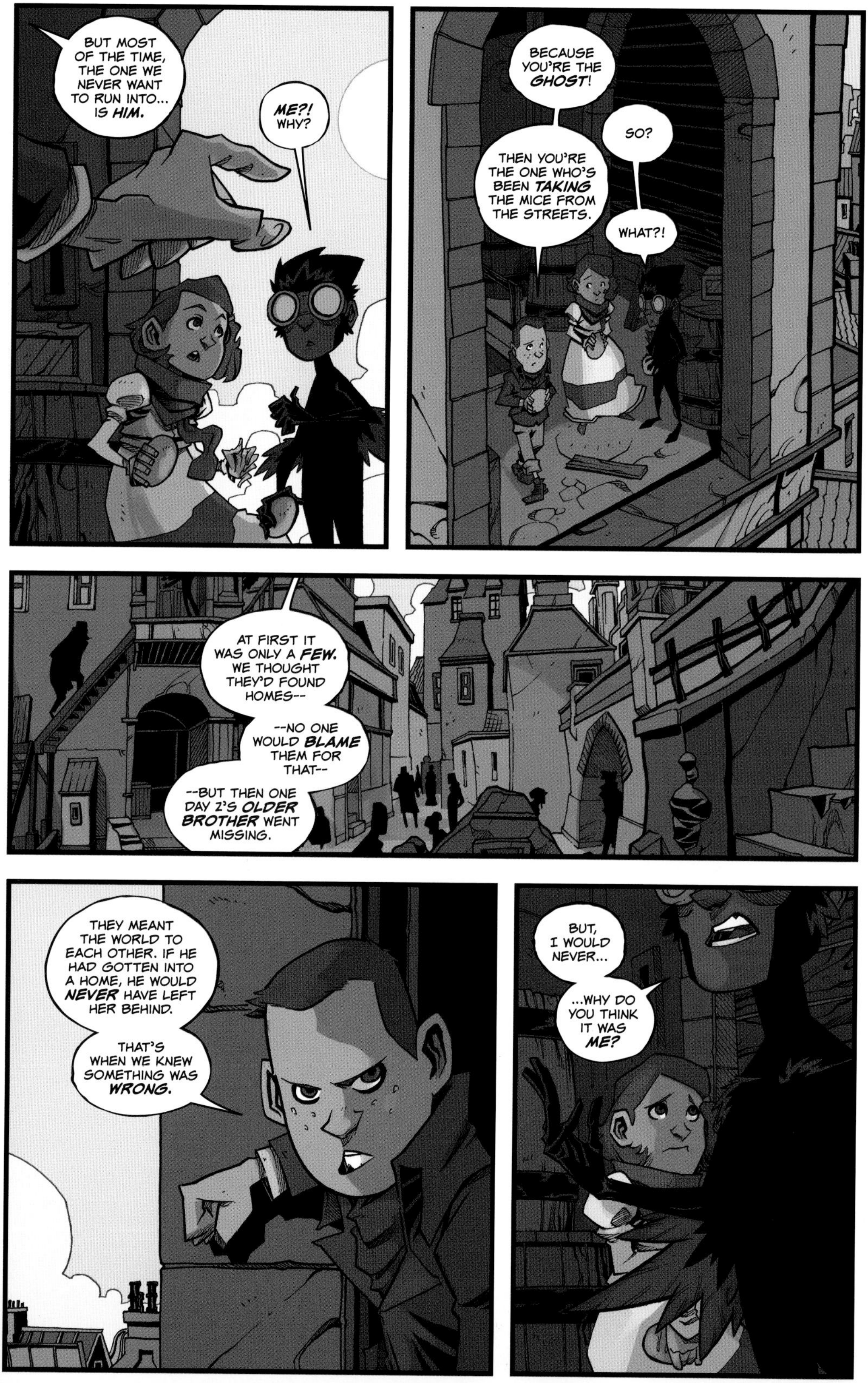
BUT MOST OF THE TIME, THE ONE WE NEVER WANT TO RUN INTO... IS HIM.
ME?! WHY?
BECAUSE YOU'RE THE GHOST!
THEN YOU'RE THE ONE WHO'S BEEN TAKING THE MICE FROM THE STREETS.
SO?
WHAT?!
AT FIRST IT WAS ONLY A FEW. WE THOUGHT THEY'D FOUND HOMES--
--NO ONE WOULD BLAME THEM FOR THAT--
--BUT THEN ONE DAY Z'S OLDER BROTHER WENT MISSING.
THEY MEANT THE WORLD TO EACH OTHER. IF HE HAD GOTTEN INTO A HOME, HE WOULD NEVER HAVE LEFT HER BEHIND.
THAT'S WHEN WE KNEW SOMETHING WAS WRONG.
BUT, I WOULD NEVER...
...WHY DO YOU THINK IT WAS ME?

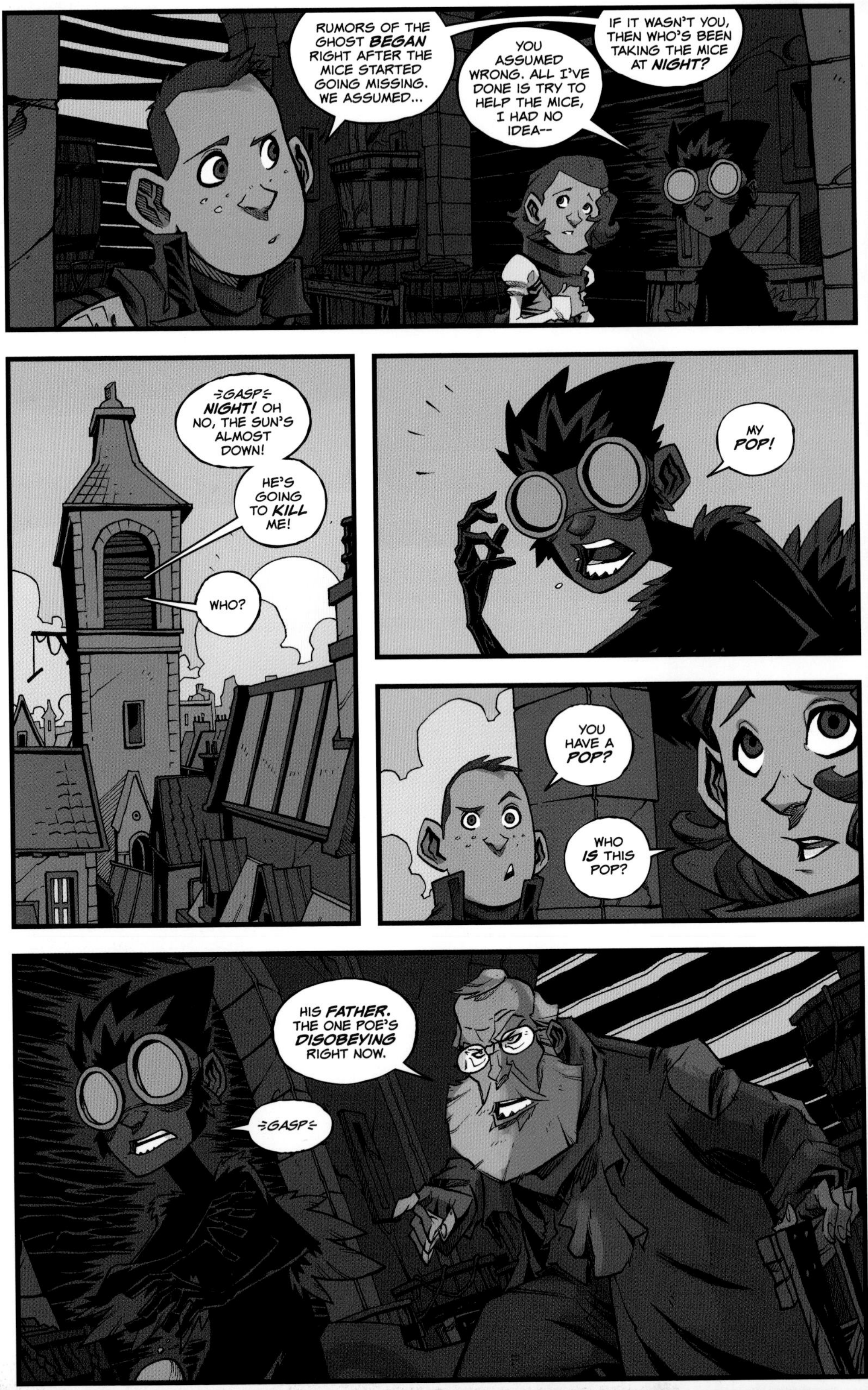
RUMORS OF THE GHOST BEGAN RIGHT AFTER THE MICE STARTED GOING MISSING. WE ASSUMED...
YOU ASSUMED WRONG. ALL I'VE DONE IS TRY TO HELP THE MICE, I HAD NO IDEA--
IF IT WASN'T YOU, THEN WHO'S BEEN TAKING THE MICE AT NIGHT?
GASP NIGHT! OH NO, THE SUN'S ALMOST DOWN!
HE'S GOING TO KILL ME!
WHO?
MY POP!
YOU HAVE A POP?
WHO IS THIS POP?
HIS FATHER. THE ONE POE'S DISOBEYING RIGHT NOW.
GASP

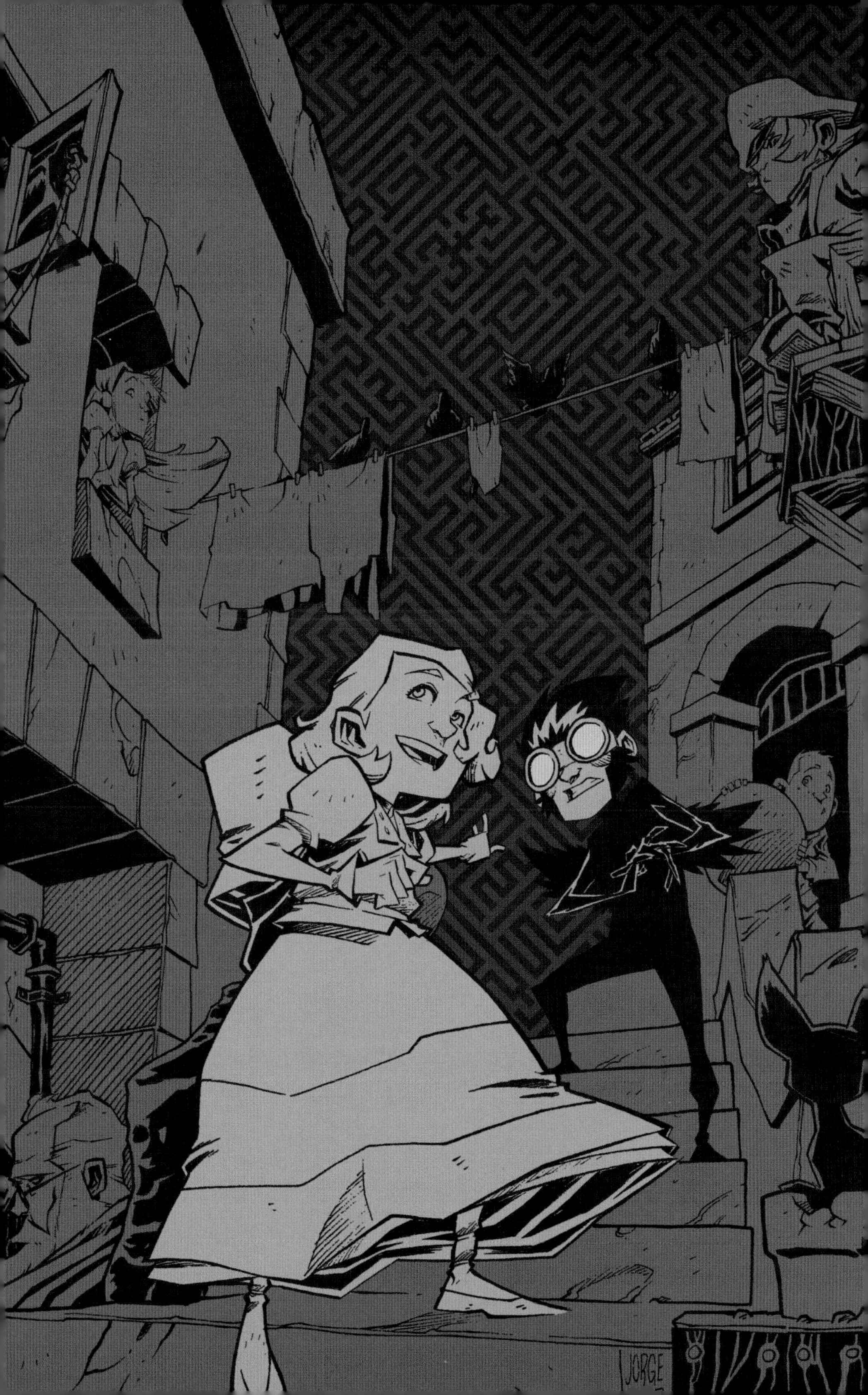
JORGE

CHAPTER
THREE

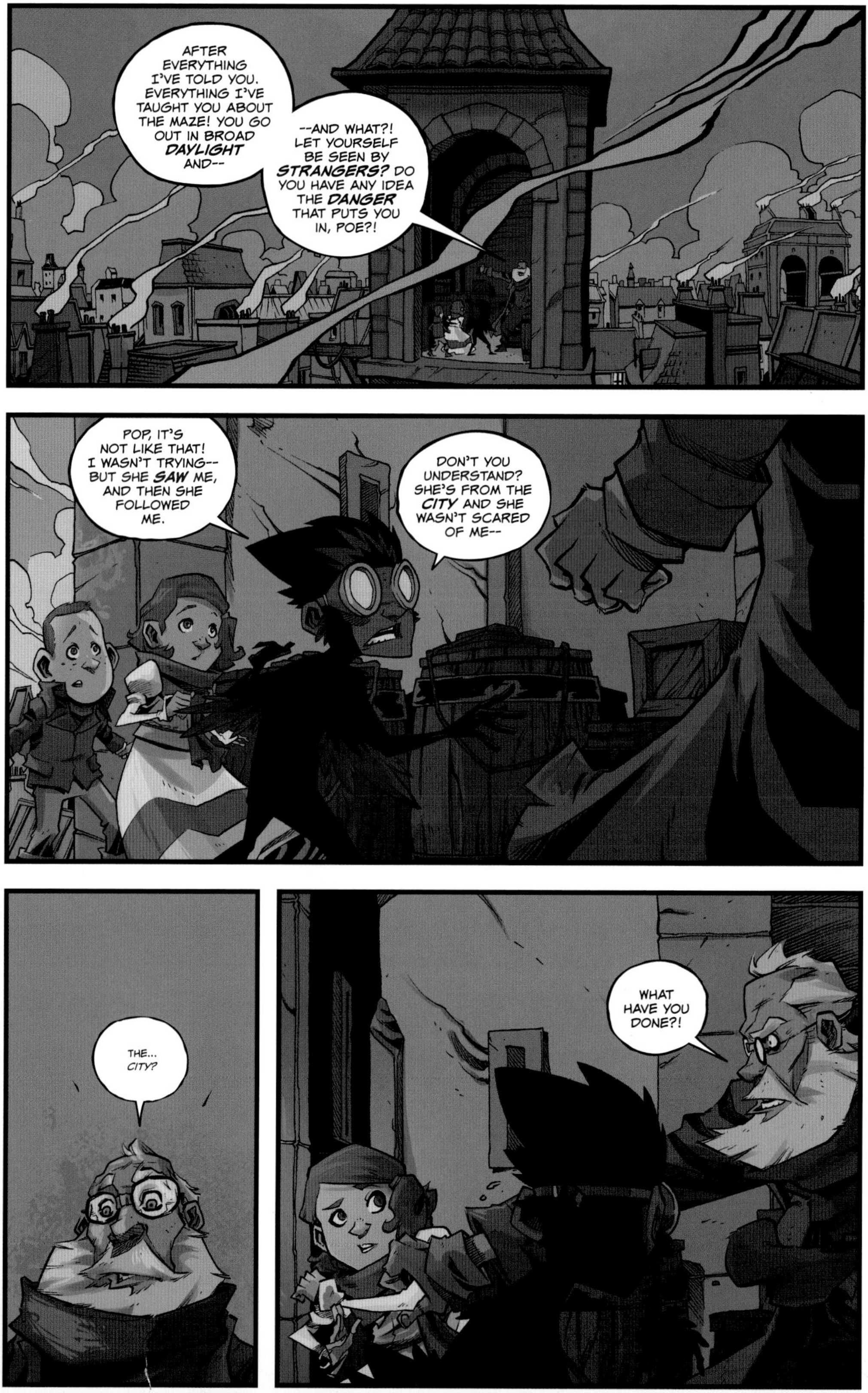
AFTER EVERYTHING I'VE TOLD YOU. EVERYTHING I'VE TAUGHT YOU ABOUT THE MAZE! YOU GO OUT IN BROAD DAYLIGHT AND--
--AND WHAT?! LET YOURSELF BE SEEN BY STRANGERS? DO YOU HAVE ANY IDEA THE DANGER THAT PUTS YOU IN, POE?!
POP, IT'S NOT LIKE THAT! I WASN'T TRYING-- BUT SHE SAW ME, AND THEN SHE FOLLOWED ME.
DON'T YOU UNDERSTAND? SHE'S FROM THE CITY AND SHE WASN'T SCARED OF ME--
THE... CITY?
WHAT HAVE YOU DONE?!

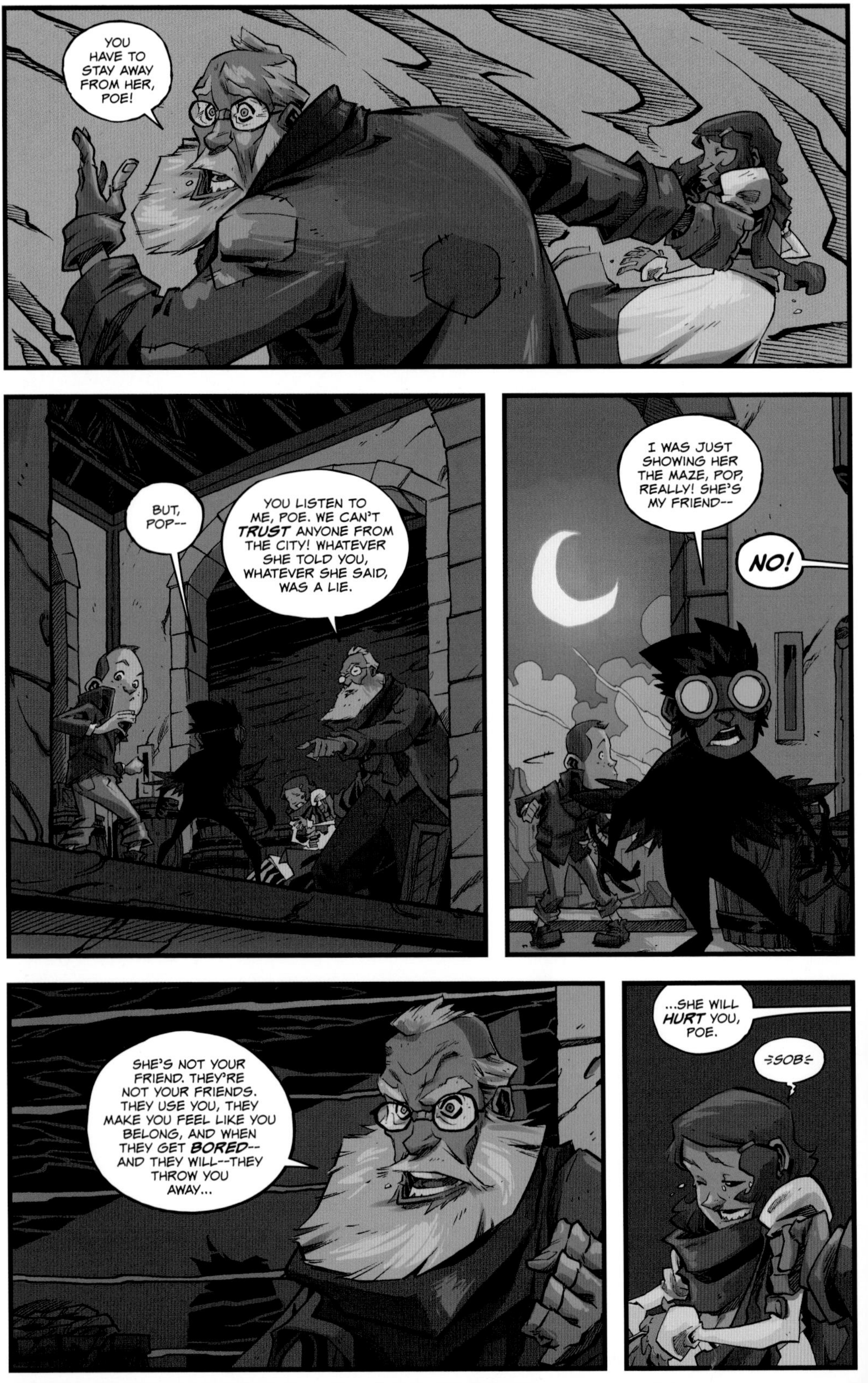
YOU HAVE TO STAY AWAY FROM HER, POE!
BUT, POP--
YOU LISTEN TO ME, POE. WE CAN'T TRUST ANYONE FROM THE CITY! WHATEVER SHE TOLD YOU, WHATEVER SHE SAID, WAS A LIE.
I WAS JUST SHOWING HER THE MAZE, POP, REALLY! SHE'S MY FRIEND--
NO!
SHE'S NOT YOUR FRIEND. THEY'RE NOT YOUR FRIENDS. THEY USE YOU, THEY MAKE YOU FEEL LIKE YOU BELONG, AND WHEN THEY GET BORED-- AND THEY WILL--THEY THROW YOU AWAY...
...SHE WILL HURT YOU, POE.
SOB

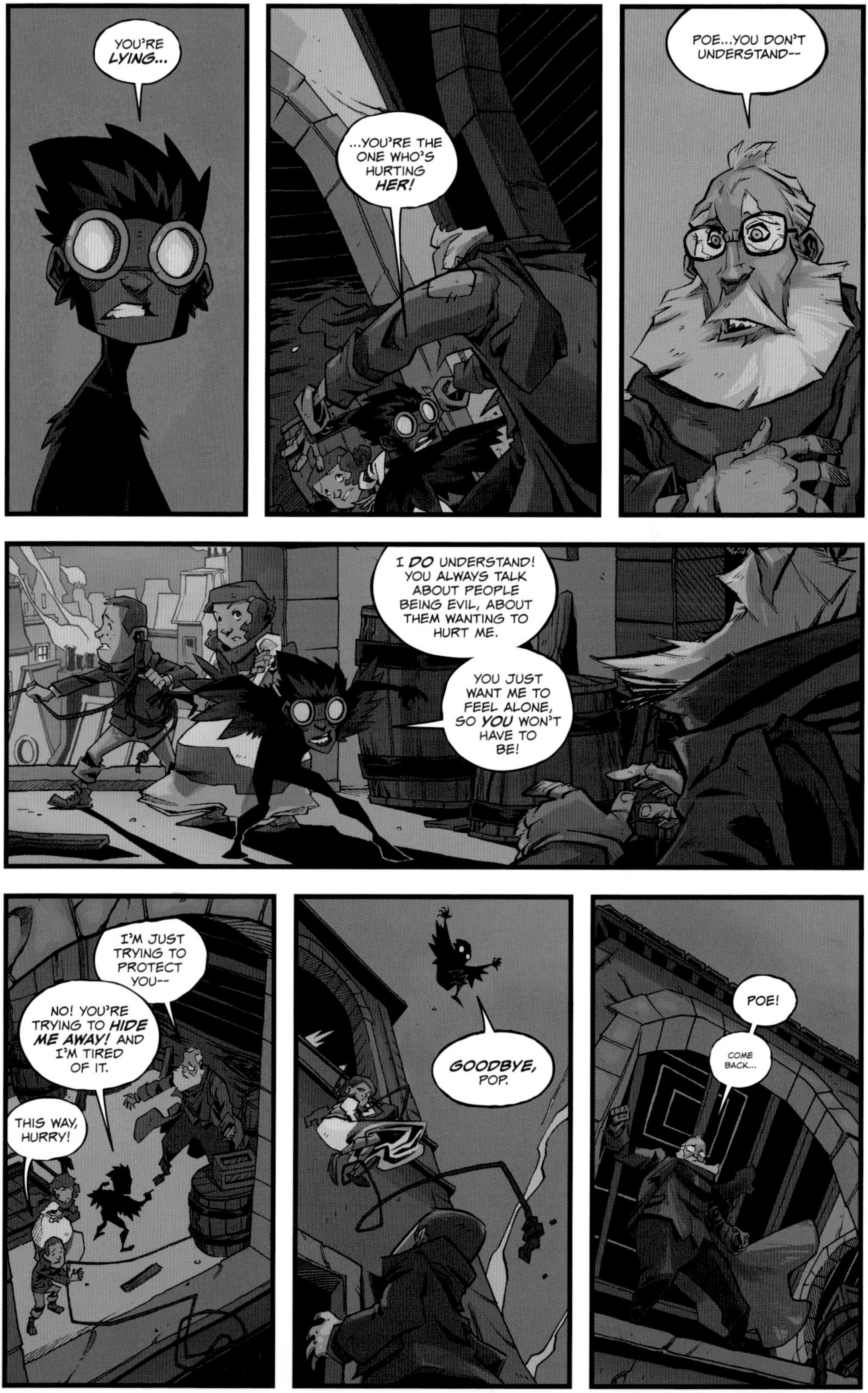
YOU'RE LYING...
...YOU'RE THE ONE WHO'S HURTING HER!
POE...YOU DON'T UNDERSTAND--
I DO UNDERSTAND! YOU ALWAYS TALK ABOUT PEOPLE BEING EVIL, ABOUT THEM WANTING TO HURT ME.
YOU JUST WANT ME TO FEEL ALONE, SO YOU WON'T HAVE TO BE!
I'M JUST TRYING TO PROTECT YOU--
NO! YOU'RE TRYING TO HIDE ME AWAY! AND I'M TIRED OF IT.
THIS WAY, HURRY!
GOODBYE, POP.
POE!
COME BACK...

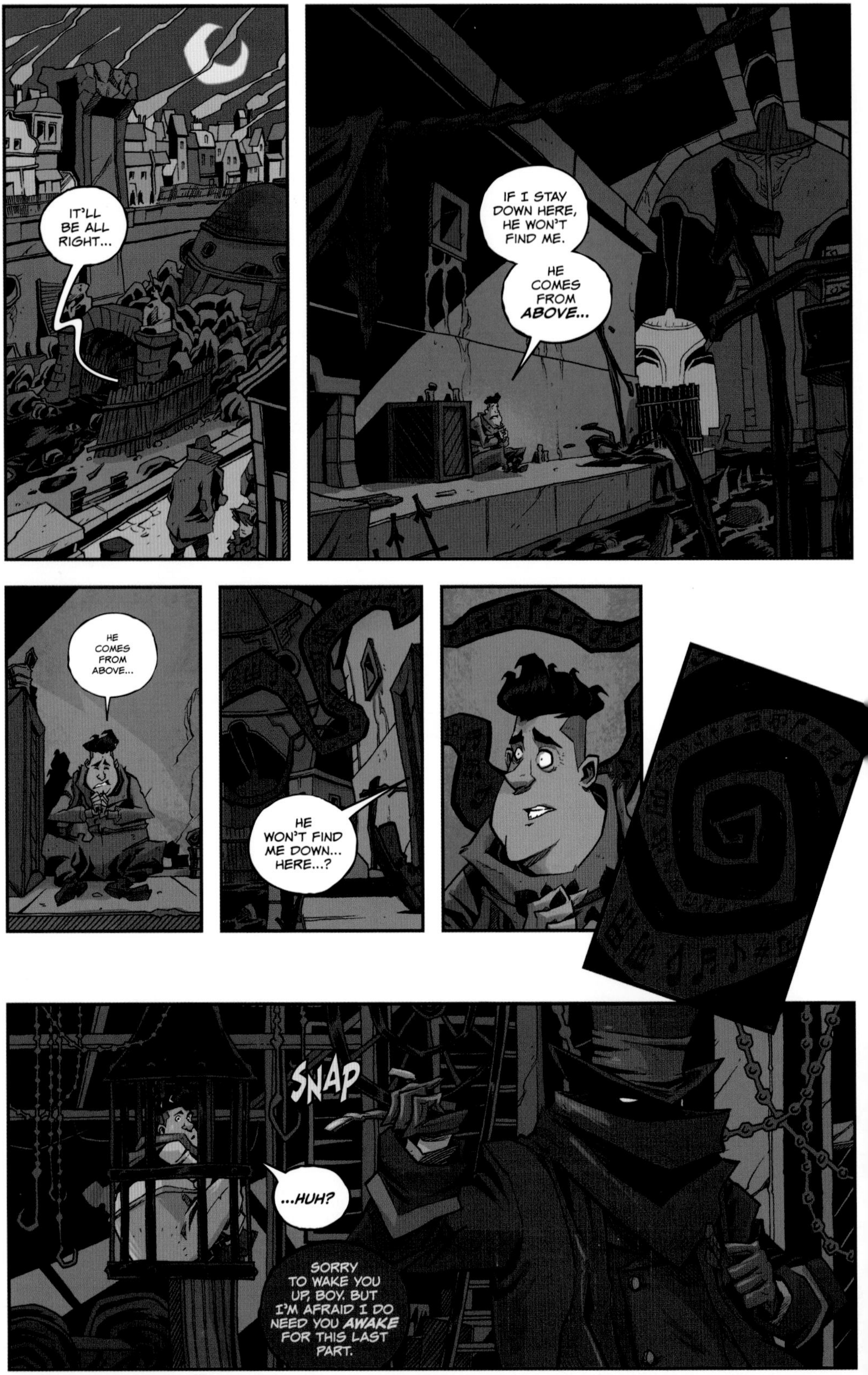
IT'LL BE ALL RIGHT...
IF I STAY DOWN HERE, HE WON'T FIND ME.
HE COMES FROM ABOVE...
HE COMES FROM ABOVE...
HE WON'T FIND ME DOWN... HERE...?
SNAP
...HUH?
SORRY TO WAKE YOU UP, BOY. BUT I'M AFRAID I DO NEED YOU AWAKE FOR THIS LAST PART.

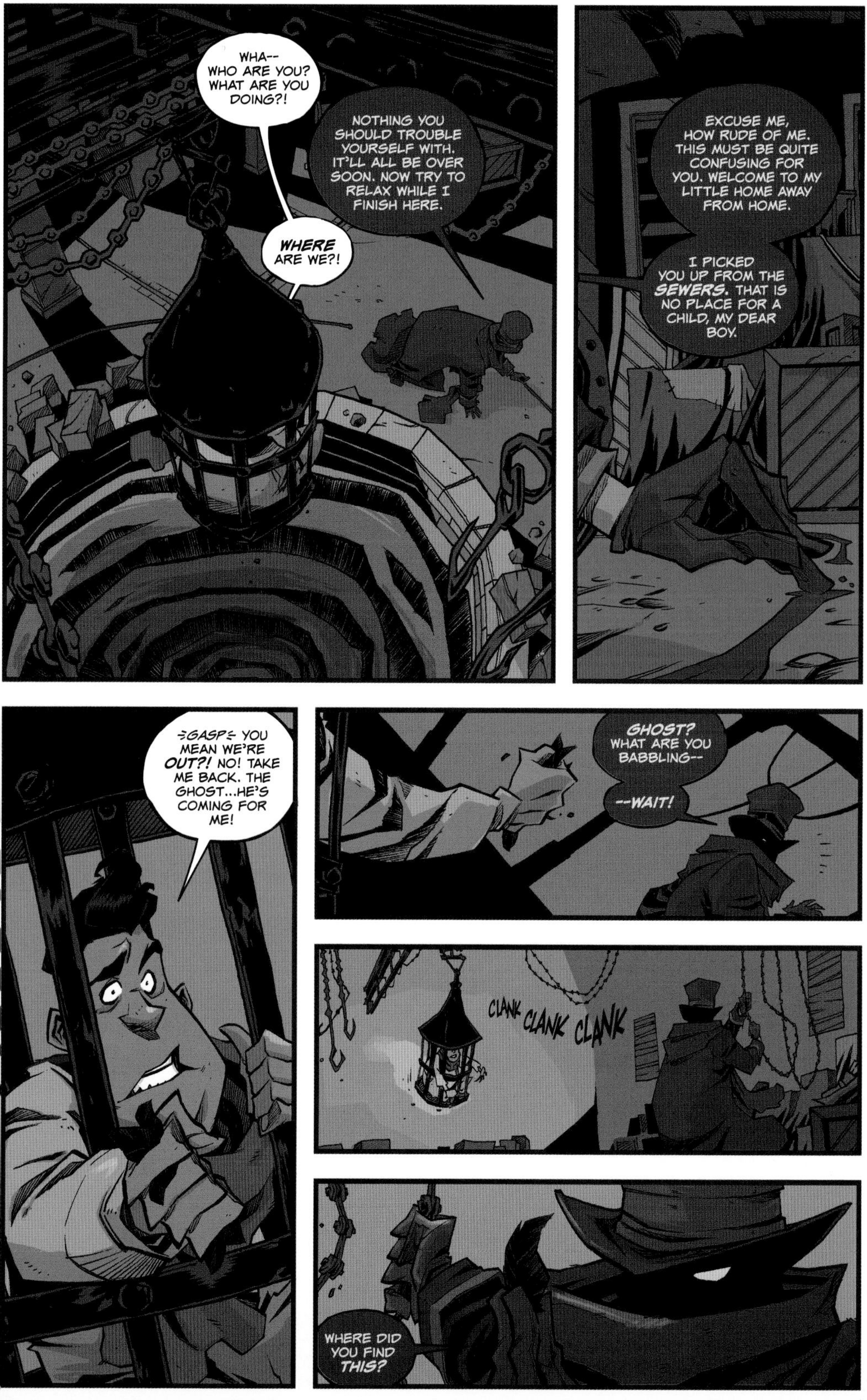
WHA-- WHO ARE YOU? WHAT ARE YOU DOING?!
NOTHING YOU SHOULD TROUBLE YOURSELF WITH. IT'LL ALL BE OVER SOON. NOW TRY TO RELAX WHILE I FINISH HERE.
WHERE ARE WE?!
EXCUSE ME, HOW RUDE OF ME. THIS MUST BE QUITE CONFUSING FOR YOU. WELCOME TO MY LITTLE HOME AWAY FROM HOME.
I PICKED YOU UP FROM THE SEWERS. THAT IS NO PLACE FOR A CHILD, MY DEAR BOY.
GASP YOU MEAN WE'RE OUT?! NO! TAKE ME BACK. THE GHOST...HE'S COMING FOR ME!
GHOST? WHAT ARE YOU BABBLING--
--WAIT!
CLANK CLANK CLANK
WHERE DID YOU FIND THIS?

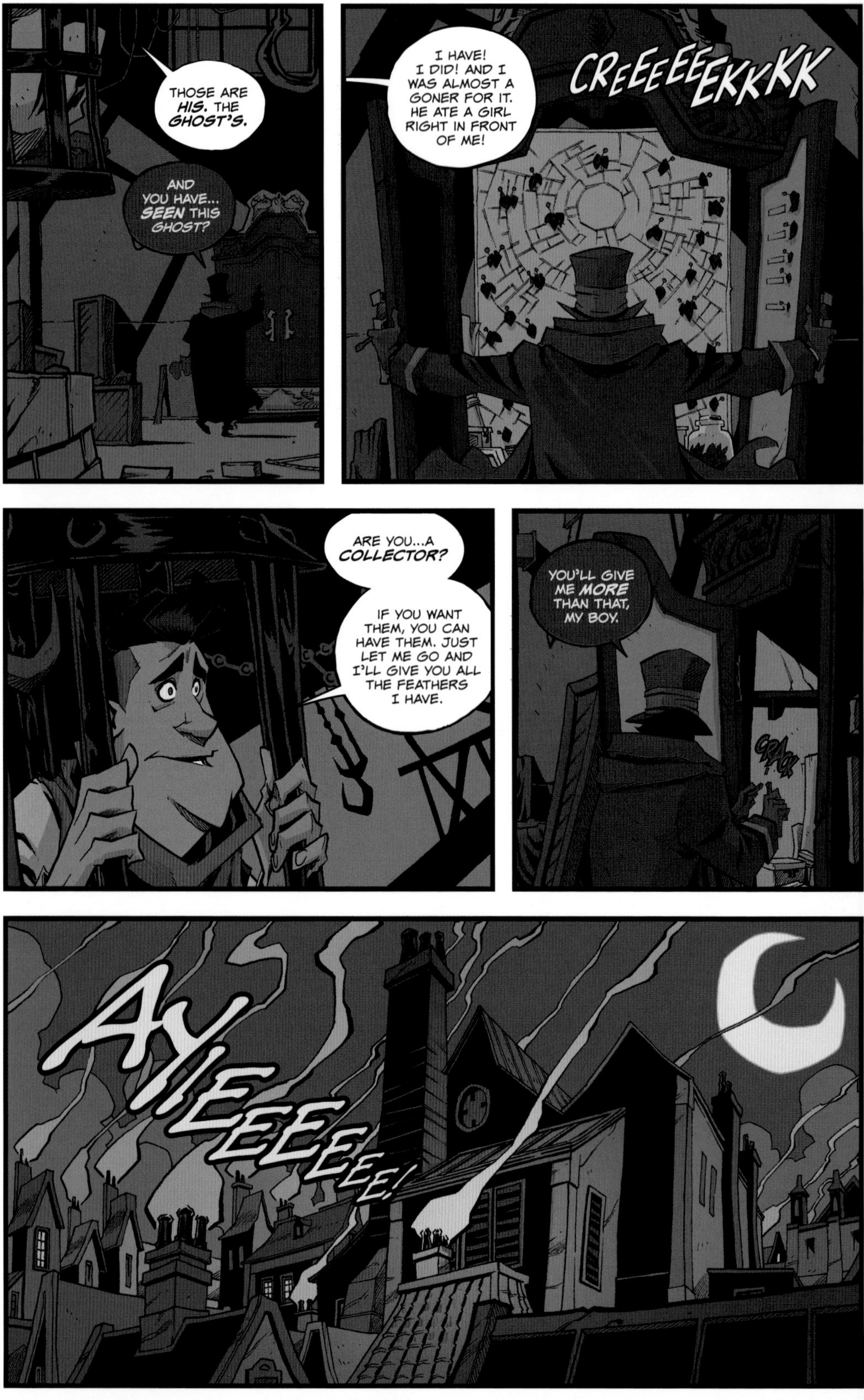
THOSE ARE HIS. THE GHOST'S.
AND YOU HAVE... SEEN THIS GHOST?
I HAVE! I DID! AND I WAS ALMOST A GONER FOR IT. HE ATE A GIRL RIGHT IN FRONT OF ME!
CREEEEEEEKKKK
ARE YOU...A COLLECTOR?
IF YOU WANT THEM, YOU CAN HAVE THEM. JUST LET ME GO AND I'LL GIVE YOU ALL THE FEATHERS I HAVE.
YOU'LL GIVE ME MORE THAN THAT, MY BOY.
AYIEEEEEEE!

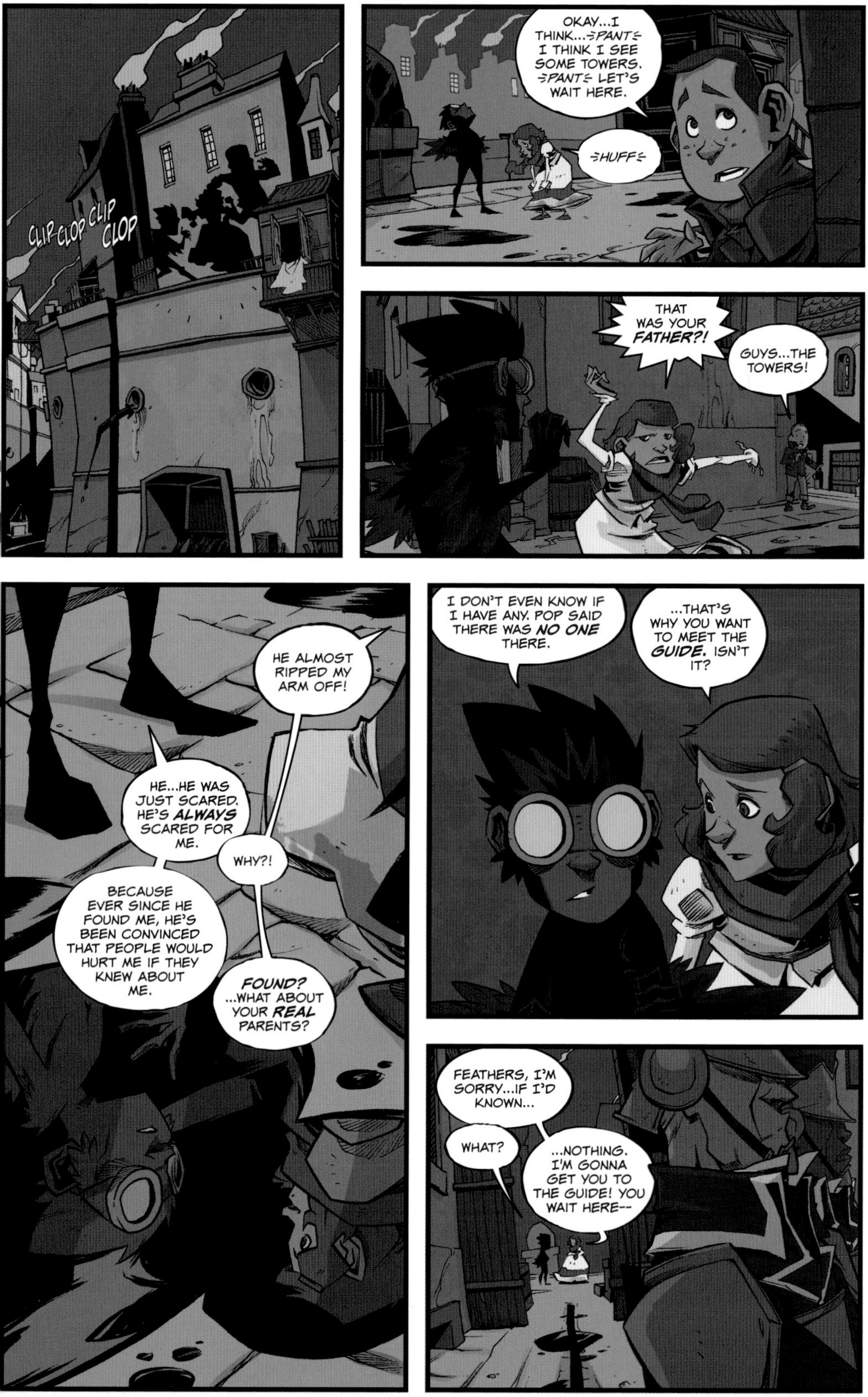
CLIP CLOP CLIP CLOP
OKAY...I THINK...=PANT= I THINK I SEE SOME TOWERS. =PANT= LET'S WAIT HERE.
=HUFF=
THAT WAS YOUR FATHER?!
GUYS...THE TOWERS!
HE ALMOST RIPPED MY ARM OFF!
HE...HE WAS JUST SCARED. HE'S ALWAYS SCARED FOR ME.
WHY?!
BECAUSE EVER SINCE HE FOUND ME, HE'S BEEN CONVINCED THAT PEOPLE WOULD HURT ME IF THEY KNEW ABOUT ME.
FOUND? ...WHAT ABOUT YOUR REAL PARENTS?
I DON'T EVEN KNOW IF I HAVE ANY. POP SAID THERE WAS NO ONE THERE.
...THAT'S WHY YOU WANT TO MEET THE GUIDE. ISN'T IT?
FEATHERS, I'M SORRY...IF I'D KNOWN...
WHAT?
...NOTHING. I'M GONNA GET YOU TO THE GUIDE! YOU WAIT HERE--

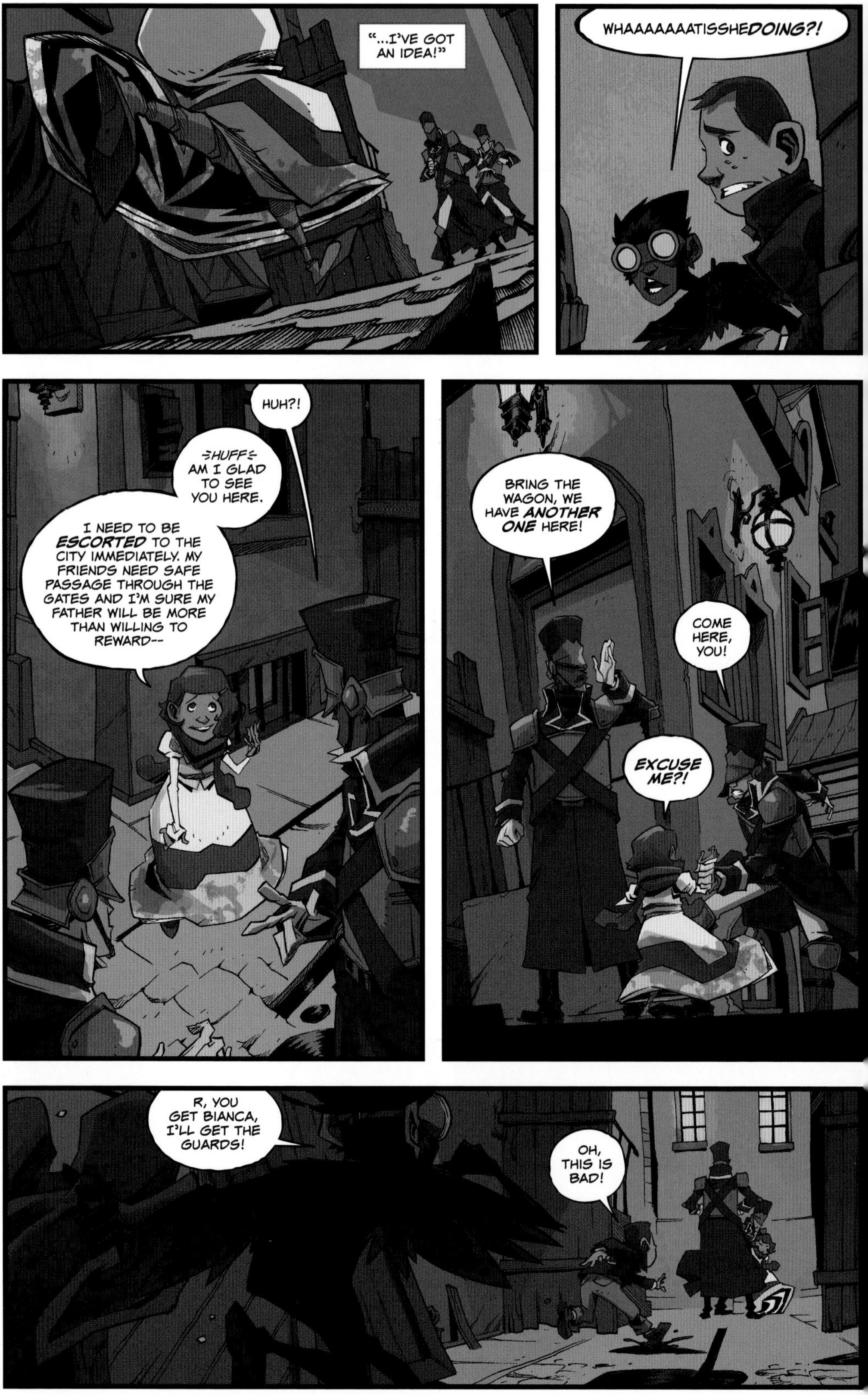
"...I'VE GOT AN IDEA!"
WHAAAAAAAATISSHEDOING?!
HUH?!
HUFF AM I GLAD TO SEE YOU HERE.
I NEED TO BE ESCORTED TO THE CITY IMMEDIATELY. MY FRIENDS NEED SAFE PASSAGE THROUGH THE GATES AND I'M SURE MY FATHER WILL BE MORE THAN WILLING TO REWARD--
BRING THE WAGON, WE HAVE ANOTHER ONE HERE!
COME HERE, YOU!
EXCUSE ME?!
R, YOU GET BIANCA, I'LL GET THE GUARDS!
OH, THIS IS BAD!

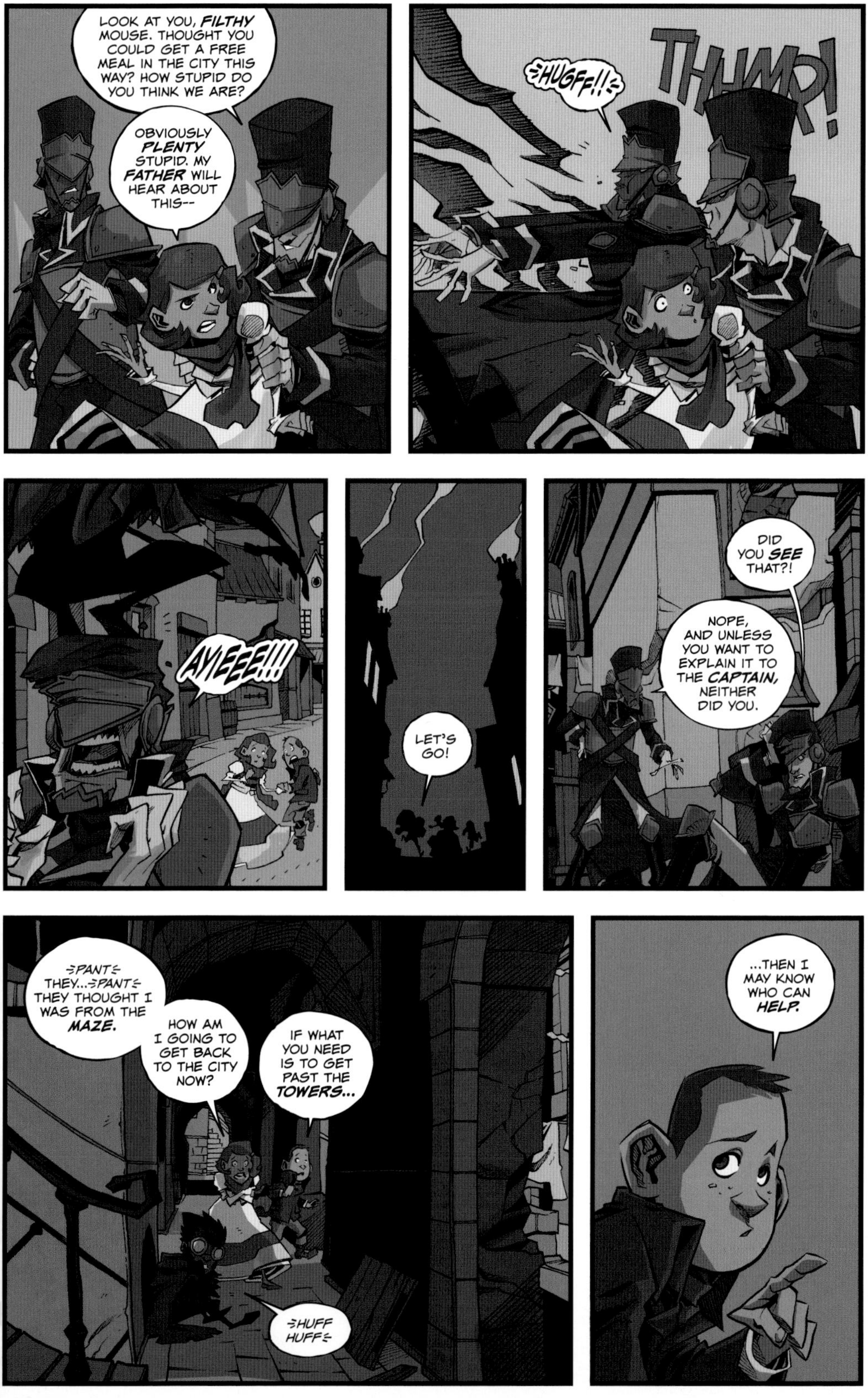
LOOK AT YOU, FILTHY MOUSE. THOUGHT YOU COULD GET A FREE MEAL IN THE CITY THIS WAY? HOW STUPID DO YOU THINK WE ARE?
OBVIOUSLY PLENTY STUPID. MY FATHER WILL HEAR ABOUT THIS--
HUGFF!!
THUMP!
AYIEEE!!!
LET'S GO!
DID YOU SEE THAT?!
NOPE, AND UNLESS YOU WANT TO EXPLAIN IT TO THE CAPTAIN, NEITHER DID YOU.
PANT THEY...PANT THEY THOUGHT I WAS FROM THE MAZE.
HOW AM I GOING TO GET BACK TO THE CITY NOW?
IF WHAT YOU NEED IS TO GET PAST THE TOWERS...
HUFF HUFF
...THEN I MAY KNOW WHO CAN HELP.

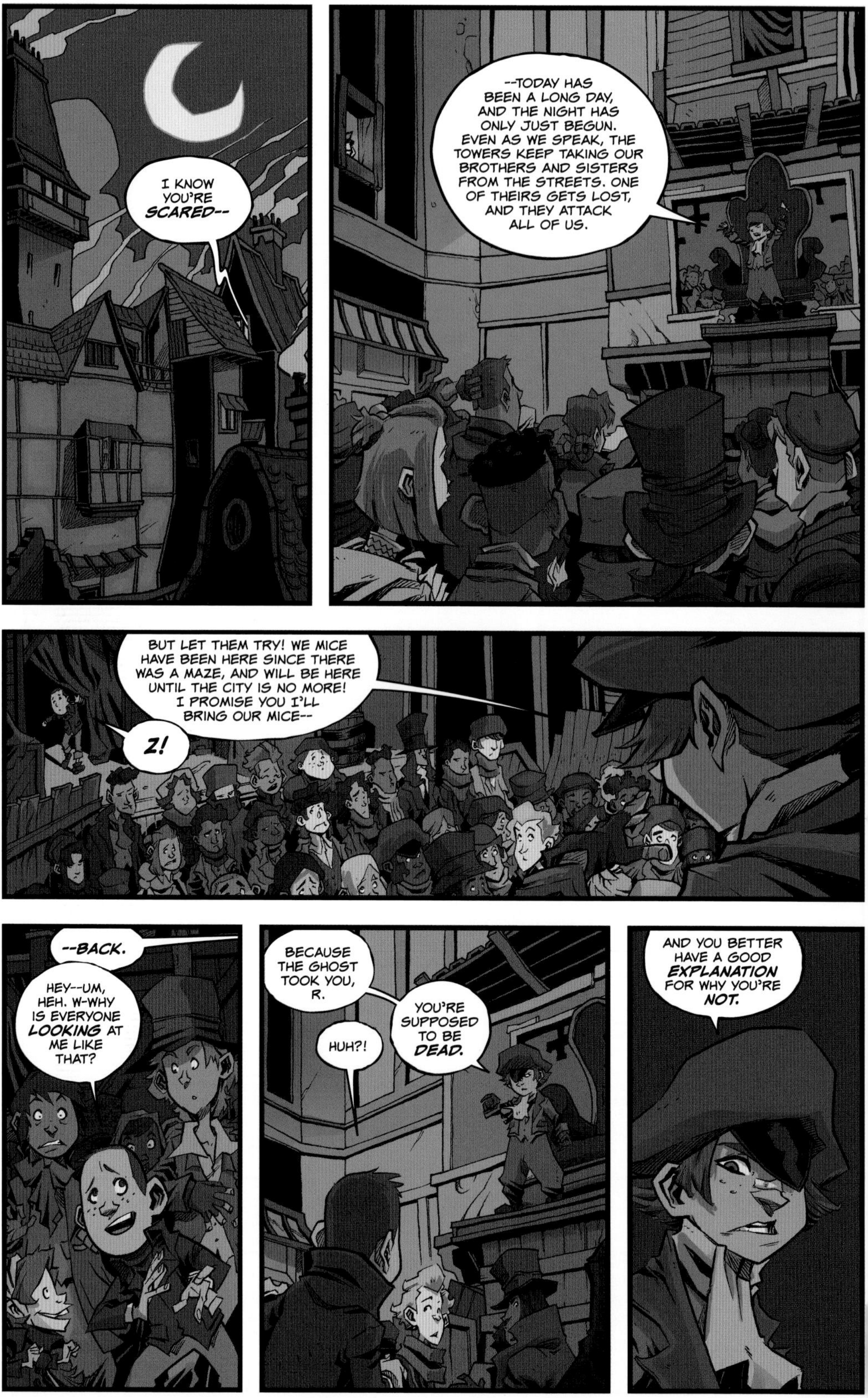
I KNOW YOU'RE SCARED--
--TODAY HAS BEEN A LONG DAY, AND THE NIGHT HAS ONLY JUST BEGUN. EVEN AS WE SPEAK, THE TOWERS KEEP TAKING OUR BROTHERS AND SISTERS FROM THE STREETS. ONE OF THEIRS GETS LOST, AND THEY ATTACK ALL OF US.
BUT LET THEM TRY! WE MICE HAVE BEEN HERE SINCE THERE WAS A MAZE, AND WILL BE HERE UNTIL THE CITY IS NO MORE! I PROMISE YOU I'LL BRING OUR MICE--
Z!
--BACK.
HEY--UM, HEH. W-WHY IS EVERYONE LOOKING AT ME LIKE THAT?
BECAUSE THE GHOST TOOK YOU, R.
HUH?!
YOU'RE SUPPOSED TO BE DEAD.
AND YOU BETTER HAVE A GOOD EXPLANATION FOR WHY YOU'RE NOT.

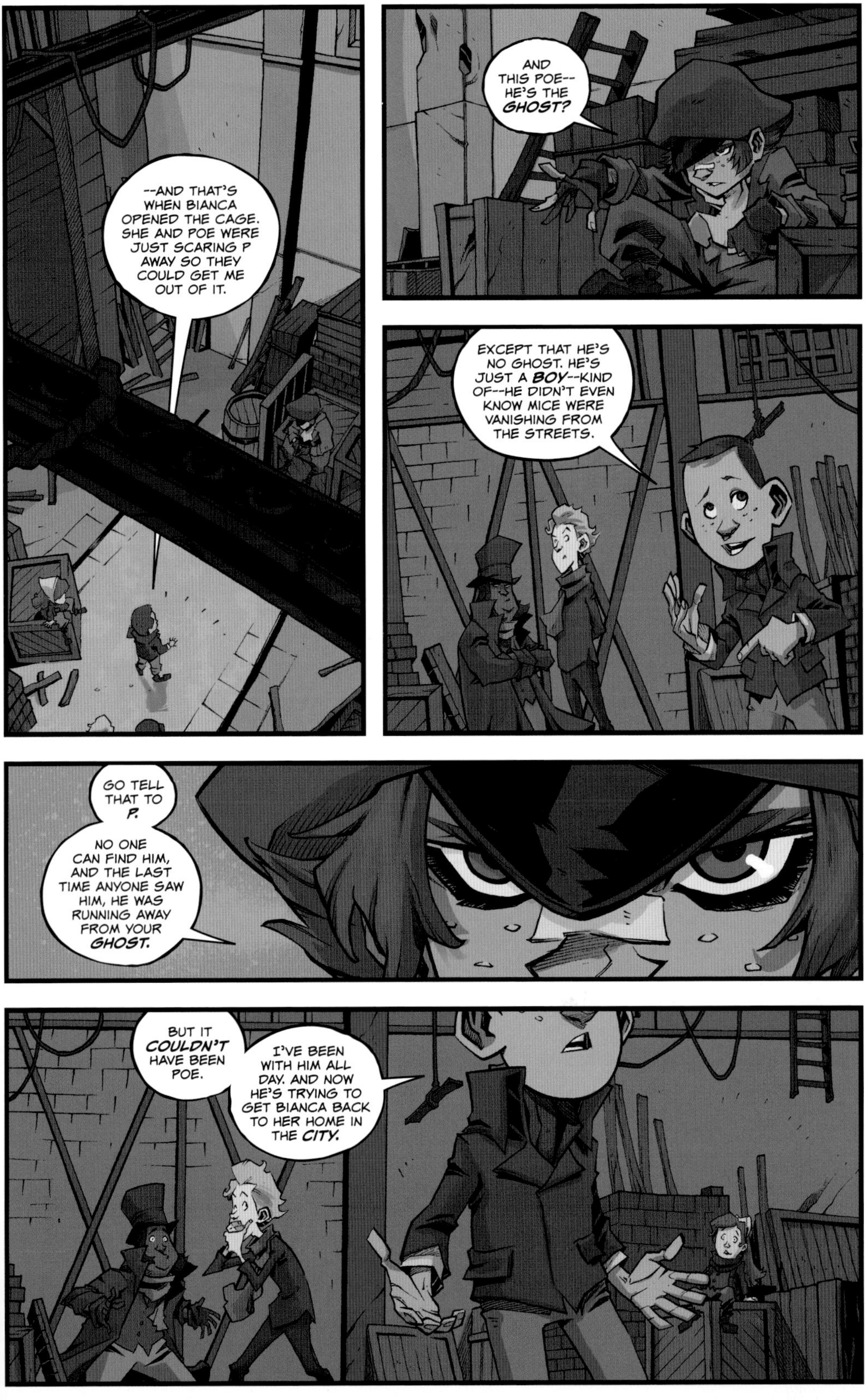
--AND THAT'S WHEN BIANCA OPENED THE CAGE. SHE AND POE WERE JUST SCARING P AWAY SO THEY COULD GET ME OUT OF IT.
AND THIS POE-- HE'S THE GHOST?
EXCEPT THAT HE'S NO GHOST. HE'S JUST A BOY--KIND OF--HE DIDN'T EVEN KNOW MICE WERE VANISHING FROM THE STREETS.
GO TELL THAT TO P.
NO ONE CAN FIND HIM, AND THE LAST TIME ANYONE SAW HIM, HE WAS RUNNING AWAY FROM YOUR GHOST.
BUT IT COULDN'T HAVE BEEN POE.
I'VE BEEN WITH HIM ALL DAY. AND NOW HE'S TRYING TO GET BIANCA BACK TO HER HOME IN THE CITY.

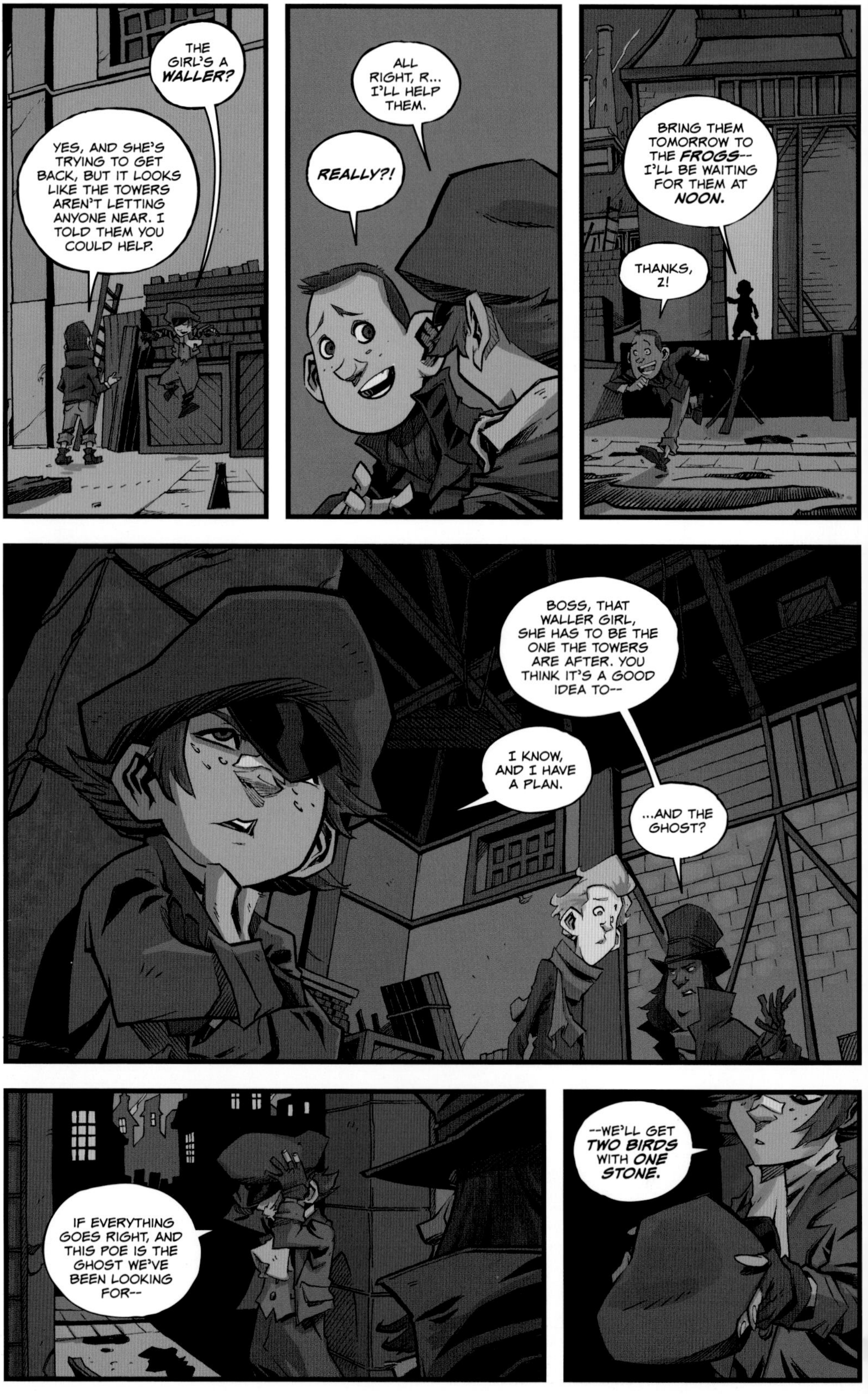
THE GIRL'S A *WALLER?*
YES, AND SHE'S TRYING TO GET BACK, BUT IT LOOKS LIKE THE TOWERS AREN'T LETTING ANYONE NEAR. I TOLD THEM YOU COULD HELP.
ALL RIGHT, R... I'LL HELP THEM.
REALLY?!
BRING THEM TOMORROW TO THE *FROGS*-- I'LL BE WAITING FOR THEM AT *NOON.*
THANKS, Z!
BOSS, THAT WALLER GIRL, SHE HAS TO BE THE ONE THE TOWERS ARE AFTER. YOU THINK IT'S A GOOD IDEA TO--
I KNOW, AND I HAVE A PLAN.
...AND THE GHOST?
IF EVERYTHING GOES RIGHT, AND THIS POE IS THE GHOST WE'VE BEEN LOOKING FOR--
--WE'LL GET *TWO BIRDS* WITH *ONE STONE.*

HE'S BEEN GONE A LONG TIME.

YOU THINK HE'S ALL RIGHT?

I'M SURE HE IS. IT WAS BETTER THIS WAY. DON'T THINK THE MICE WOULD REACT TOO WELL IF I'D GONE WITH HIM.

AND THIS Z GIRL, WILL SHE HELP?

I--DON'T KNOW.

...

I NEVER THOUGHT I WOULD *MISS* IT THIS MUCH.

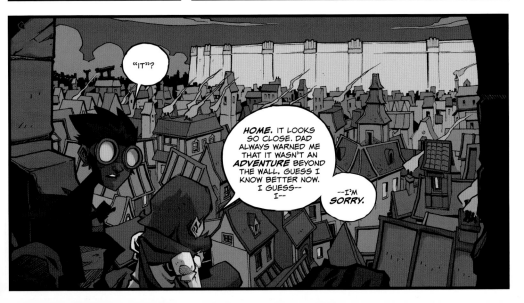

"IT"?

HOME. IT LOOKS SO CLOSE. DAD ALWAYS WARNED ME THAT IT WASN'T AN *ADVENTURE* BEYOND THE WALL. GUESS I KNOW BETTER NOW. I GUESS-- I--

--I'M *SORRY.*

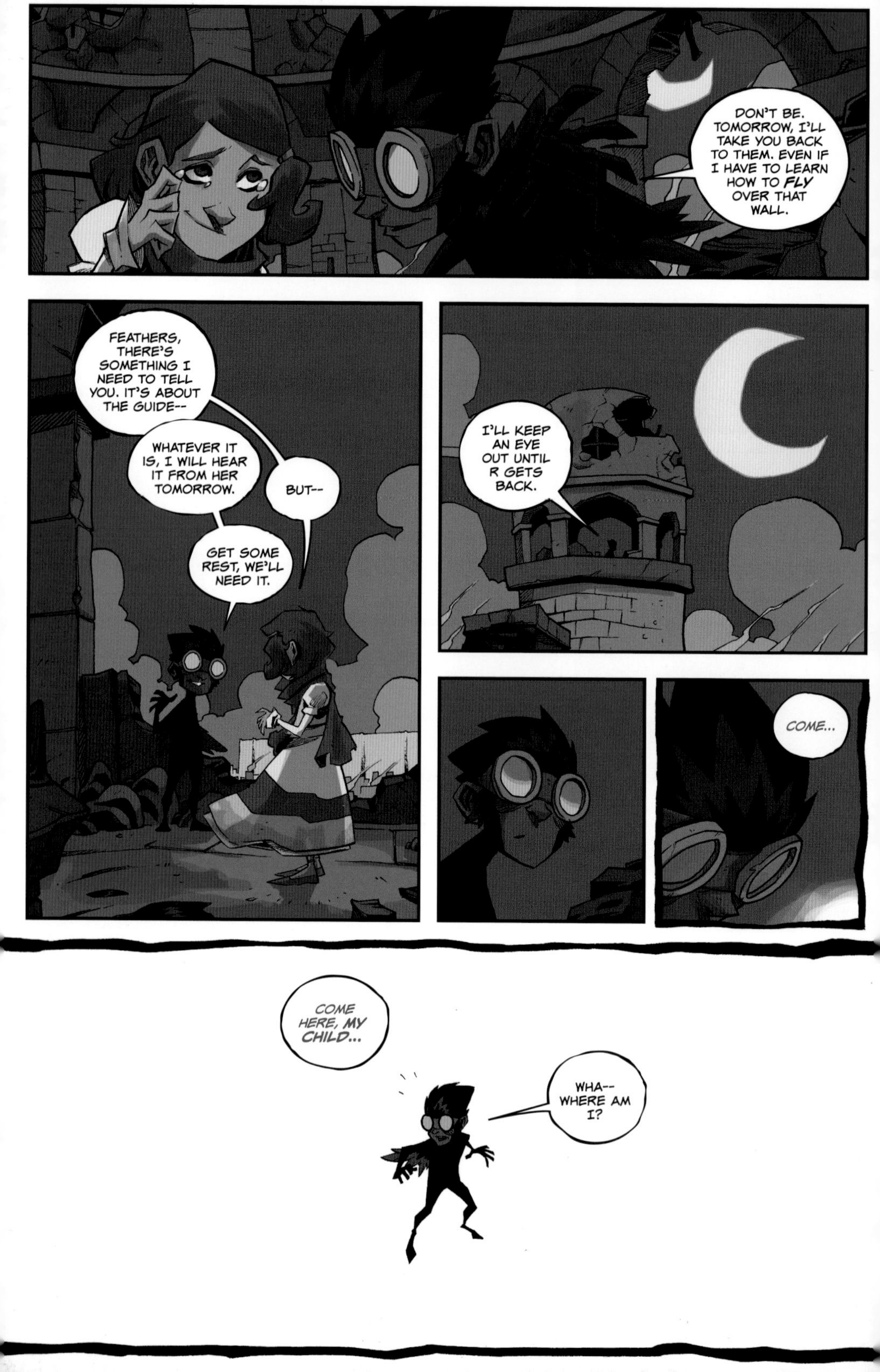
DON'T BE. TOMORROW, I'LL TAKE YOU BACK TO THEM. EVEN IF I HAVE TO LEARN HOW TO FLY OVER THAT WALL.
FEATHERS, THERE'S SOMETHING I NEED TO TELL YOU. IT'S ABOUT THE GUIDE--
WHATEVER IT IS, I WILL HEAR IT FROM HER TOMORROW.
BUT--
GET SOME REST, WE'LL NEED IT.
I'LL KEEP AN EYE OUT UNTIL R GETS BACK.
COME...
COME HERE, MY CHILD...
WHA-- WHERE AM I?

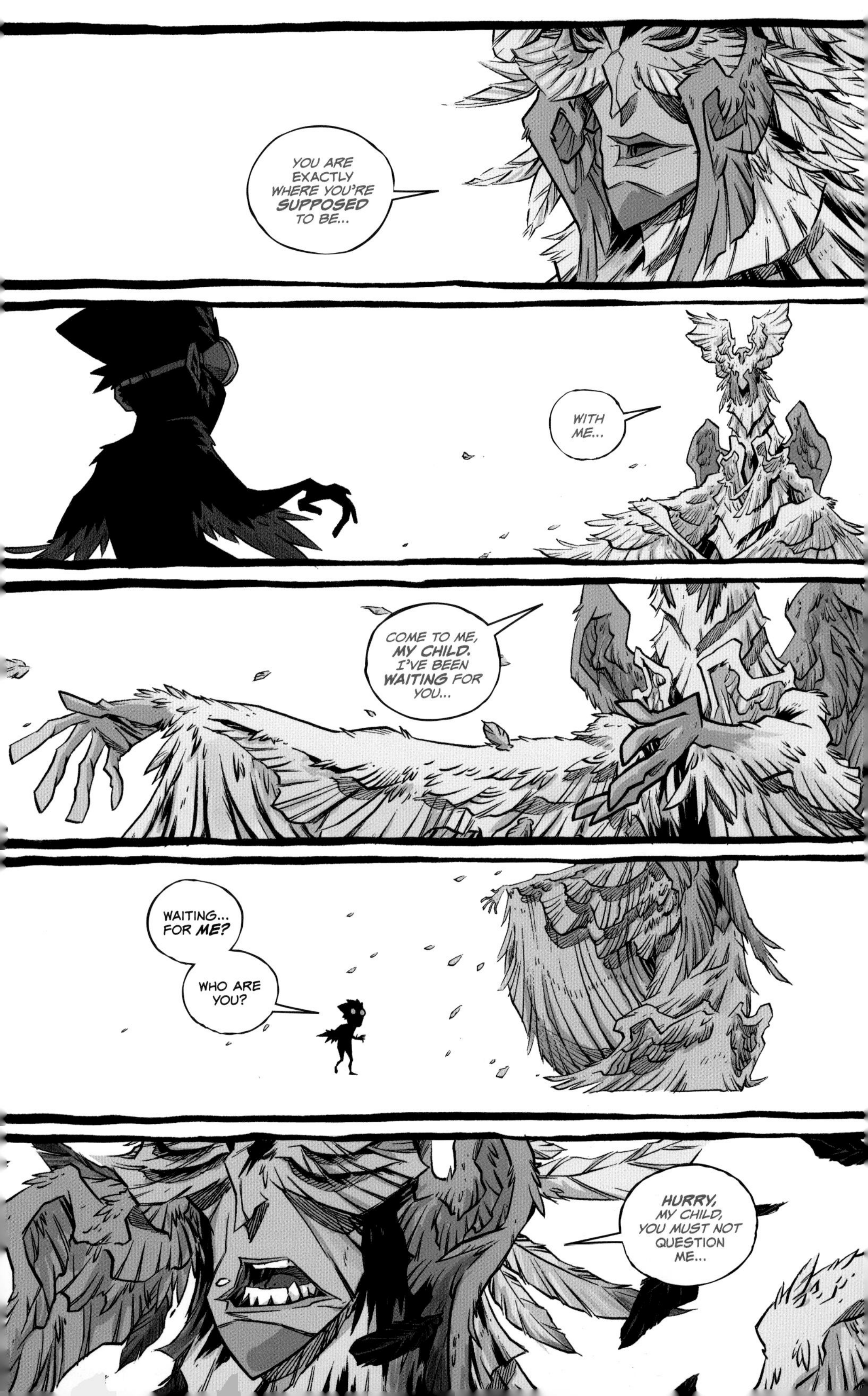
YOU ARE EXACTLY WHERE YOU'RE SUPPOSED TO BE...
WITH ME...
COME TO ME, MY CHILD. I'VE BEEN WAITING FOR YOU...
WAITING... FOR ME?
WHO ARE YOU?
HURRY, MY CHILD, YOU MUST NOT QUESTION ME...

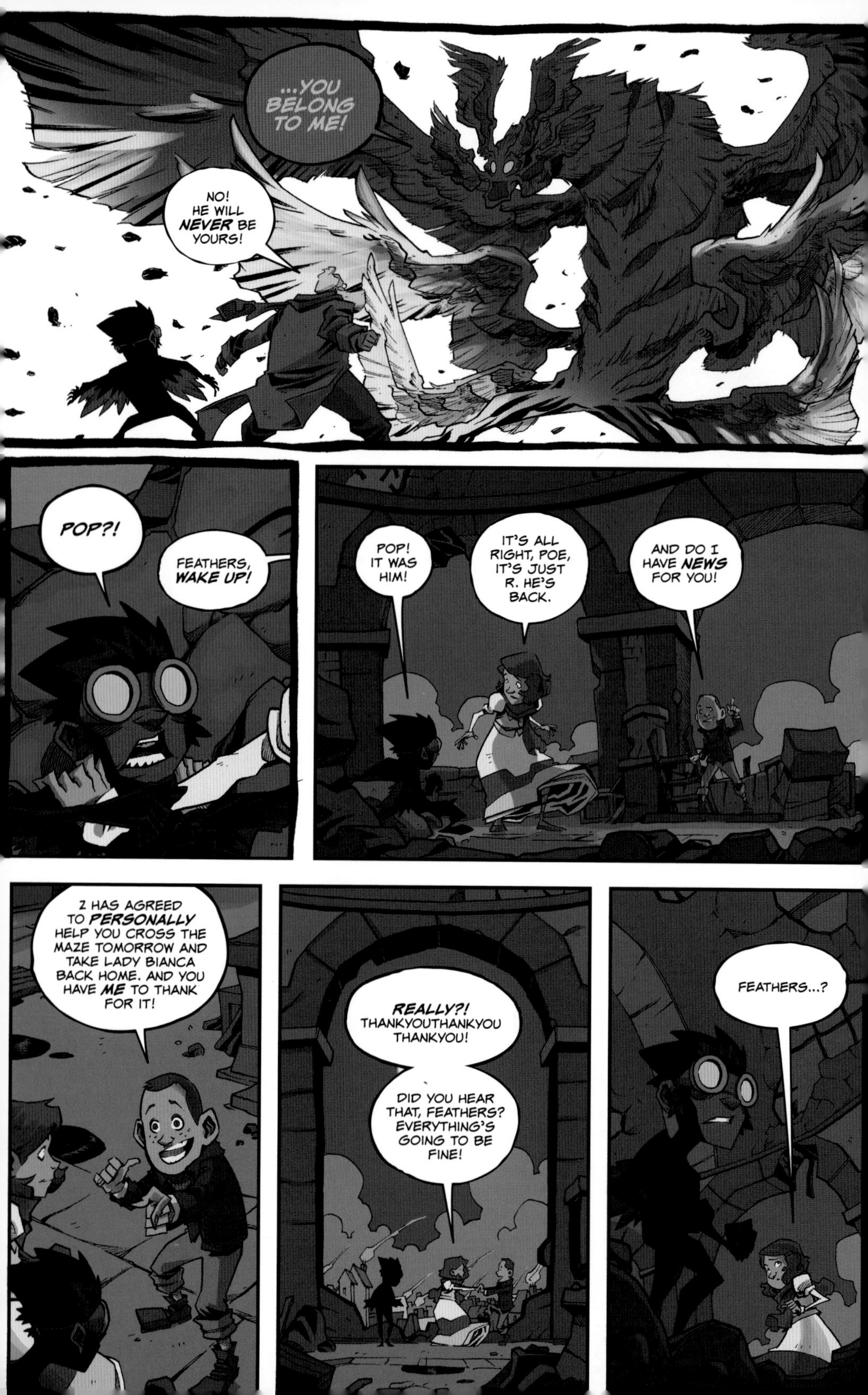
...YOU BELONG TO ME!
NO! HE WILL NEVER BE YOURS!
POP?!
FEATHERS, WAKE UP!
POP! IT WAS HIM!
IT'S ALL RIGHT, POE, IT'S JUST R. HE'S BACK.
AND DO I HAVE NEWS FOR YOU!
Z HAS AGREED TO PERSONALLY HELP YOU CROSS THE MAZE TOMORROW AND TAKE LADY BIANCA BACK HOME. AND YOU HAVE ME TO THANK FOR IT!
REALLY?! THANKYOUTHANKYOU THANKYOU!
DID YOU HEAR THAT, FEATHERS? EVERYTHING'S GOING TO BE FINE!
FEATHERS...?

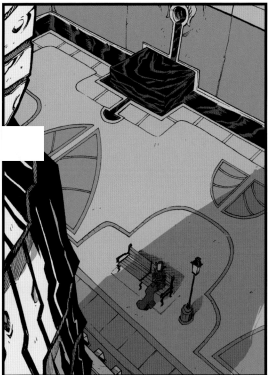

ELEANOR!

SEBASTIAN?!

WE'VE BEEN LOOKING EVERYWHERE FOR YOU!

HAS SHE COME BACK? PLEASE, TELL ME SHE'S *BACK!*

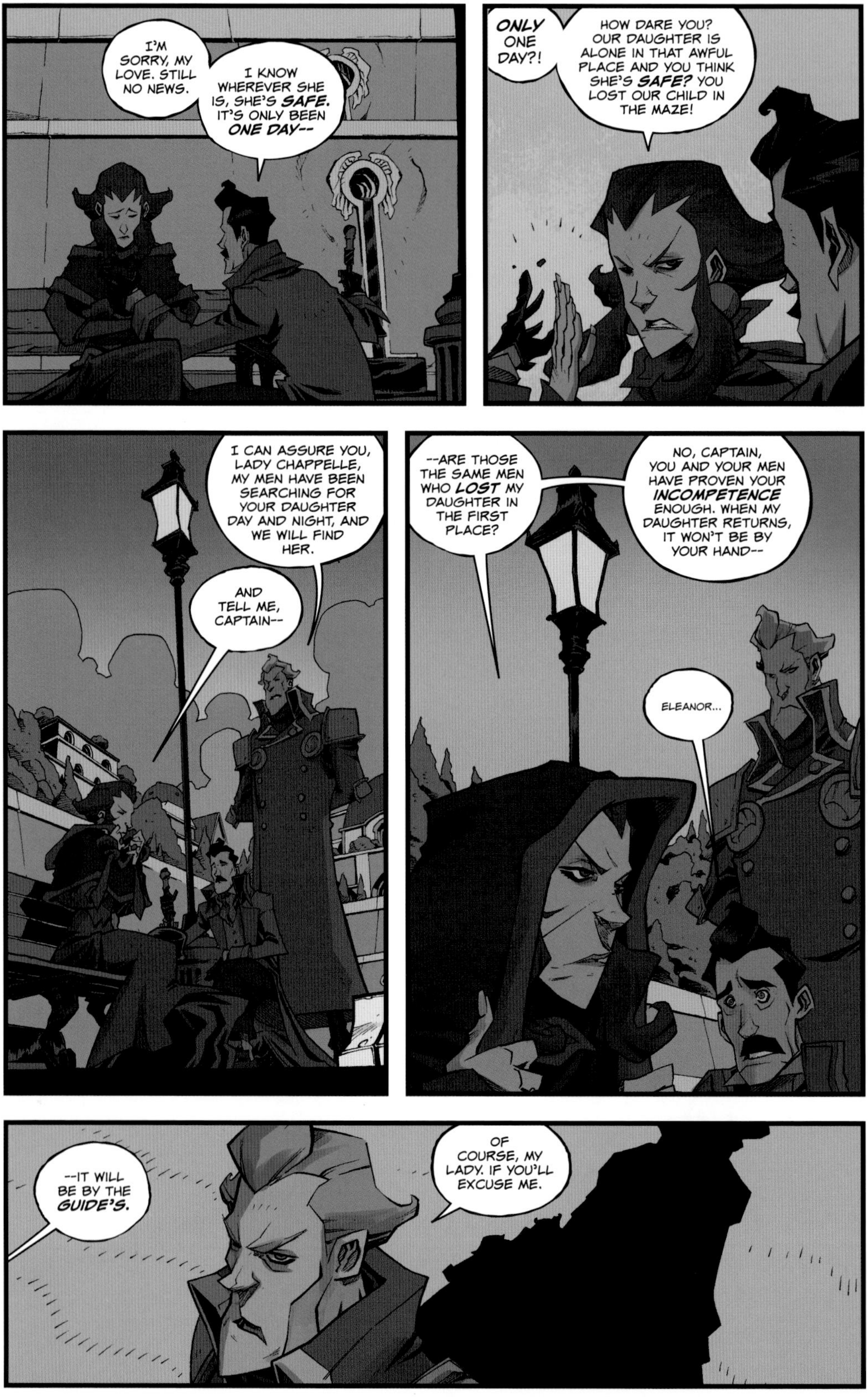
I'M SORRY, MY LOVE. STILL NO NEWS.
I KNOW WHEREVER SHE IS, SHE'S SAFE. IT'S ONLY BEEN ONE DAY--
ONLY ONE DAY?!
HOW DARE YOU? OUR DAUGHTER IS ALONE IN THAT AWFUL PLACE AND YOU THINK SHE'S SAFE? YOU LOST OUR CHILD IN THE MAZE!
I CAN ASSURE YOU, LADY CHAPPELLE, MY MEN HAVE BEEN SEARCHING FOR YOUR DAUGHTER DAY AND NIGHT, AND WE WILL FIND HER.
AND TELL ME, CAPTAIN--
--ARE THOSE THE SAME MEN WHO LOST MY DAUGHTER IN THE FIRST PLACE?
NO, CAPTAIN, YOU AND YOUR MEN HAVE PROVEN YOUR INCOMPETENCE ENOUGH. WHEN MY DAUGHTER RETURNS, IT WON'T BE BY YOUR HAND--
ELEANOR...
--IT WILL BE BY THE GUIDE'S.
OF COURSE, MY LADY. IF YOU'LL EXCUSE ME.

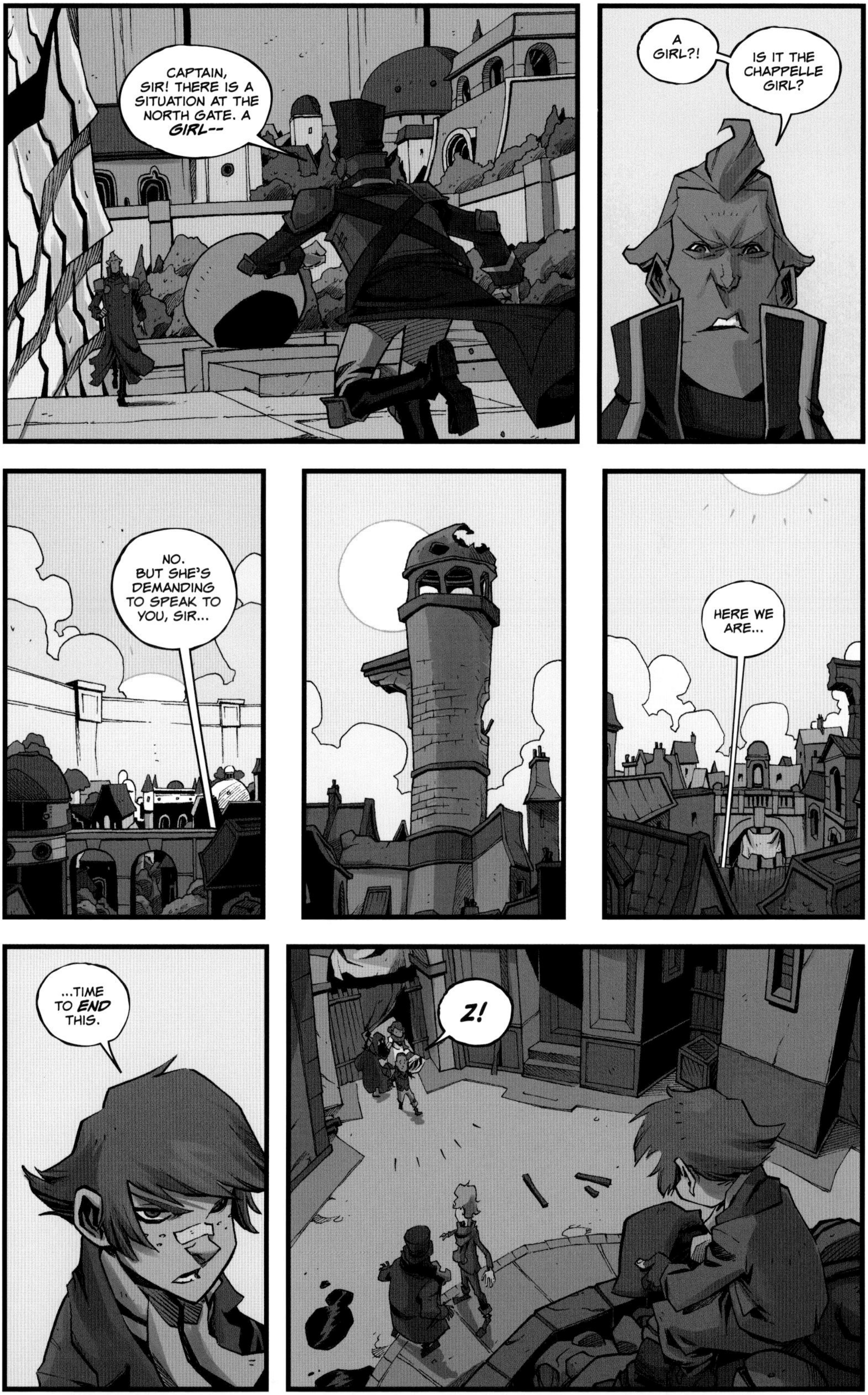
CAPTAIN, SIR! THERE IS A SITUATION AT THE NORTH GATE. A GIRL--
A GIRL?!
IS IT THE CHAPPELLE GIRL?
NO. BUT SHE'S DEMANDING TO SPEAK TO YOU, SIR...
HERE WE ARE...
...TIME TO END THIS.
Z!

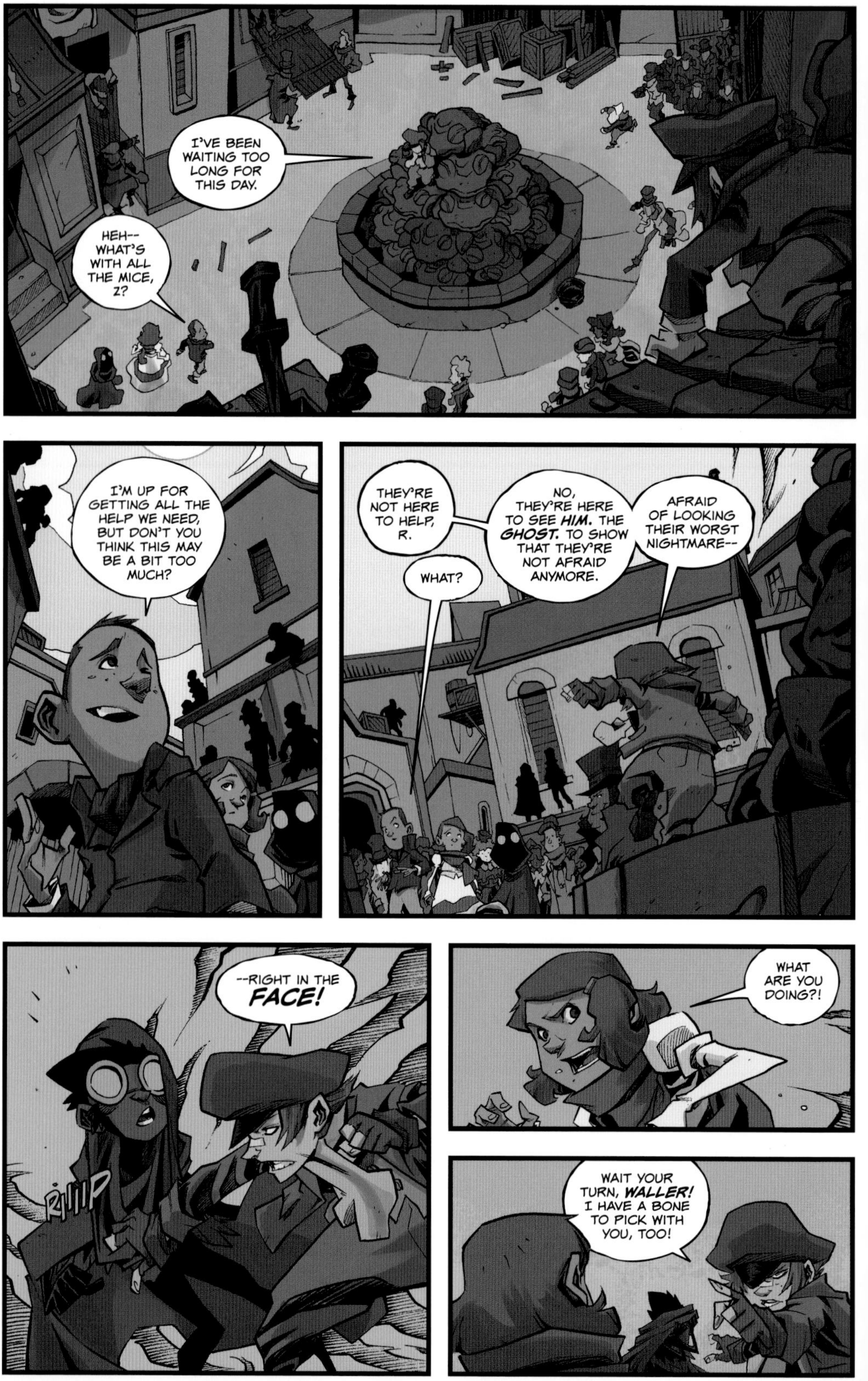
I'VE BEEN WAITING TOO LONG FOR THIS DAY.
HEH-- WHAT'S WITH ALL THE MICE, Z?
I'M UP FOR GETTING ALL THE HELP WE NEED, BUT DON'T YOU THINK THIS MAY BE A BIT TOO MUCH?
THEY'RE NOT HERE TO HELP, R.
WHAT?
NO, THEY'RE HERE TO SEE *HIM*. THE *GHOST*. TO SHOW THAT THEY'RE NOT AFRAID ANYMORE.
AFRAID OF LOOKING THEIR WORST NIGHTMARE--
--RIGHT IN THE *FACE!*
RIIIP
WHAT ARE YOU DOING?!
WAIT YOUR TURN, *WALLER!* I HAVE A BONE TO PICK WITH YOU, TOO!

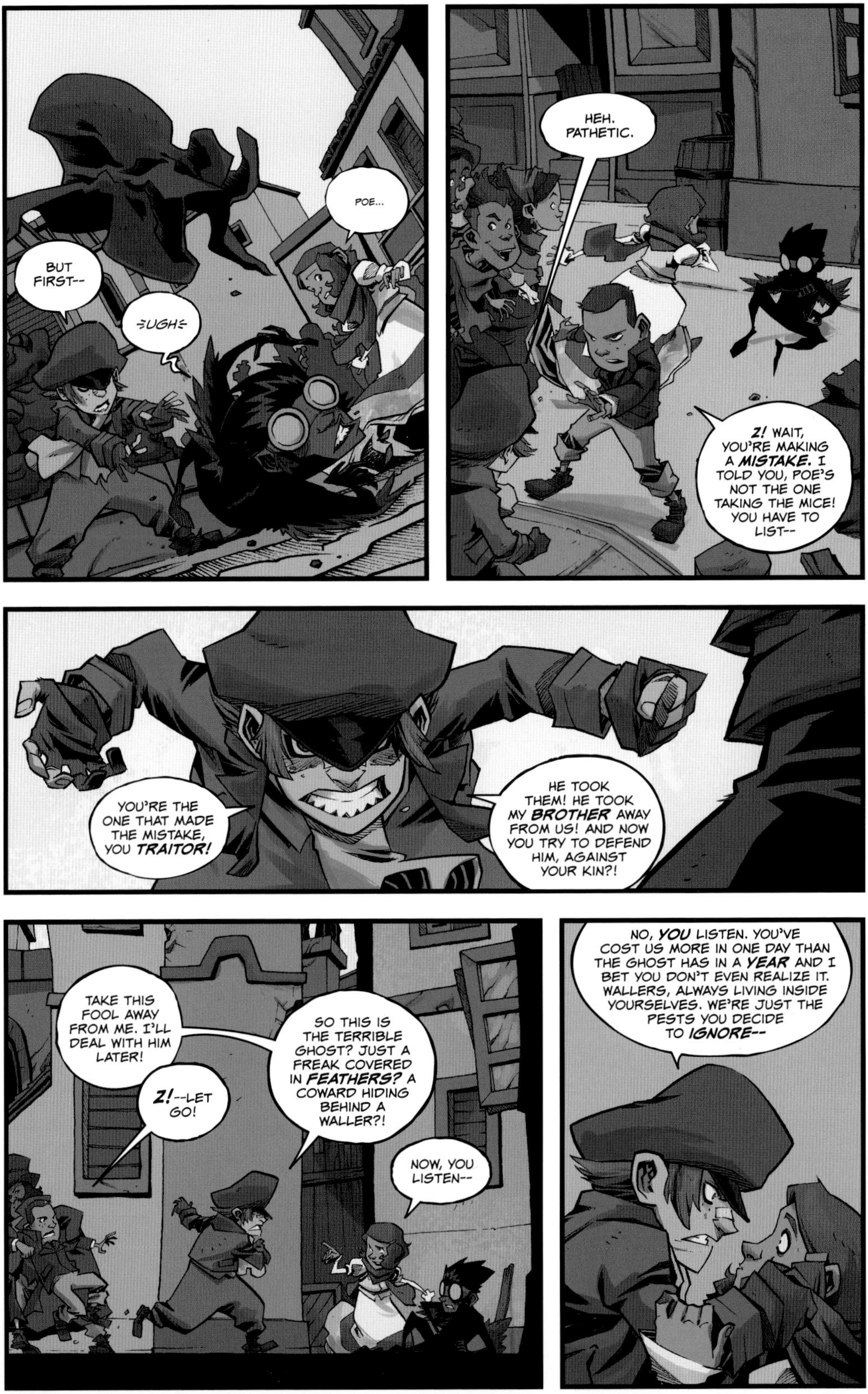
POE...
BUT FIRST--
=UGH=
HEH. PATHETIC.
Z! WAIT, YOU'RE MAKING A MISTAKE. I TOLD YOU, POE'S NOT THE ONE TAKING THE MICE! YOU HAVE TO LIST--
YOU'RE THE ONE THAT MADE THE MISTAKE, YOU TRAITOR!
HE TOOK THEM! HE TOOK MY BROTHER AWAY FROM US! AND NOW YOU TRY TO DEFEND HIM, AGAINST YOUR KIN?!
TAKE THIS FOOL AWAY FROM ME. I'LL DEAL WITH HIM LATER!
Z!--LET GO!
SO THIS IS THE TERRIBLE GHOST? JUST A FREAK COVERED IN FEATHERS? A COWARD HIDING BEHIND A WALLER?!
NOW, YOU LISTEN--
NO, YOU LISTEN. YOU'VE COST US MORE IN ONE DAY THAN THE GHOST HAS IN A YEAR AND I BET YOU DON'T EVEN REALIZE IT. WALLERS, ALWAYS LIVING INSIDE YOURSELVES. WE'RE JUST THE PESTS YOU DECIDE TO IGNORE--

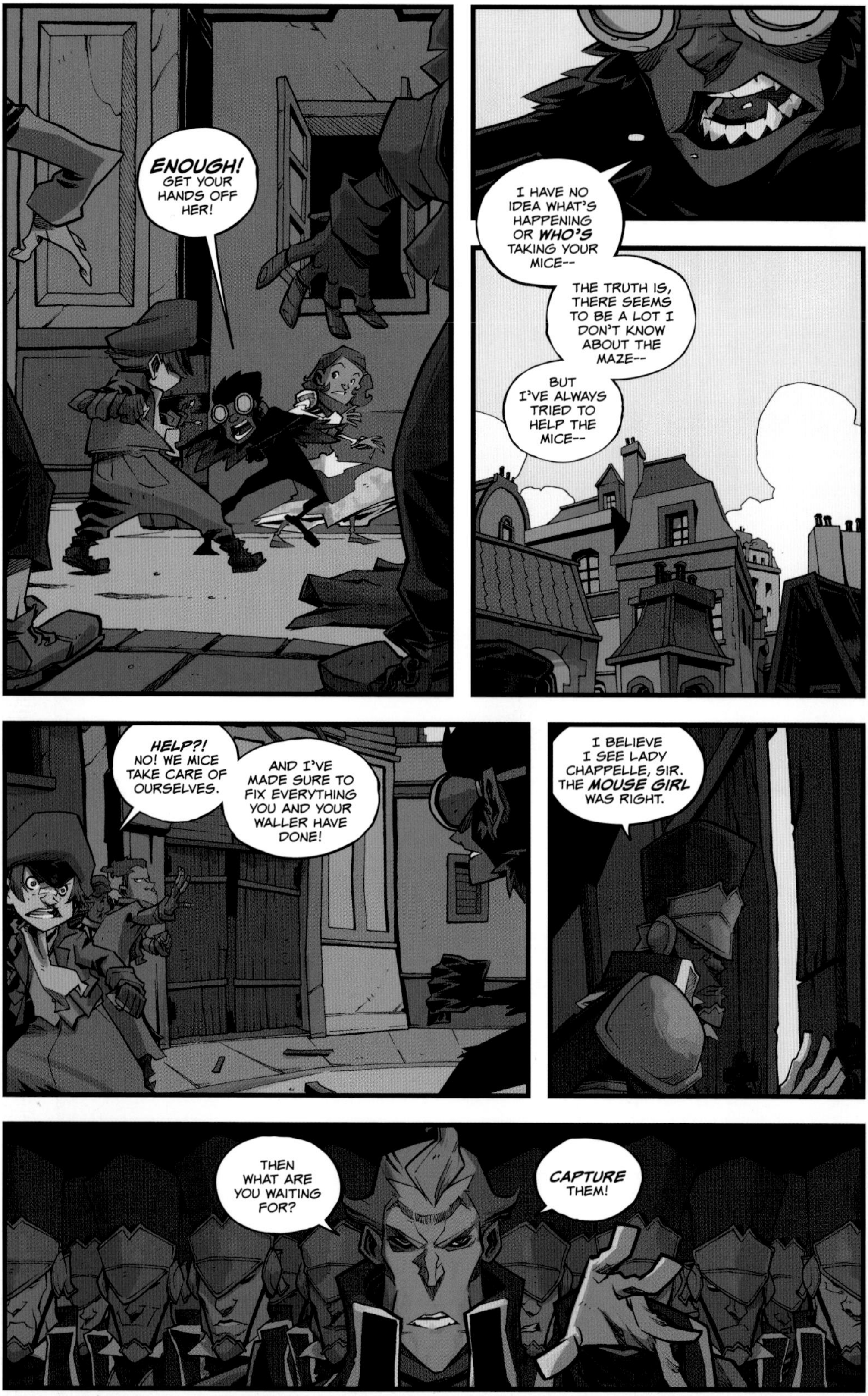
ENOUGH! GET YOUR HANDS OFF HER!
I HAVE NO IDEA WHAT'S HAPPENING OR WHO'S TAKING YOUR MICE--
THE TRUTH IS, THERE SEEMS TO BE A LOT I DON'T KNOW ABOUT THE MAZE--
BUT I'VE ALWAYS TRIED TO HELP THE MICE--
HELP?! NO! WE MICE TAKE CARE OF OURSELVES.
AND I'VE MADE SURE TO FIX EVERYTHING YOU AND YOUR WALLER HAVE DONE!
I BELIEVE I SEE LADY CHAPPELLE, SIR. THE MOUSE GIRL WAS RIGHT.
THEN WHAT ARE YOU WAITING FOR?
CAPTURE THEM!

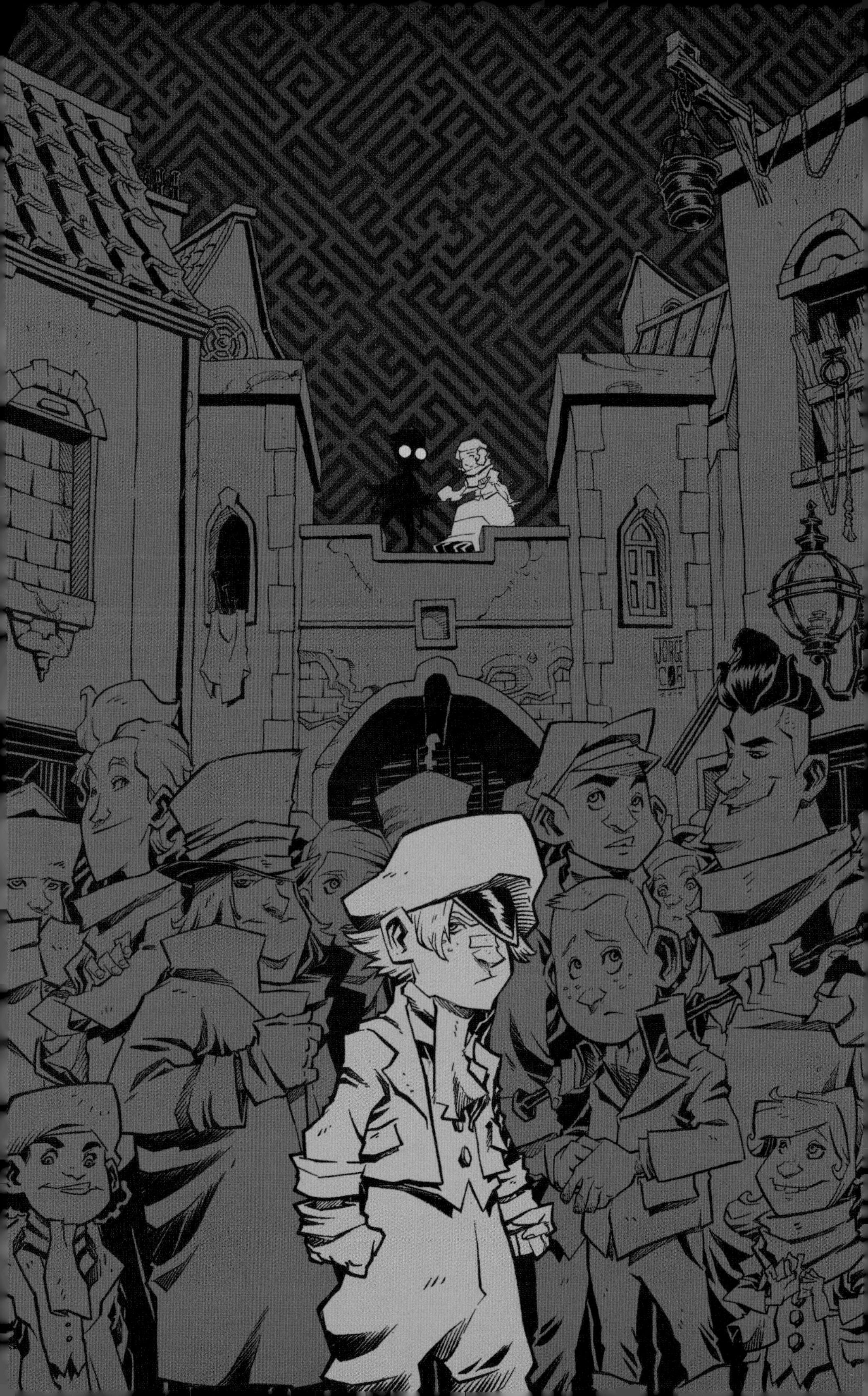
JORGE
COR

CHAPTER
FOUR

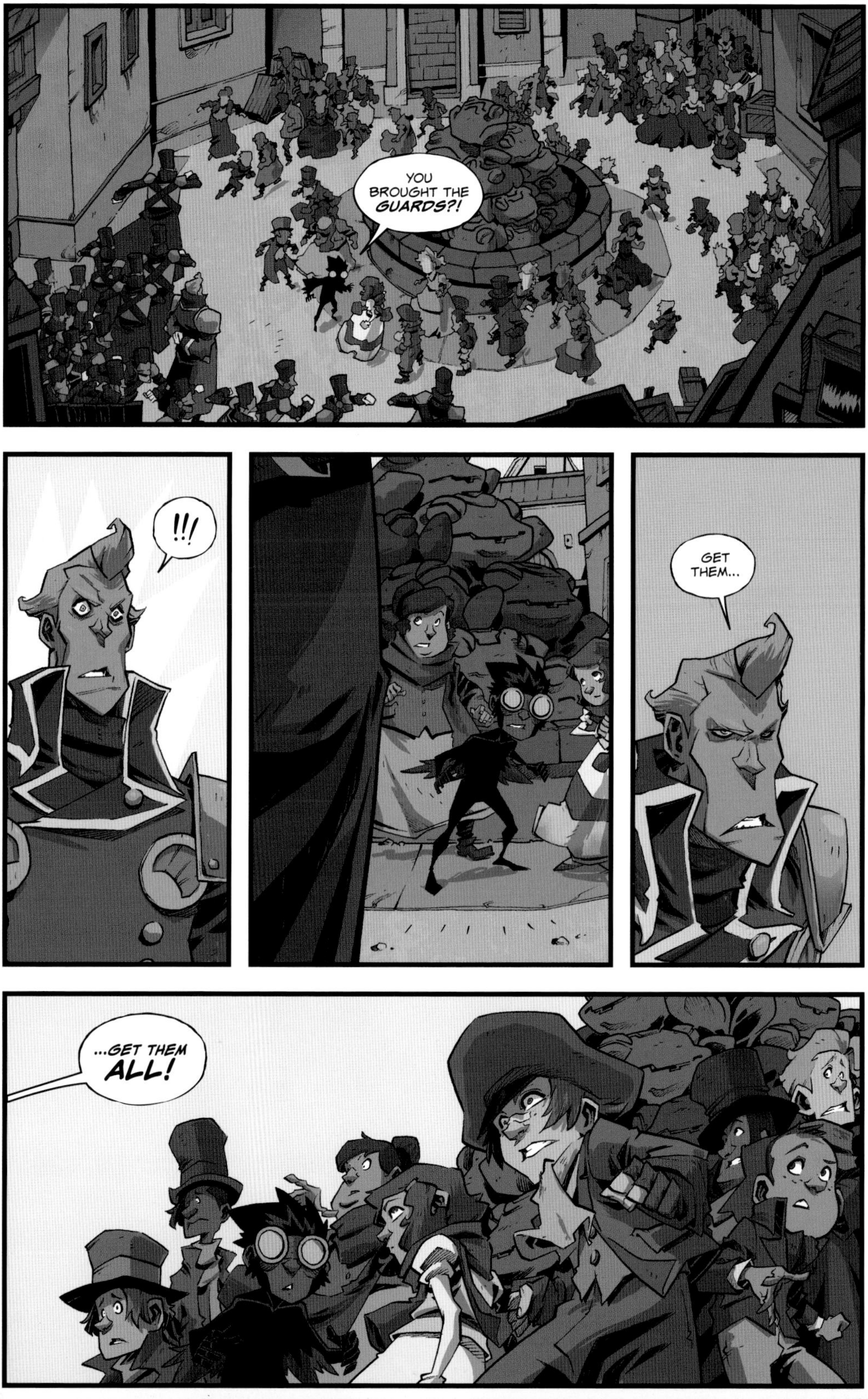
YOU BROUGHT THE GUARDS?!
!!!
GET THEM...
...GET THEM ALL!

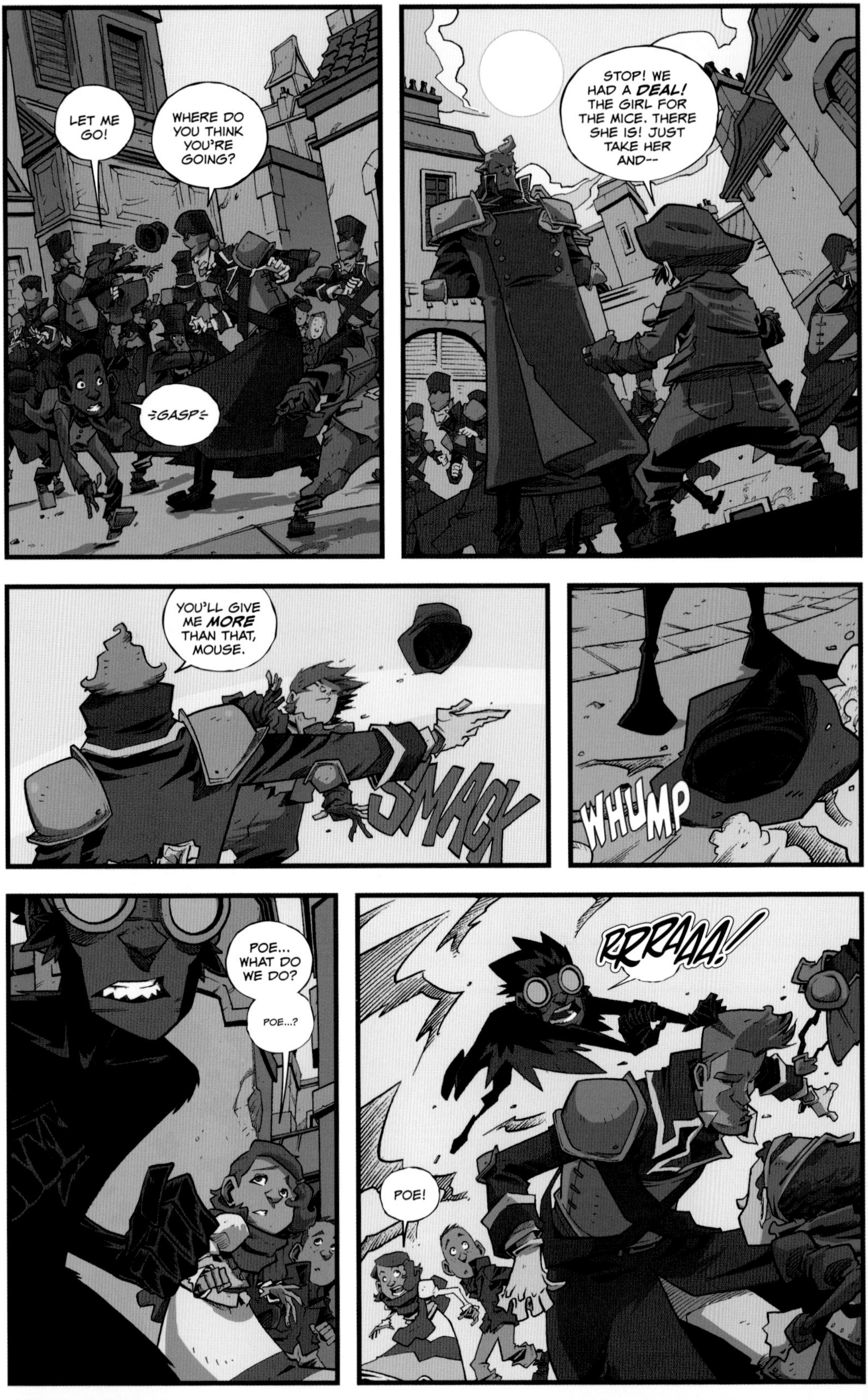
LET ME GO!
WHERE DO YOU THINK YOU'RE GOING?
≡GASP≡
STOP! WE HAD A *DEAL!* THE GIRL FOR THE MICE. THERE SHE IS! JUST TAKE HER AND--
YOU'LL GIVE ME *MORE* THAN THAT, MOUSE.
SMACK
WHUMP
POE... WHAT DO WE DO?
POE...?
RRRAAAA!
POE!

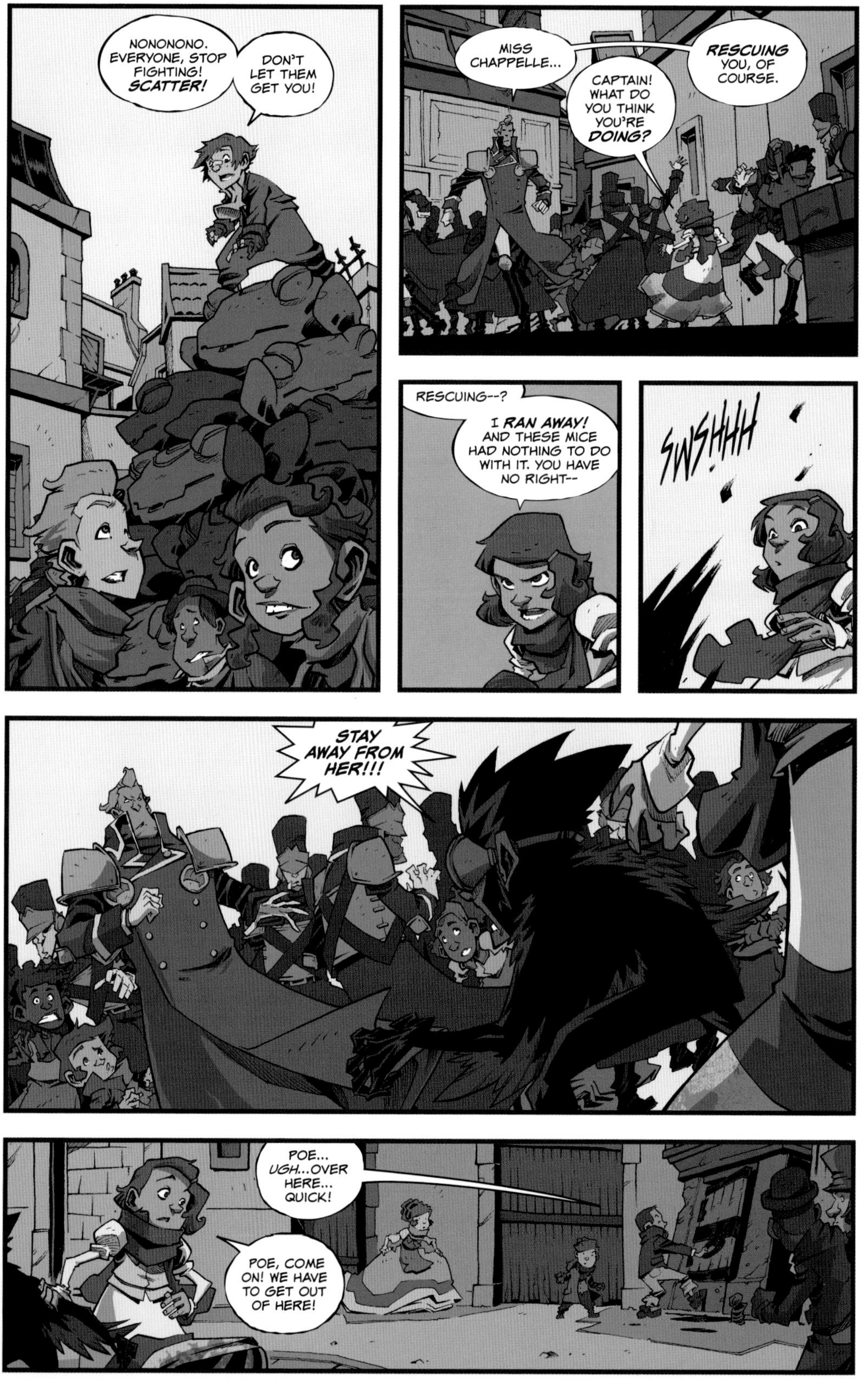
NONONONO. EVERYONE, STOP FIGHTING! SCATTER!
DON'T LET THEM GET YOU!
MISS CHAPPELLE...
RESCUING YOU, OF COURSE.
CAPTAIN! WHAT DO YOU THINK YOU'RE DOING?
RESCUING--?
I RAN AWAY! AND THESE MICE HAD NOTHING TO DO WITH IT. YOU HAVE NO RIGHT--
SWSHHH
STAY AWAY FROM HER!!!
POE... UGH...OVER HERE... QUICK!
POE, COME ON! WE HAVE TO GET OUT OF HERE!

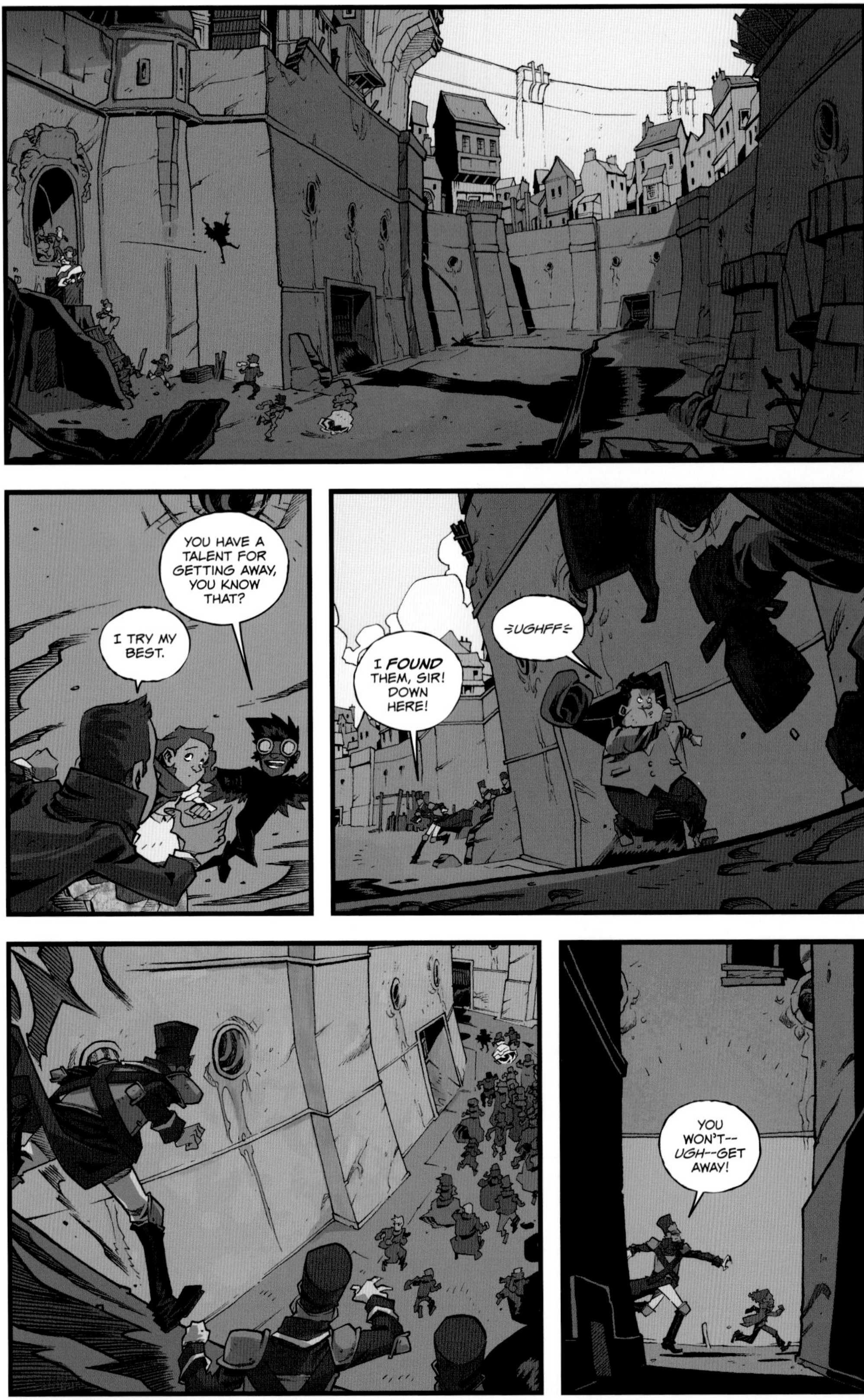
YOU HAVE A TALENT FOR GETTING AWAY, YOU KNOW THAT?
I TRY MY BEST.
I *FOUND* THEM, SIR! DOWN HERE!
=UGHFF=
YOU WON'T-- *UGH*--GET AWAY!

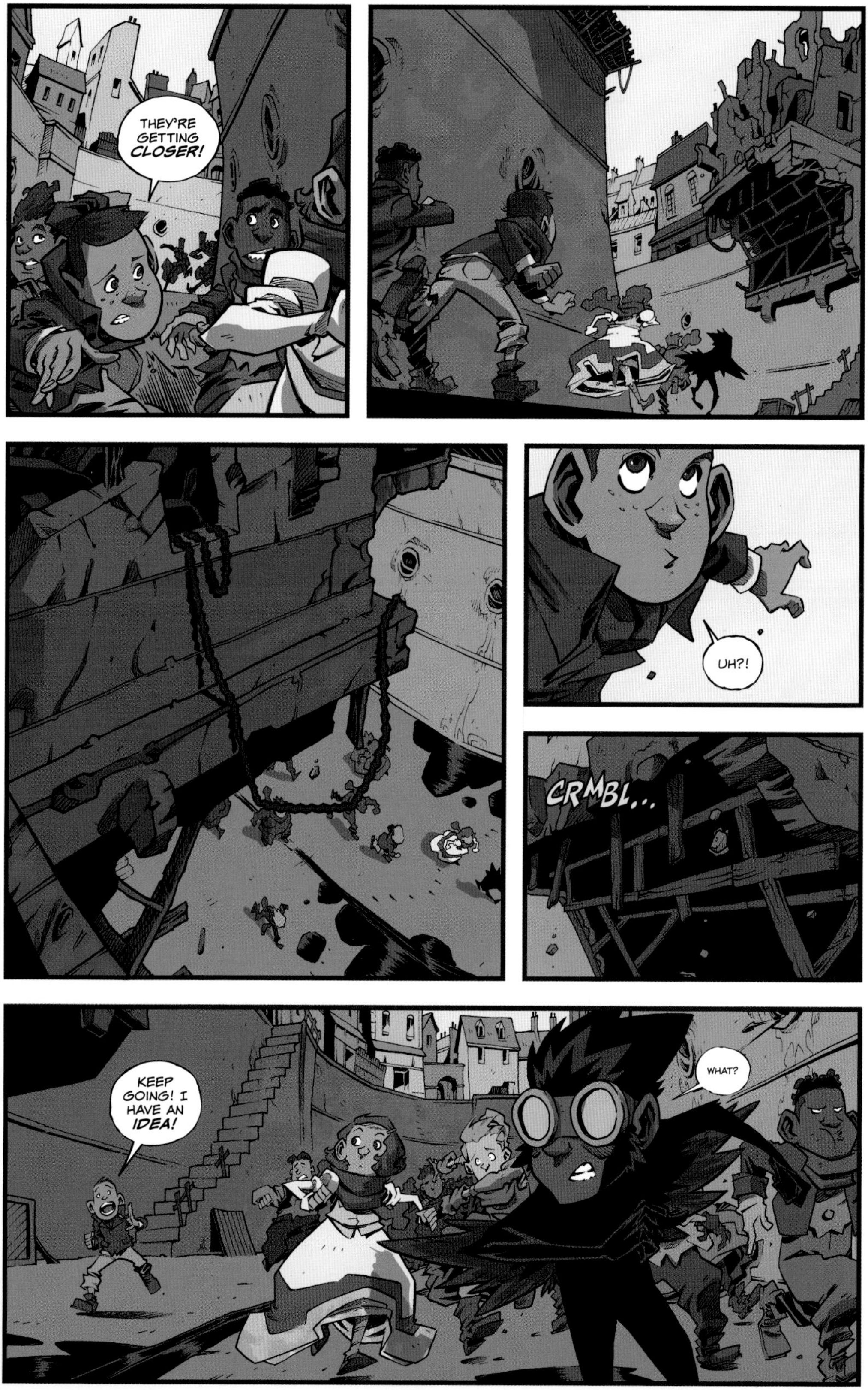
THEY'RE GETTING CLOSER!
UH?!
CRMBL...
KEEP GOING! I HAVE AN IDEA!
WHAT?

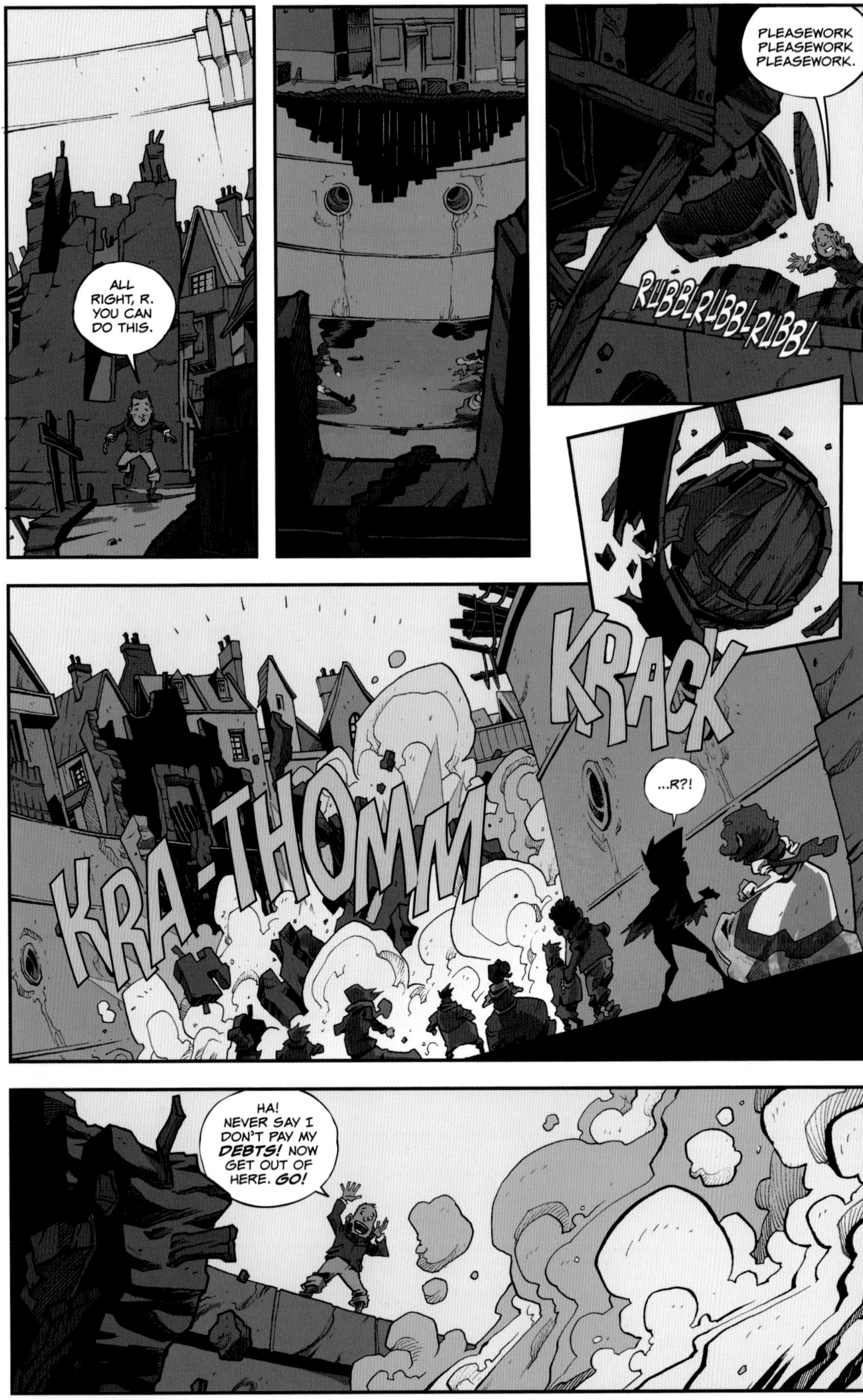

ALL RIGHT, R. YOU CAN DO THIS.
PLEASEWORK PLEASEWORK PLEASEWORK.
RUBBL RUBBL RUBBL
KRACK
KRA-THOMM
...R?!
HA! NEVER SAY I DON'T PAY MY DEBTS! NOW GET OUT OF HERE. GO!

IT'S NOT LOOKING GOOD, SIR.

NO ONE'S MISSING SO FAR, BUT MANY OF OUR MEN ARE INJURED.

WE MANAGED TO CATCH MOST OF THE MICE, BUT *NEITHER* MISS CHAPPELLE NOR THAT Z GIRL SEEM TO BE AMONG THEM.

...THEY DROPPED A HOUSE ON US...

I KNOW, BUDDY.

AND NOW WE HAVE *THAT* IN THE WAY.

I'M JUST NOT SURE HOW WE'RE GOING TO FIND THEM, SIR.

...SIR?

≶OUGHFF≶

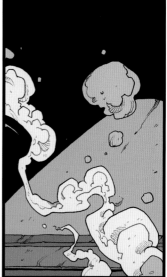

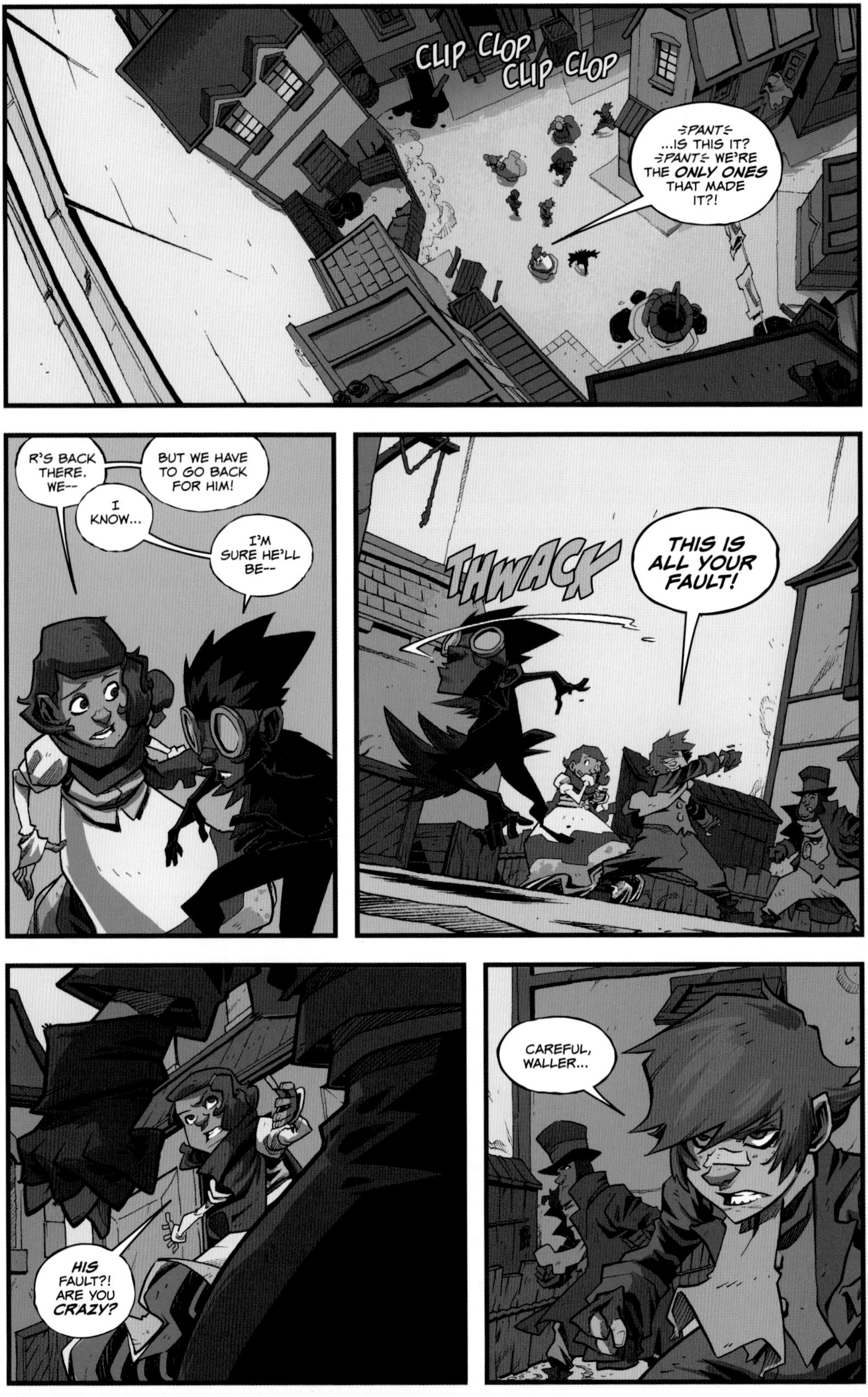
CLIP CLOP
CLIP CLOP
=PANT= ...IS THIS IT? =PANT= WE'RE THE ONLY ONES THAT MADE IT?!
R'S BACK THERE. WE--
BUT WE HAVE TO GO BACK FOR HIM!
I KNOW...
I'M SURE HE'LL BE--
THWACK
THIS IS ALL YOUR FAULT!
HIS FAULT?! ARE YOU CRAZY?
CAREFUL, WALLER...

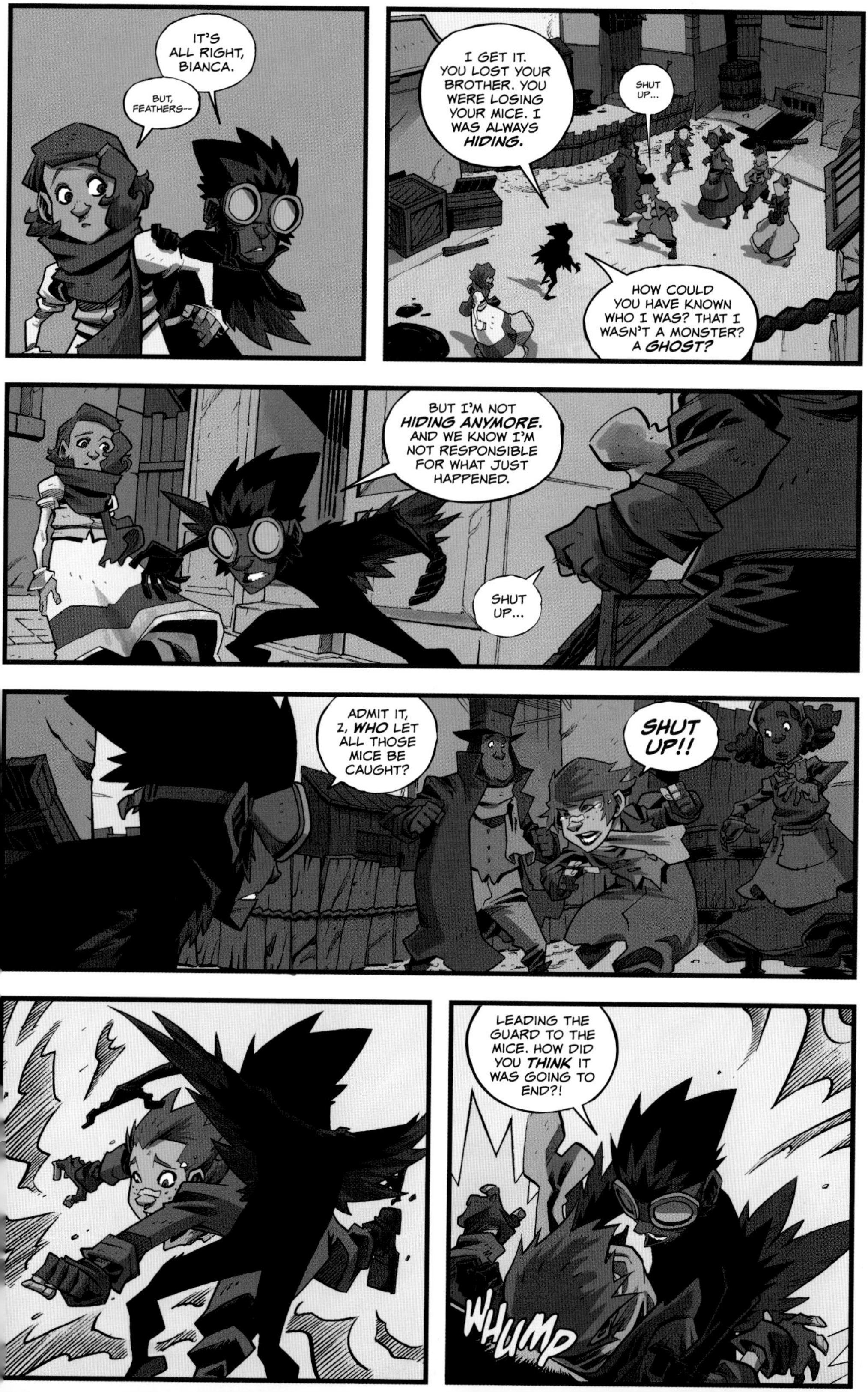

IT'S ALL RIGHT, BIANCA.
BUT, FEATHERS--
I GET IT. YOU LOST YOUR BROTHER. YOU WERE LOSING YOUR MICE. I WAS ALWAYS *HIDING.*
SHUT UP...
HOW COULD YOU HAVE KNOWN WHO I WAS? THAT I WASN'T A MONSTER? A *GHOST?*
BUT I'M NOT *HIDING ANYMORE.* AND WE KNOW I'M NOT RESPONSIBLE FOR WHAT JUST HAPPENED.
SHUT UP...
ADMIT IT, Z, *WHO* LET ALL THOSE MICE BE CAUGHT?
SHUT UP!!
LEADING THE GUARD TO THE MICE. HOW DID YOU *THINK* IT WAS GOING TO END?!
WHUMP

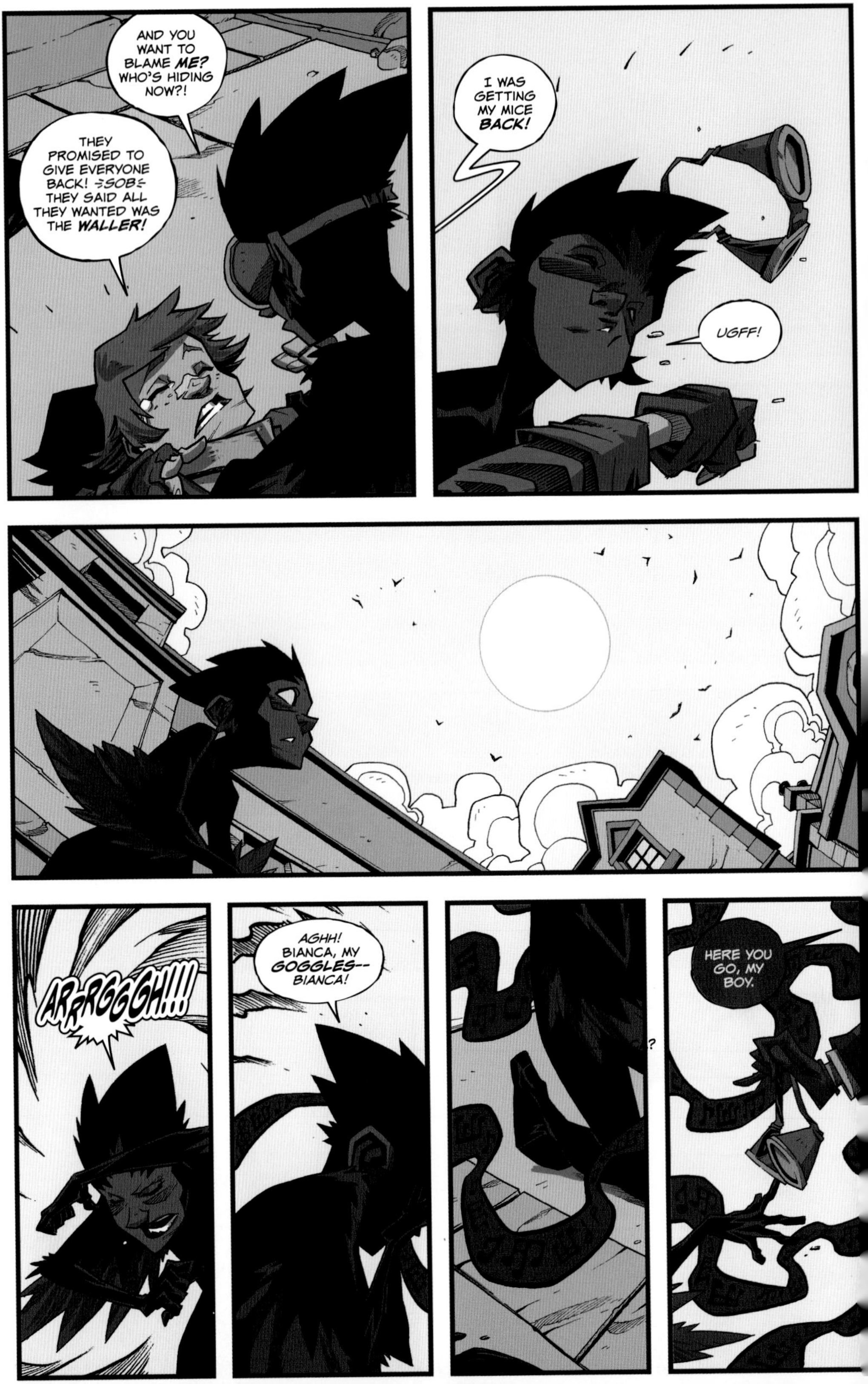
AND YOU WANT TO BLAME ME? WHO'S HIDING NOW?!
THEY PROMISED TO GIVE EVERYONE BACK! =SOB= THEY SAID ALL THEY WANTED WAS THE WALLER!
I WAS GETTING MY MICE BACK!
UGFF!
ARRRGGGH!!!!
AGHH! BIANCA, MY GOGGLES-- BIANCA!
?
HERE YOU GO, MY BOY.

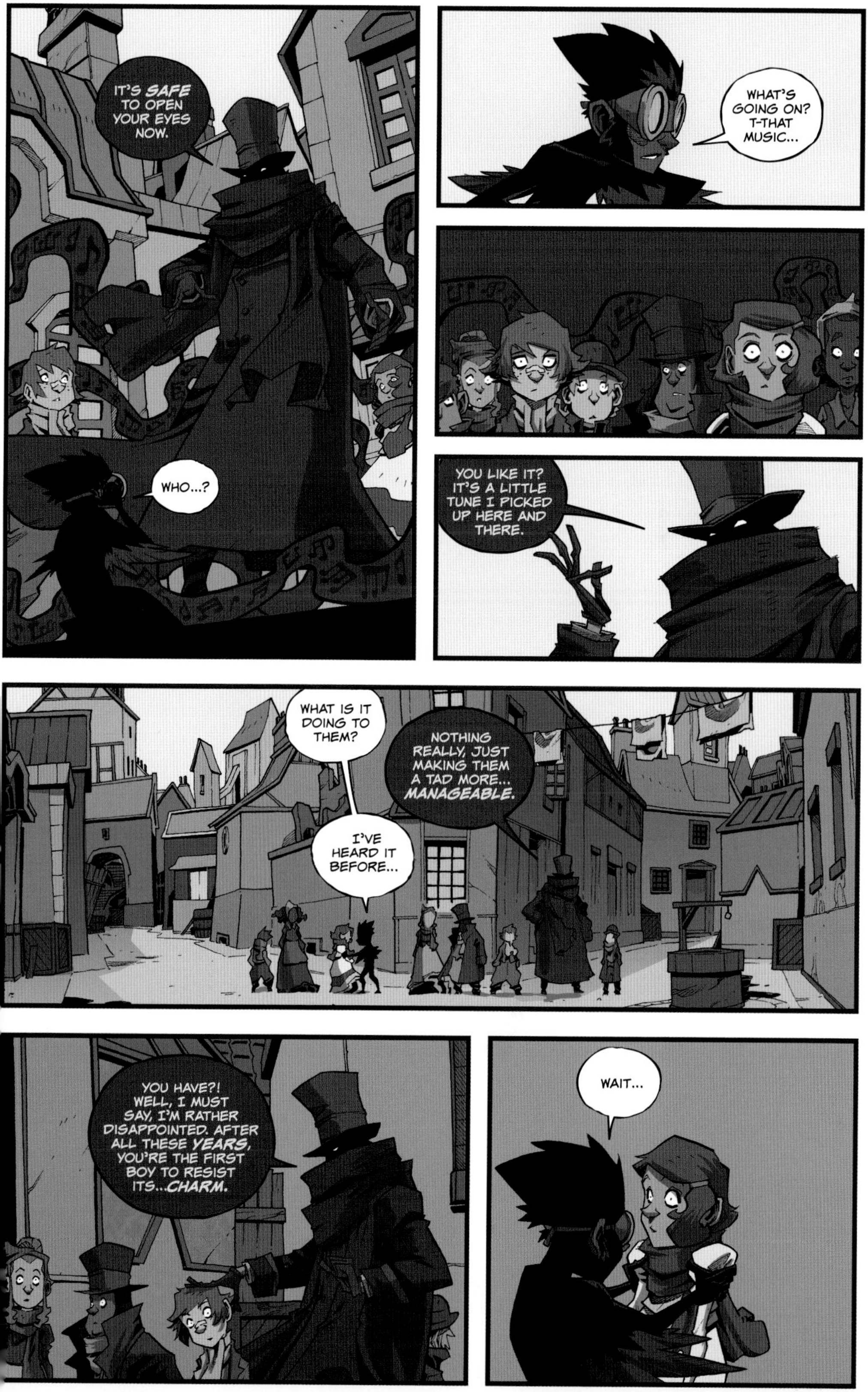
IT'S SAFE TO OPEN YOUR EYES NOW.
WHO...?
WHAT'S GOING ON? T-THAT MUSIC...
YOU LIKE IT? IT'S A LITTLE TUNE I PICKED UP HERE AND THERE.
WHAT IS IT DOING TO THEM?
NOTHING REALLY, JUST MAKING THEM A TAD MORE... MANAGEABLE.
I'VE HEARD IT BEFORE...
YOU HAVE?! WELL, I MUST SAY, I'M RATHER DISAPPOINTED. AFTER ALL THESE YEARS, YOU'RE THE FIRST BOY TO RESIST ITS...CHARM.
WAIT...

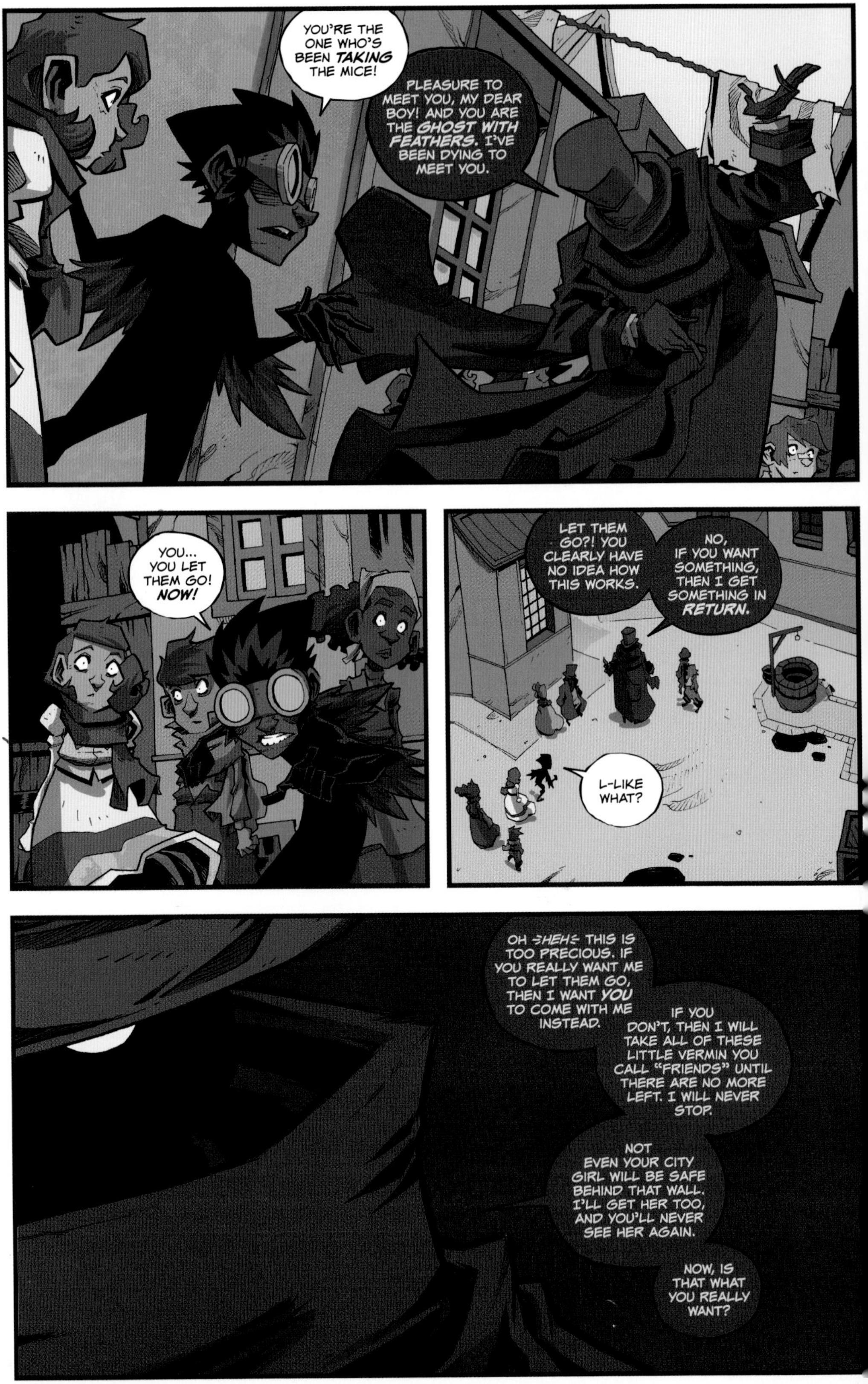
YOU'RE THE ONE WHO'S BEEN TAKING THE MICE!
PLEASURE TO MEET YOU, MY DEAR BOY! AND YOU ARE THE GHOST WITH FEATHERS. I'VE BEEN DYING TO MEET YOU.
YOU... YOU LET THEM GO! NOW!
LET THEM GO?! YOU CLEARLY HAVE NO IDEA HOW THIS WORKS.
NO, IF YOU WANT SOMETHING, THEN I GET SOMETHING IN RETURN.
L-LIKE WHAT?
OH =HEH= THIS IS TOO PRECIOUS. IF YOU REALLY WANT ME TO LET THEM GO, THEN I WANT YOU TO COME WITH ME INSTEAD.
IF YOU DON'T, THEN I WILL TAKE ALL OF THESE LITTLE VERMIN YOU CALL "FRIENDS" UNTIL THERE ARE NO MORE LEFT. I WILL NEVER STOP.
NOT EVEN YOUR CITY GIRL WILL BE SAFE BEHIND THAT WALL. I'LL GET HER TOO, AND YOU'LL NEVER SEE HER AGAIN.
NOW, IS THAT WHAT YOU REALLY WANT?

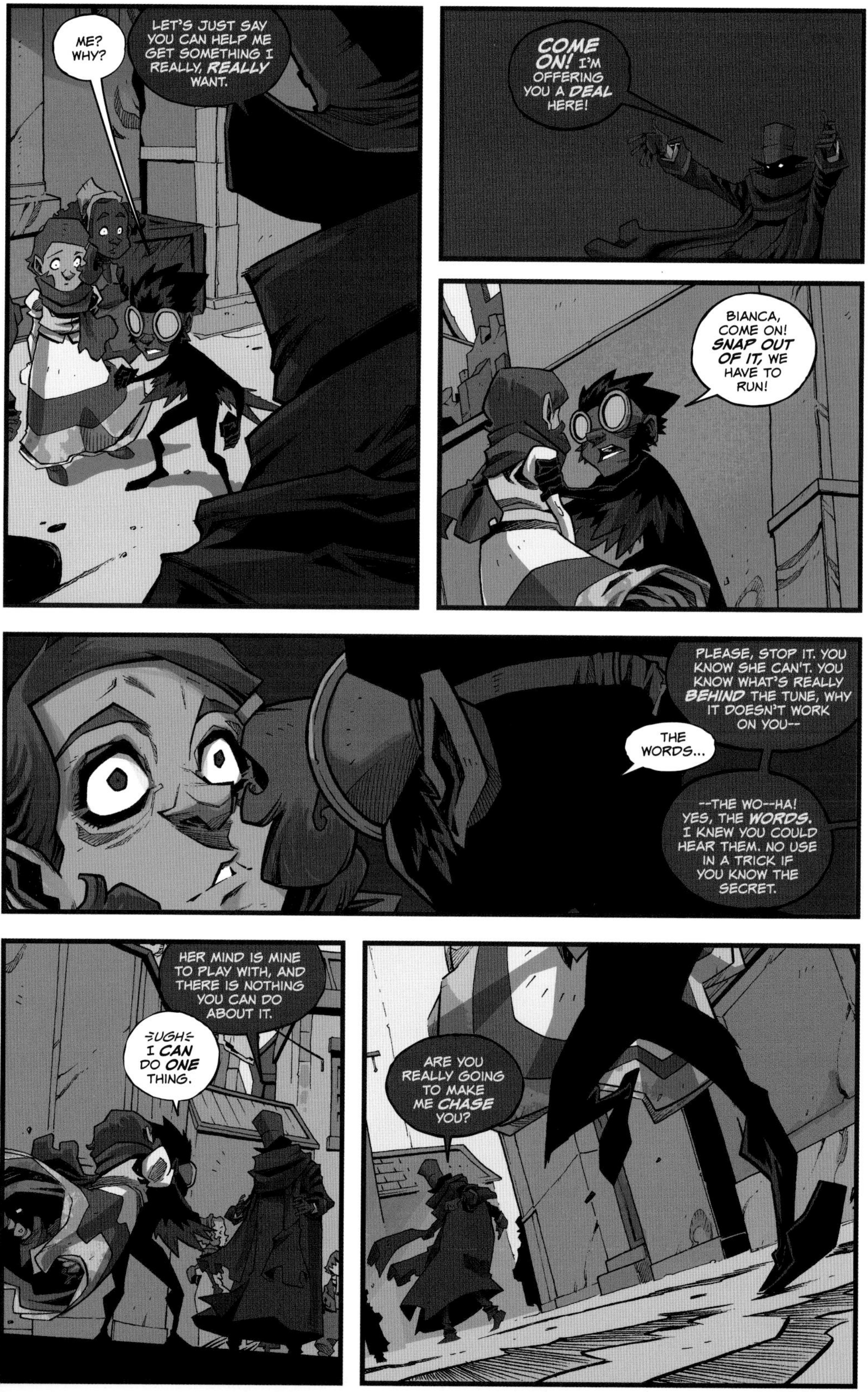

ME? WHY?
LET'S JUST SAY YOU CAN HELP ME GET SOMETHING I REALLY, REALLY WANT.
COME ON! I'M OFFERING YOU A DEAL HERE!
BIANCA, COME ON! SNAP OUT OF IT, WE HAVE TO RUN!
PLEASE, STOP IT. YOU KNOW SHE CAN'T. YOU KNOW WHAT'S REALLY BEHIND THE TUNE, WHY IT DOESN'T WORK ON YOU--
THE WORDS...
--THE WO--HA! YES, THE WORDS. I KNEW YOU COULD HEAR THEM. NO USE IN A TRICK IF YOU KNOW THE SECRET.
HER MIND IS MINE TO PLAY WITH, AND THERE IS NOTHING YOU CAN DO ABOUT IT.
UGH I CAN DO ONE THING.
ARE YOU REALLY GOING TO MAKE ME CHASE YOU?

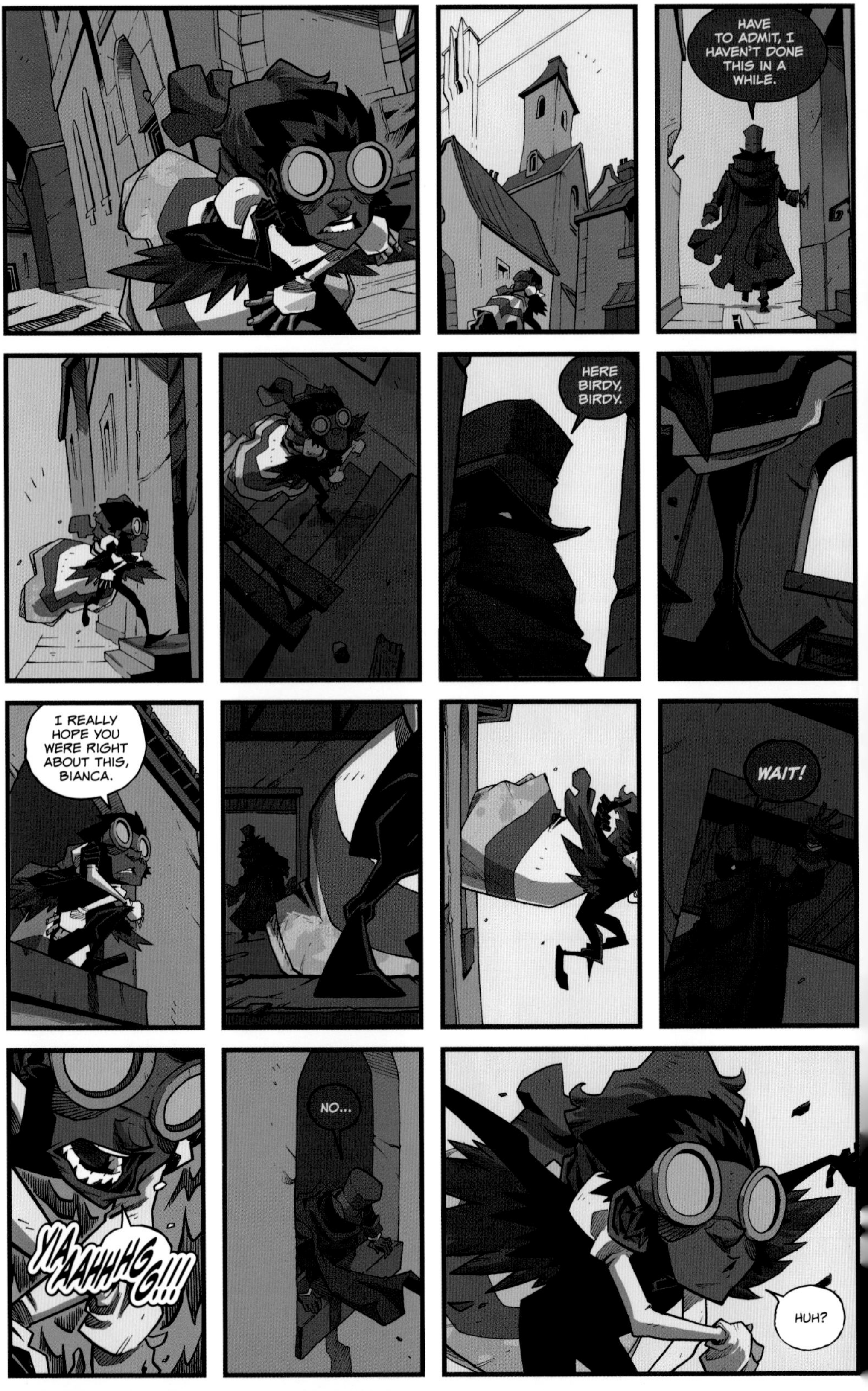
HAVE TO ADMIT, I HAVEN'T DONE THIS IN A WHILE.
HERE BIRDY, BIRDY.
I REALLY HOPE YOU WERE RIGHT ABOUT THIS, BIANCA.
WAIT!
YIAAAHHHG!!!
NO...
HUH?

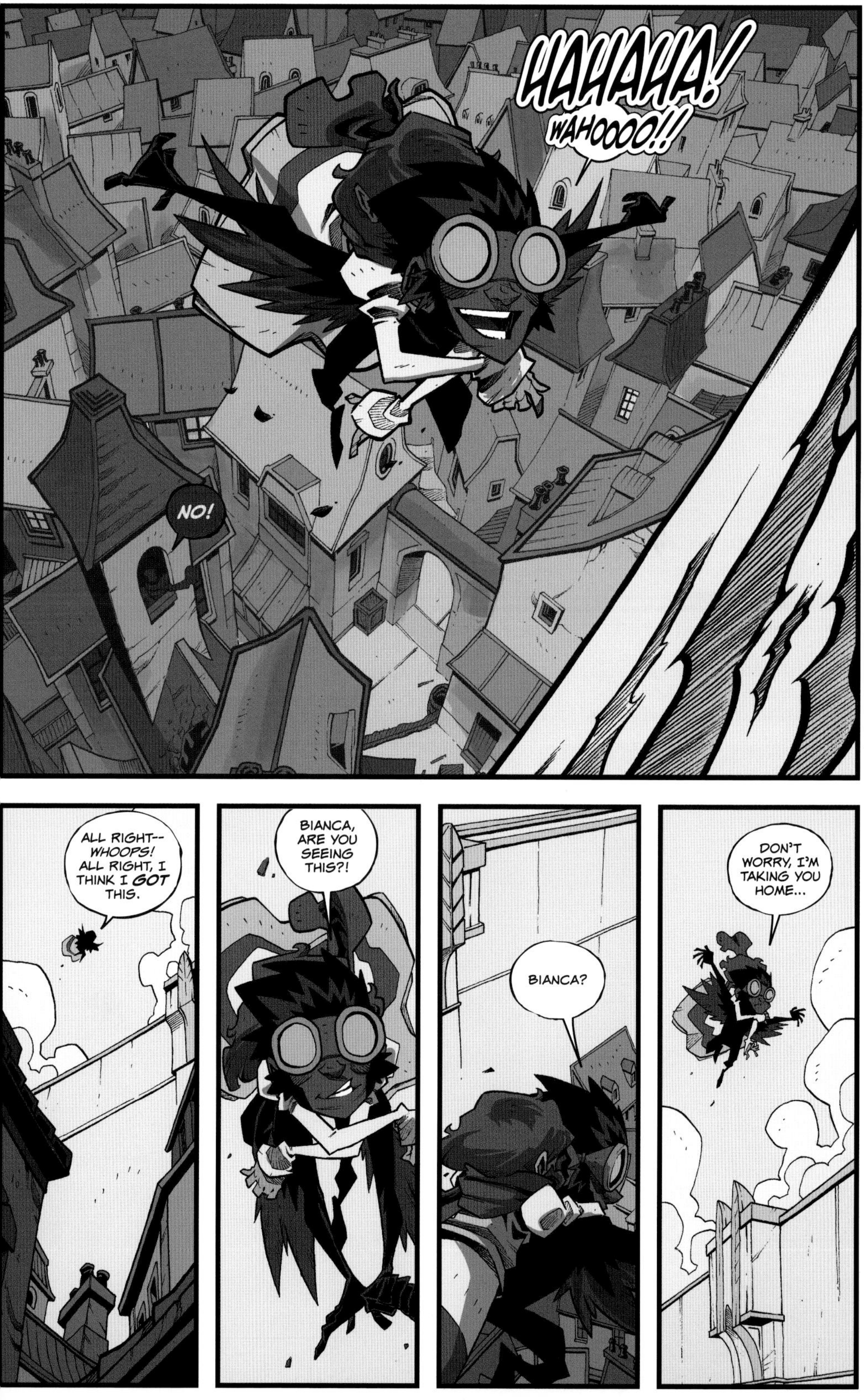
HAHAHA!
WAHOOOO!!
NO!
ALL RIGHT--
WHOOPS!
ALL RIGHT, I THINK I GOT THIS.
BIANCA, ARE YOU SEEING THIS?!
BIANCA?
DON'T WORRY, I'M TAKING YOU HOME...

≳HMMN≲
W-WHAT? WHERE ARE WE?

HOLY--
WOAAA!!

CALM DOWN! YOU'RE GOING TO MAKE US FALL!

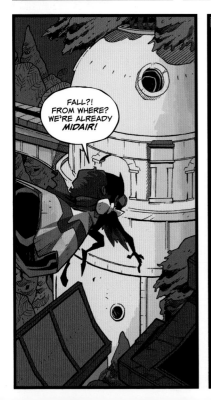

FALL?! FROM WHERE? WE'RE ALREADY MIDAIR!

WAIT, HOLD ON.

WHAT WAS THAT?! YOU WERE FLYING!

I KNOW! YOU WERE RIGHT!

BUT...WHAT HAPPENED? Z AND THE MICE-- LAST THING I REMEMBER, YOU WERE SCREAMING ABOUT SOMETHING, AND THEN... MUSIC...

IT WAS HIM, THE MAN WHO'S BEEN TAKING THE MICE. I SAW HIM. HE ALMOST TOOK YOU, TOO. WE BARELY MADE IT OUT.

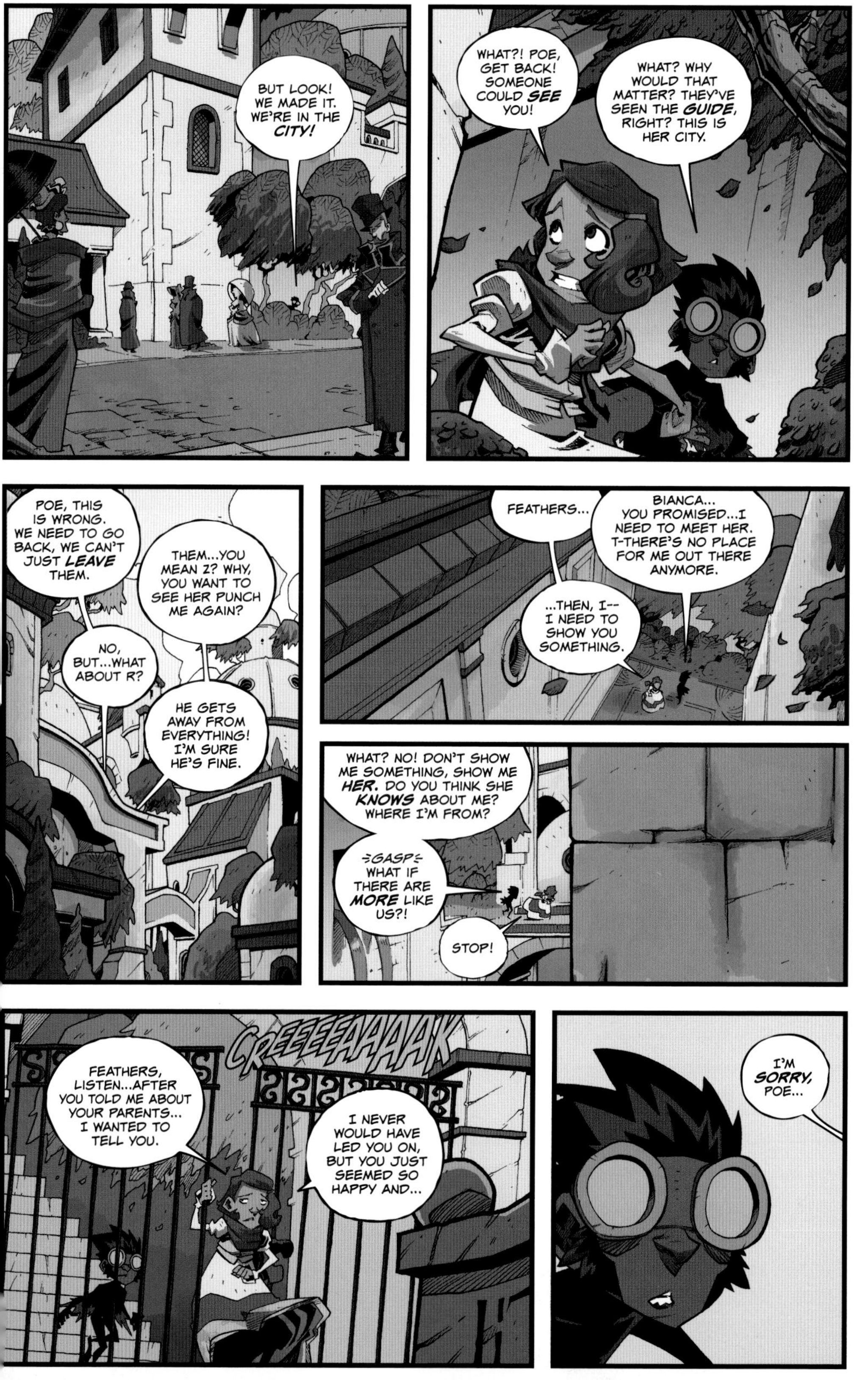
BUT LOOK! WE MADE IT. WE'RE IN THE CITY!
WHAT?! POE, GET BACK! SOMEONE COULD SEE YOU!
WHAT? WHY WOULD THAT MATTER? THEY'VE SEEN THE GUIDE, RIGHT? THIS IS HER CITY.
POE, THIS IS WRONG. WE NEED TO GO BACK, WE CAN'T JUST LEAVE THEM.
THEM...YOU MEAN Z? WHY, YOU WANT TO SEE HER PUNCH ME AGAIN?
NO, BUT...WHAT ABOUT R?
HE GETS AWAY FROM EVERYTHING! I'M SURE HE'S FINE.
FEATHERS...
...THEN, I-- I NEED TO SHOW YOU SOMETHING.
BIANCA... YOU PROMISED...I NEED TO MEET HER. T-THERE'S NO PLACE FOR ME OUT THERE ANYMORE.
WHAT? NO! DON'T SHOW ME SOMETHING, SHOW ME HER. DO YOU THINK SHE KNOWS ABOUT ME? WHERE I'M FROM?
GASP WHAT IF THERE ARE MORE LIKE US?!
STOP!
CREEEEAAAAK
FEATHERS, LISTEN...AFTER YOU TOLD ME ABOUT YOUR PARENTS... I WANTED TO TELL YOU.
I NEVER WOULD HAVE LED YOU ON, BUT YOU JUST SEEMED SO HAPPY AND...
I'M SORRY, POE...

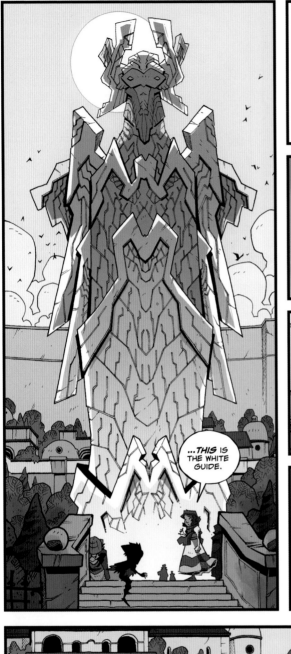

...*THIS* IS THE WHITE GUIDE.

COME...

...I'M HERE.

POE, WAIT!

YOU'VE COME TO ME...

IS THAT...

--THE GUIDE?

THIS IS MY PLACE...

THE GUIDE!

SHE'S BACK...

THE GUIDE HAS RETURNED!

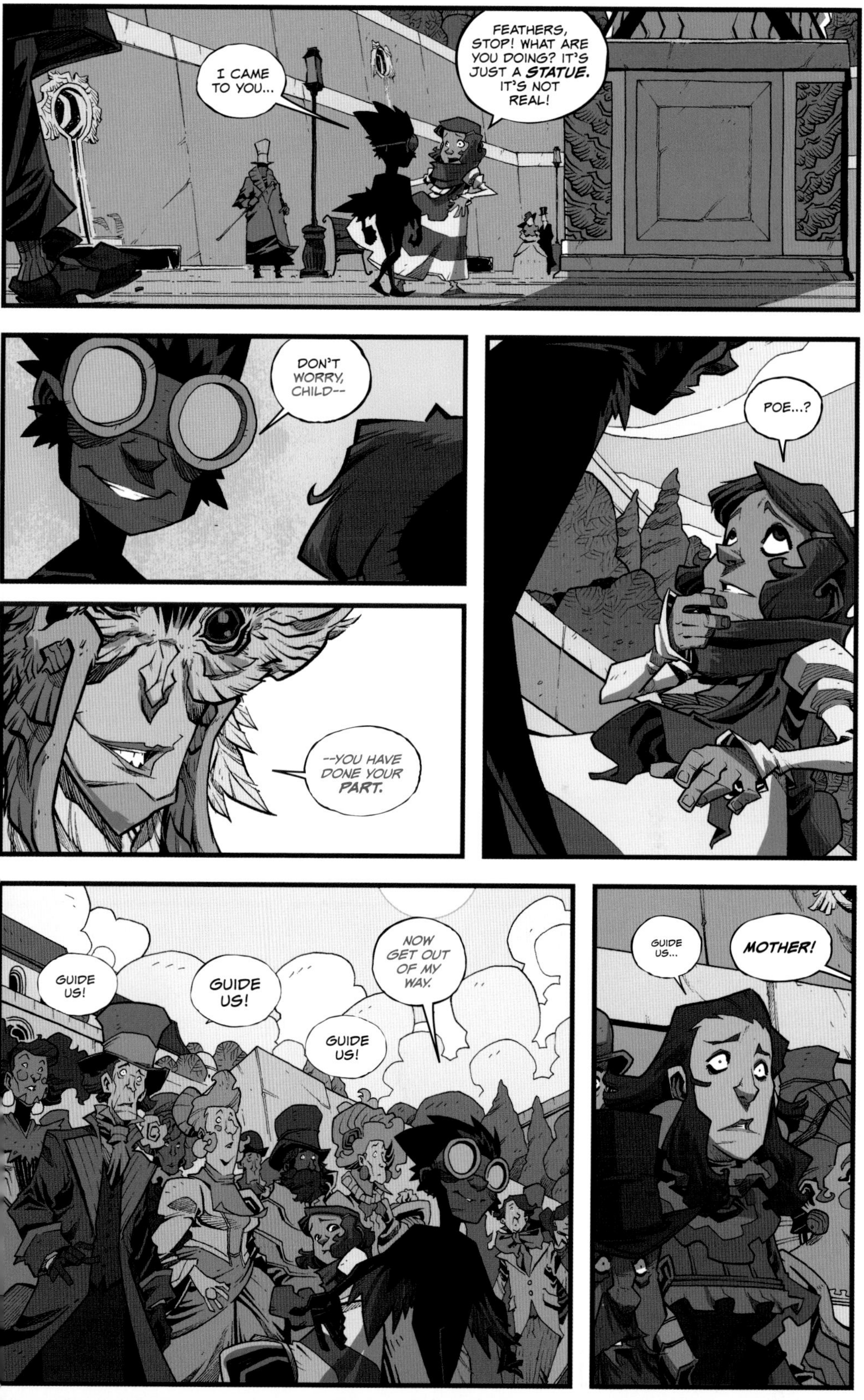
I CAME TO YOU...
FEATHERS, STOP! WHAT ARE YOU DOING? IT'S JUST A STATUE. IT'S NOT REAL!
DON'T WORRY, CHILD--
--YOU HAVE DONE YOUR PART.
POE...?
GUIDE US!
GUIDE US!
GUIDE US!
NOW GET OUT OF MY WAY.
GUIDE US...
MOTHER!

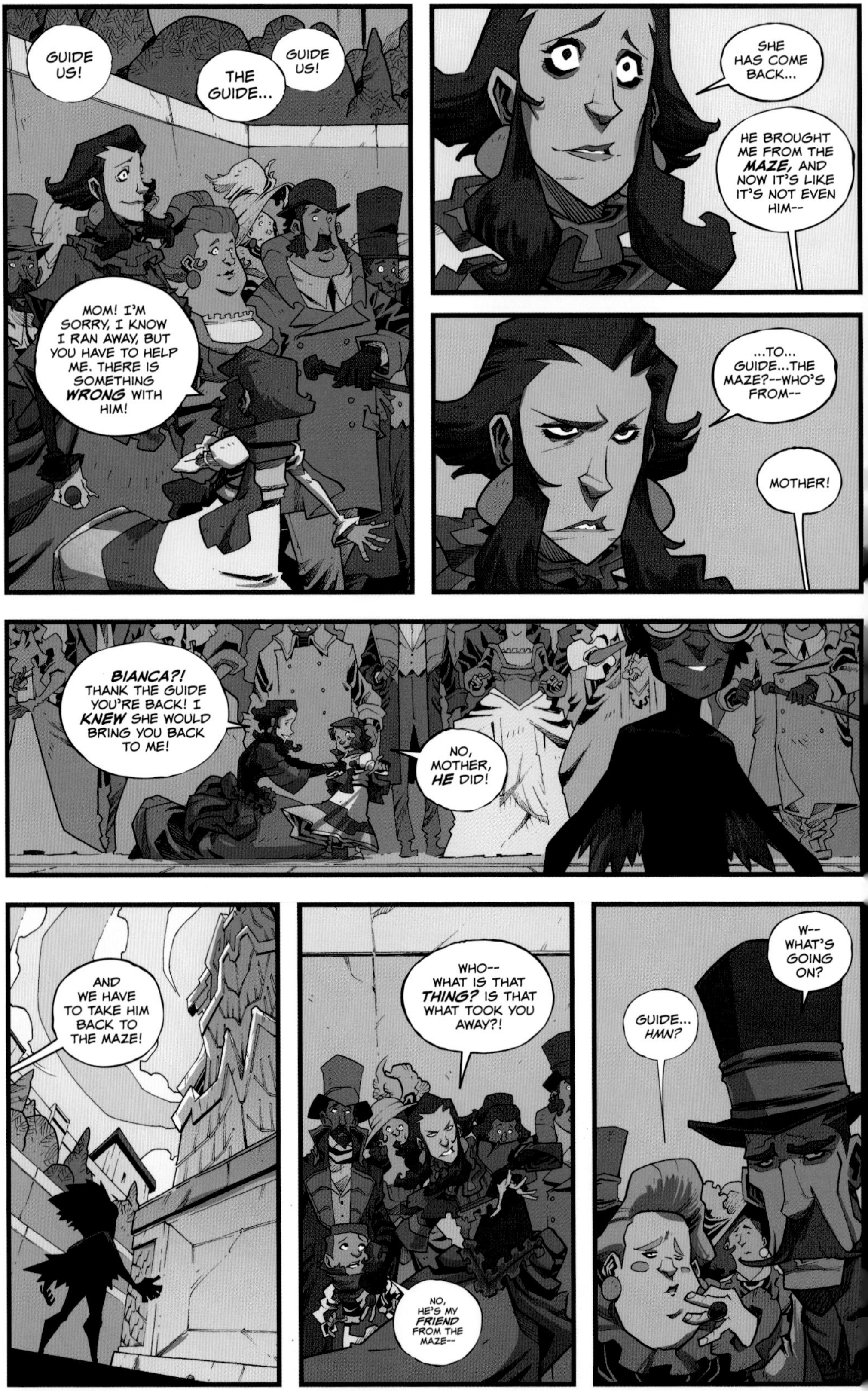
GUIDE US!
THE GUIDE...
GUIDE US!
MOM! I'M SORRY, I KNOW I RAN AWAY, BUT YOU HAVE TO HELP ME. THERE IS SOMETHING WRONG WITH HIM!
SHE HAS COME BACK...
HE BROUGHT ME FROM THE MAZE, AND NOW IT'S LIKE IT'S NOT EVEN HIM--
...TO... GUIDE...THE MAZE?--WHO'S FROM--
MOTHER!
BIANCA?! THANK THE GUIDE YOU'RE BACK! I KNEW SHE WOULD BRING YOU BACK TO ME!
NO, MOTHER, HE DID!
AND WE HAVE TO TAKE HIM BACK TO THE MAZE!
WHO-- WHAT IS THAT THING? IS THAT WHAT TOOK YOU AWAY?!
NO, HE'S MY FRIEND FROM THE MAZE--
W-- WHAT'S GOING ON?
GUIDE... HMN?

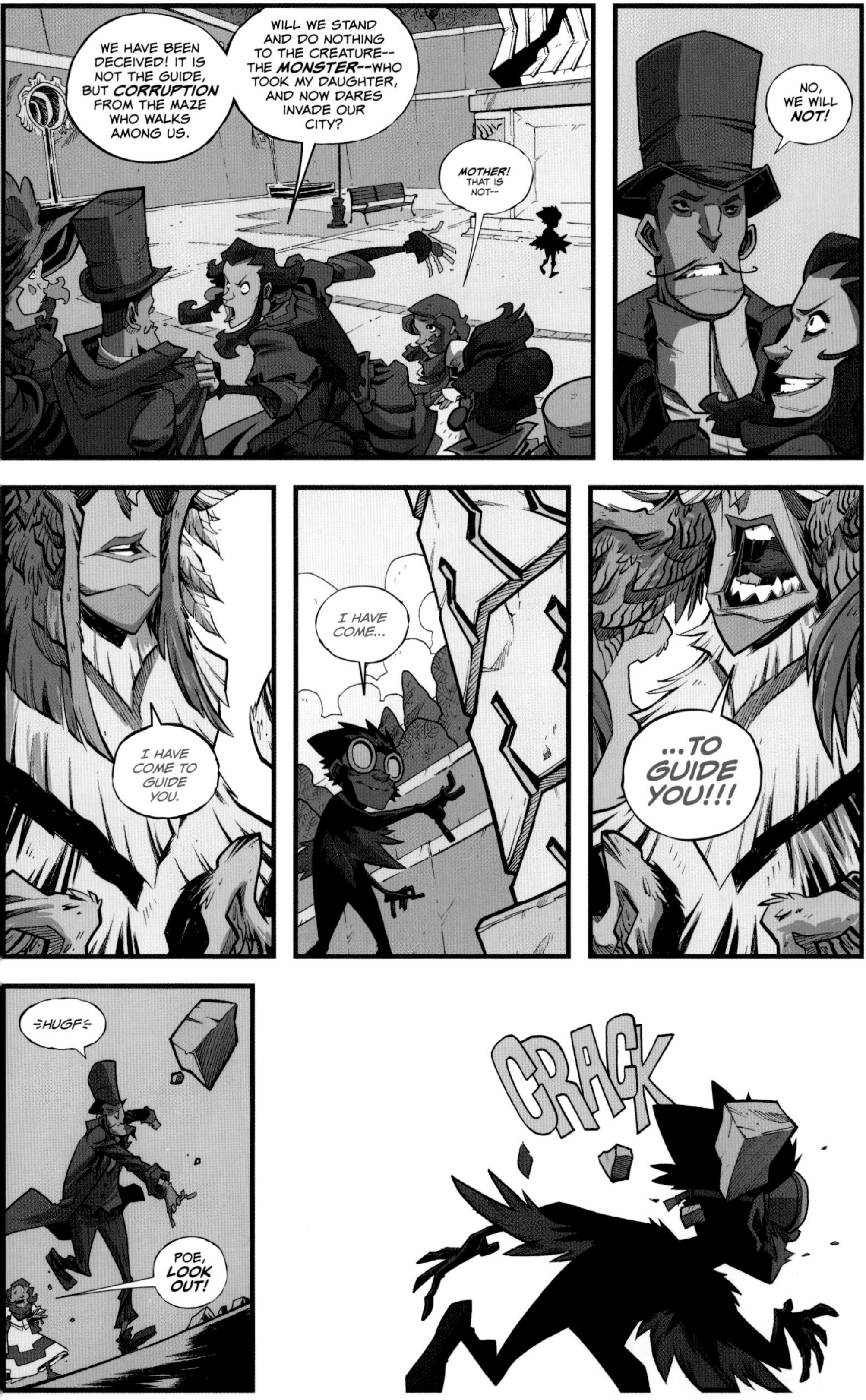
WE HAVE BEEN DECEIVED! IT IS NOT THE GUIDE, BUT CORRUPTION FROM THE MAZE WHO WALKS AMONG US.
WILL WE STAND AND DO NOTHING TO THE CREATURE-- THE MONSTER--WHO TOOK MY DAUGHTER, AND NOW DARES INVADE OUR CITY?
MOTHER! THAT IS NOT--
NO, WE WILL NOT!
I HAVE COME TO GUIDE YOU.
I HAVE COME...
...TO GUIDE YOU!!!
HUGF
POE, LOOK OUT!
CRACK

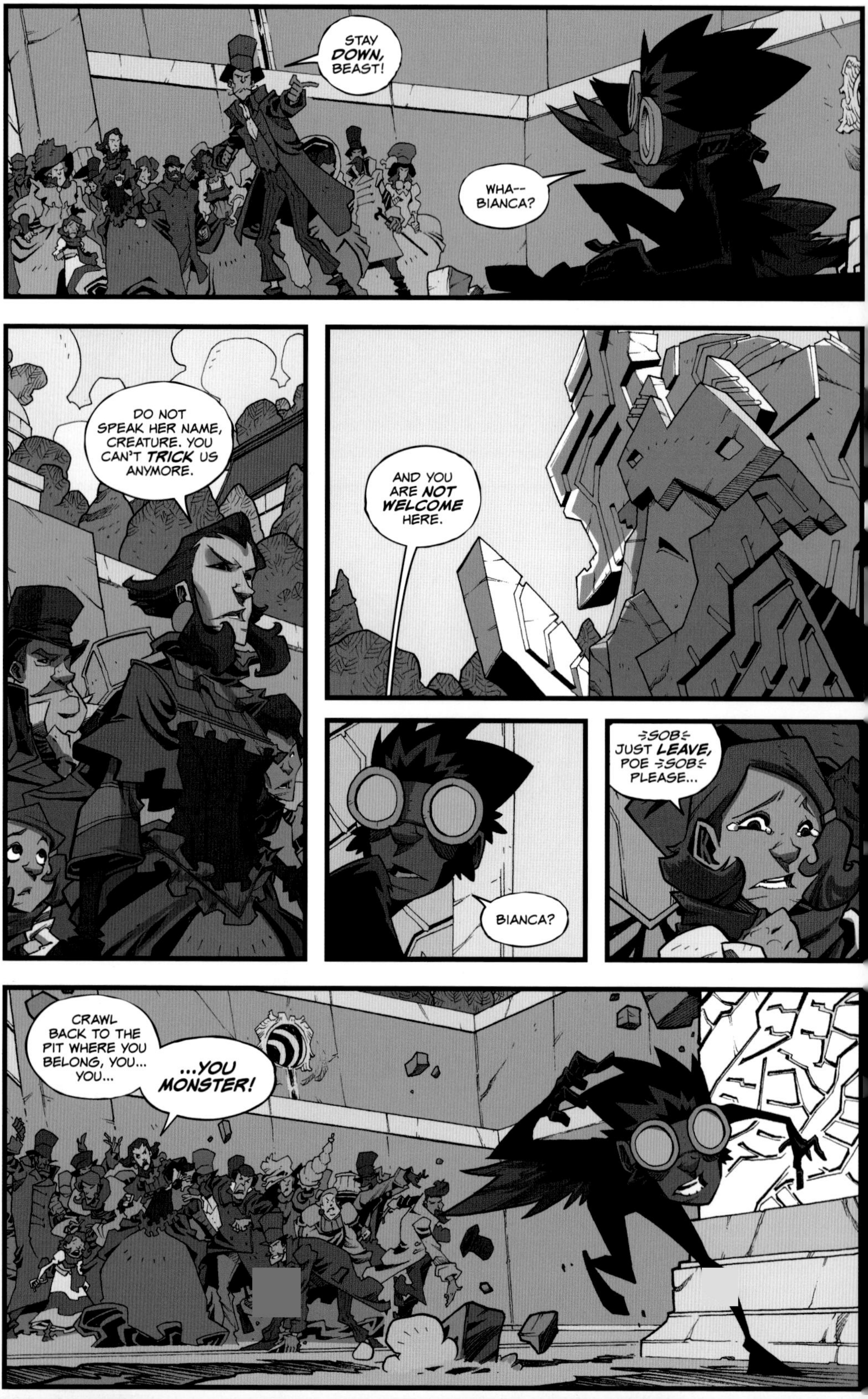
STAY DOWN, BEAST!
WHA-- BIANCA?
DO NOT SPEAK HER NAME, CREATURE. YOU CAN'T TRICK US ANYMORE.
AND YOU ARE NOT WELCOME HERE.
BIANCA?
≈SOB≈ JUST LEAVE, POE ≈SOB≈ PLEASE...
CRAWL BACK TO THE PIT WHERE YOU BELONG, YOU... YOU...
...YOU MONSTER!

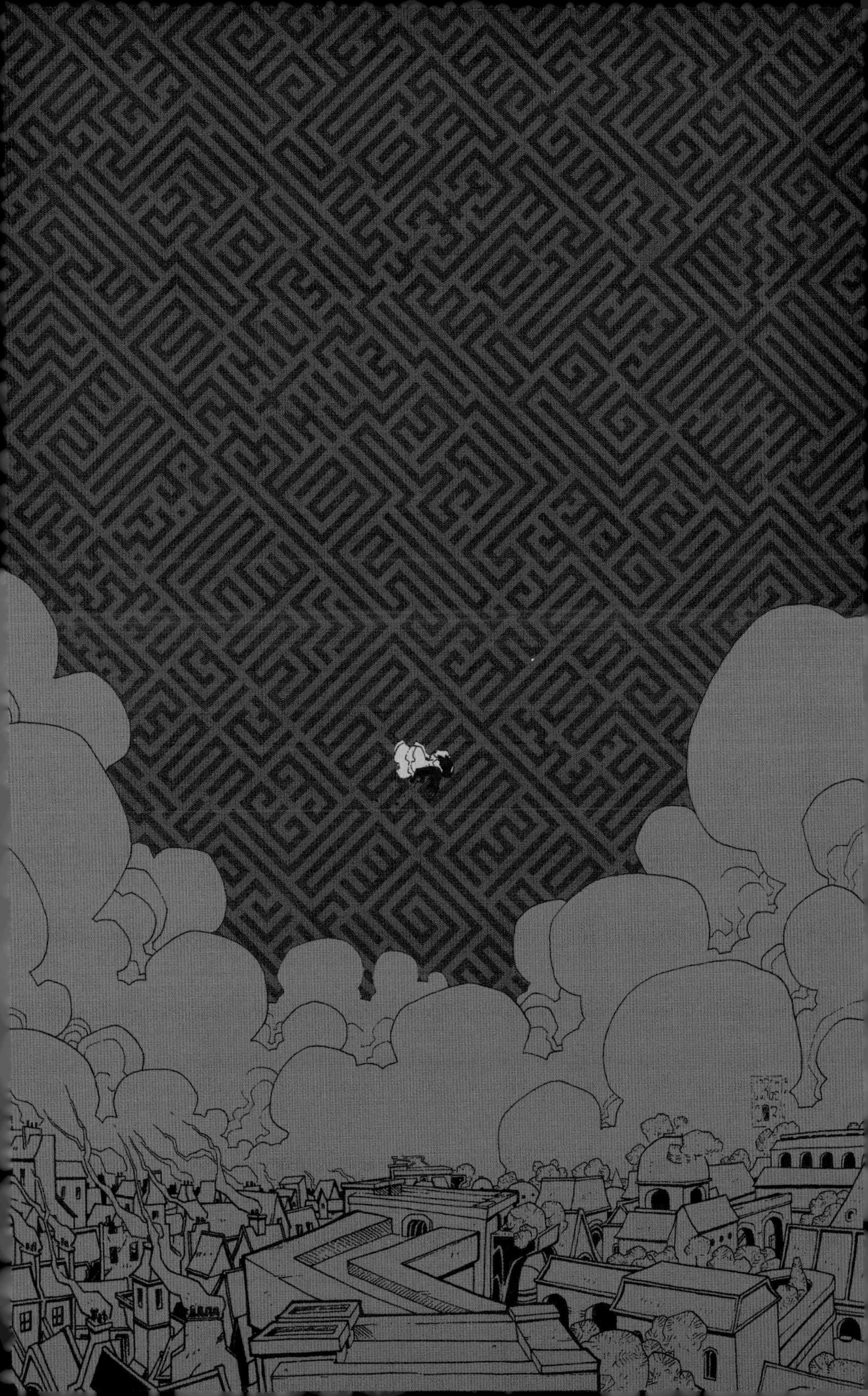

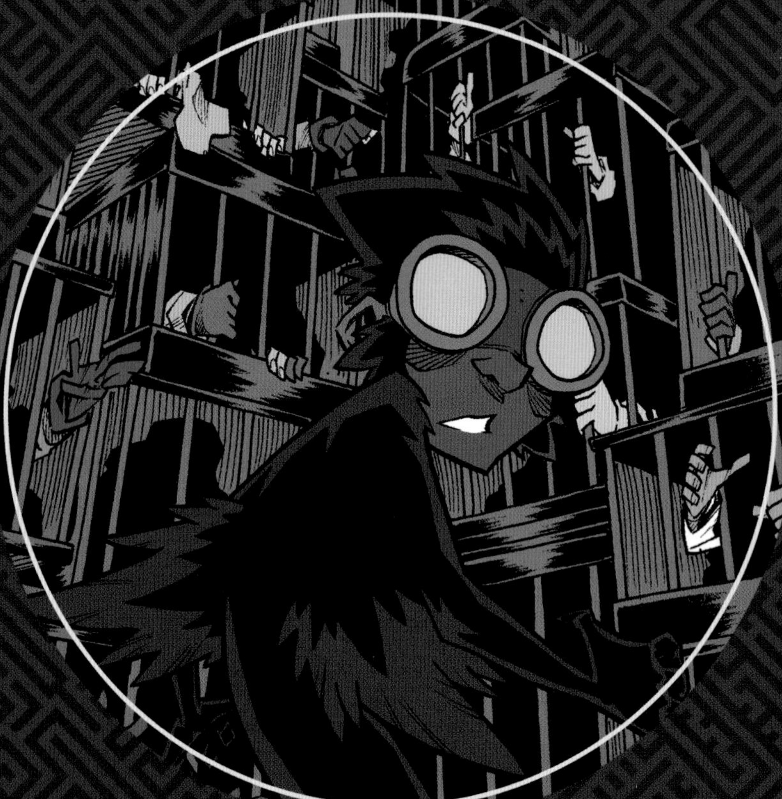

CHAPTER FIVE

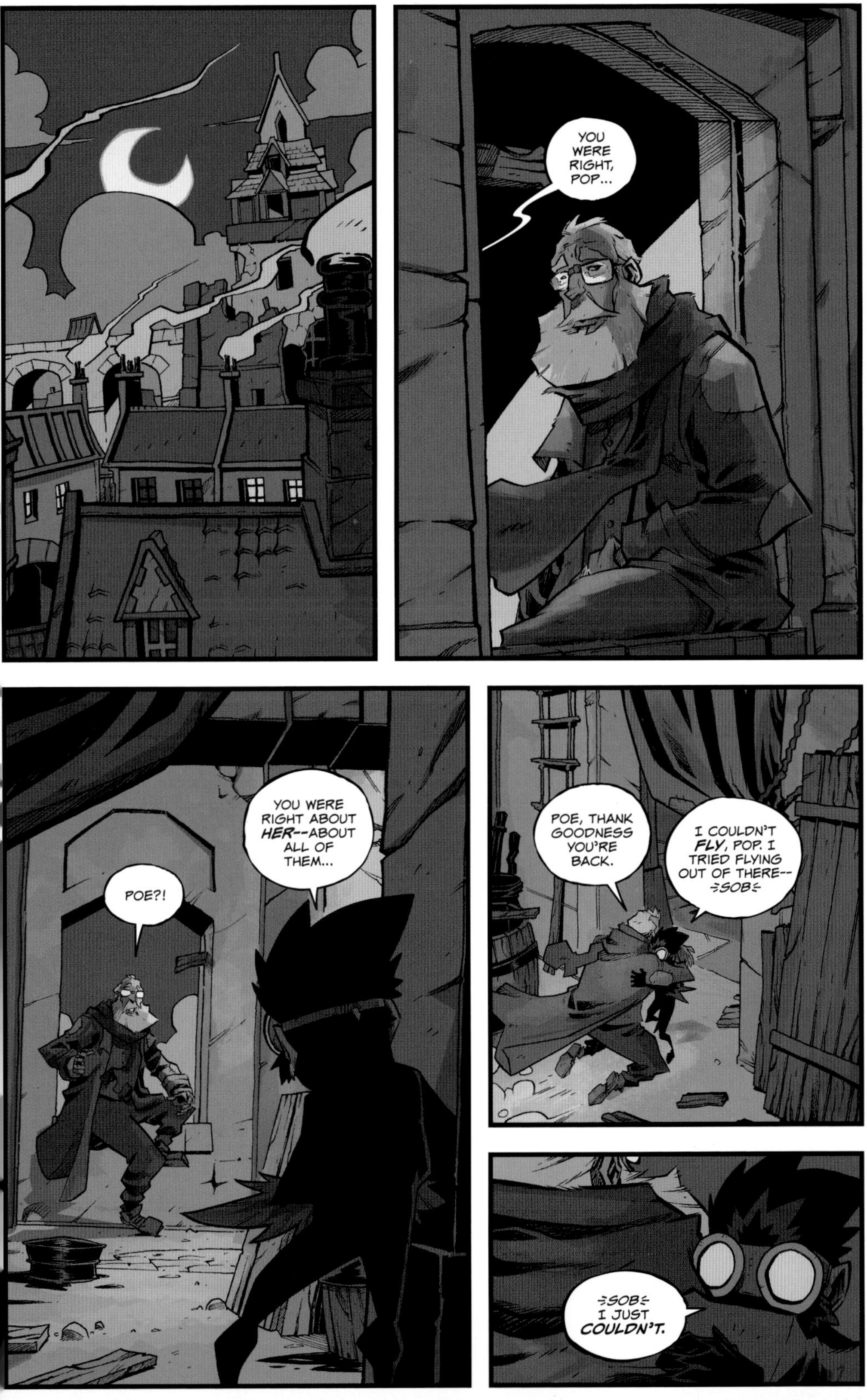
YOU WERE RIGHT, POP...
POE?!
YOU WERE RIGHT ABOUT HER--ABOUT ALL OF THEM...
POE, THANK GOODNESS YOU'RE BACK.
I COULDN'T FLY, POP. I TRIED FLYING OUT OF THERE-- SOB
SOB I JUST COULDN'T.

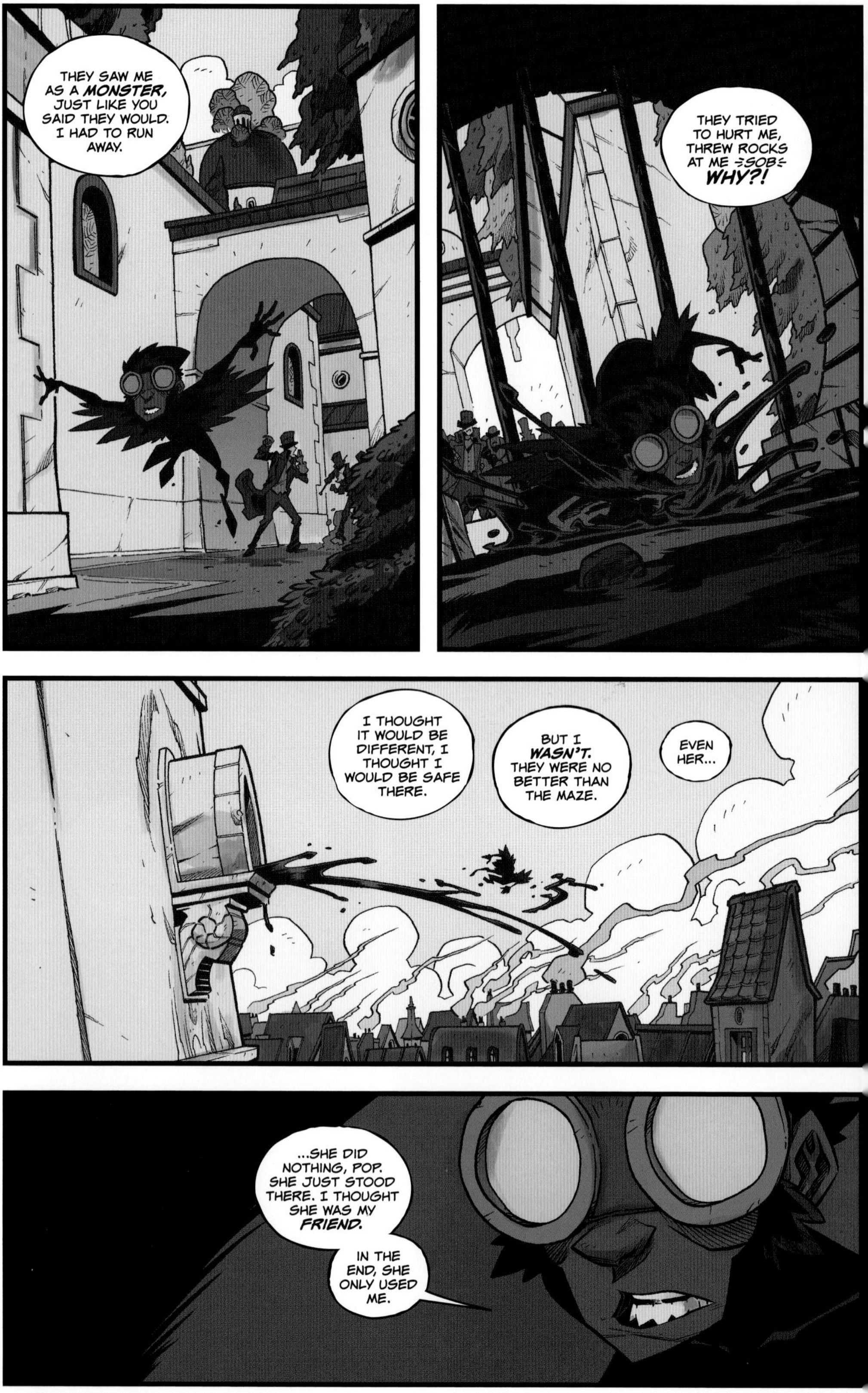
THEY SAW ME AS A MONSTER, JUST LIKE YOU SAID THEY WOULD. I HAD TO RUN AWAY.
THEY TRIED TO HURT ME, THREW ROCKS AT ME =SOB= WHY?!
I THOUGHT IT WOULD BE DIFFERENT, I THOUGHT I WOULD BE SAFE THERE.
BUT I WASN'T. THEY WERE NO BETTER THAN THE MAZE.
EVEN HER...
...SHE DID NOTHING, POP. SHE JUST STOOD THERE. I THOUGHT SHE WAS MY FRIEND.
IN THE END, SHE ONLY USED ME.

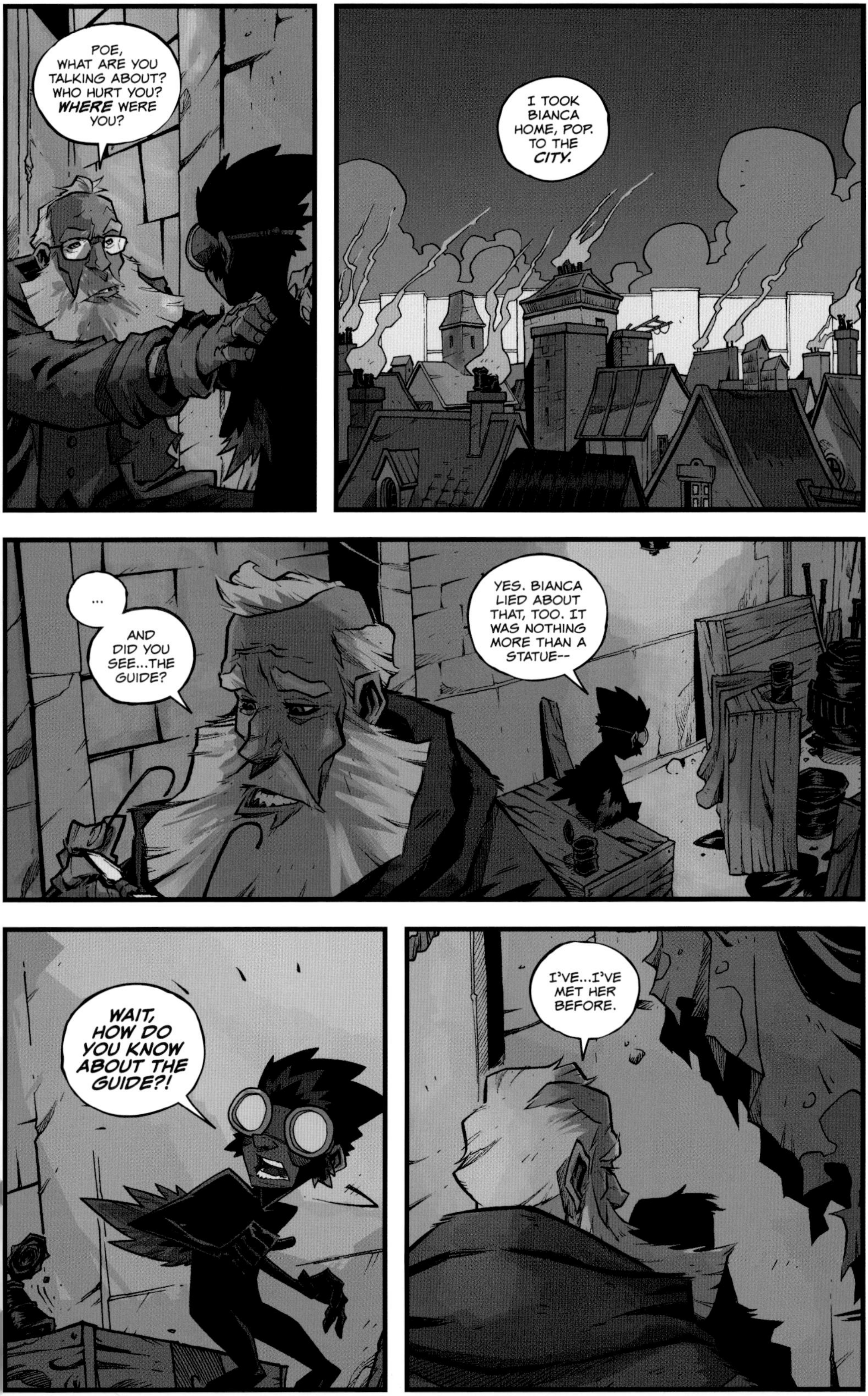
POE, WHAT ARE YOU TALKING ABOUT? WHO HURT YOU? WHERE WERE YOU?
I TOOK BIANCA HOME, POP. TO THE CITY.
...
AND DID YOU SEE...THE GUIDE?
YES. BIANCA LIED ABOUT THAT, TOO. IT WAS NOTHING MORE THAN A STATUE--
WAIT, HOW DO YOU KNOW ABOUT THE GUIDE?!
I'VE...I'VE MET HER BEFORE.

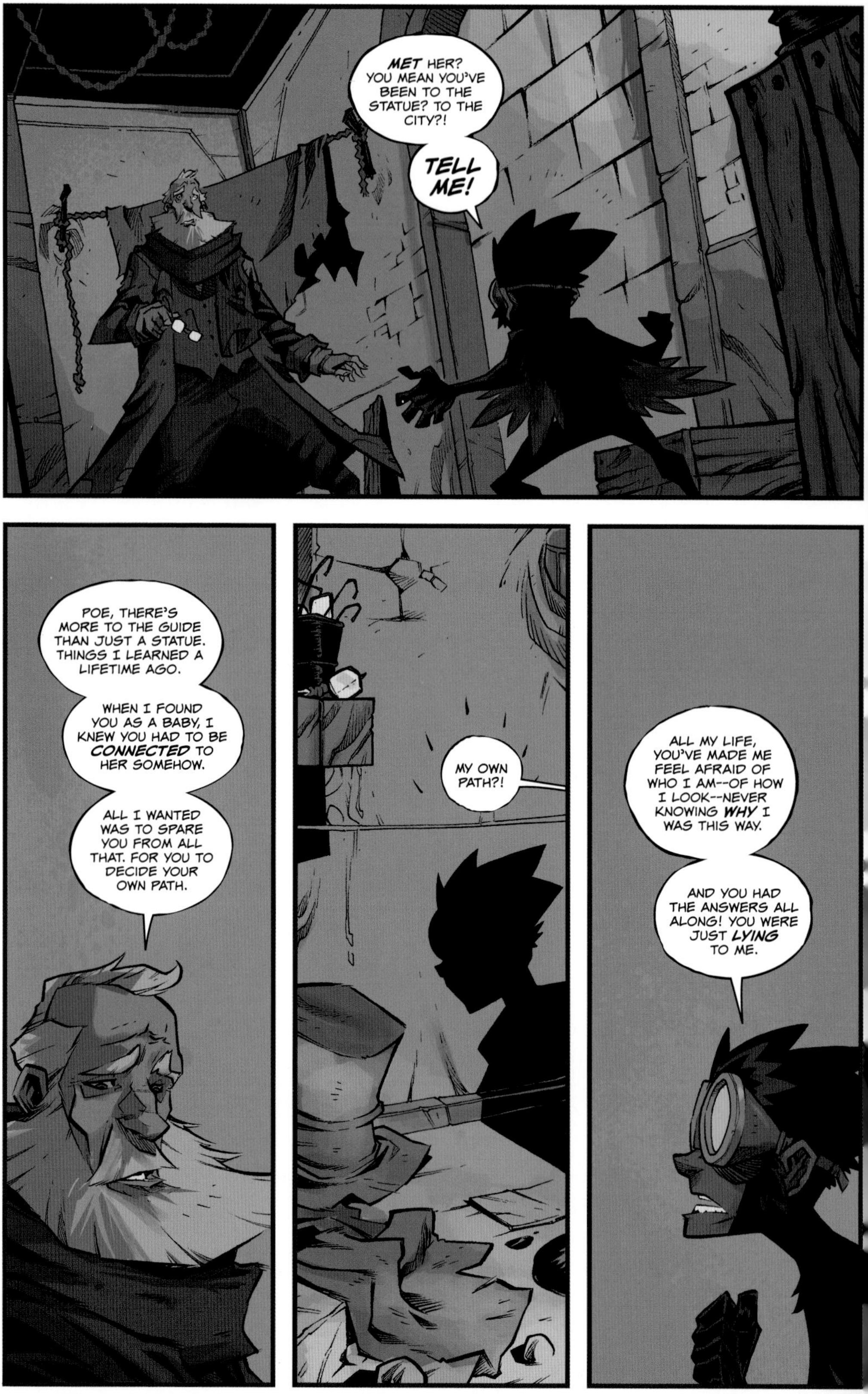
MET HER? YOU MEAN YOU'VE BEEN TO THE STATUE? TO THE CITY?!
TELL ME!
POE, THERE'S MORE TO THE GUIDE THAN JUST A STATUE. THINGS I LEARNED A LIFETIME AGO.
WHEN I FOUND YOU AS A BABY, I KNEW YOU HAD TO BE CONNECTED TO HER SOMEHOW.
ALL I WANTED WAS TO SPARE YOU FROM ALL THAT. FOR YOU TO DECIDE YOUR OWN PATH.
MY OWN PATH?!
ALL MY LIFE, YOU'VE MADE ME FEEL AFRAID OF WHO I AM--OF HOW I LOOK--NEVER KNOWING WHY I WAS THIS WAY.
AND YOU HAD THE ANSWERS ALL ALONG! YOU WERE JUST LYING TO ME.

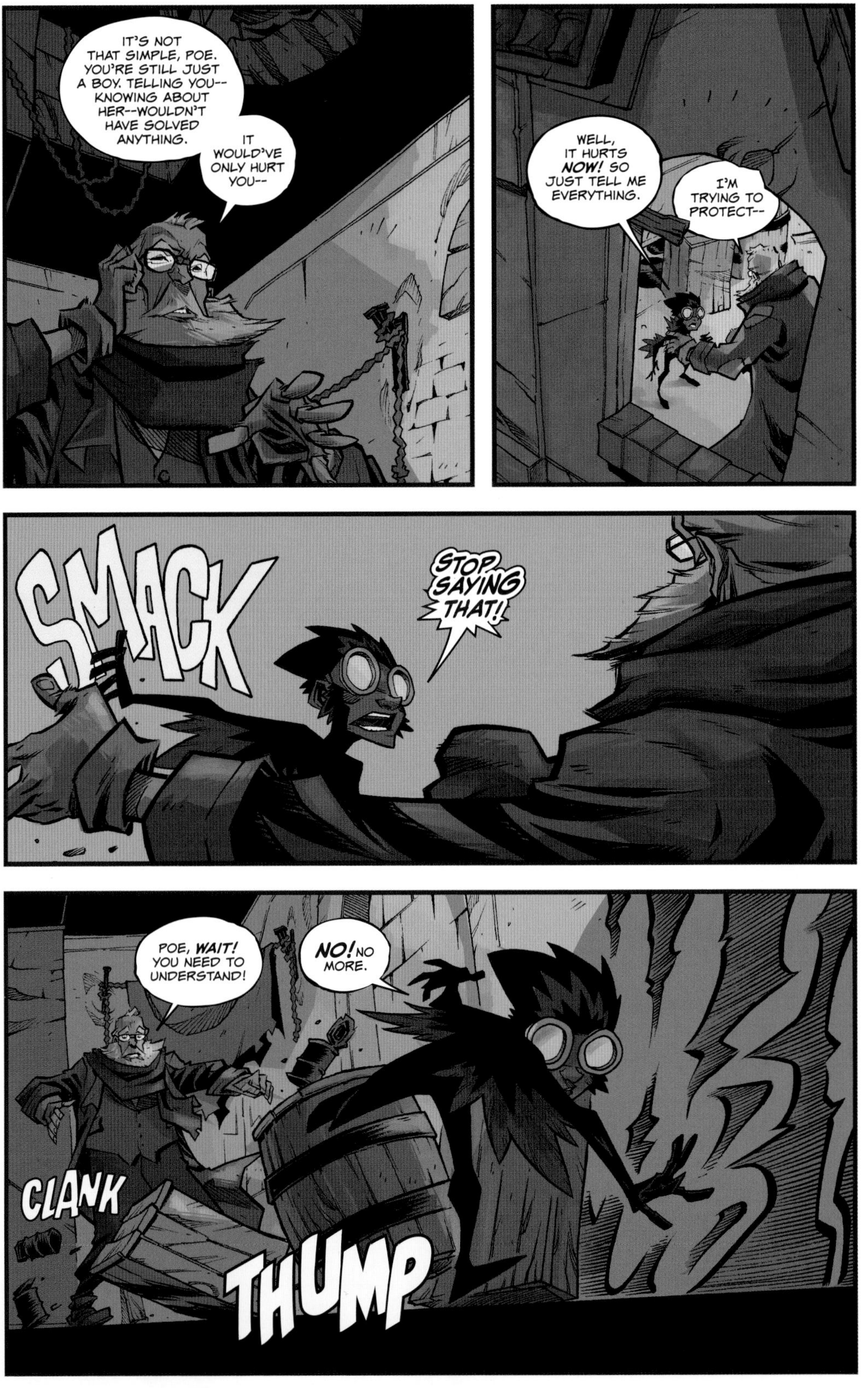
IT'S NOT THAT SIMPLE, POE. YOU'RE STILL JUST A BOY. TELLING YOU--KNOWING ABOUT HER--WOULDN'T HAVE SOLVED ANYTHING.
IT WOULD'VE ONLY HURT YOU--
WELL, IT HURTS NOW! SO JUST TELL ME EVERYTHING.
I'M TRYING TO PROTECT--
SMACK
STOP SAYING THAT!
POE, WAIT! YOU NEED TO UNDERSTAND!
NO! NO MORE.
CLANK
THUMP

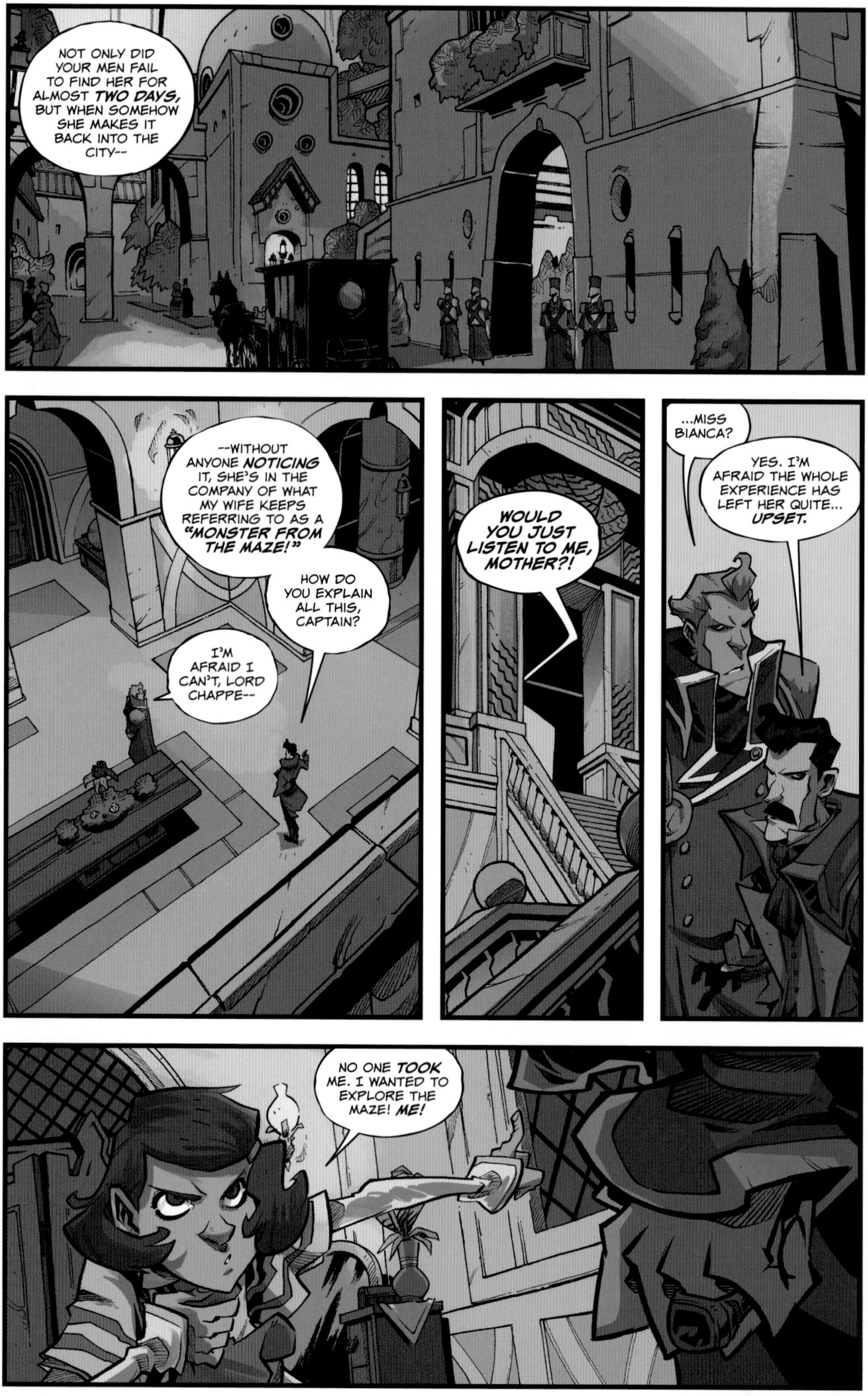
NOT ONLY DID YOUR MEN FAIL TO FIND HER FOR ALMOST **TWO DAYS,** BUT WHEN SOMEHOW SHE MAKES IT BACK INTO THE CITY--
--WITHOUT ANYONE **NOTICING** IT, SHE'S IN THE COMPANY OF WHAT MY WIFE KEEPS REFERRING TO AS A **"MONSTER FROM THE MAZE!"**
HOW DO YOU EXPLAIN ALL THIS, CAPTAIN?
I'M AFRAID I CAN'T, LORD CHAPPE--
WOULD YOU JUST LISTEN TO ME, MOTHER?!
...MISS BIANCA?
YES. I'M AFRAID THE WHOLE EXPERIENCE HAS LEFT HER QUITE... **UPSET.**
NO ONE **TOOK** ME. I WANTED TO EXPLORE THE MAZE! **ME!**

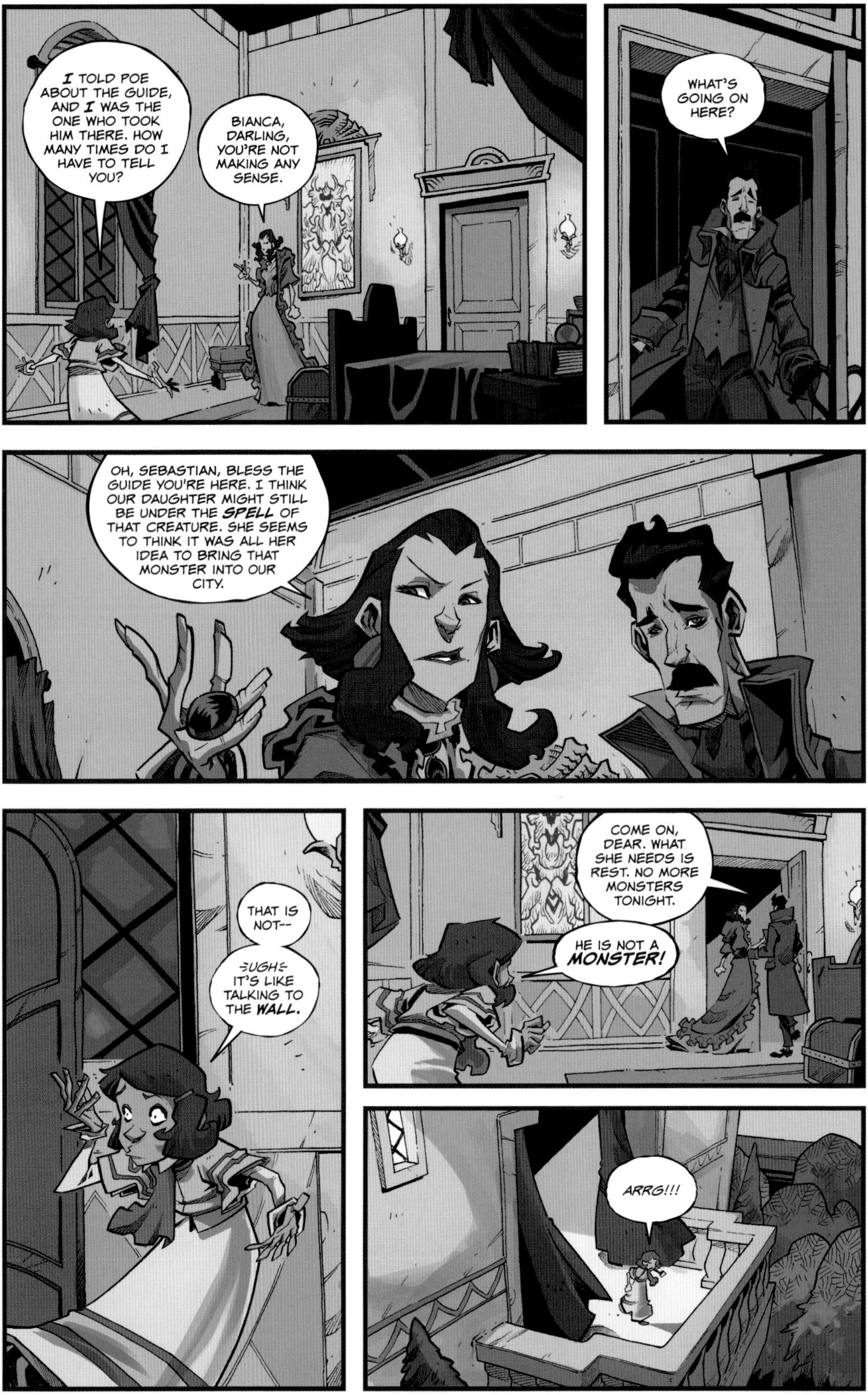
I TOLD POE ABOUT THE GUIDE, AND I WAS THE ONE WHO TOOK HIM THERE. HOW MANY TIMES DO I HAVE TO TELL YOU?
BIANCA, DARLING, YOU'RE NOT MAKING ANY SENSE.
WHAT'S GOING ON HERE?
OH, SEBASTIAN, BLESS THE GUIDE YOU'RE HERE. I THINK OUR DAUGHTER MIGHT STILL BE UNDER THE SPELL OF THAT CREATURE. SHE SEEMS TO THINK IT WAS ALL HER IDEA TO BRING THAT MONSTER INTO OUR CITY.
THAT IS NOT--
UGH IT'S LIKE TALKING TO THE WALL.
COME ON, DEAR. WHAT SHE NEEDS IS REST. NO MORE MONSTERS TONIGHT.
HE IS NOT A MONSTER!
ARRG!!!

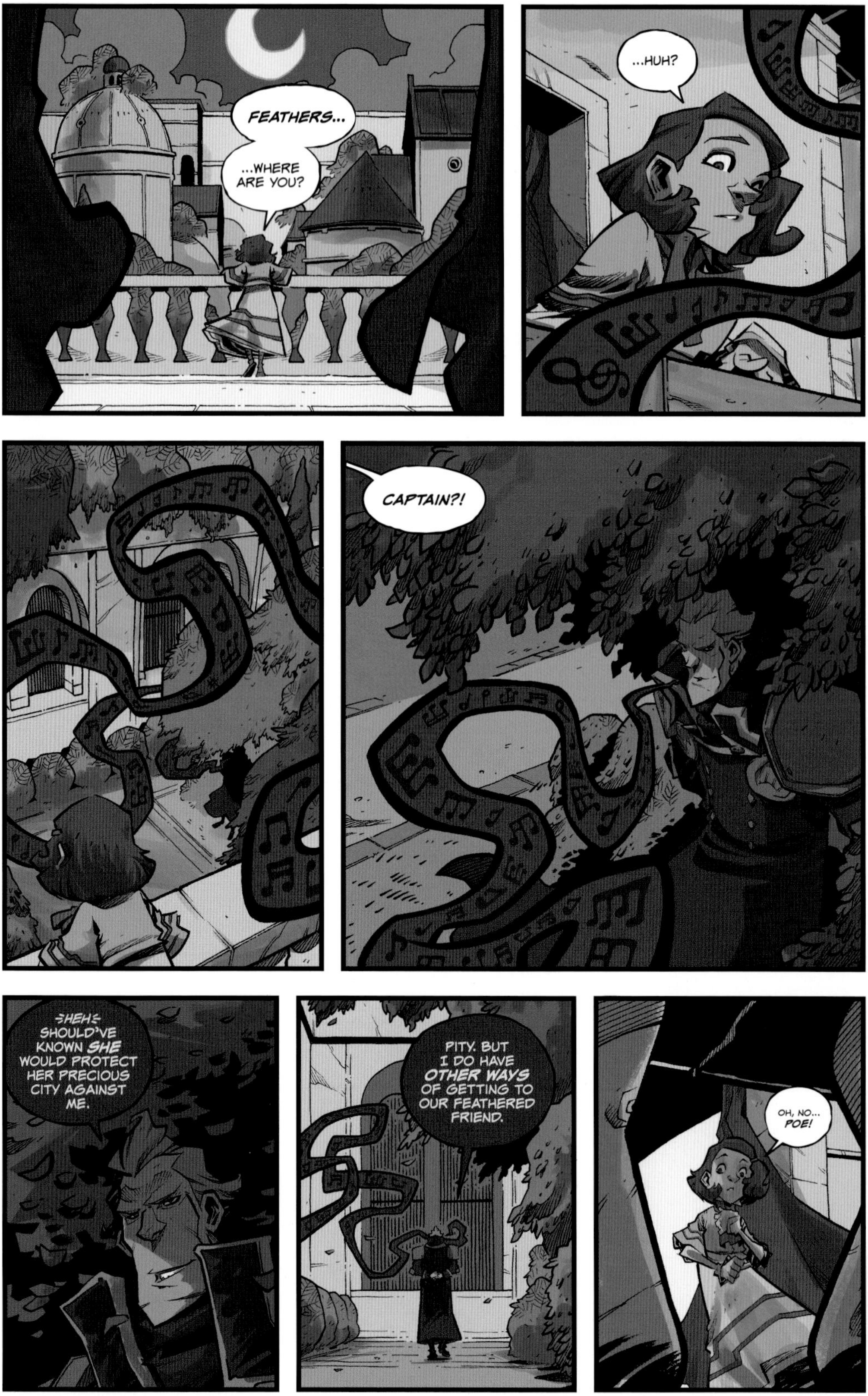
FEATHERS...
...WHERE ARE YOU?
...HUH?
CAPTAIN?!
HEH
SHOULD'VE KNOWN SHE WOULD PROTECT HER PRECIOUS CITY AGAINST ME.
PITY. BUT I DO HAVE OTHER WAYS OF GETTING TO OUR FEATHERED FRIEND.
OH, NO... POE!

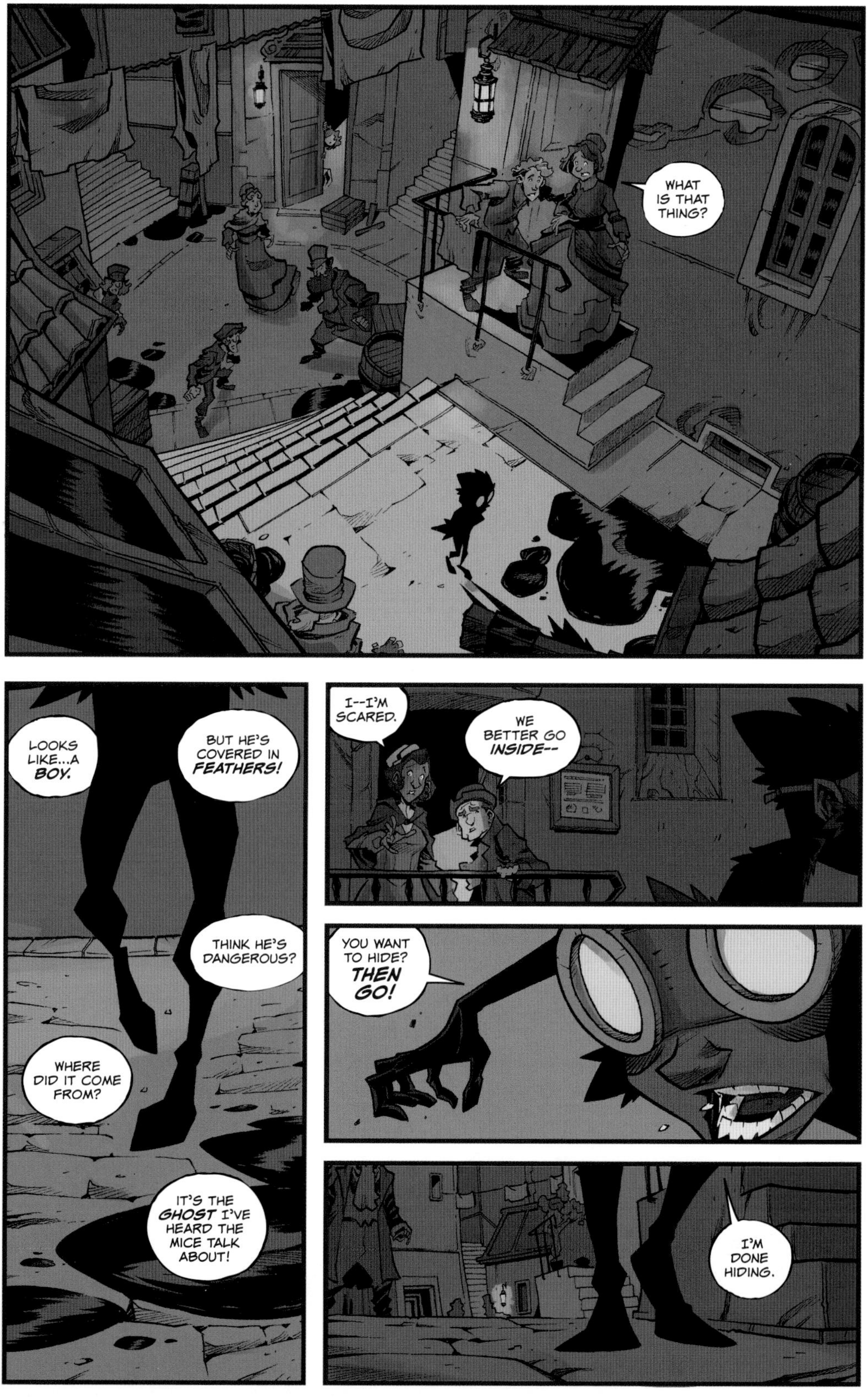
WHAT IS THAT THING?
LOOKS LIKE...A BOY.
BUT HE'S COVERED IN FEATHERS!
THINK HE'S DANGEROUS?
WHERE DID IT COME FROM?
IT'S THE GHOST I'VE HEARD THE MICE TALK ABOUT!
I--I'M SCARED.
WE BETTER GO INSIDE--
YOU WANT TO HIDE? THEN GO!
I'M DONE HIDING.

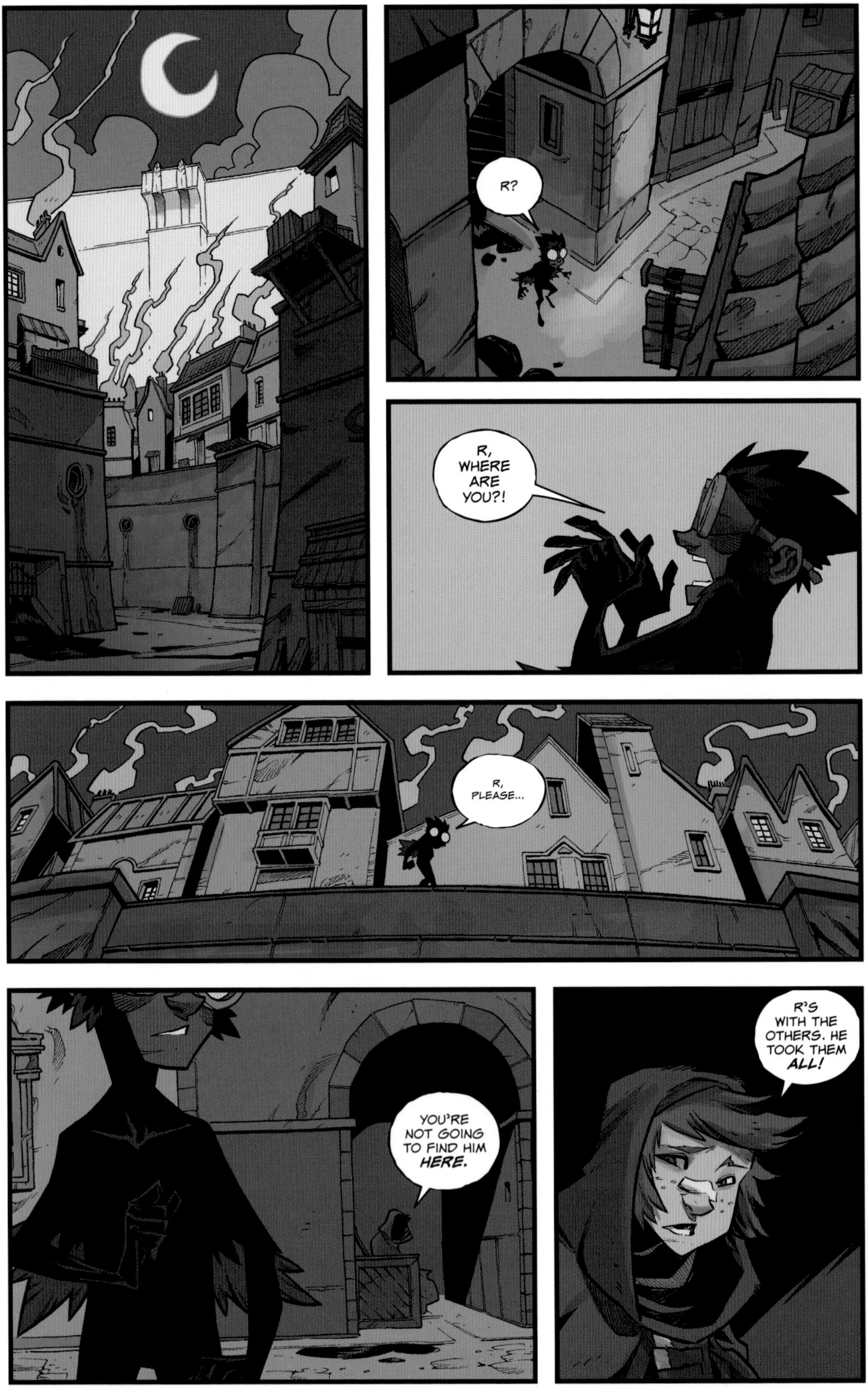
R?
R, WHERE ARE YOU?!
R, PLEASE...
YOU'RE NOT GOING TO FIND HIM *HERE.*
R'S WITH THE OTHERS. HE TOOK THEM *ALL!*

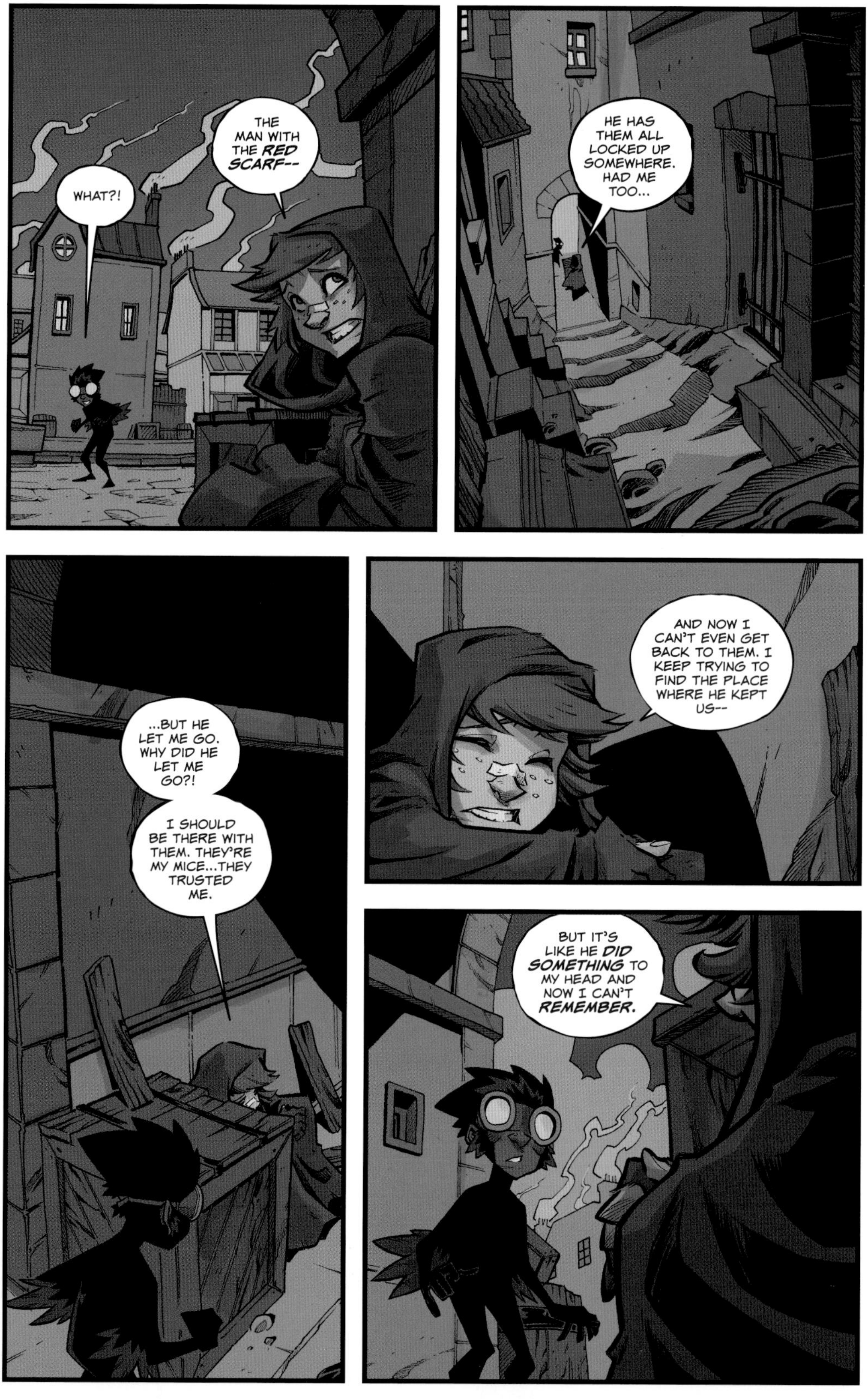
WHAT?!
THE MAN WITH THE RED SCARF--
HE HAS THEM ALL LOCKED UP SOMEWHERE. HAD ME TOO...
...BUT HE LET ME GO. WHY DID HE LET ME GO?!
I SHOULD BE THERE WITH THEM. THEY'RE MY MICE...THEY TRUSTED ME.
AND NOW I CAN'T EVEN GET BACK TO THEM. I KEEP TRYING TO FIND THE PLACE WHERE HE KEPT US--
BUT IT'S LIKE HE DID SOMETHING TO MY HEAD AND NOW I CAN'T REMEMBER.

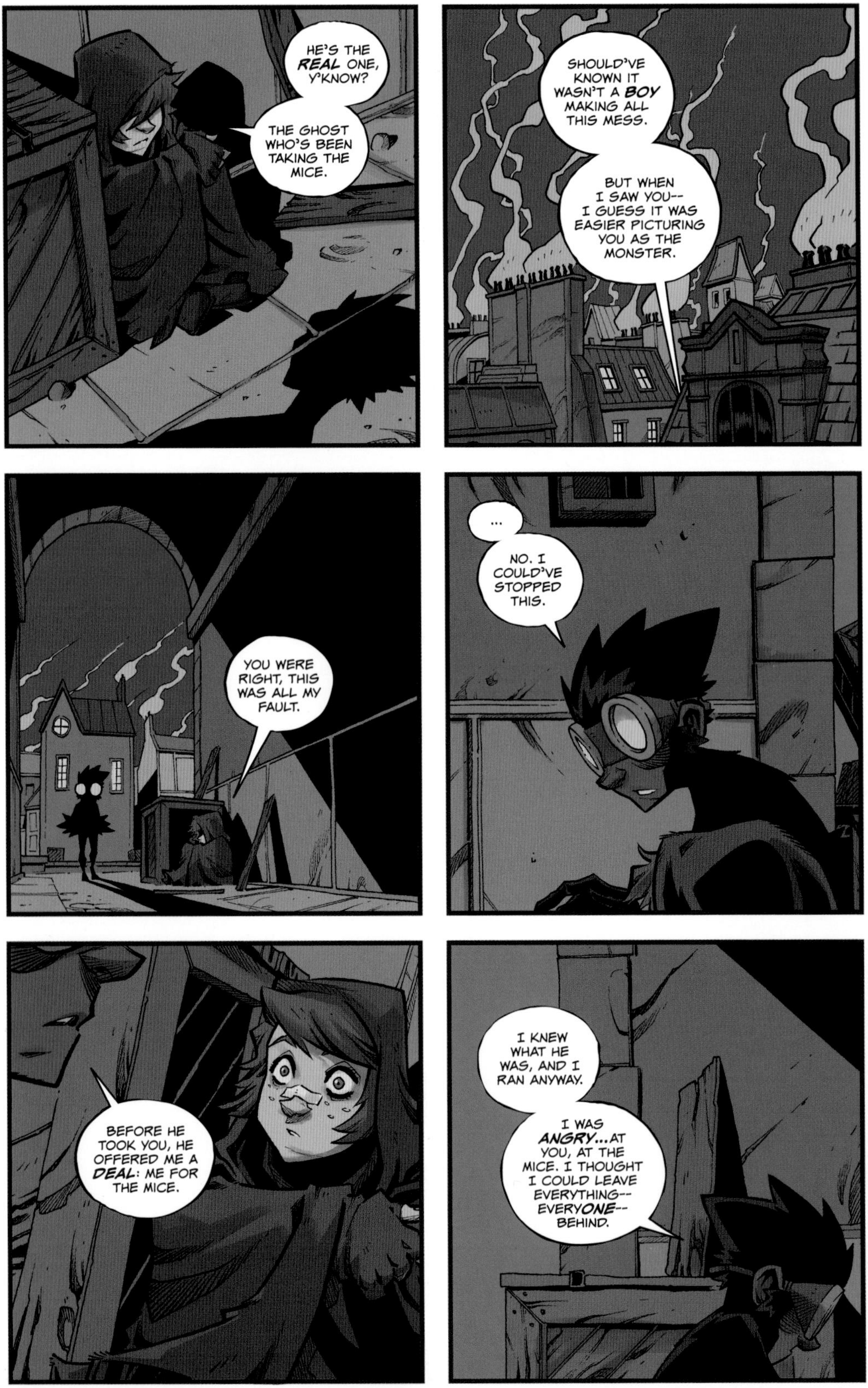
HE'S THE *REAL* ONE, Y'KNOW?
THE GHOST WHO'S BEEN TAKING THE MICE.
SHOULD'VE KNOWN IT WASN'T A *BOY* MAKING ALL THIS MESS.
BUT WHEN I SAW YOU-- I GUESS IT WAS EASIER PICTURING YOU AS THE MONSTER.
YOU WERE RIGHT, THIS WAS ALL MY FAULT.
...
NO. I COULD'VE STOPPED THIS.
BEFORE HE TOOK YOU, HE OFFERED ME A *DEAL*: ME FOR THE MICE.
I KNEW WHAT HE WAS, AND I RAN ANYWAY.
I WAS *ANGRY*... AT YOU, AT THE MICE. I THOUGHT I COULD LEAVE EVERYTHING-- EVERY*ONE*-- BEHIND.

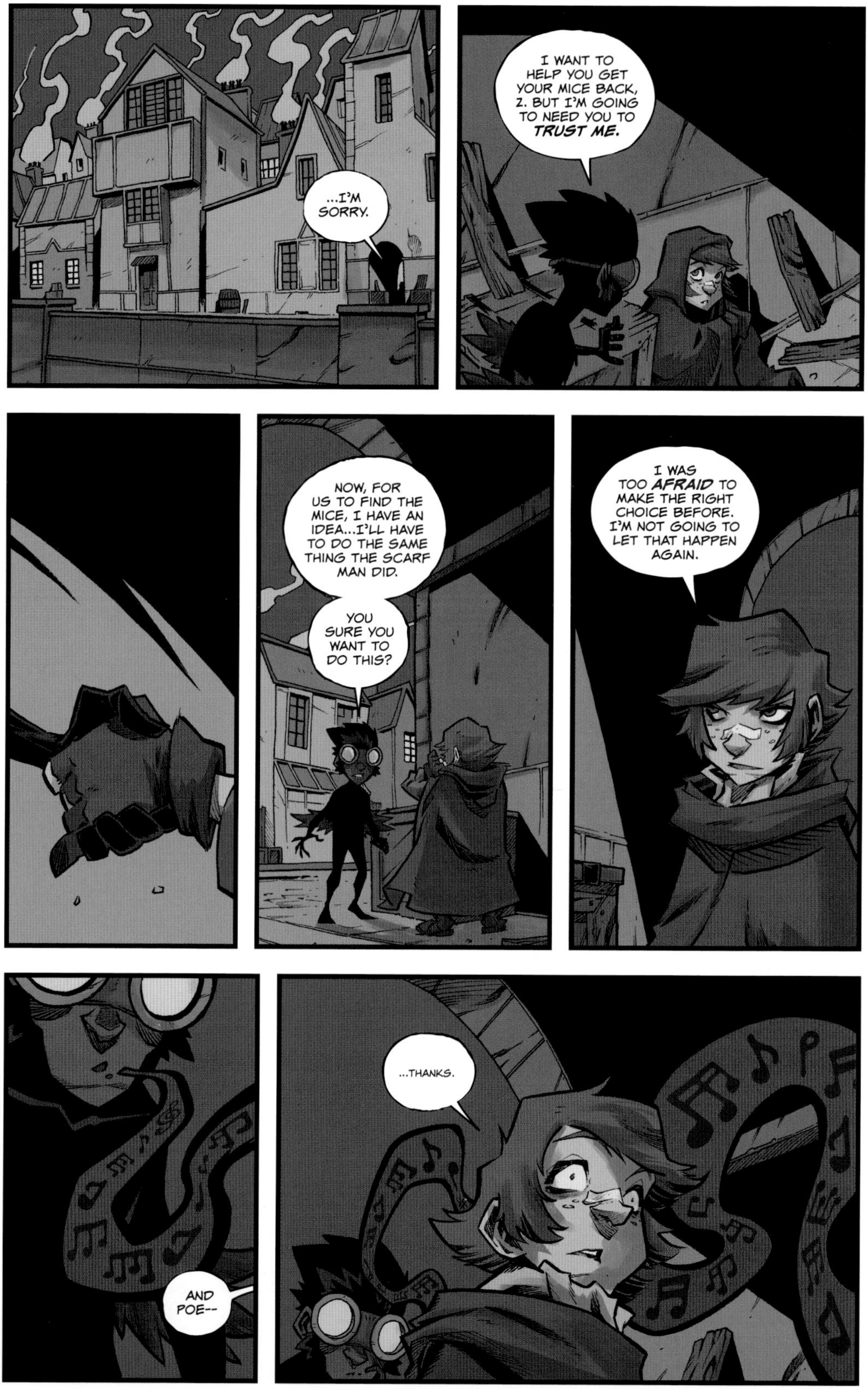
...I'M SORRY.
I WANT TO HELP YOU GET YOUR MICE BACK, Z. BUT I'M GOING TO NEED YOU TO *TRUST ME.*
NOW, FOR US TO FIND THE MICE, I HAVE AN IDEA...I'LL HAVE TO DO THE SAME THING THE SCARF MAN DID.
YOU SURE YOU WANT TO DO THIS?
I WAS TOO *AFRAID* TO MAKE THE RIGHT CHOICE BEFORE. I'M NOT GOING TO LET THAT HAPPEN AGAIN.
AND POE--
...THANKS.

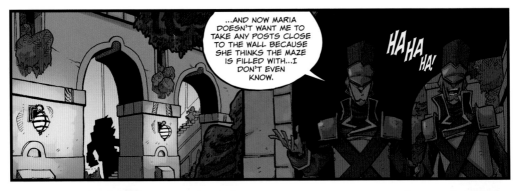

...AND NOW MARIA DOESN'T WANT ME TO TAKE ANY POSTS CLOSE TO THE WALL BECAUSE SHE THINKS THE MAZE IS FILLED WITH...I DON'T EVEN KNOW.

HA HA HA!

≥HUMPH≤ HOW DID YOU GET THROUGH THESE?

BIANCA--

WHAT DO YOU THINK YOU'RE DOING?

FATHER!

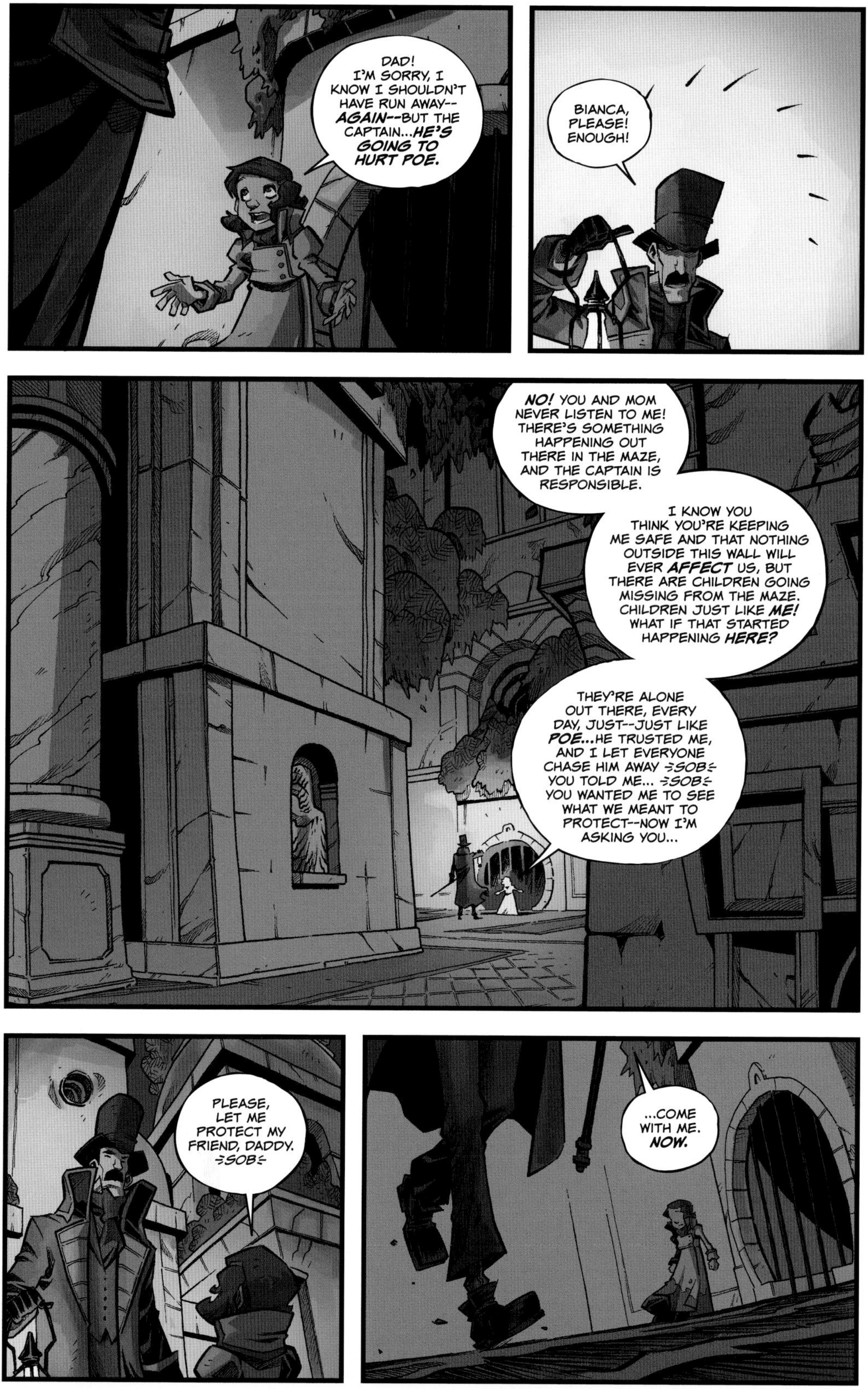
DAD! I'M SORRY, I KNOW I SHOULDN'T HAVE RUN AWAY--AGAIN--BUT THE CAPTAIN...HE'S GOING TO HURT POE.
BIANCA, PLEASE! ENOUGH!
NO! YOU AND MOM NEVER LISTEN TO ME! THERE'S SOMETHING HAPPENING OUT THERE IN THE MAZE, AND THE CAPTAIN IS RESPONSIBLE.
I KNOW YOU THINK YOU'RE KEEPING ME SAFE AND THAT NOTHING OUTSIDE THIS WALL WILL EVER AFFECT US, BUT THERE ARE CHILDREN GOING MISSING FROM THE MAZE. CHILDREN JUST LIKE ME! WHAT IF THAT STARTED HAPPENING HERE?
THEY'RE ALONE OUT THERE, EVERY DAY, JUST--JUST LIKE POE...HE TRUSTED ME, AND I LET EVERYONE CHASE HIM AWAY =SOB= YOU TOLD ME... =SOB= YOU WANTED ME TO SEE WHAT WE MEANT TO PROTECT--NOW I'M ASKING YOU...
PLEASE, LET ME PROTECT MY FRIEND, DADDY. =SOB=
...COME WITH ME. NOW.

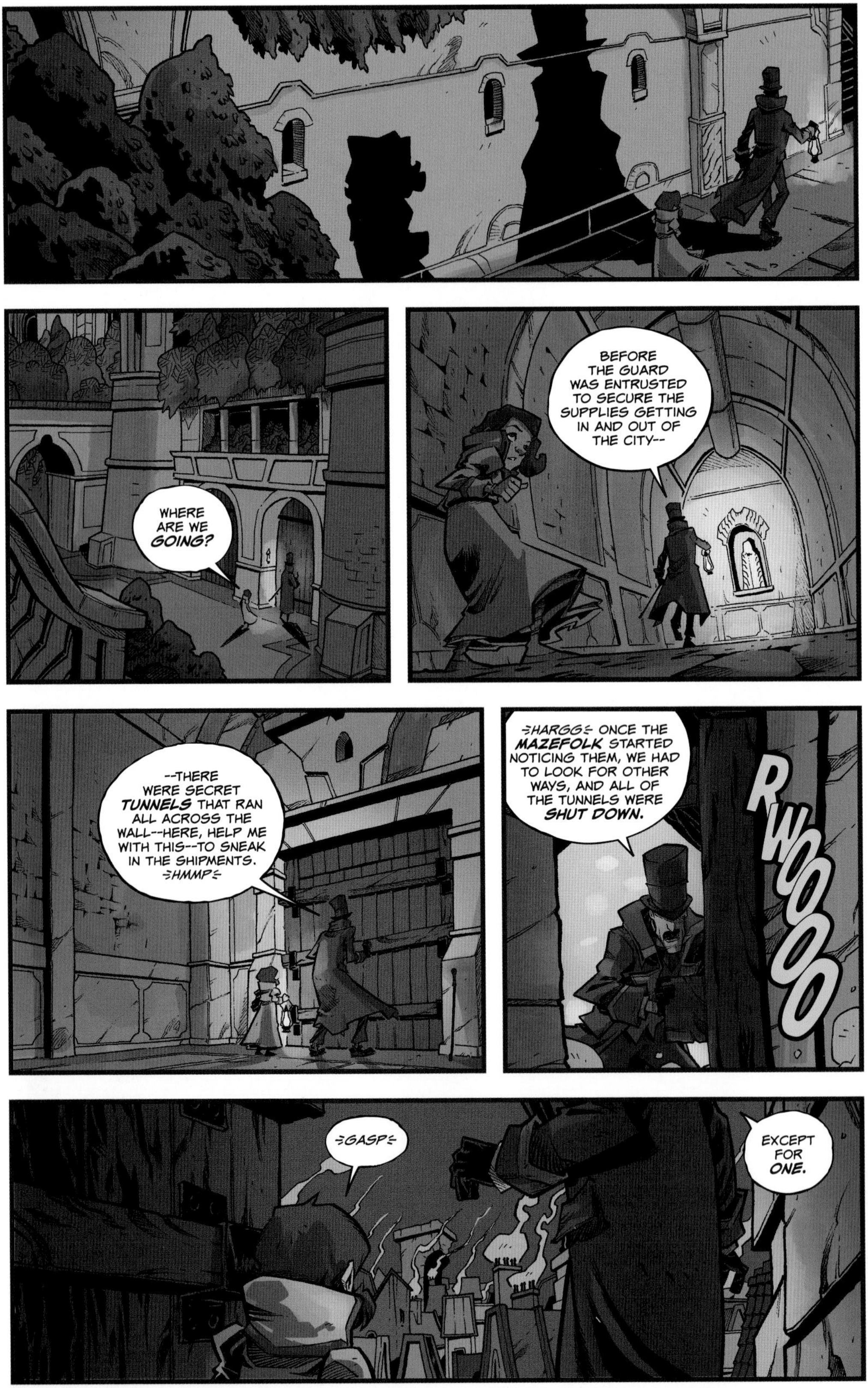
WHERE ARE WE GOING?
BEFORE THE GUARD WAS ENTRUSTED TO SECURE THE SUPPLIES GETTING IN AND OUT OF THE CITY--
--THERE WERE SECRET TUNNELS THAT RAN ALL ACROSS THE WALL--HERE, HELP ME WITH THIS--TO SNEAK IN THE SHIPMENTS. ≈HMMP≈
≈HARGG≈ ONCE THE MAZEFOLK STARTED NOTICING THEM, WE HAD TO LOOK FOR OTHER WAYS, AND ALL OF THE TUNNELS WERE SHUT DOWN.
RWOOOO
≈GASP≈
EXCEPT FOR ONE.

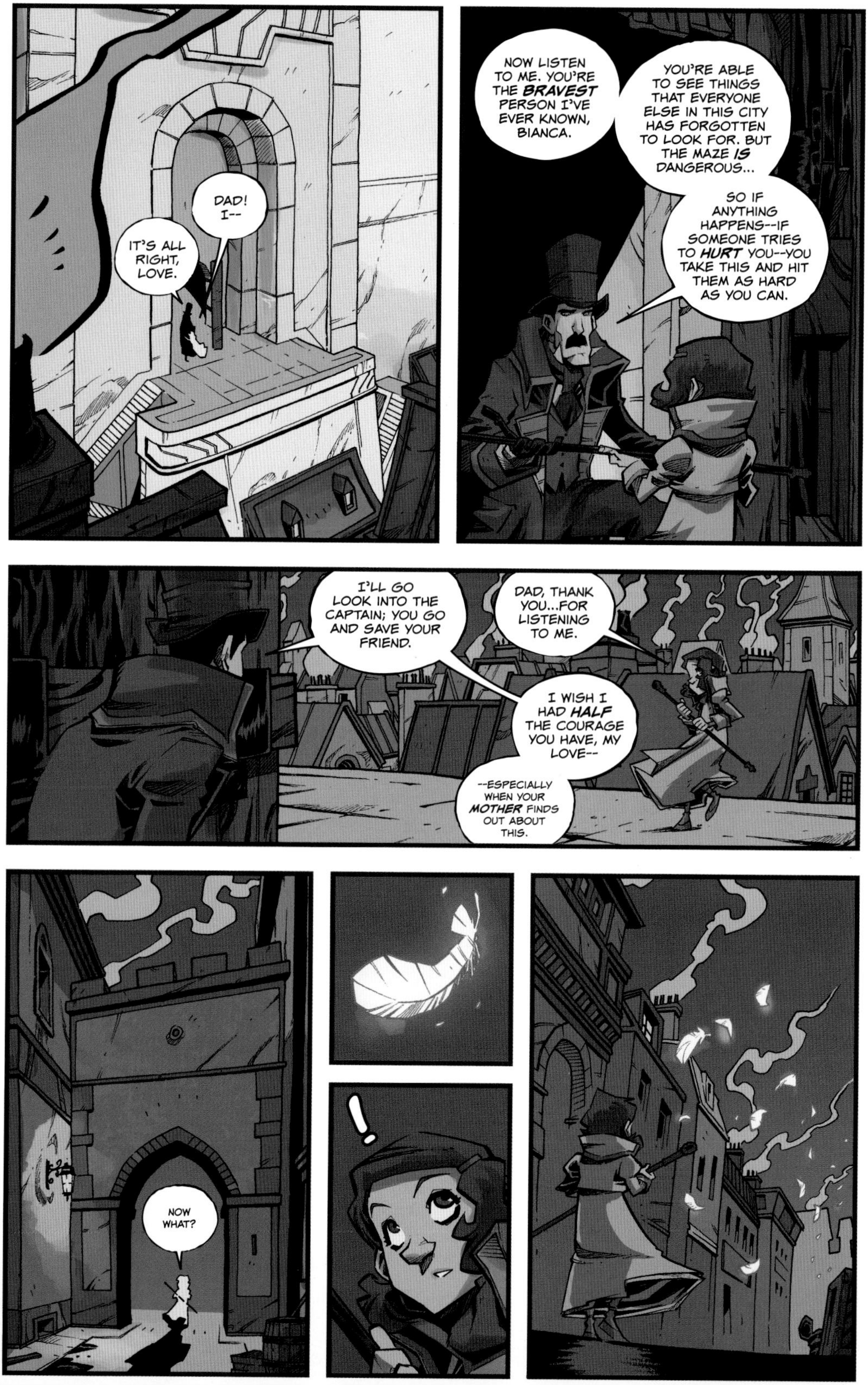
DAD! I--
IT'S ALL RIGHT, LOVE.
NOW LISTEN TO ME. YOU'RE THE BRAVEST PERSON I'VE EVER KNOWN, BIANCA.
YOU'RE ABLE TO SEE THINGS THAT EVERYONE ELSE IN THIS CITY HAS FORGOTTEN TO LOOK FOR. BUT THE MAZE IS DANGEROUS...
SO IF ANYTHING HAPPENS--IF SOMEONE TRIES TO HURT YOU--YOU TAKE THIS AND HIT THEM AS HARD AS YOU CAN.
I'LL GO LOOK INTO THE CAPTAIN; YOU GO AND SAVE YOUR FRIEND.
DAD, THANK YOU...FOR LISTENING TO ME.
I WISH I HAD HALF THE COURAGE YOU HAVE, MY LOVE--
--ESPECIALLY WHEN YOUR MOTHER FINDS OUT ABOUT THIS.
NOW WHAT?
!

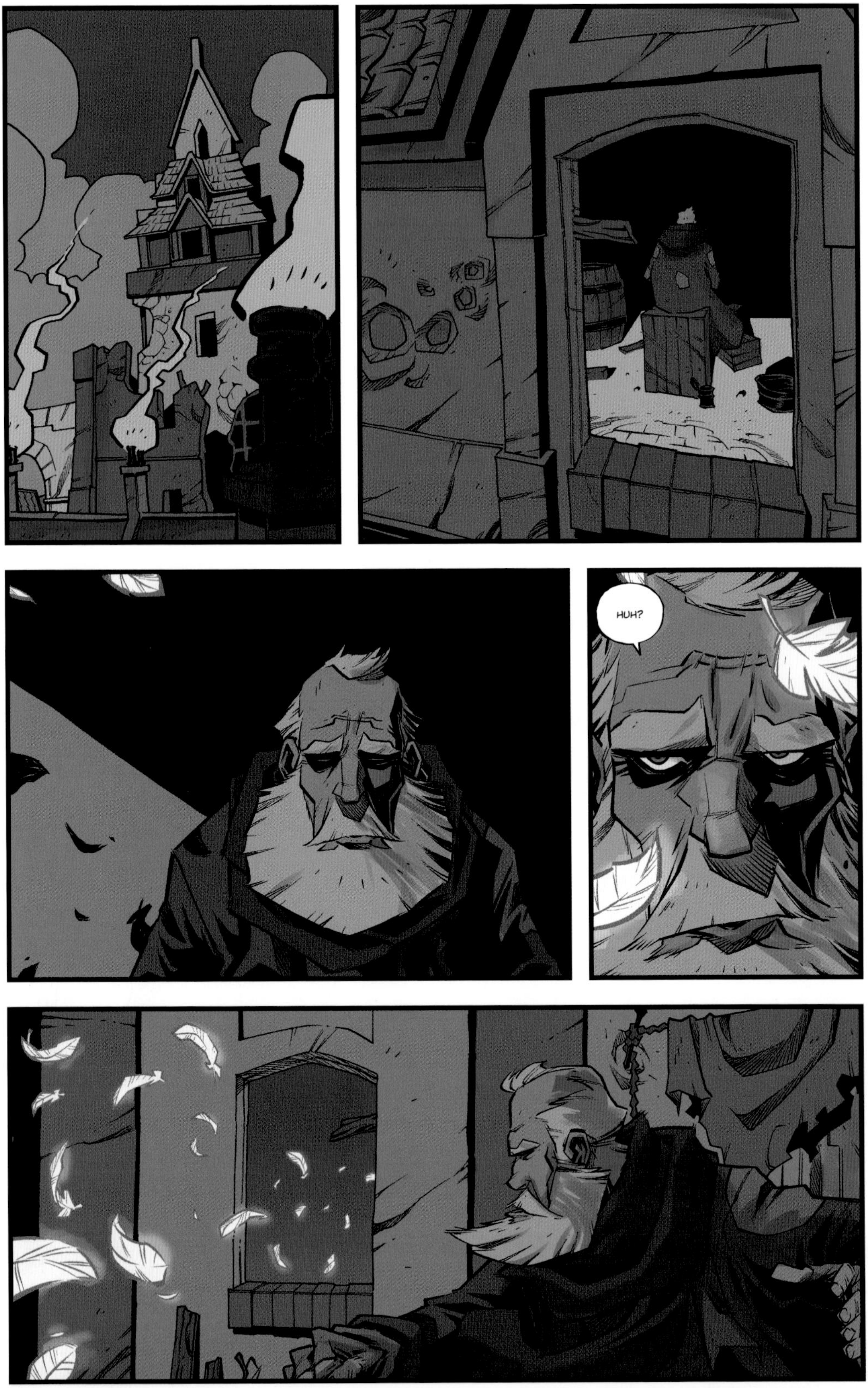
HUH?

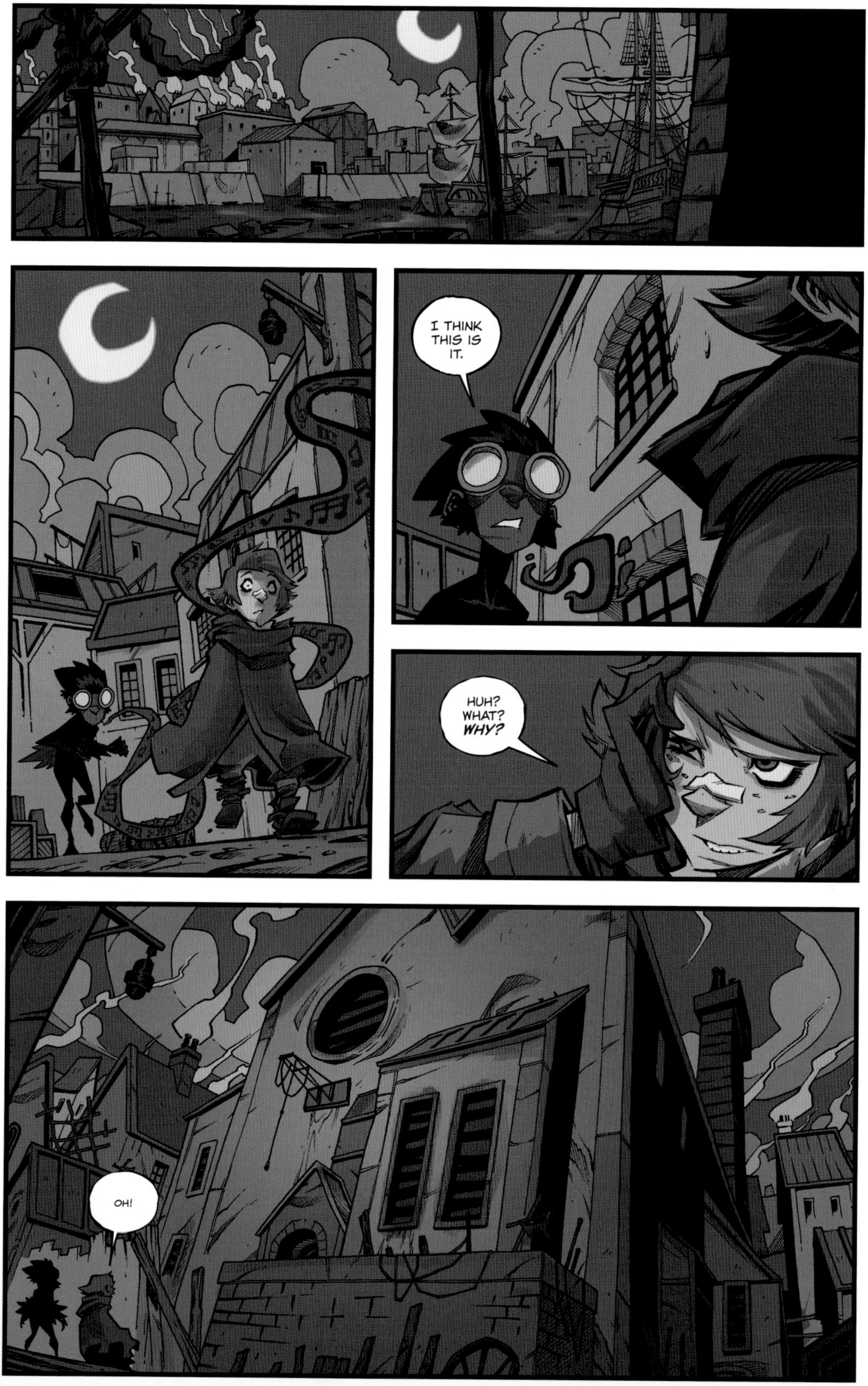
I THINK THIS IS IT.
HUH? WHAT? WHY?
OH!

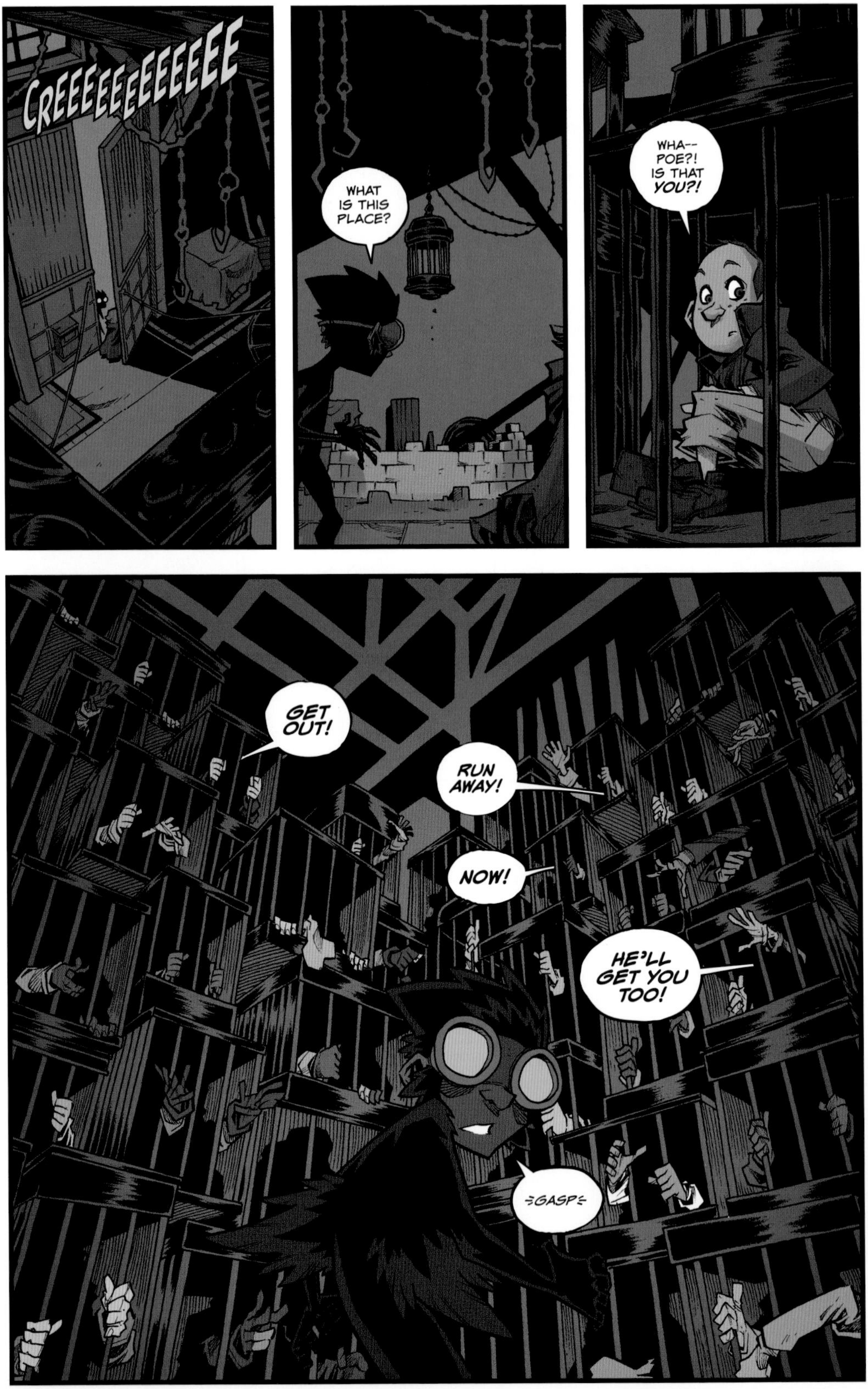
CREEEEEEEEEEEE
WHAT IS THIS PLACE?
WHA-- POE?! IS THAT YOU?!
GET OUT!
RUN AWAY!
NOW!
HE'LL GET YOU TOO!
GASP

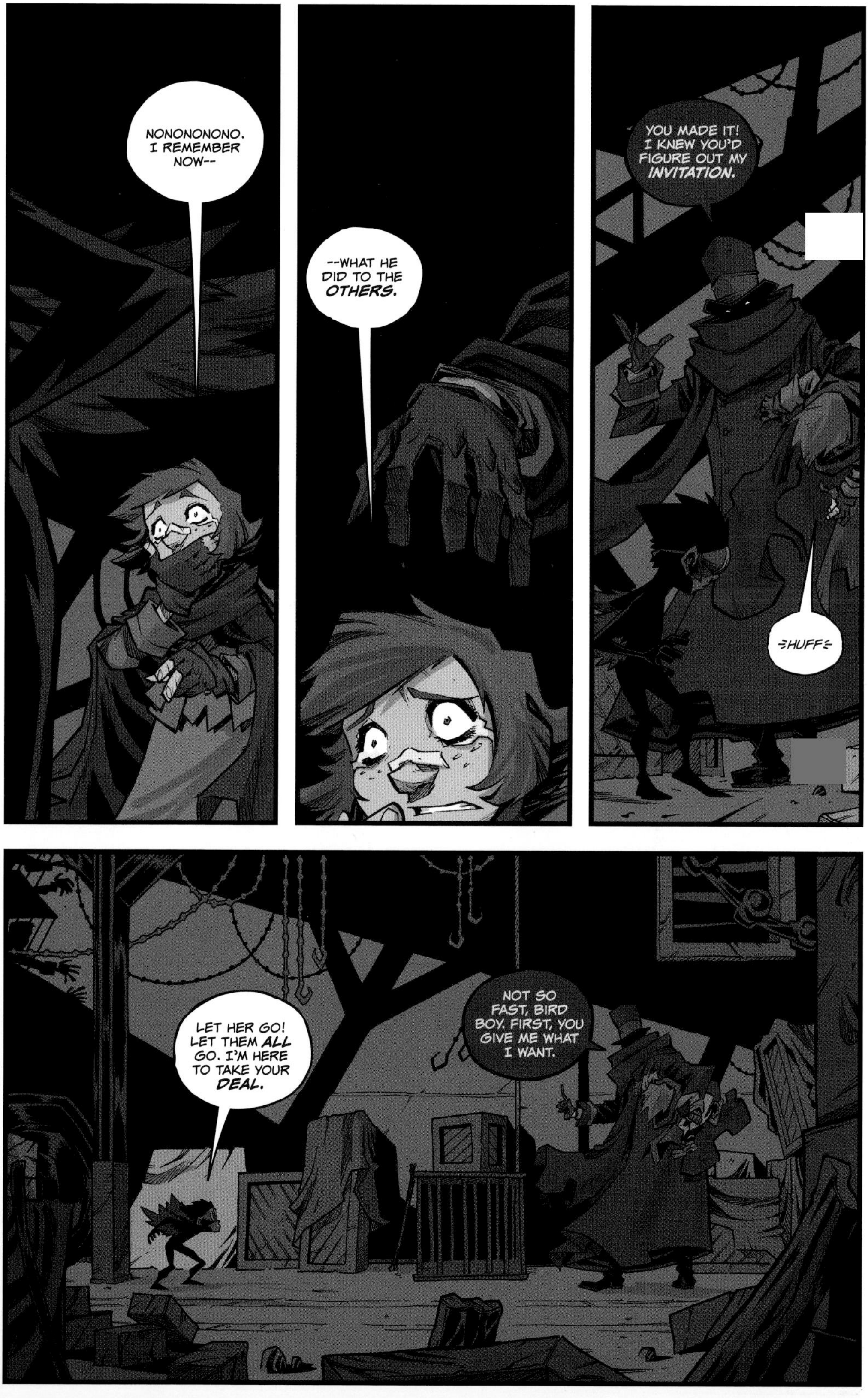
NONONONONO. I REMEMBER NOW--
--WHAT HE DID TO THE OTHERS.
YOU MADE IT! I KNEW YOU'D FIGURE OUT MY INVITATION.
≈HUFF≈
LET HER GO! LET THEM ALL GO. I'M HERE TO TAKE YOUR DEAL.
NOT SO FAST, BIRD BOY. FIRST, YOU GIVE ME WHAT I WANT.

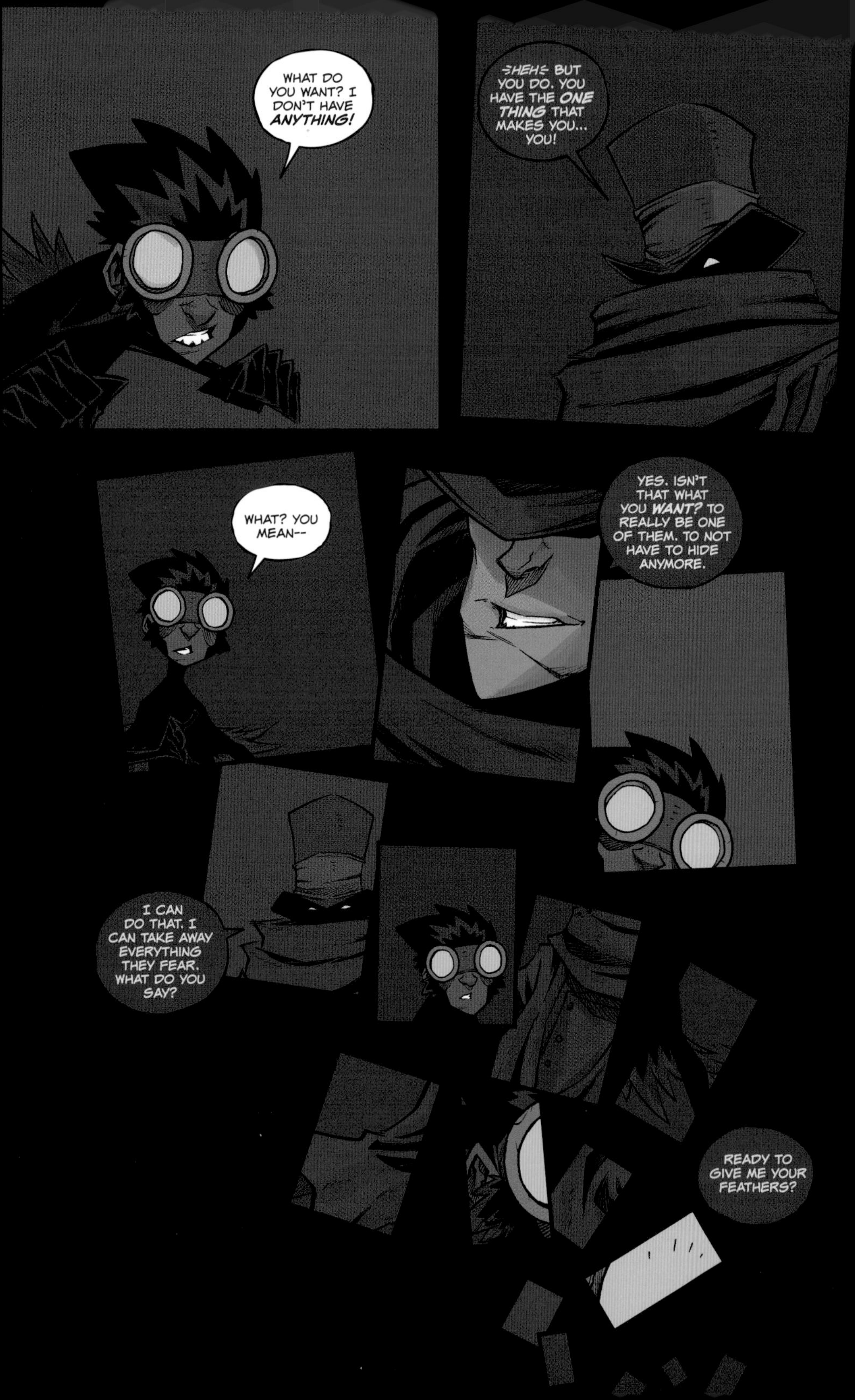
WHAT DO YOU WANT? I DON'T HAVE *ANYTHING!*
=HEH= BUT YOU DO. YOU HAVE THE *ONE THING* THAT MAKES YOU... YOU!
WHAT? YOU MEAN--
YES. ISN'T THAT WHAT YOU *WANT?* TO REALLY BE ONE OF THEM. TO NOT HAVE TO HIDE ANYMORE.
I CAN DO THAT. I CAN TAKE AWAY EVERYTHING THEY FEAR. WHAT DO YOU SAY?
READY TO GIVE ME YOUR FEATHERS?

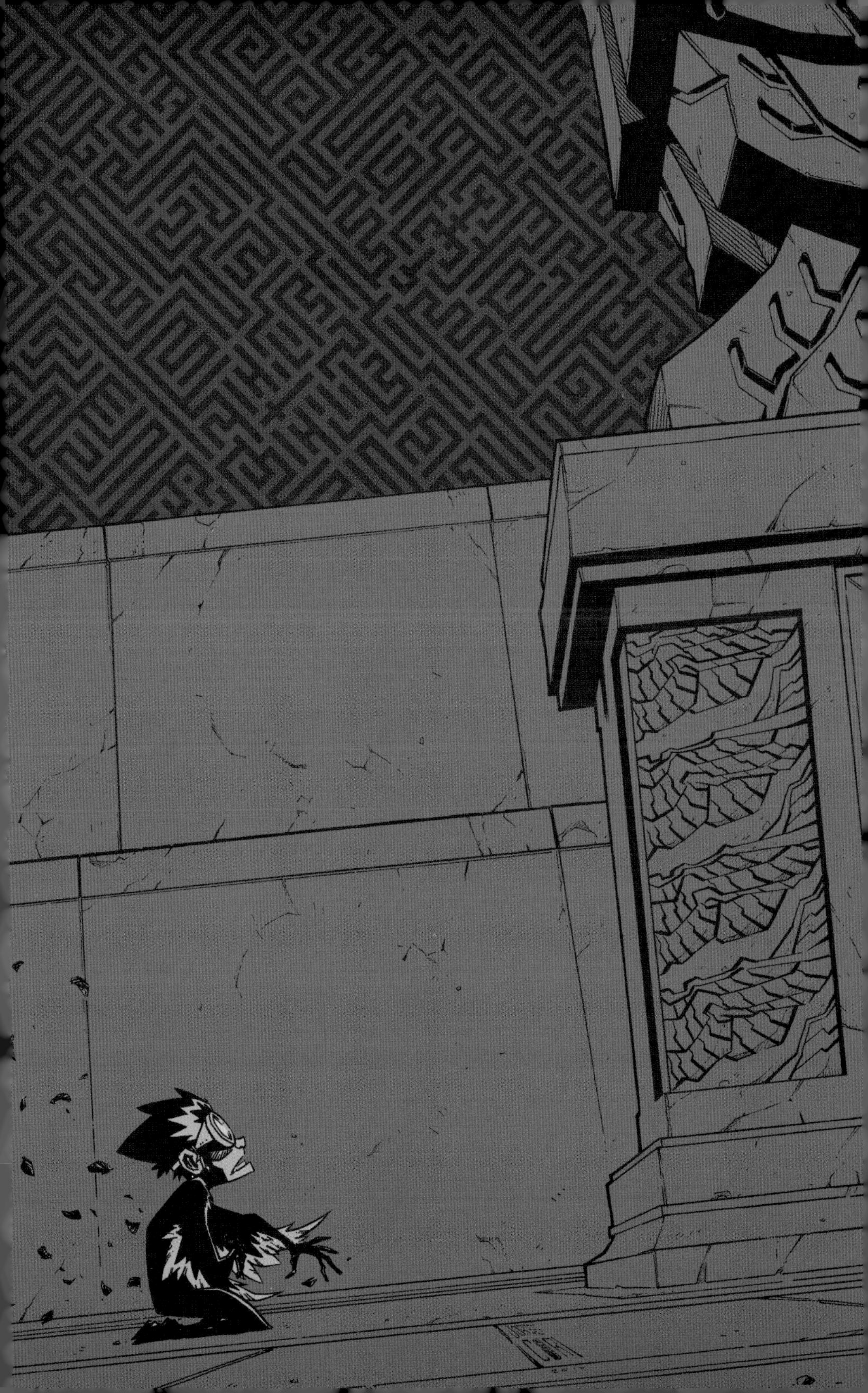

CHAPTER
SIX

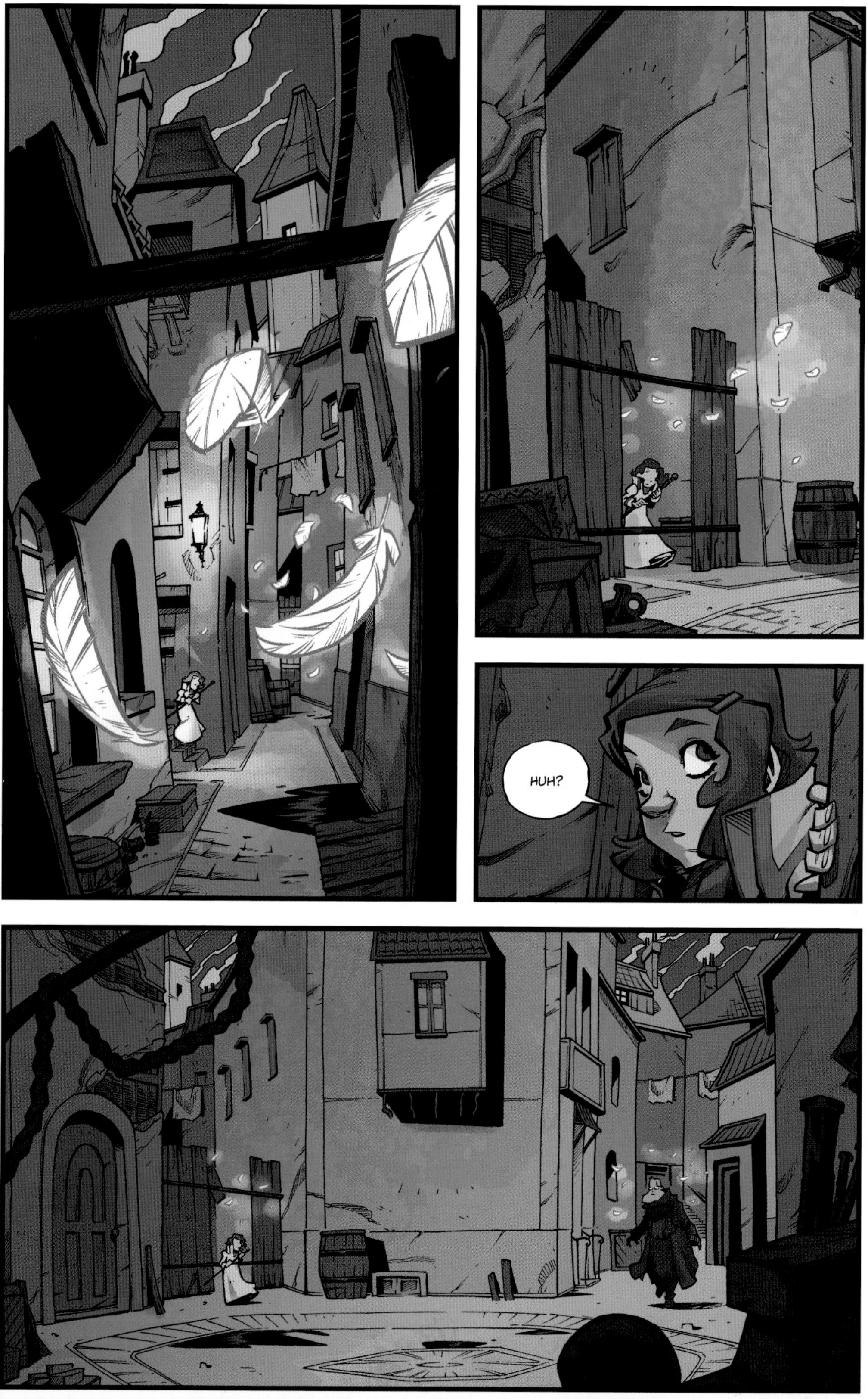
HUH?

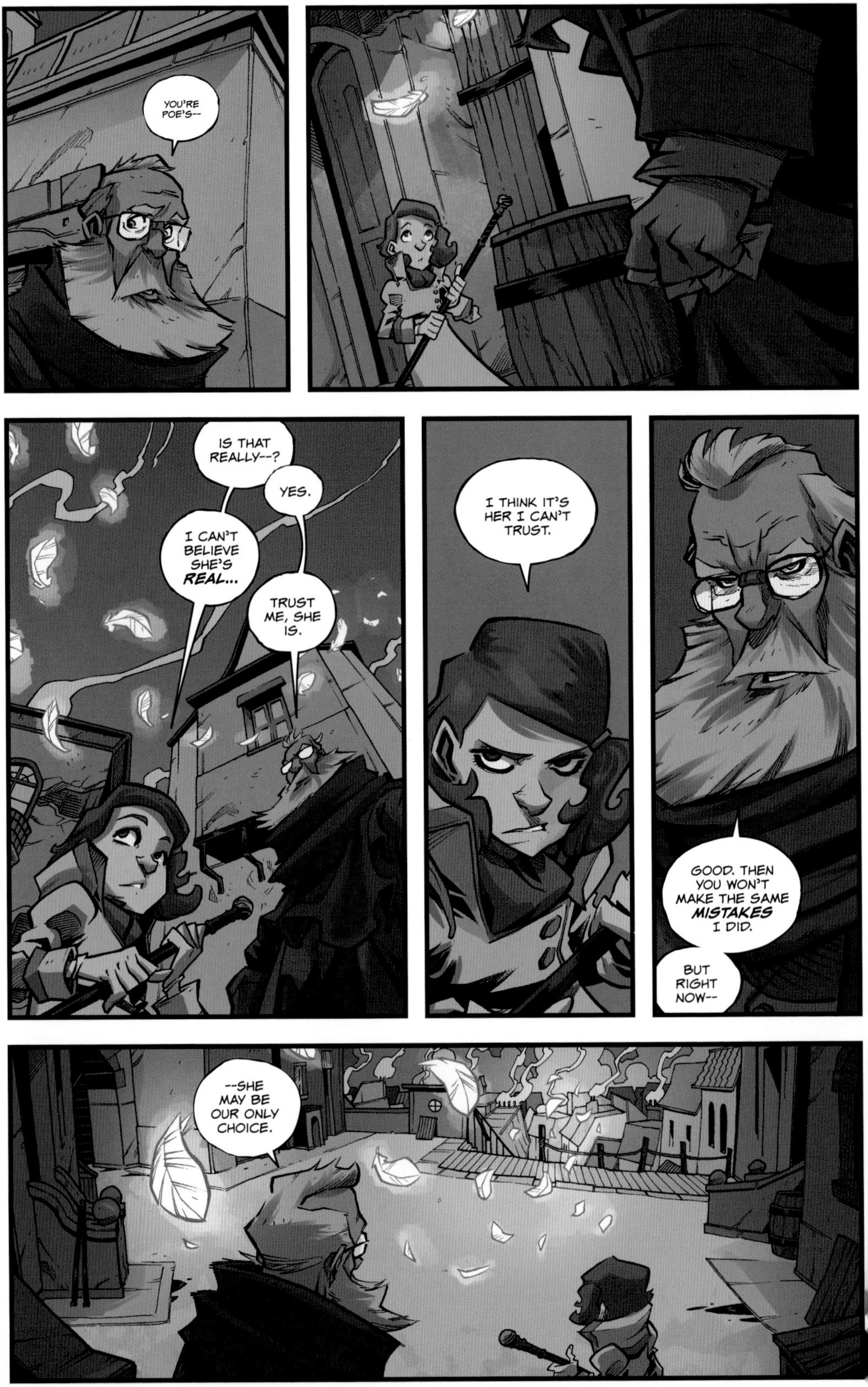
YOU'RE POE'S--
IS THAT REALLY--?
YES.
I CAN'T BELIEVE SHE'S REAL...
TRUST ME, SHE IS.
I THINK IT'S HER I CAN'T TRUST.
GOOD. THEN YOU WON'T MAKE THE SAME MISTAKES I DID.
BUT RIGHT NOW--
--SHE MAY BE OUR ONLY CHOICE.

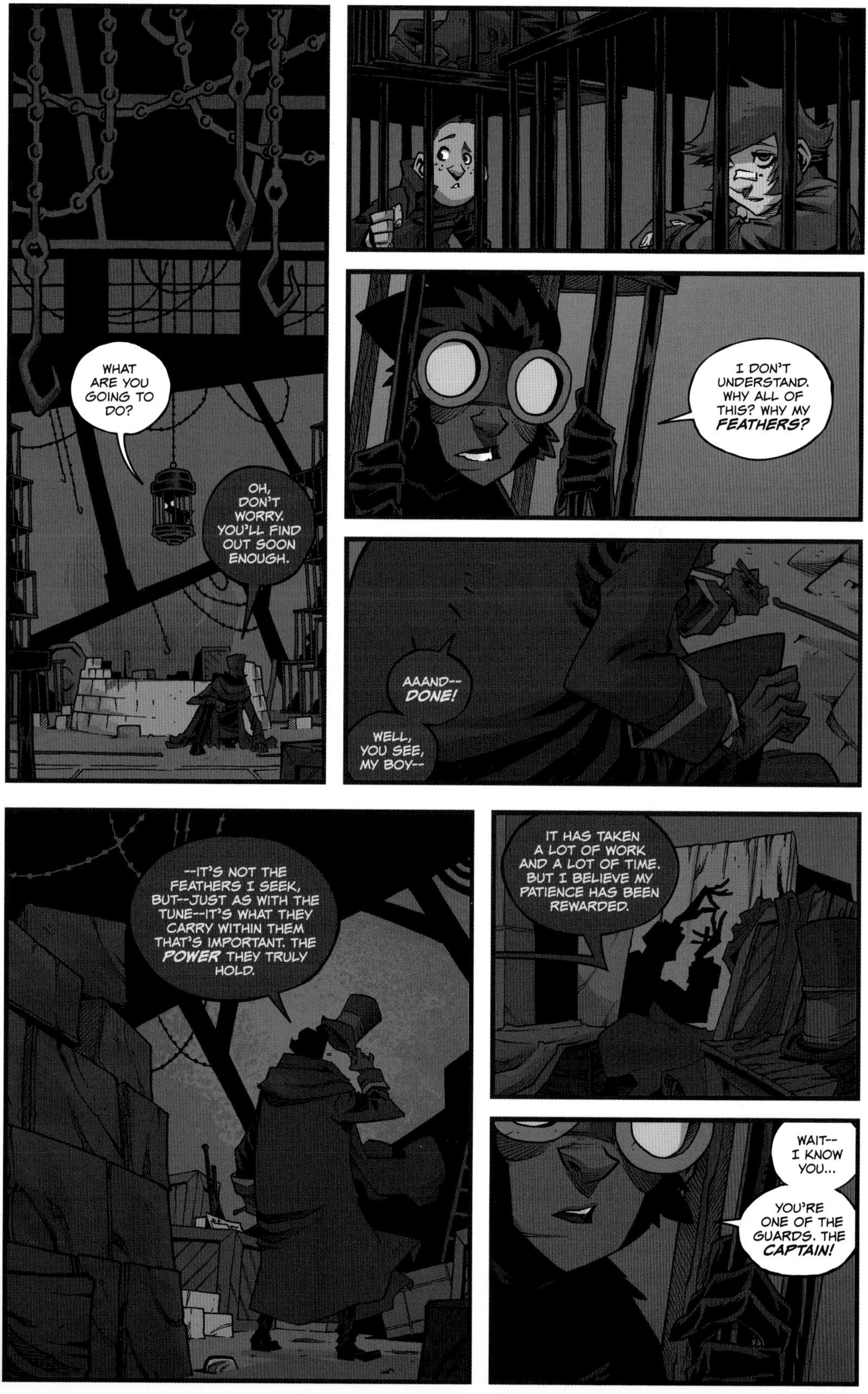
WHAT ARE YOU GOING TO DO?
OH, DON'T WORRY. YOU'LL FIND OUT SOON ENOUGH.
I DON'T UNDERSTAND. WHY ALL OF THIS? WHY MY FEATHERS?
AAAND-- DONE!
WELL, YOU SEE, MY BOY--
--IT'S NOT THE FEATHERS I SEEK, BUT--JUST AS WITH THE TUNE--IT'S WHAT THEY CARRY WITHIN THEM THAT'S IMPORTANT. THE POWER THEY TRULY HOLD.
IT HAS TAKEN A LOT OF WORK AND A LOT OF TIME. BUT I BELIEVE MY PATIENCE HAS BEEN REWARDED.
WAIT-- I KNOW YOU...
YOU'RE ONE OF THE GUARDS. THE CAPTAIN!

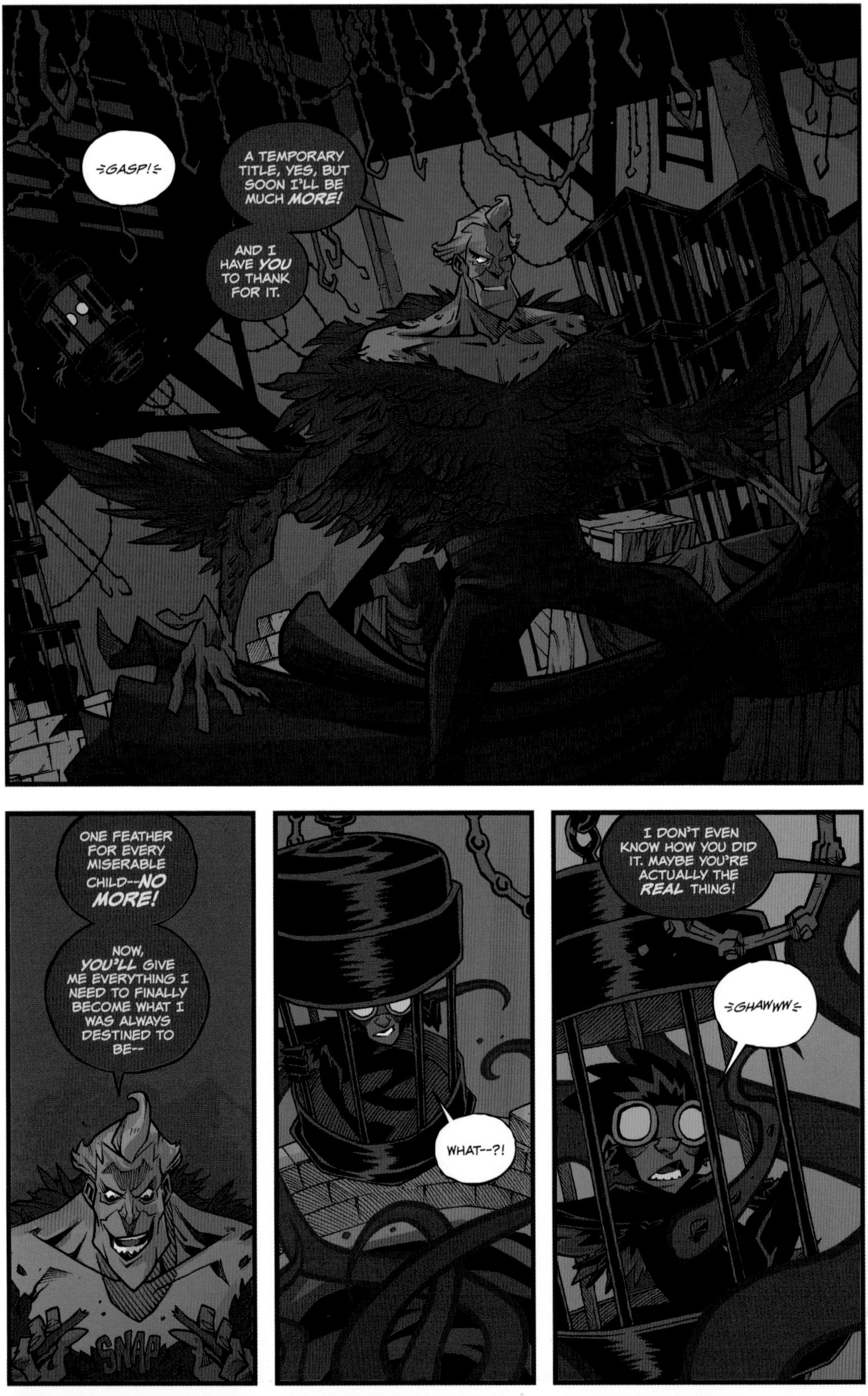

GASP!
A TEMPORARY TITLE, YES, BUT SOON I'LL BE MUCH MORE!
AND I HAVE YOU TO THANK FOR IT.
ONE FEATHER FOR EVERY MISERABLE CHILD--NO MORE!
NOW, YOU'LL GIVE ME EVERYTHING I NEED TO FINALLY BECOME WHAT I WAS ALWAYS DESTINED TO BE--
SNAP
WHAT--?!
I DON'T EVEN KNOW HOW YOU DID IT. MAYBE YOU'RE ACTUALLY THE REAL THING!
GHAWWW

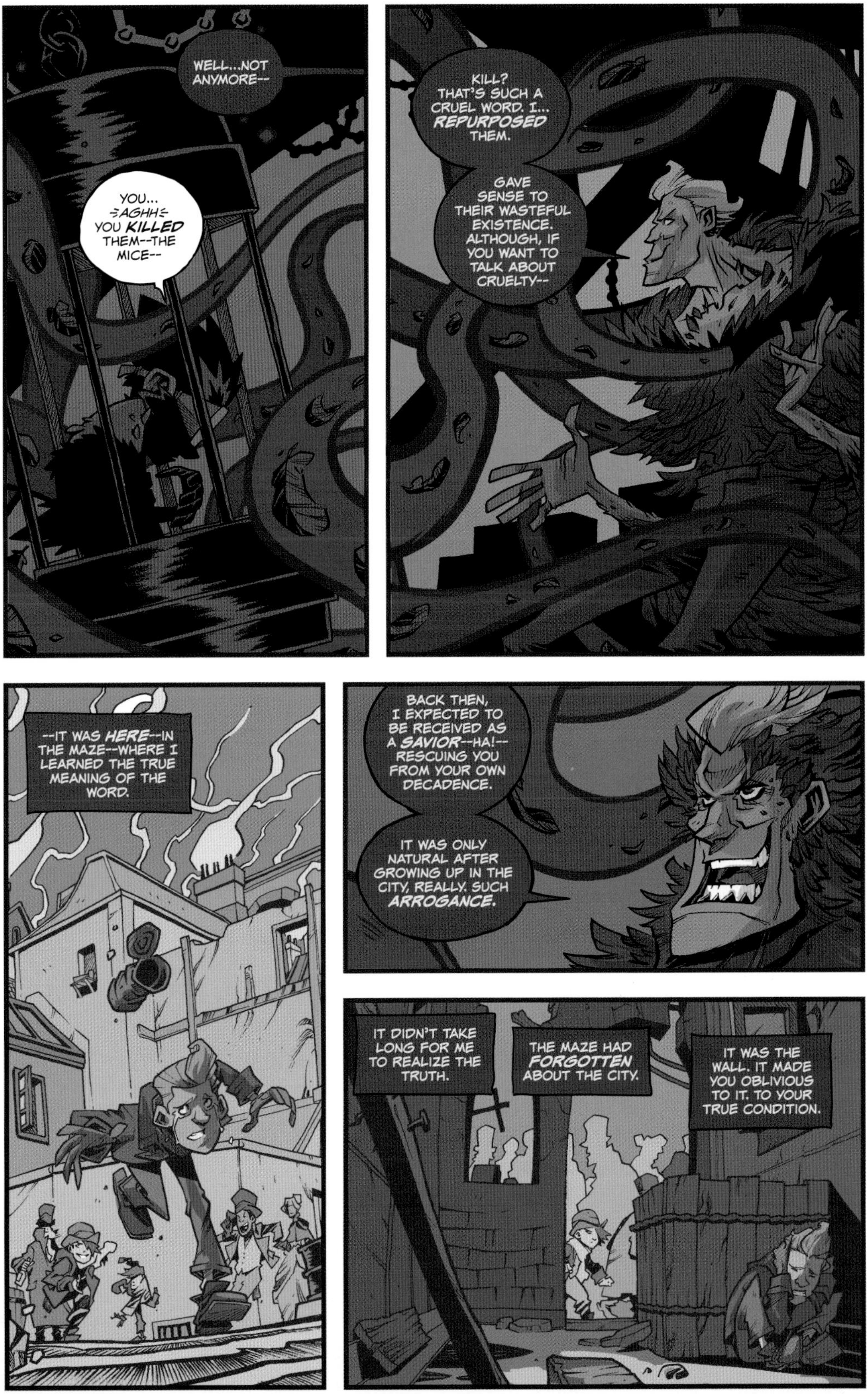
WELL...NOT ANYMORE--
YOU... =AGHH= YOU KILLED THEM--THE MICE--
KILL? THAT'S SUCH A CRUEL WORD. I... REPURPOSED THEM.
GAVE SENSE TO THEIR WASTEFUL EXISTENCE. ALTHOUGH, IF YOU WANT TO TALK ABOUT CRUELTY--
--IT WAS HERE--IN THE MAZE--WHERE I LEARNED THE TRUE MEANING OF THE WORD.
BACK THEN, I EXPECTED TO BE RECEIVED AS A SAVIOR--HA!--RESCUING YOU FROM YOUR OWN DECADENCE.
IT WAS ONLY NATURAL AFTER GROWING UP IN THE CITY, REALLY. SUCH ARROGANCE.
IT DIDN'T TAKE LONG FOR ME TO REALIZE THE TRUTH.
THE MAZE HAD FORGOTTEN ABOUT THE CITY.
IT WAS THE WALL. IT MADE YOU OBLIVIOUS TO IT. TO YOUR TRUE CONDITION.

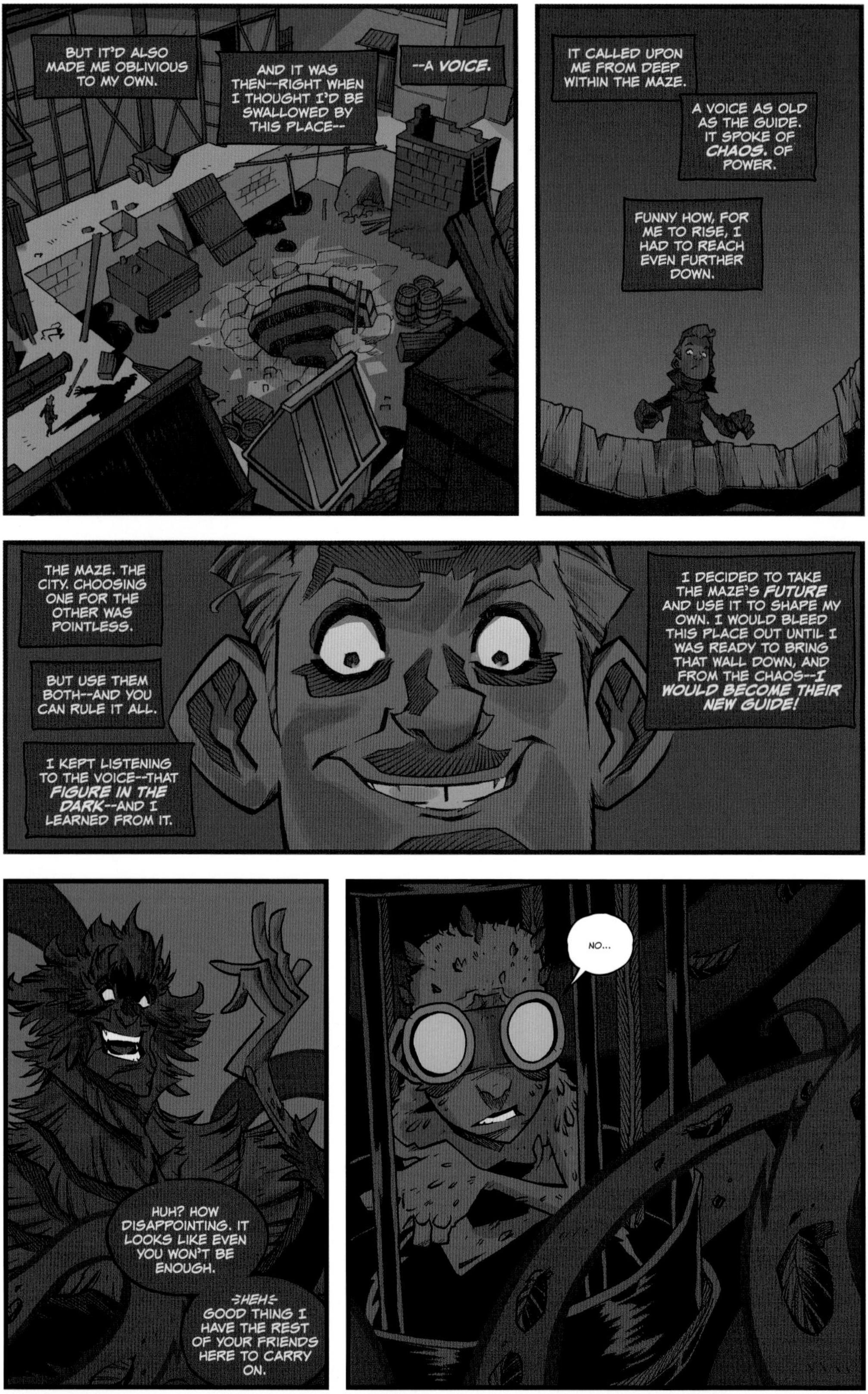
BUT IT'D ALSO MADE ME OBLIVIOUS TO MY OWN.
AND IT WAS THEN--RIGHT WHEN I THOUGHT I'D BE SWALLOWED BY THIS PLACE--
--A *VOICE.*
IT CALLED UPON ME FROM DEEP WITHIN THE MAZE.
A VOICE AS OLD AS THE GUIDE. IT SPOKE OF *CHAOS.* OF POWER.
FUNNY HOW, FOR ME TO RISE, I HAD TO REACH EVEN FURTHER DOWN.
THE MAZE. THE CITY. CHOOSING ONE FOR THE OTHER WAS POINTLESS.
BUT USE THEM BOTH--AND YOU CAN RULE IT ALL.
I KEPT LISTENING TO THE VOICE--THAT *FIGURE IN THE DARK*--AND I LEARNED FROM IT.
I DECIDED TO TAKE THE MAZE'S *FUTURE* AND USE IT TO SHAPE MY OWN. I WOULD BLEED THIS PLACE OUT UNTIL I WAS READY TO BRING THAT WALL DOWN, AND FROM THE CHAOS--*I WOULD BECOME THEIR NEW GUIDE!*
HUH? HOW DISAPPOINTING. IT LOOKS LIKE EVEN YOU WON'T BE ENOUGH.
HEH GOOD THING I HAVE THE REST OF YOUR FRIENDS HERE TO CARRY ON.
NO...

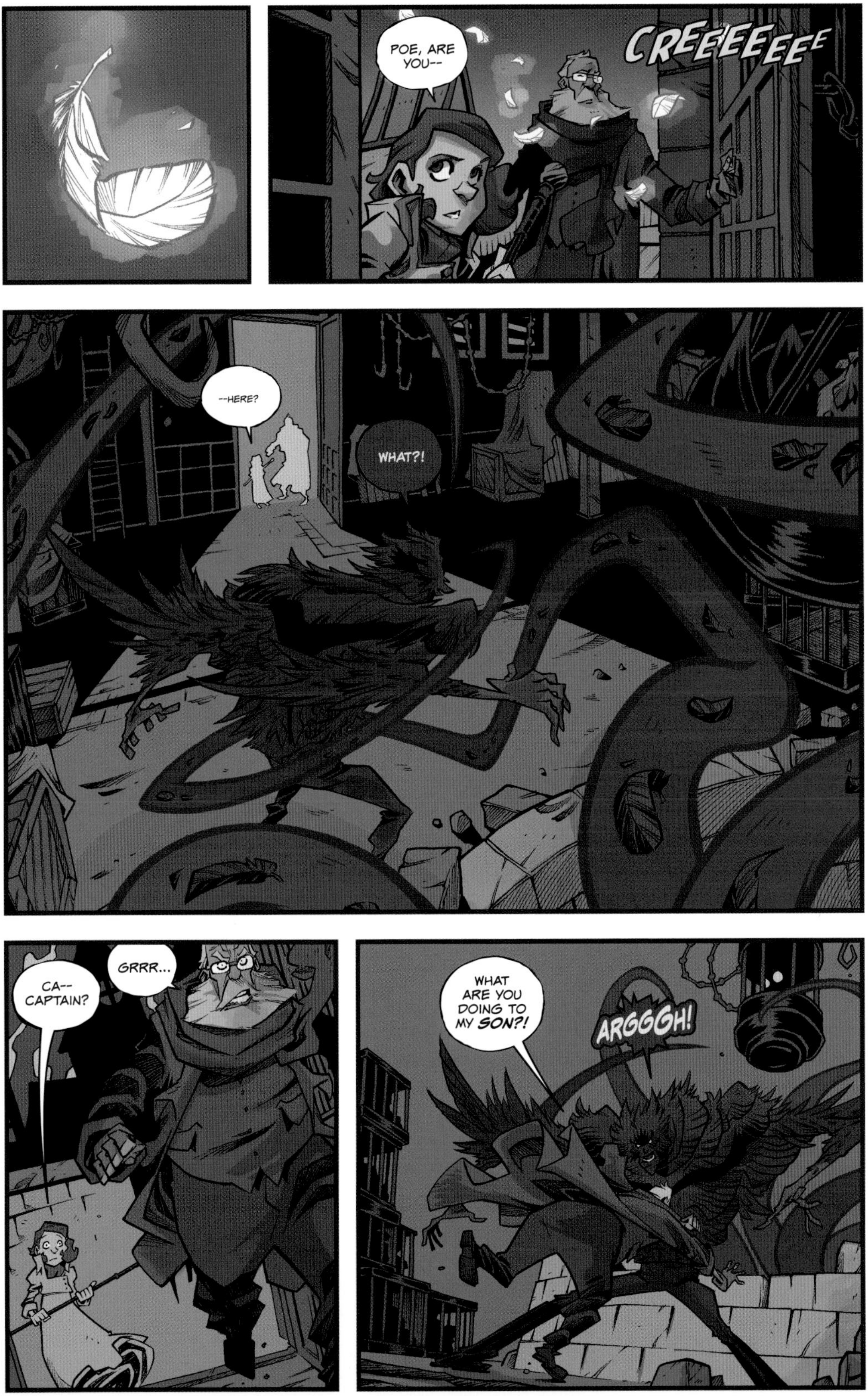
CREEEEEEE
POE, ARE YOU--
--HERE?
WHAT?!
CA-- CAPTAIN?
GRRR...
WHAT ARE YOU DOING TO MY SON?!
ARGGGH!

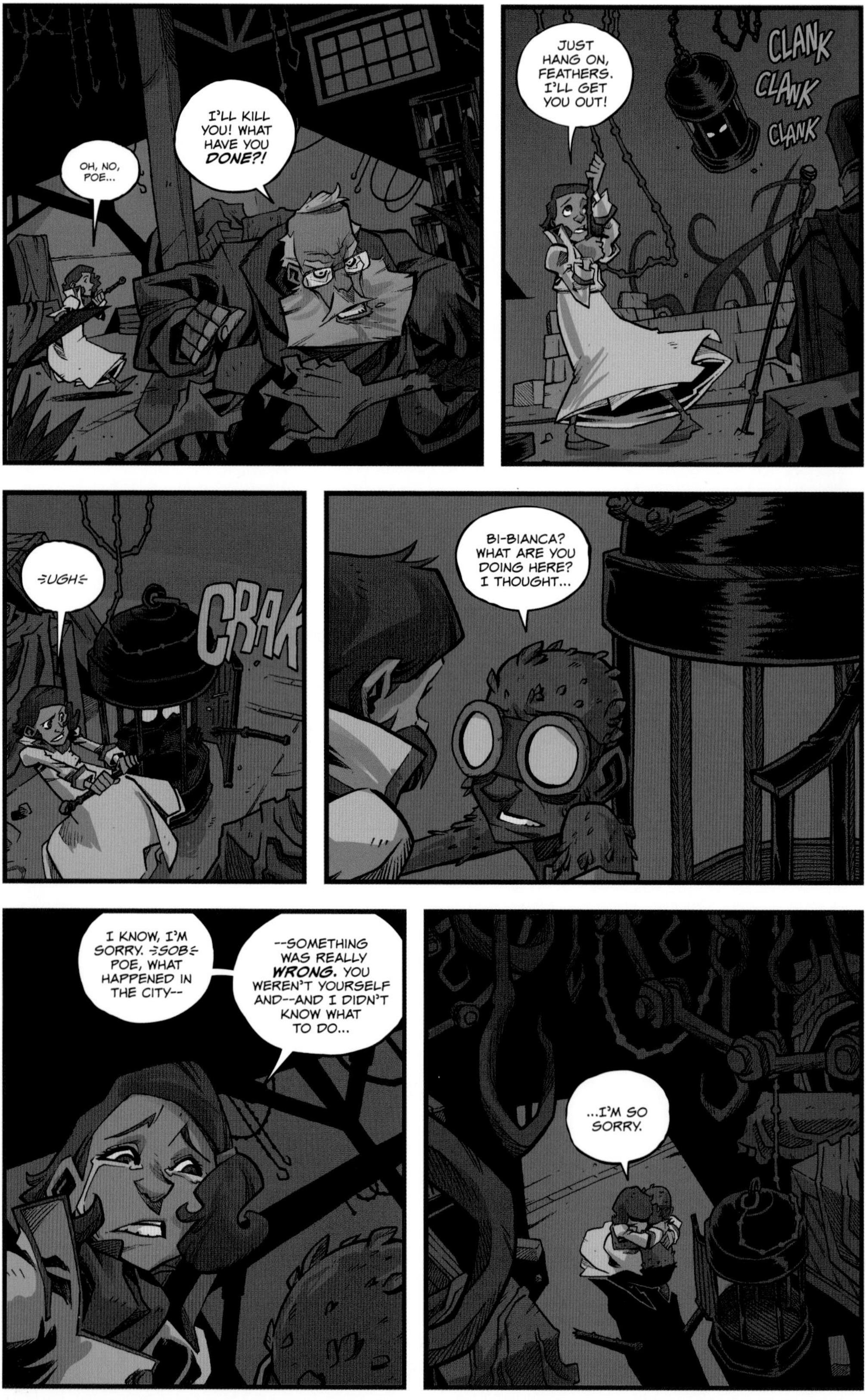
OH, NO, POE...
I'LL KILL YOU! WHAT HAVE YOU DONE?!
JUST HANG ON, FEATHERS. I'LL GET YOU OUT!
CLANK
CLANK
CLANK
UGH
CRAK
BI-BIANCA? WHAT ARE YOU DOING HERE? I THOUGHT...
I KNOW, I'M SORRY. SOB POE, WHAT HAPPENED IN THE CITY--
--SOMETHING WAS REALLY WRONG. YOU WEREN'T YOURSELF AND--AND I DIDN'T KNOW WHAT TO DO...
...I'M SO SORRY.

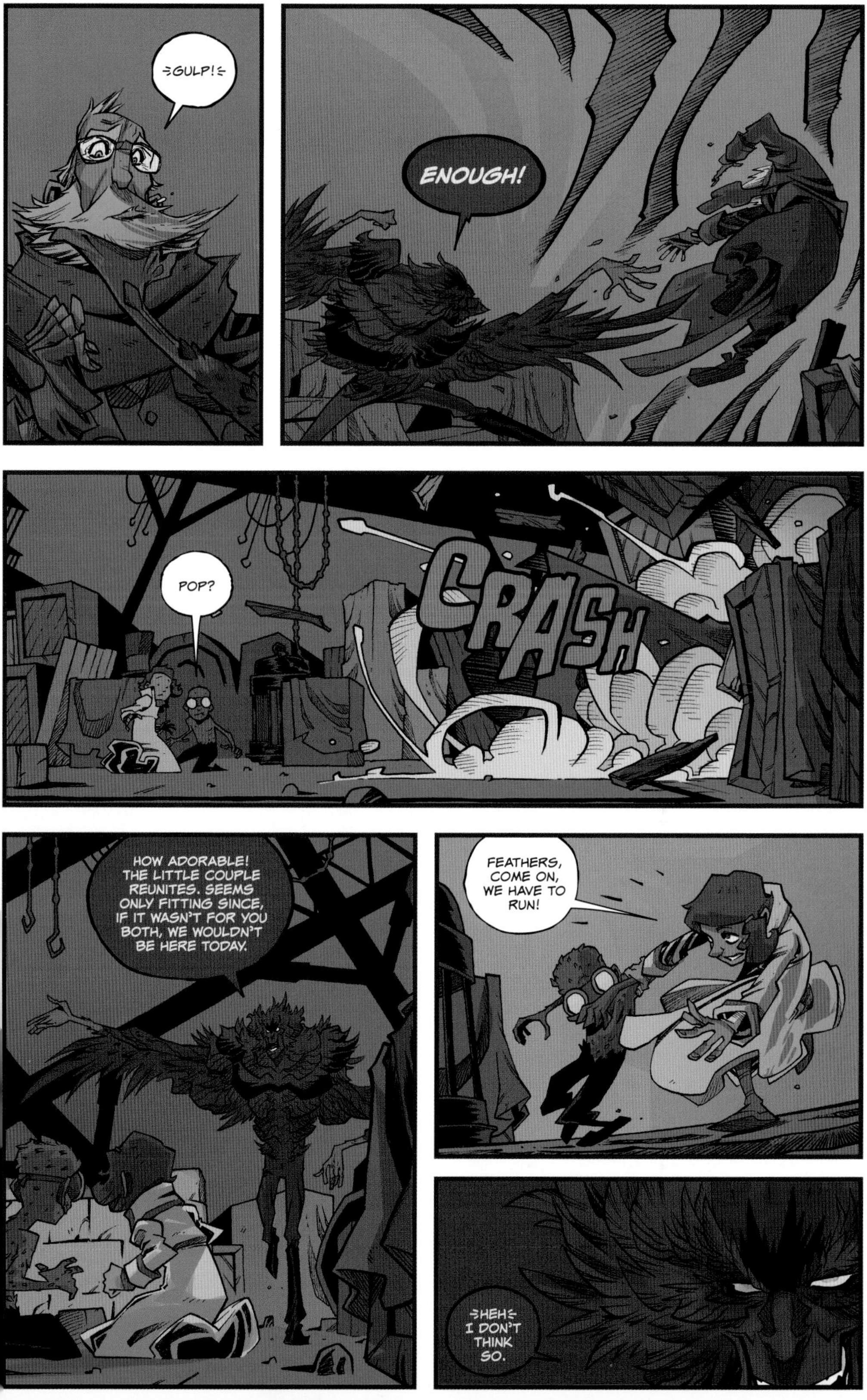

GULP!
ENOUGH!
POP?
CRASH
HOW ADORABLE! THE LITTLE COUPLE REUNITES. SEEMS ONLY FITTING SINCE, IF IT WASN'T FOR YOU BOTH, WE WOULDN'T BE HERE TODAY.
FEATHERS, COME ON, WE HAVE TO RUN!
HEH I DON'T THINK SO.

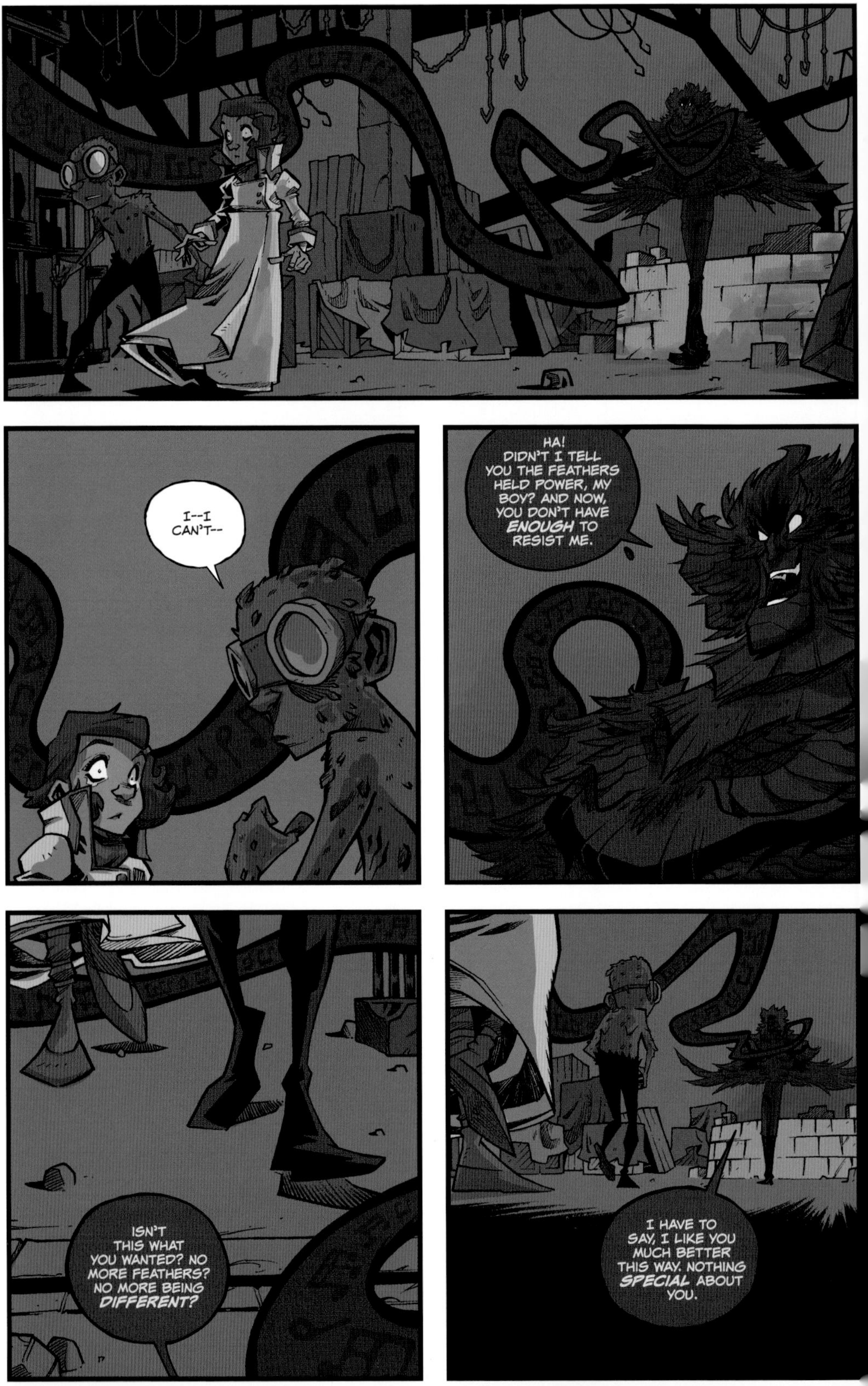
I--I CAN'T--
HA! DIDN'T I TELL YOU THE FEATHERS HELD POWER, MY BOY? AND NOW, YOU DON'T HAVE ENOUGH TO RESIST ME.
ISN'T THIS WHAT YOU WANTED? NO MORE FEATHERS? NO MORE BEING DIFFERENT?
I HAVE TO SAY, I LIKE YOU MUCH BETTER THIS WAY. NOTHING SPECIAL ABOUT YOU.

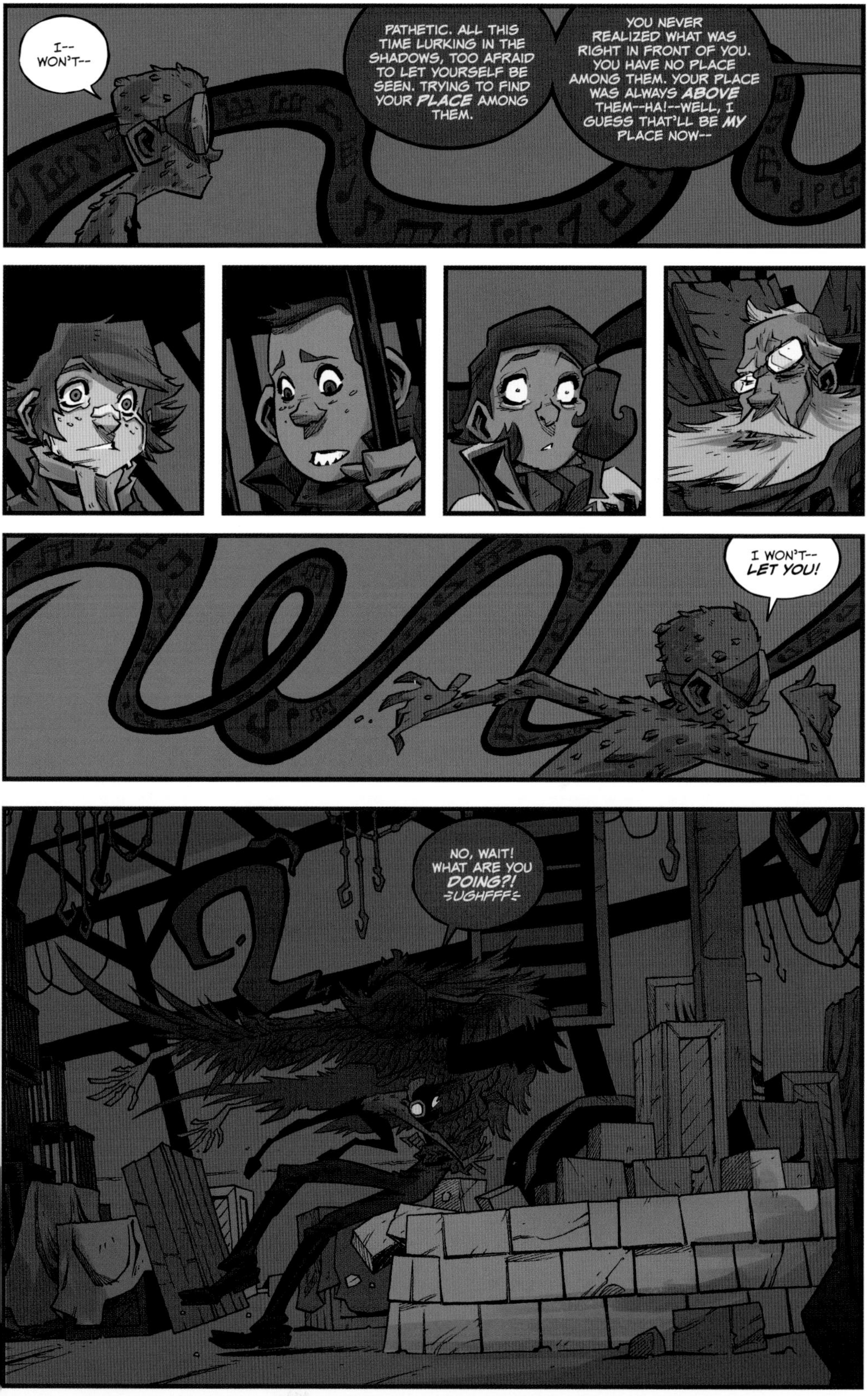
I-- WON'T--
PATHETIC. ALL THIS TIME LURKING IN THE SHADOWS, TOO AFRAID TO LET YOURSELF BE SEEN. TRYING TO FIND YOUR *PLACE* AMONG THEM.
YOU NEVER REALIZED WHAT WAS RIGHT IN FRONT OF YOU. YOU HAVE NO PLACE AMONG THEM. YOUR PLACE WAS ALWAYS *ABOVE* THEM--HA!--WELL, I GUESS THAT'LL BE *MY* PLACE NOW--
I WON'T-- *LET YOU!*
NO, WAIT! WHAT ARE YOU *DOING?!* UGHFFF

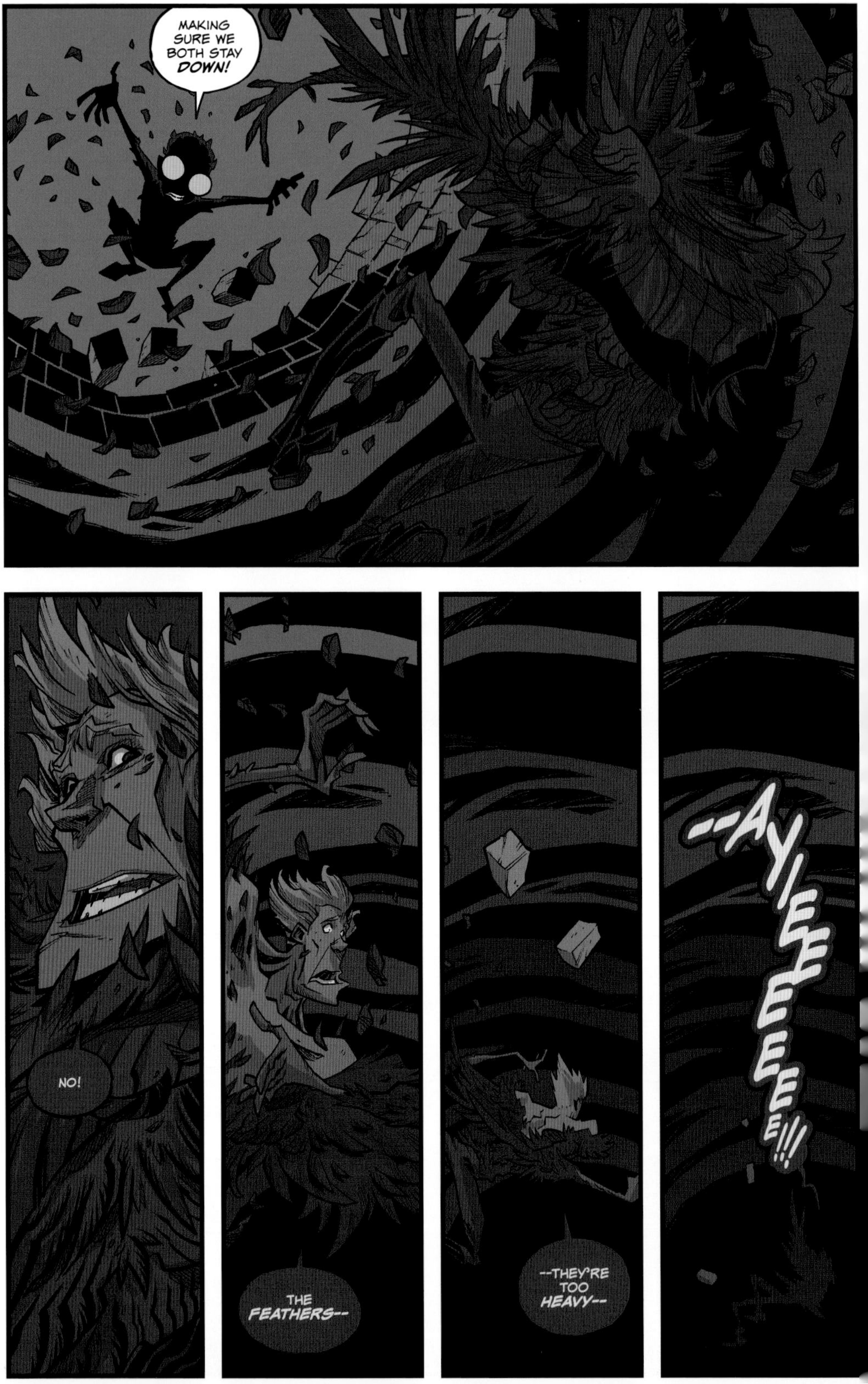
MAKING SURE WE BOTH STAY *DOWN!*
NO!
THE *FEATHERS--*
--THEY'RE TOO *HEAVY--*
--AYIEEEEEEE!!!

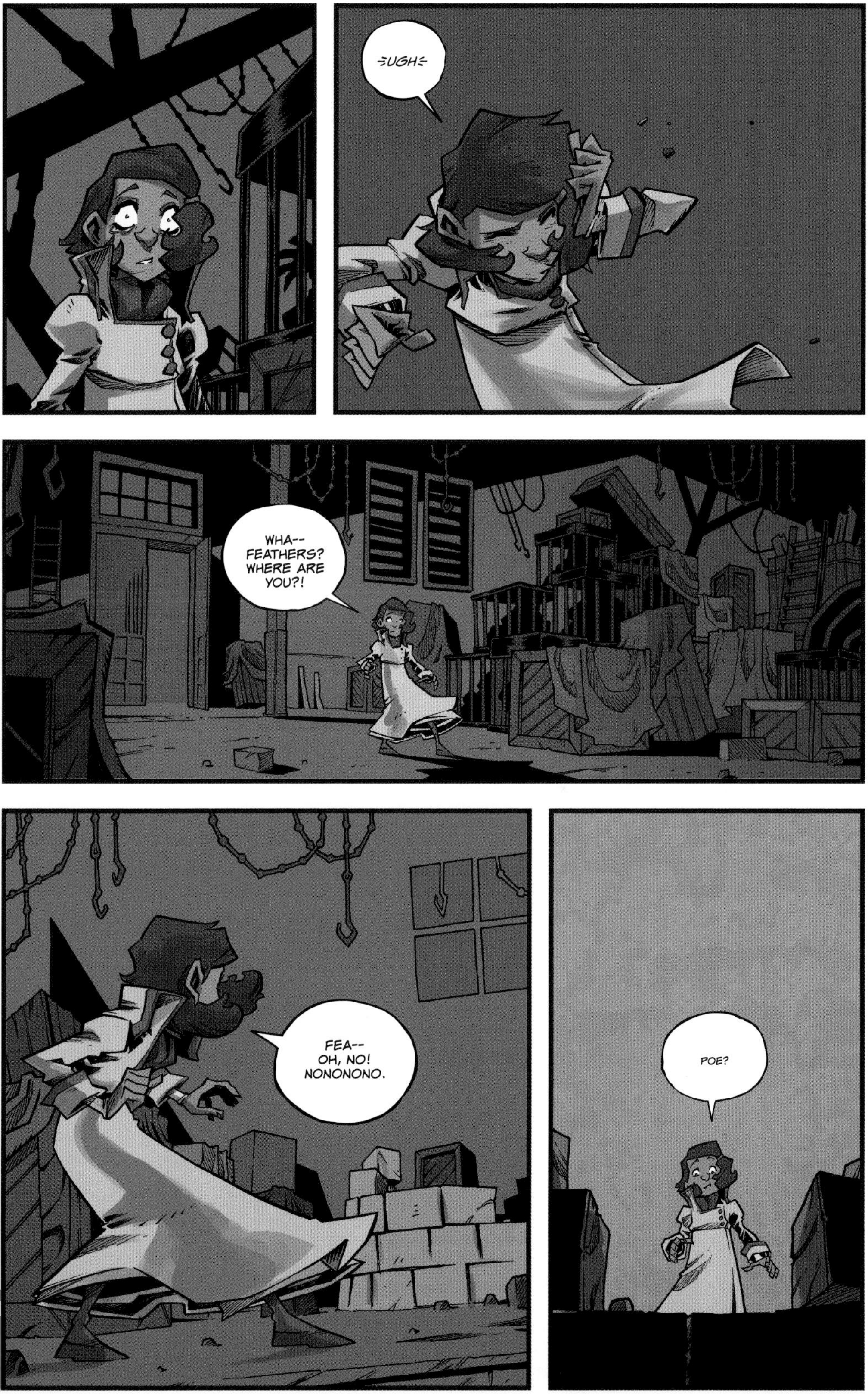
=UGH=
WHA-- FEATHERS? WHERE ARE YOU?!
FEA-- OH, NO! NONONONO.
POE?

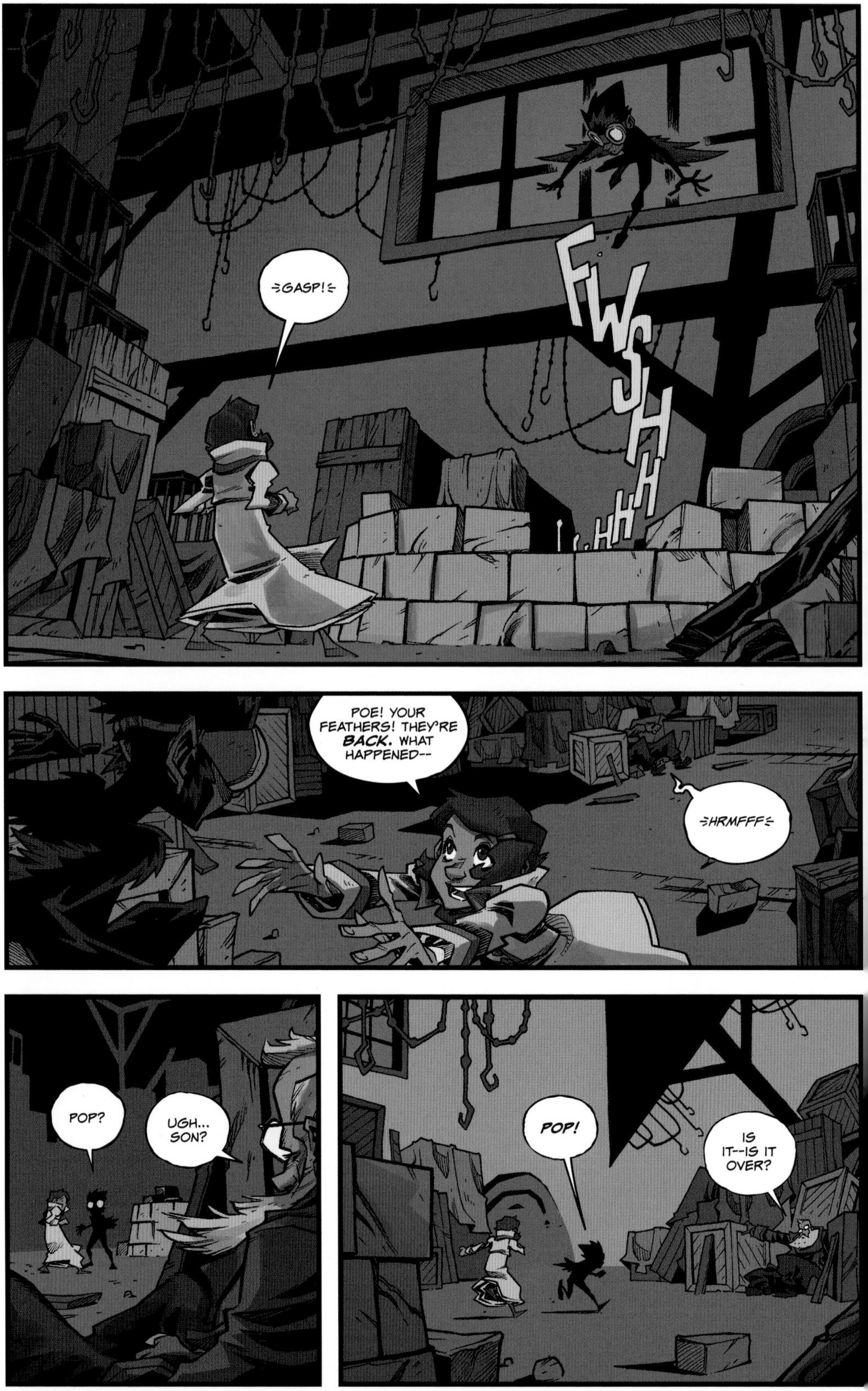

=GASP!=
FWSHHHHH
POE! YOUR FEATHERS! THEY'RE BACK. WHAT HAPPENED--
=HRMFFF=
POP?
UGH... SON?
POP!
IS IT--IS IT OVER?

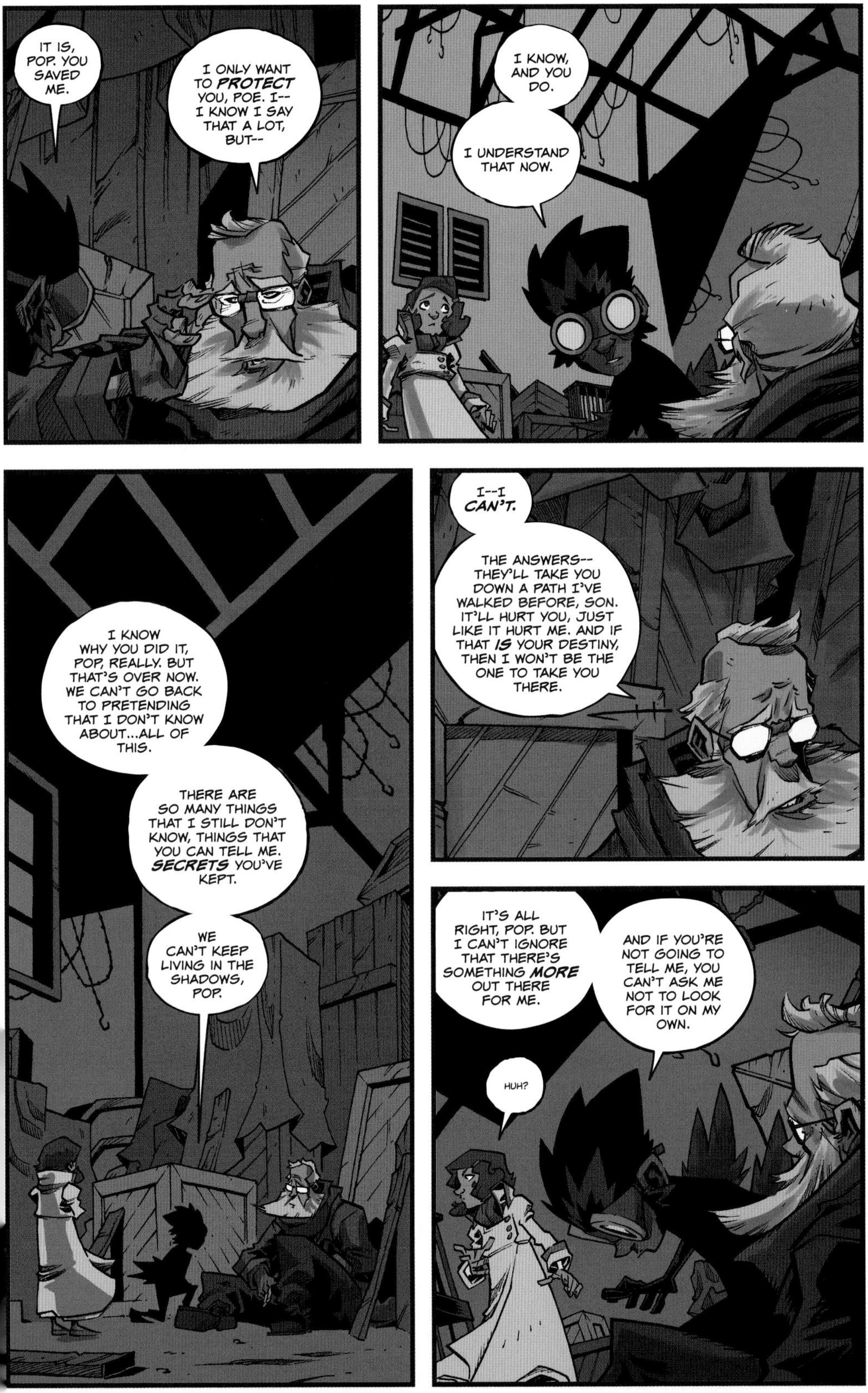
IT IS, POP. YOU SAVED ME.
I ONLY WANT TO *PROTECT* YOU, POE. I-- I KNOW I SAY THAT A LOT, BUT--
I KNOW, AND YOU DO.
I UNDERSTAND THAT NOW.
I KNOW WHY YOU DID IT, POP, REALLY. BUT THAT'S OVER NOW. WE CAN'T GO BACK TO PRETENDING THAT I DON'T KNOW ABOUT...ALL OF THIS.
THERE ARE SO MANY THINGS THAT I STILL DON'T KNOW, THINGS THAT YOU CAN TELL ME. *SECRETS* YOU'VE KEPT.
WE CAN'T KEEP LIVING IN THE SHADOWS, POP.
I--I *CAN'T.*
THE ANSWERS-- THEY'LL TAKE YOU DOWN A PATH I'VE WALKED BEFORE, SON. IT'LL HURT YOU, JUST LIKE IT HURT ME. AND IF THAT *IS* YOUR DESTINY, THEN I WON'T BE THE ONE TO TAKE YOU THERE.
IT'S ALL RIGHT, POP. BUT I CAN'T IGNORE THAT THERE'S SOMETHING *MORE* OUT THERE FOR ME.
AND IF YOU'RE NOT GOING TO TELL ME, YOU CAN'T ASK ME NOT TO LOOK FOR IT ON MY OWN.
HUH?

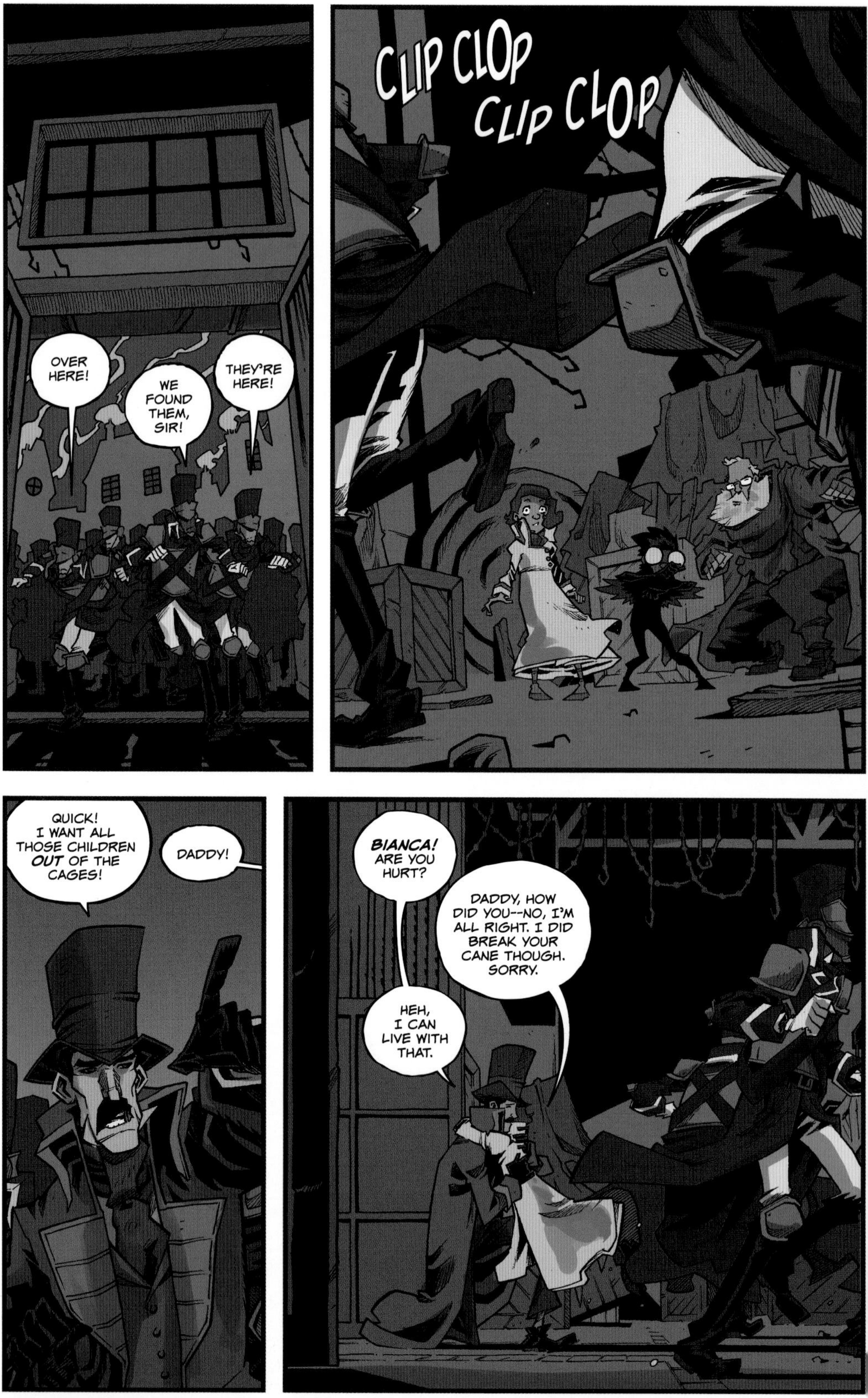

OVER HERE!
WE FOUND THEM, SIR!
THEY'RE HERE!
CLIP CLOP
CLIP CLOP
QUICK! I WANT ALL THOSE CHILDREN OUT OF THE CAGES!
DADDY!
BIANCA! ARE YOU HURT?
DADDY, HOW DID YOU--NO, I'M ALL RIGHT. I DID BREAK YOUR CANE THOUGH. SORRY.
HEH, I CAN LIVE WITH THAT.

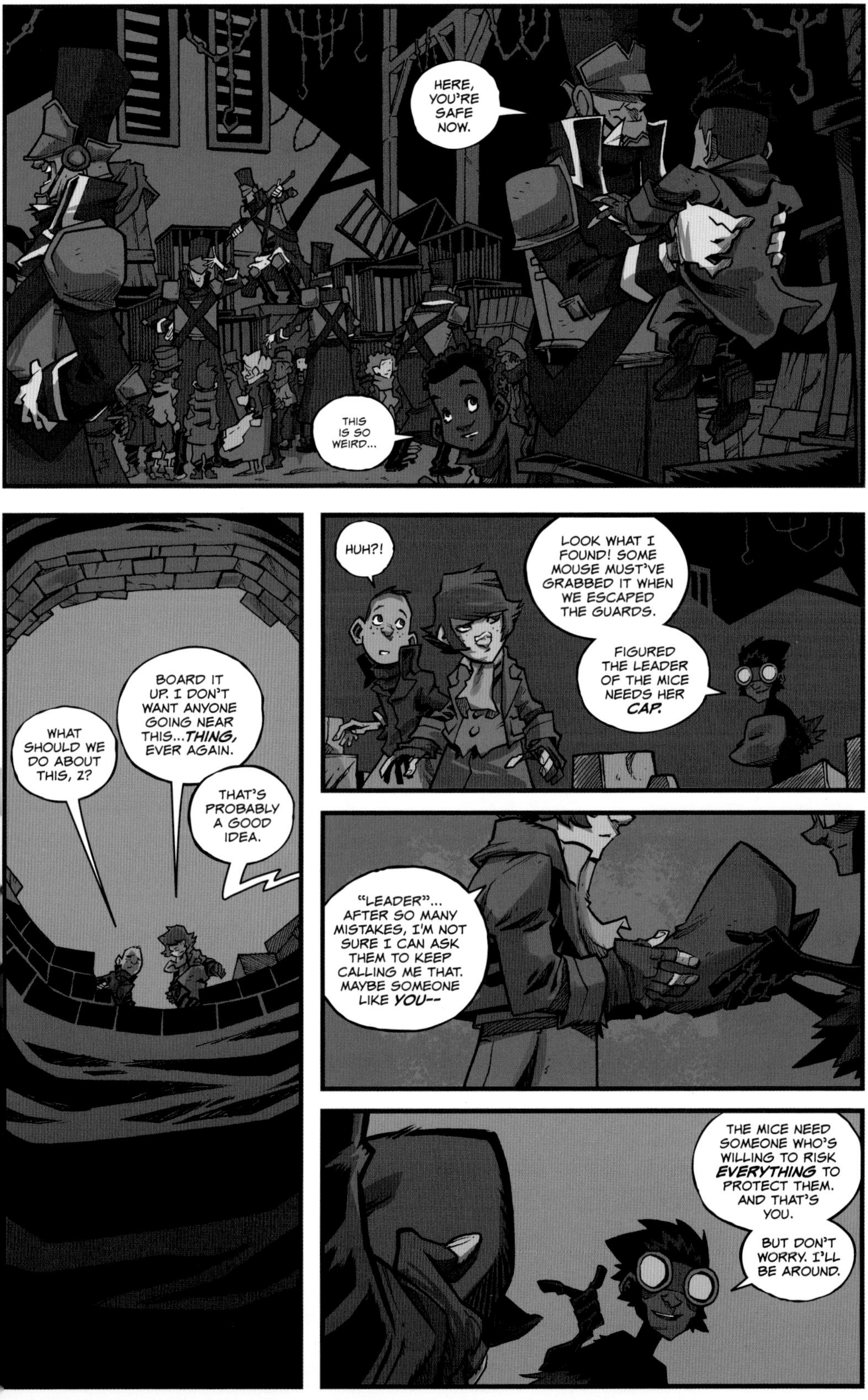
HERE, YOU'RE SAFE NOW.
THIS IS SO WEIRD...
WHAT SHOULD WE DO ABOUT THIS, Z?
BOARD IT UP. I DON'T WANT ANYONE GOING NEAR THIS...THING, EVER AGAIN.
THAT'S PROBABLY A GOOD IDEA.
HUH?!
LOOK WHAT I FOUND! SOME MOUSE MUST'VE GRABBED IT WHEN WE ESCAPED THE GUARDS.
FIGURED THE LEADER OF THE MICE NEEDS HER CAP.
"LEADER"... AFTER SO MANY MISTAKES, I'M NOT SURE I CAN ASK THEM TO KEEP CALLING ME THAT. MAYBE SOMEONE LIKE YOU--
THE MICE NEED SOMEONE WHO'S WILLING TO RISK EVERYTHING TO PROTECT THEM. AND THAT'S YOU.
BUT DON'T WORRY. I'LL BE AROUND.

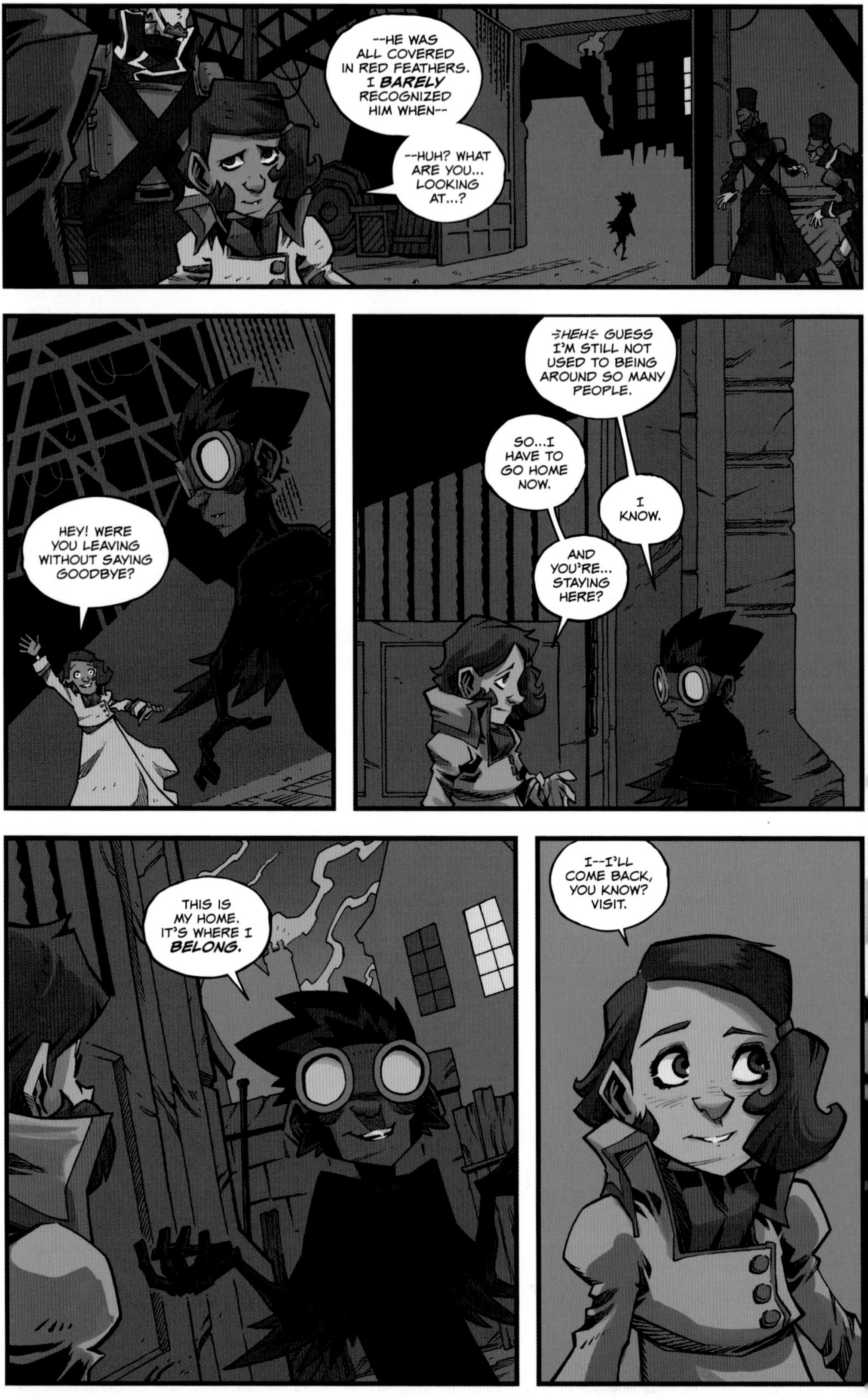
--HE WAS ALL COVERED IN RED FEATHERS. I **BARELY** RECOGNIZED HIM WHEN--
--HUH? WHAT ARE YOU... LOOKING AT...?
HEY! WERE YOU LEAVING WITHOUT SAYING GOODBYE?
=HEH= GUESS I'M STILL NOT USED TO BEING AROUND SO MANY PEOPLE.
SO...I HAVE TO GO HOME NOW.
I KNOW.
AND YOU'RE... STAYING HERE?
THIS IS MY HOME. IT'S WHERE I **BELONG.**
I--I'LL COME BACK, YOU KNOW? VISIT.

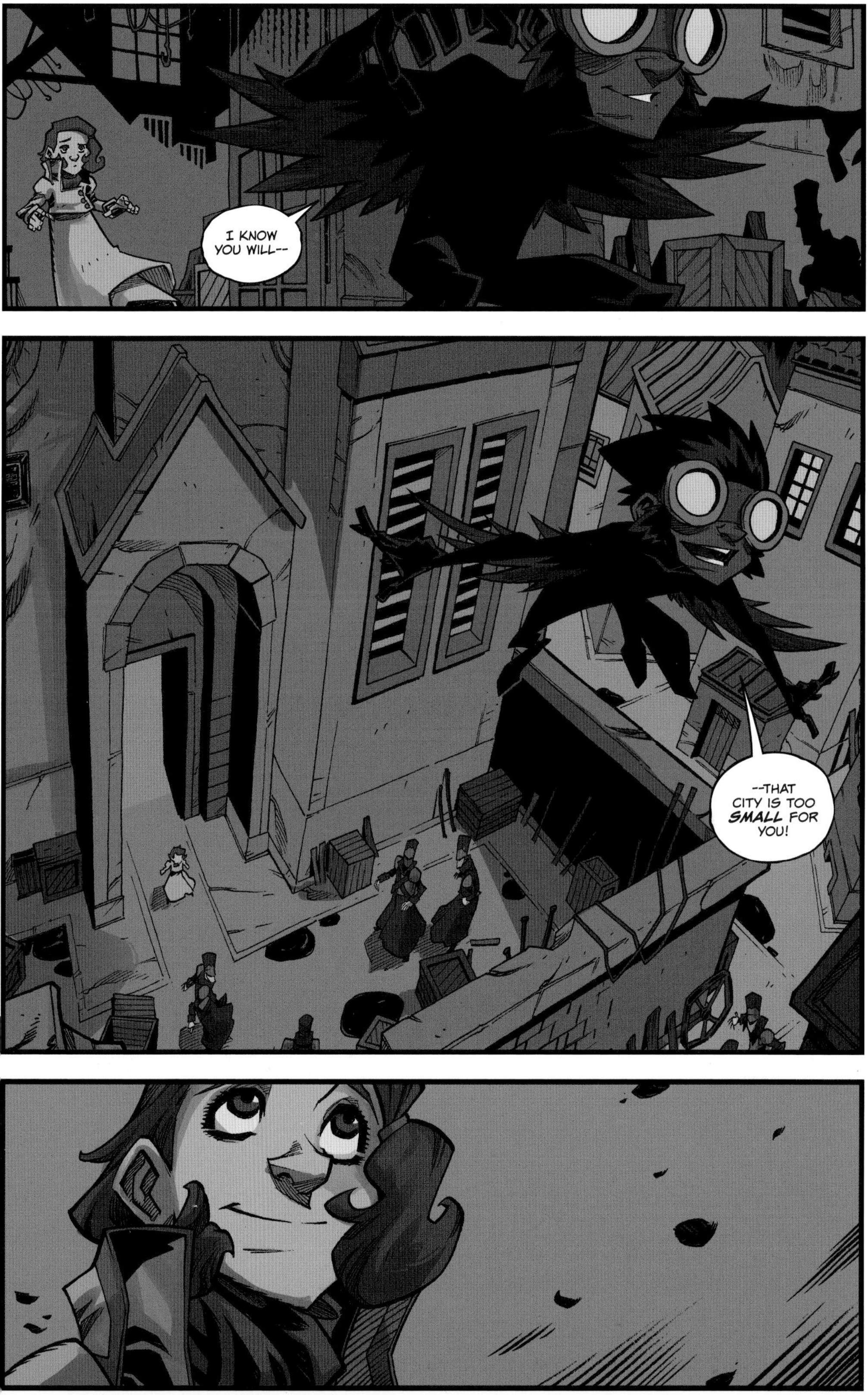
I KNOW YOU WILL--
--THAT CITY IS TOO SMALL FOR YOU!

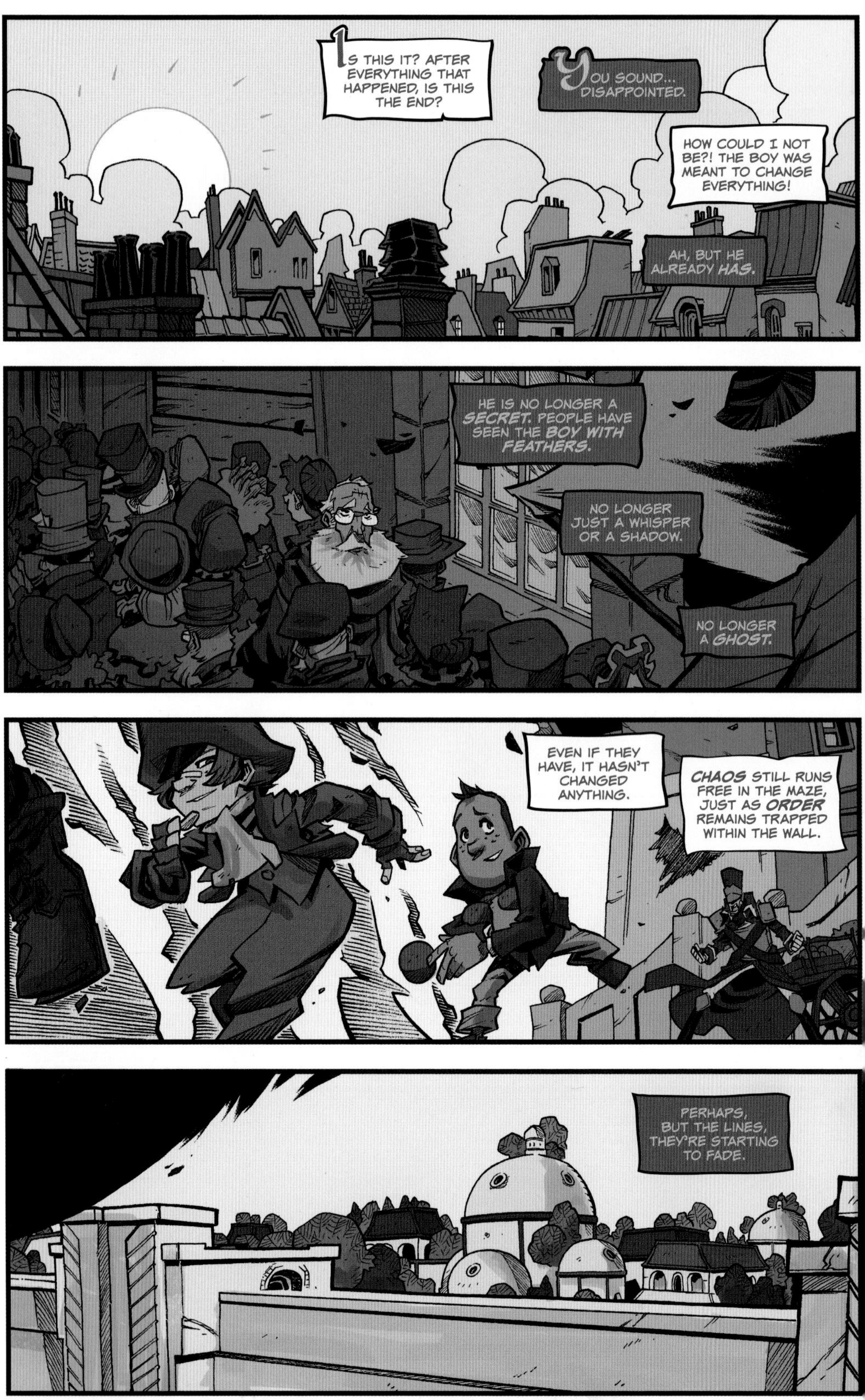
IS THIS IT? AFTER EVERYTHING THAT HAPPENED, IS THIS THE END?
YOU SOUND... DISAPPOINTED.
HOW COULD I NOT BE?! THE BOY WAS MEANT TO CHANGE EVERYTHING!
AH, BUT HE ALREADY HAS.
HE IS NO LONGER A SECRET. PEOPLE HAVE SEEN THE BOY WITH FEATHERS.
NO LONGER JUST A WHISPER OR A SHADOW.
NO LONGER A GHOST.
EVEN IF THEY HAVE, IT HASN'T CHANGED ANYTHING.
CHAOS STILL RUNS FREE IN THE MAZE, JUST AS ORDER REMAINS TRAPPED WITHIN THE WALL.
PERHAPS, BUT THE LINES, THEY'RE STARTING TO FADE.

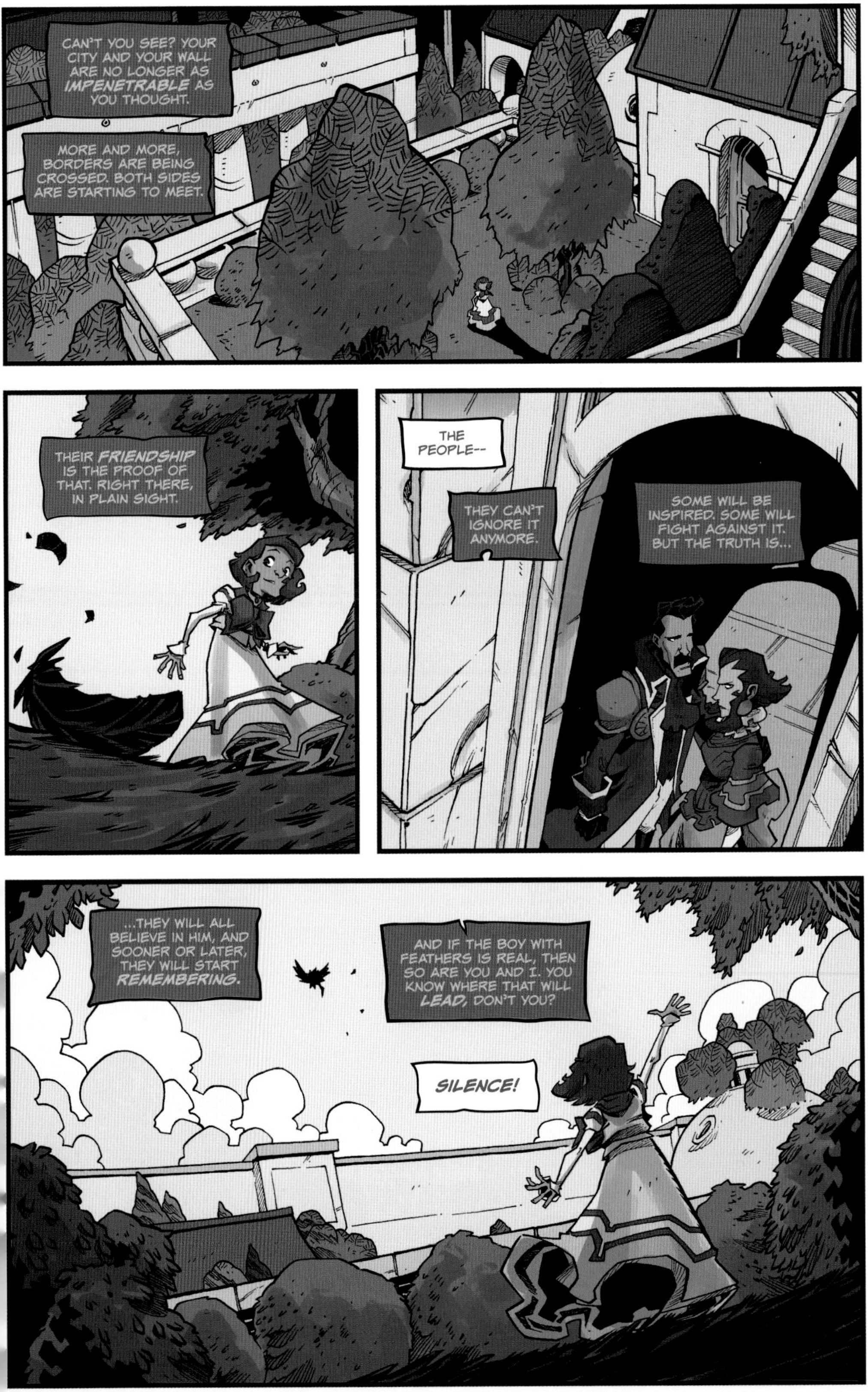
CAN'T YOU SEE? YOUR CITY AND YOUR WALL ARE NO LONGER AS IMPENETRABLE AS YOU THOUGHT.
MORE AND MORE, BORDERS ARE BEING CROSSED. BOTH SIDES ARE STARTING TO MEET.
THEIR FRIENDSHIP IS THE PROOF OF THAT. RIGHT THERE, IN PLAIN SIGHT.
THE PEOPLE--
THEY CAN'T IGNORE IT ANYMORE.
SOME WILL BE INSPIRED. SOME WILL FIGHT AGAINST IT. BUT THE TRUTH IS...
...THEY WILL ALL BELIEVE IN HIM, AND SOONER OR LATER, THEY WILL START REMEMBERING.
AND IF THE BOY WITH FEATHERS IS REAL, THEN SO ARE YOU AND I. YOU KNOW WHERE THAT WILL LEAD, DON'T YOU?
SILENCE!

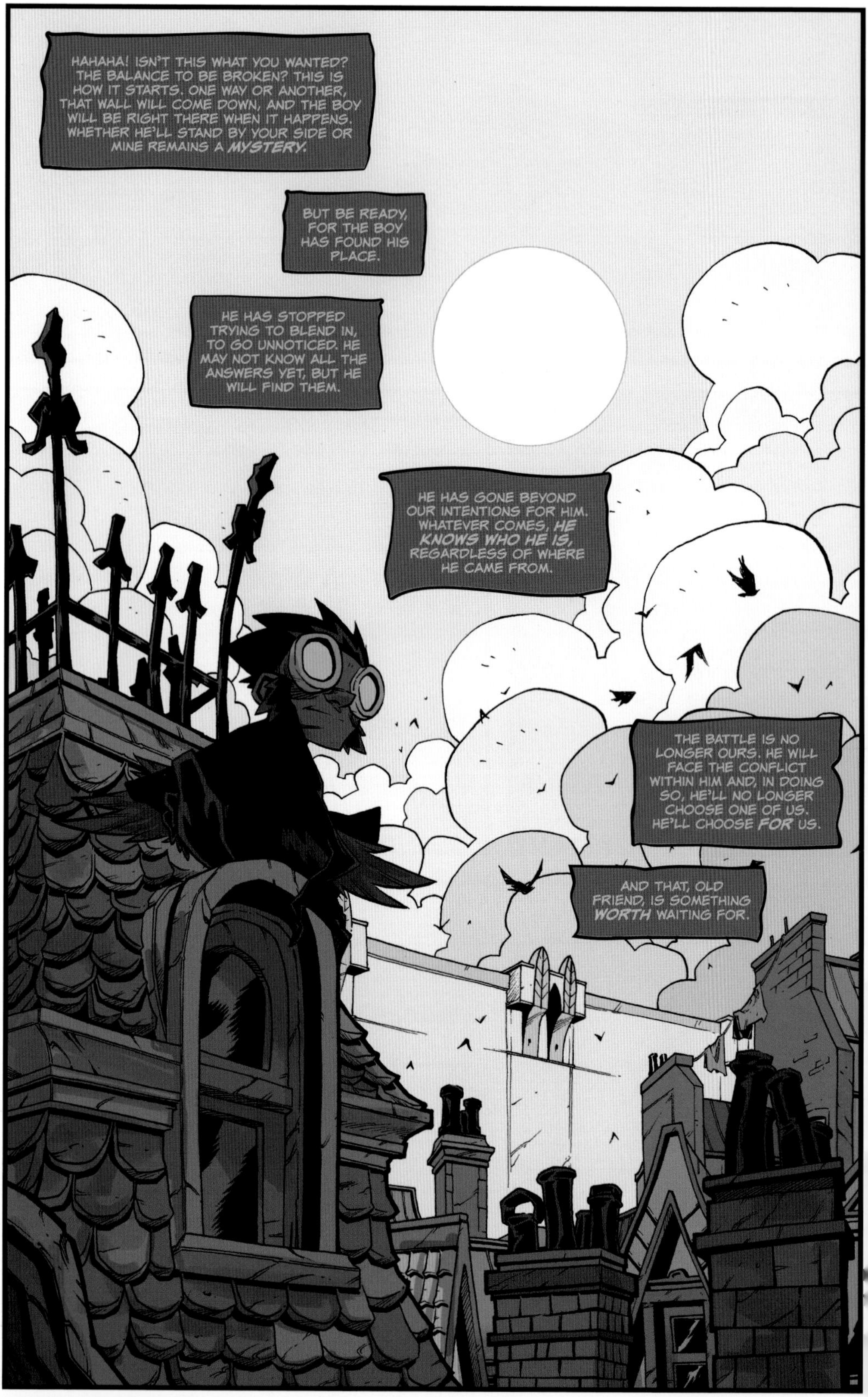
HAHAHA! ISN'T THIS WHAT YOU WANTED? THE BALANCE TO BE BROKEN? THIS IS HOW IT STARTS. ONE WAY OR ANOTHER, THAT WALL WILL COME DOWN, AND THE BOY WILL BE RIGHT THERE WHEN IT HAPPENS. WHETHER HE'LL STAND BY YOUR SIDE OR MINE REMAINS A *MYSTERY.*
BUT BE READY, FOR THE BOY HAS FOUND HIS PLACE.
HE HAS STOPPED TRYING TO BLEND IN, TO GO UNNOTICED. HE MAY NOT KNOW ALL THE ANSWERS YET, BUT HE WILL FIND THEM.
HE HAS GONE BEYOND OUR INTENTIONS FOR HIM. WHATEVER COMES, *HE KNOWS WHO HE IS,* REGARDLESS OF WHERE HE CAME FROM.
THE BATTLE IS NO LONGER OURS. HE WILL FACE THE CONFLICT WITHIN HIM AND, IN DOING SO, HE'LL NO LONGER CHOOSE ONE OF US. HE'LL CHOOSE *FOR* US.
AND THAT, OLD FRIEND, IS SOMETHING *WORTH* WAITING FOR.

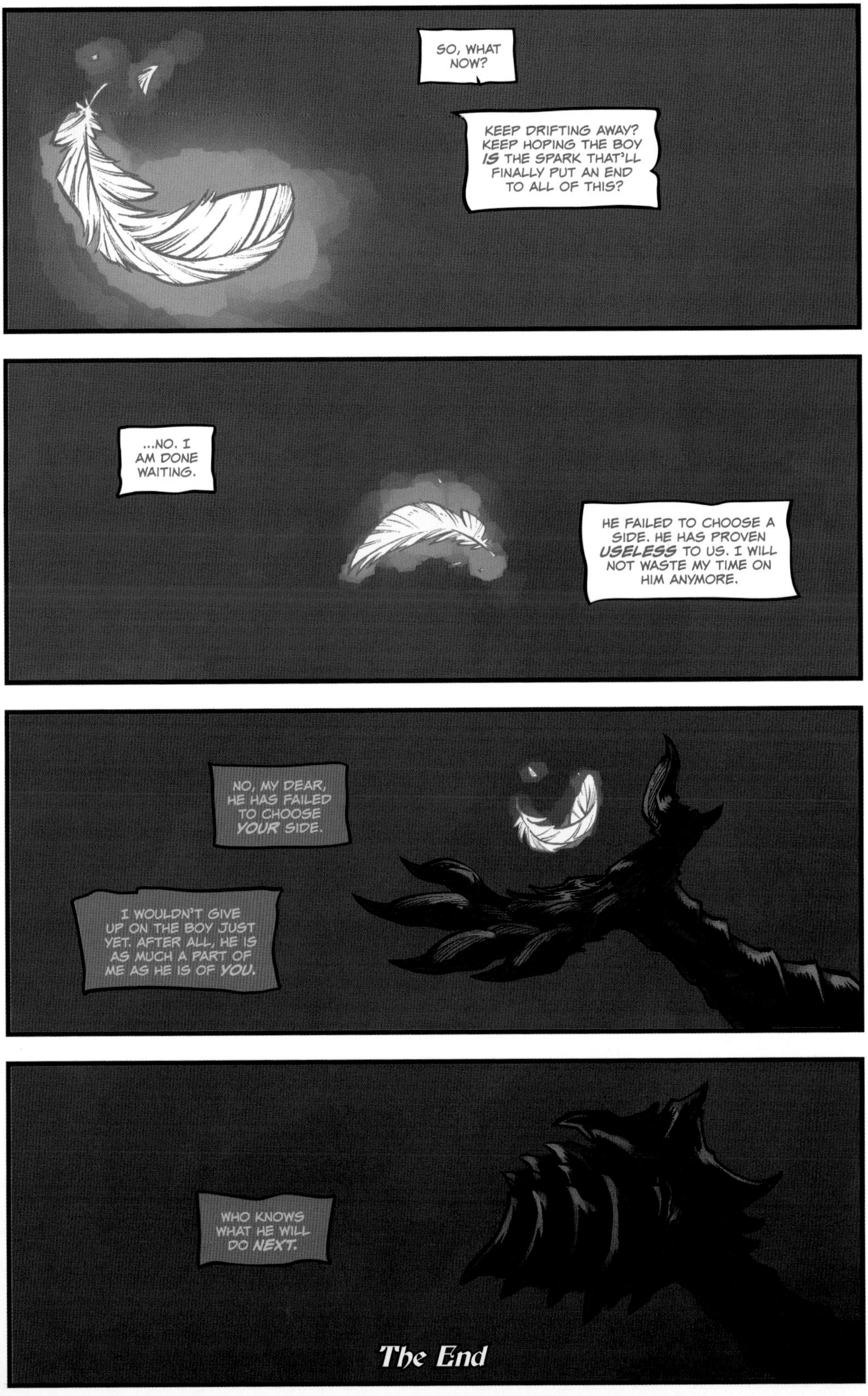
SO, WHAT NOW?
KEEP DRIFTING AWAY? KEEP HOPING THE BOY *IS* THE SPARK THAT'LL FINALLY PUT AN END TO ALL OF THIS?
...NO. I AM DONE WAITING.
HE FAILED TO CHOOSE A SIDE. HE HAS PROVEN *USELESS* TO US. I WILL NOT WASTE MY TIME ON HIM ANYMORE.
NO, MY DEAR, HE HAS FAILED TO CHOOSE *YOUR* SIDE.
I WOULDN'T GIVE UP ON THE BOY JUST YET. AFTER ALL, HE IS AS MUCH A PART OF ME AS HE IS OF *YOU*.
WHO KNOWS WHAT HE WILL DO *NEXT*.
The End

COVER
GALLERY

ISSUE ONE COVER

JORGE CORONA

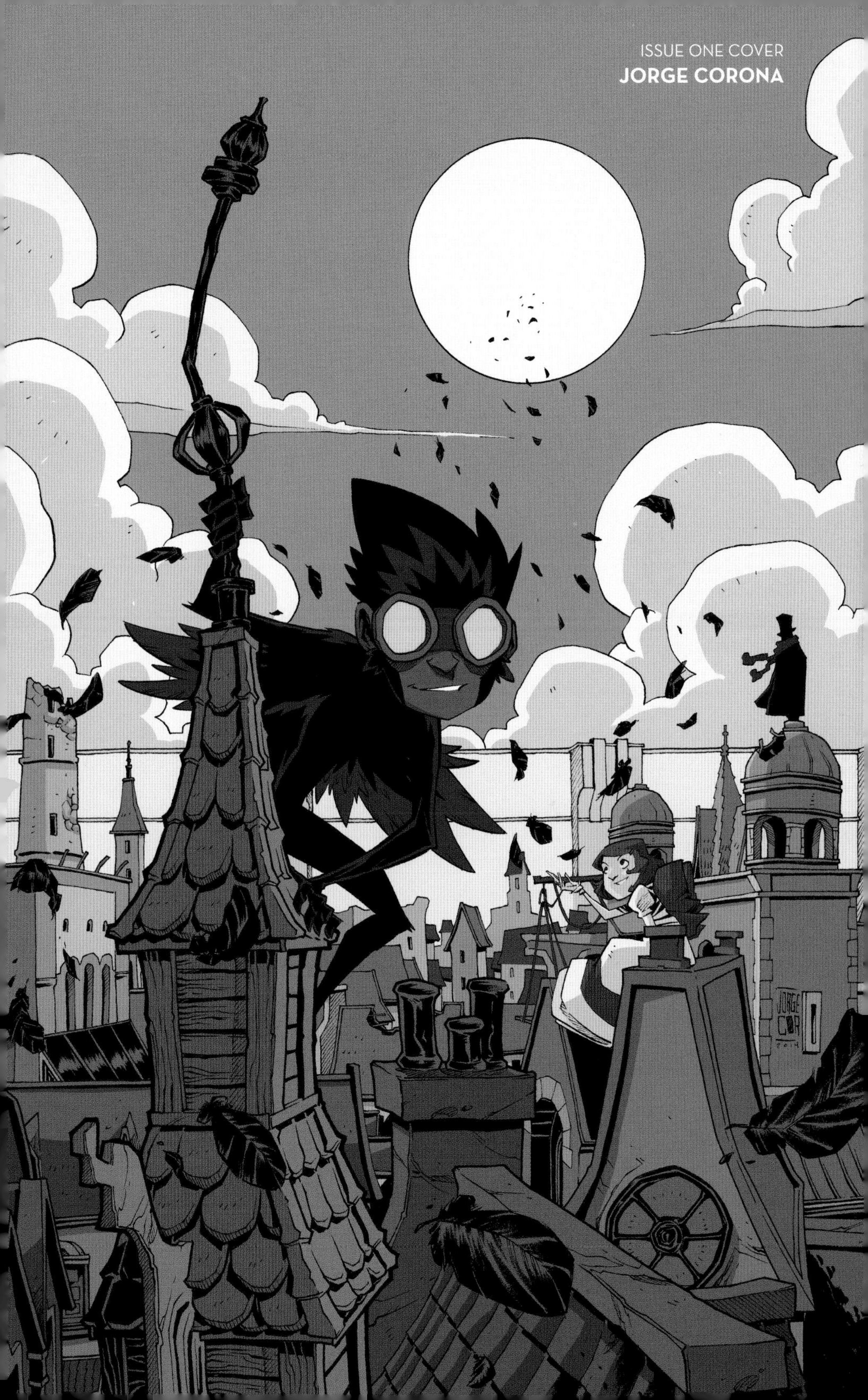
JORGE
COR

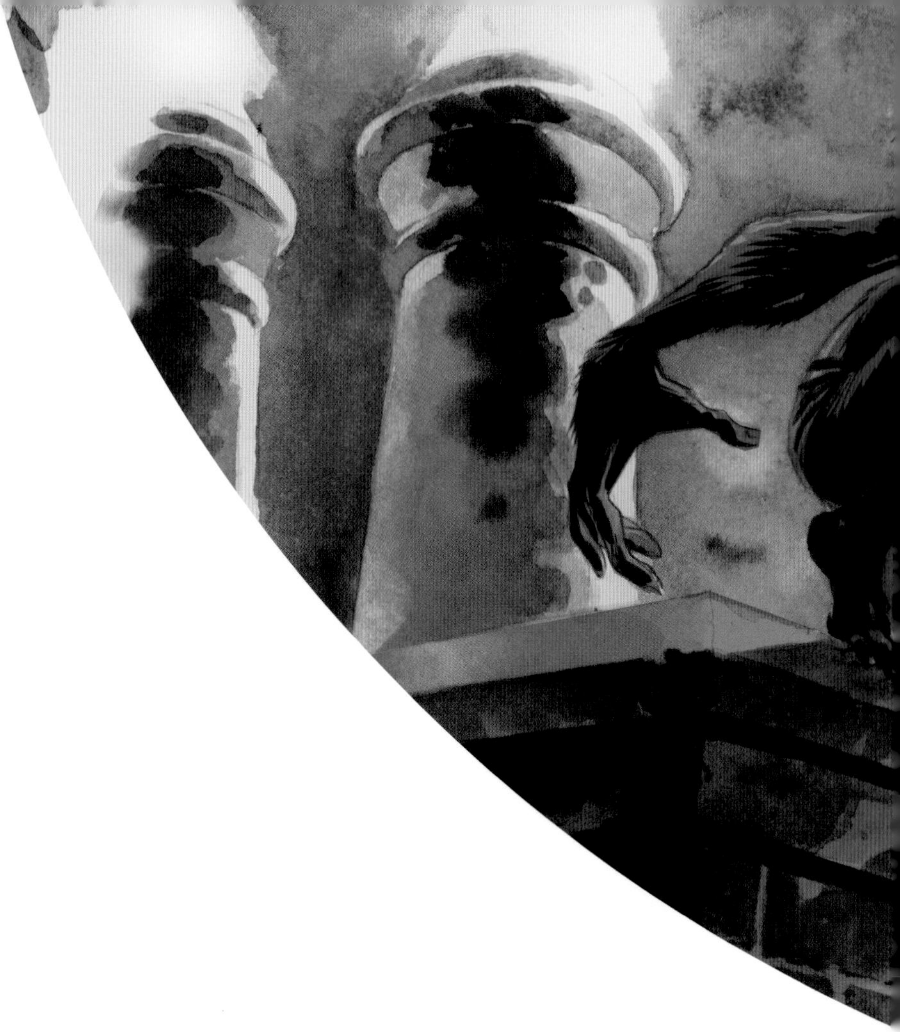

ISSUE ONE BOOM! TEN YEARS VARIANT COVER
RAMÓN K. PÉREZ

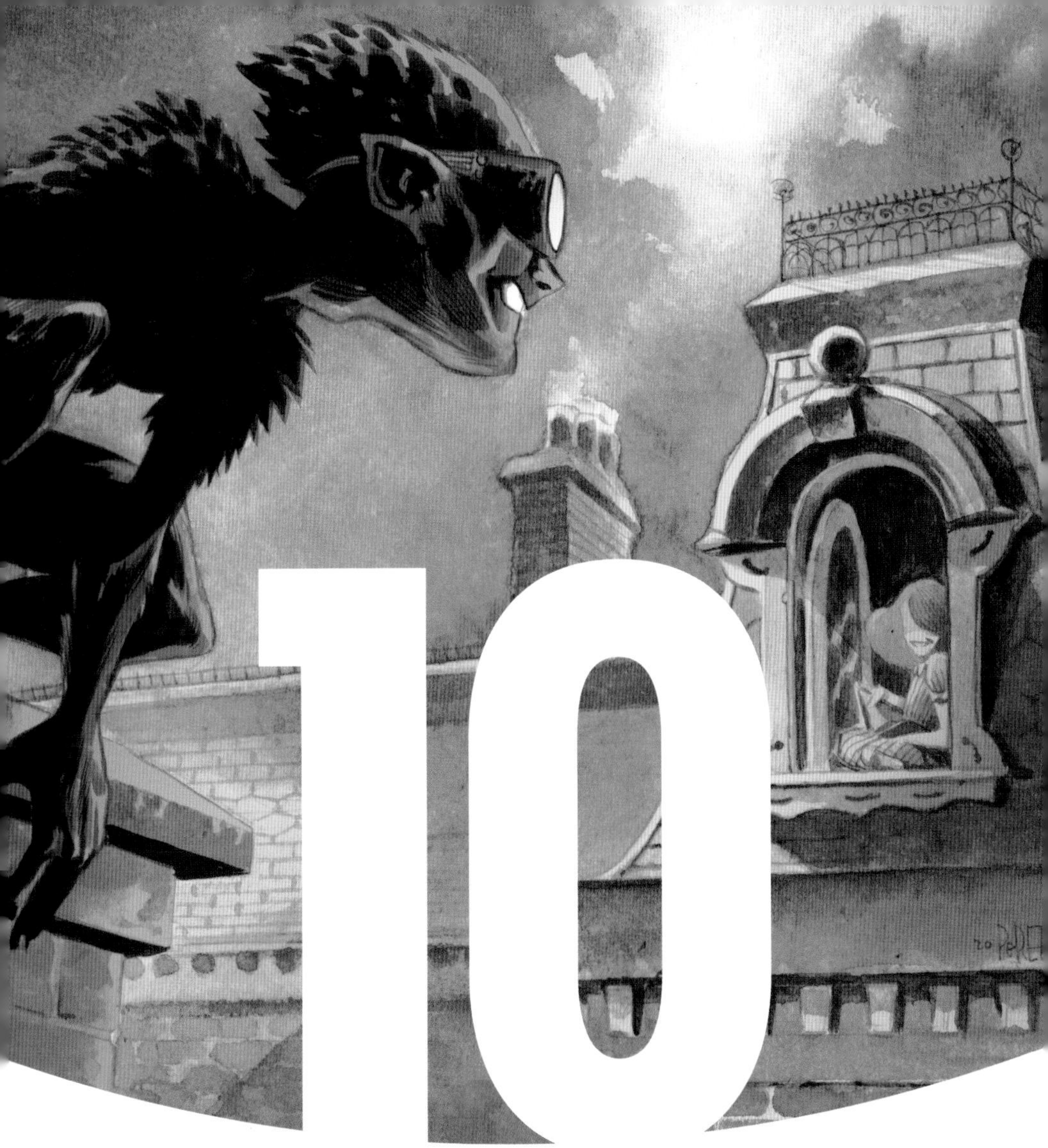

10

ISSUE ONE VARIANT COVER

KEN NIIMURA

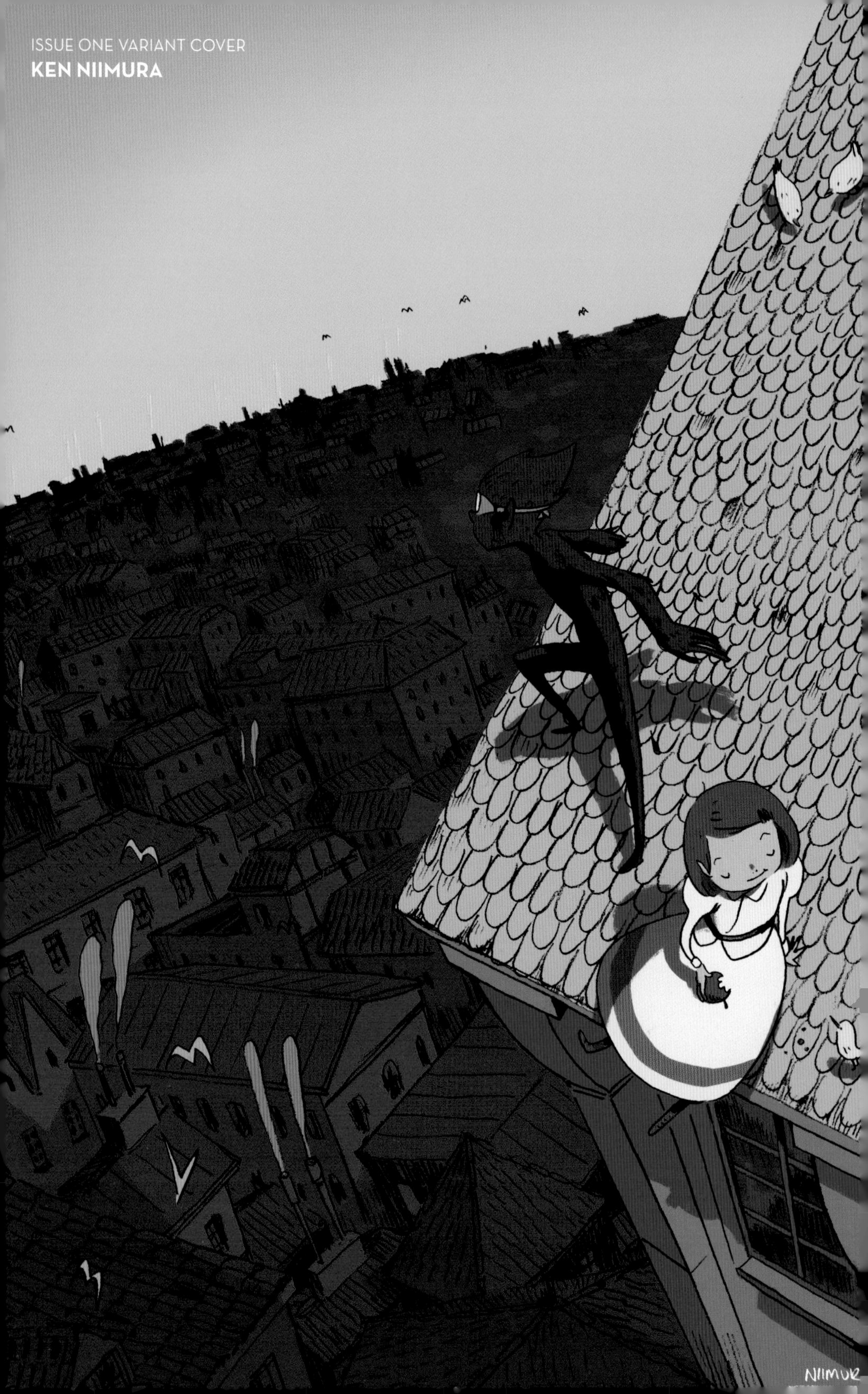

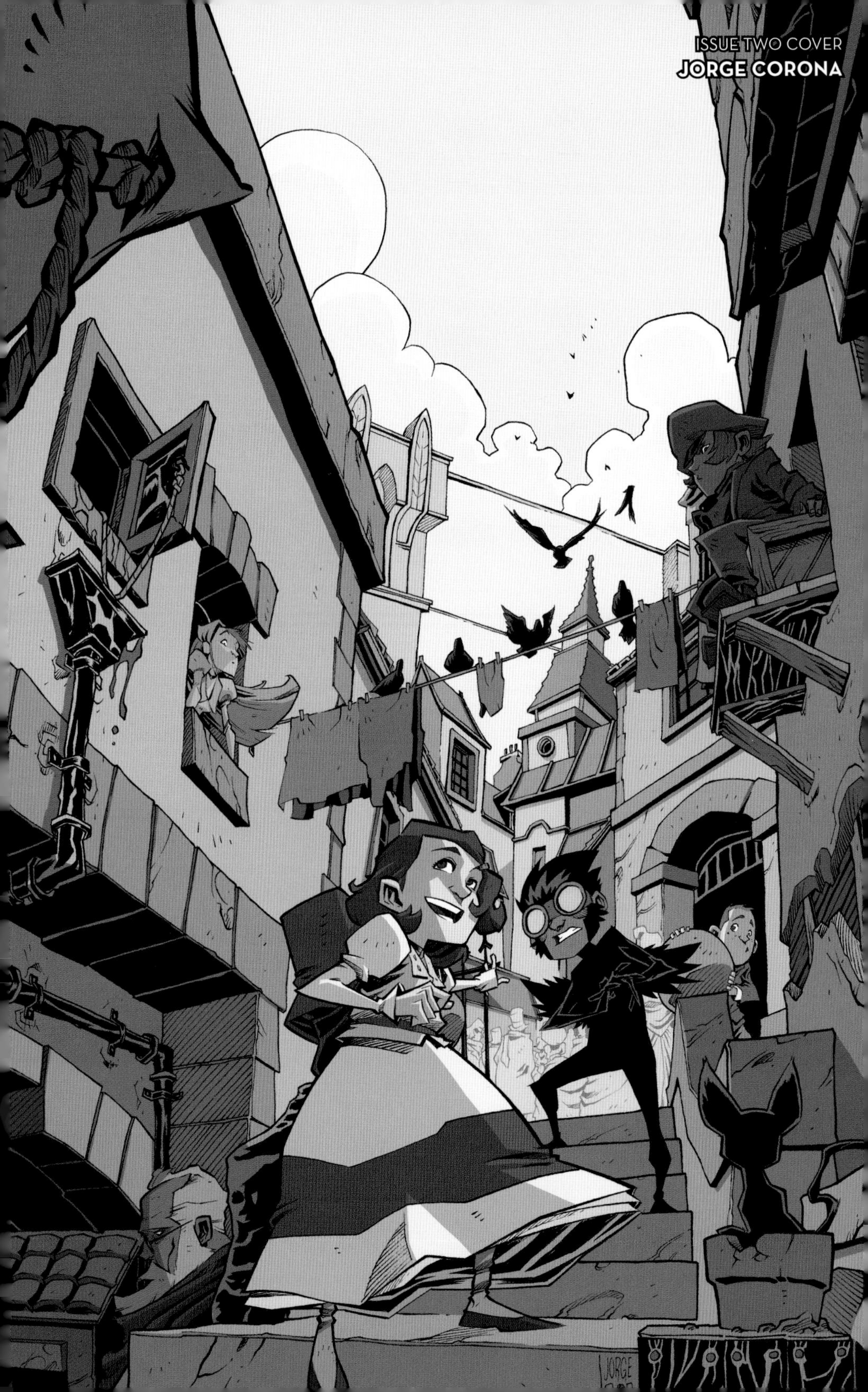
JORGE

ISSUE TWO COVER
JORGE CORONA

ISSUE THREE COVER
JORGE CORONA

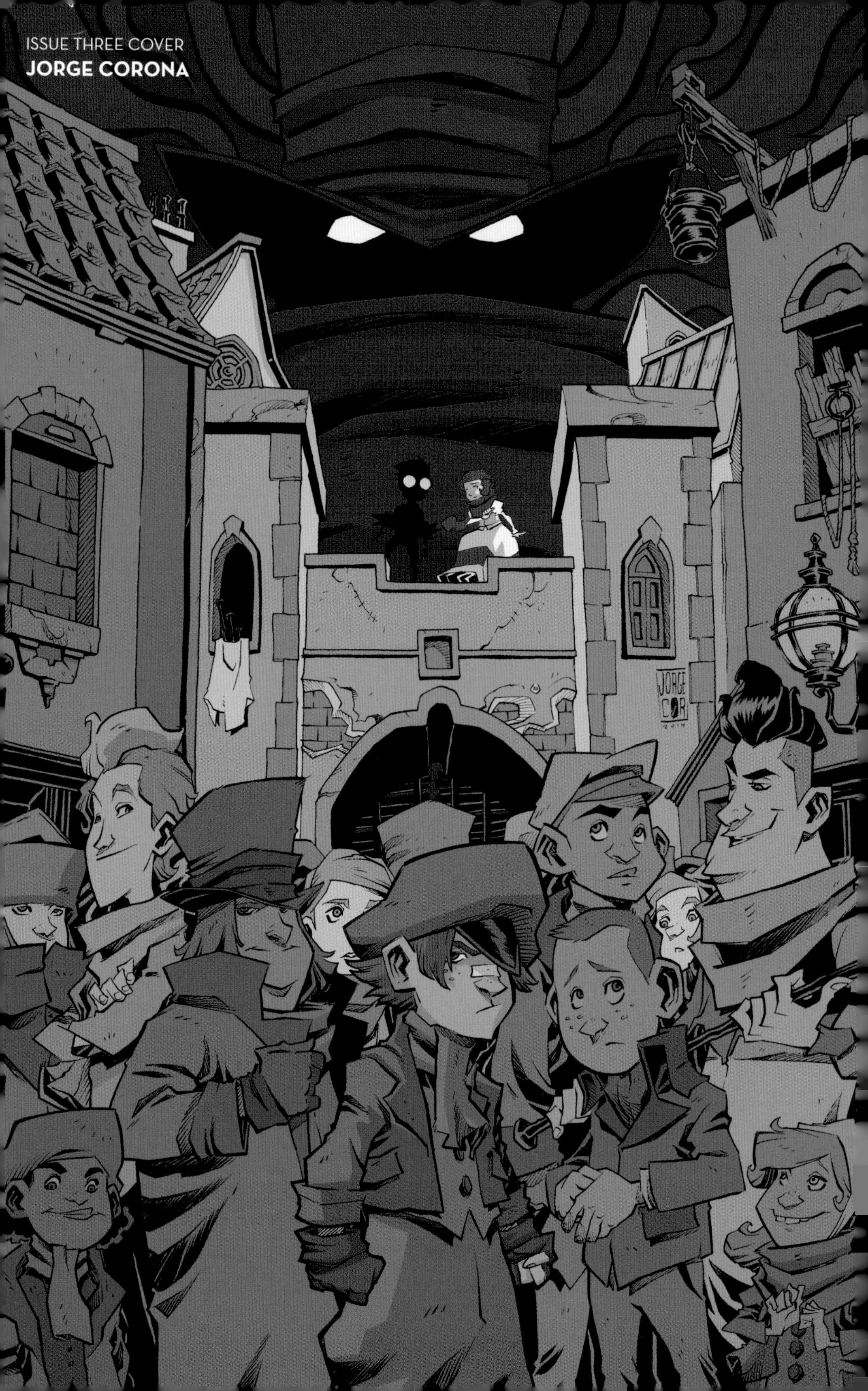
JORGE
COR
2014

ISSUE FOUR COVER
JORGE CORONA

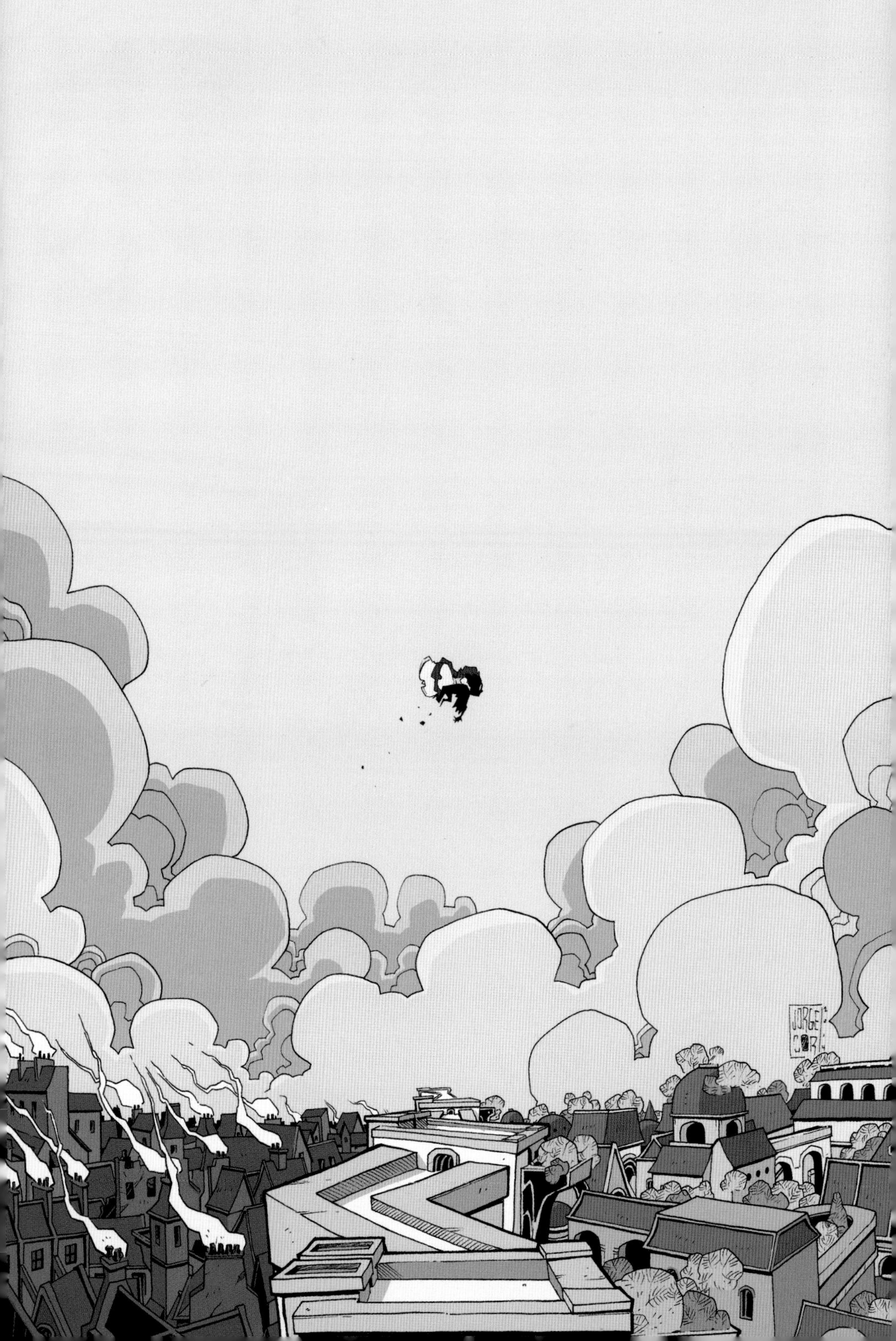
JORGE CORONA

ISSUE FIVE COVER
JORGE CORONA

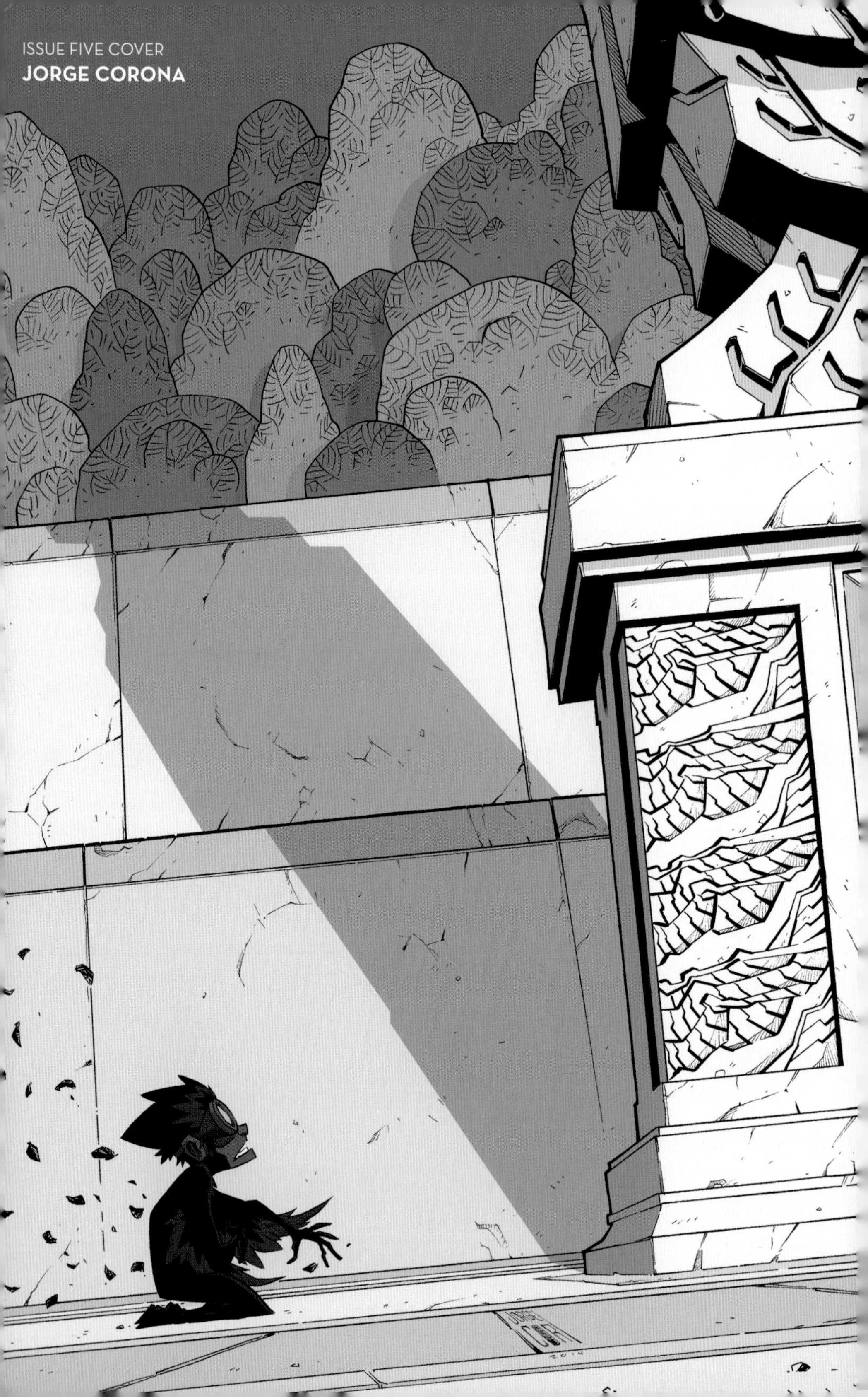

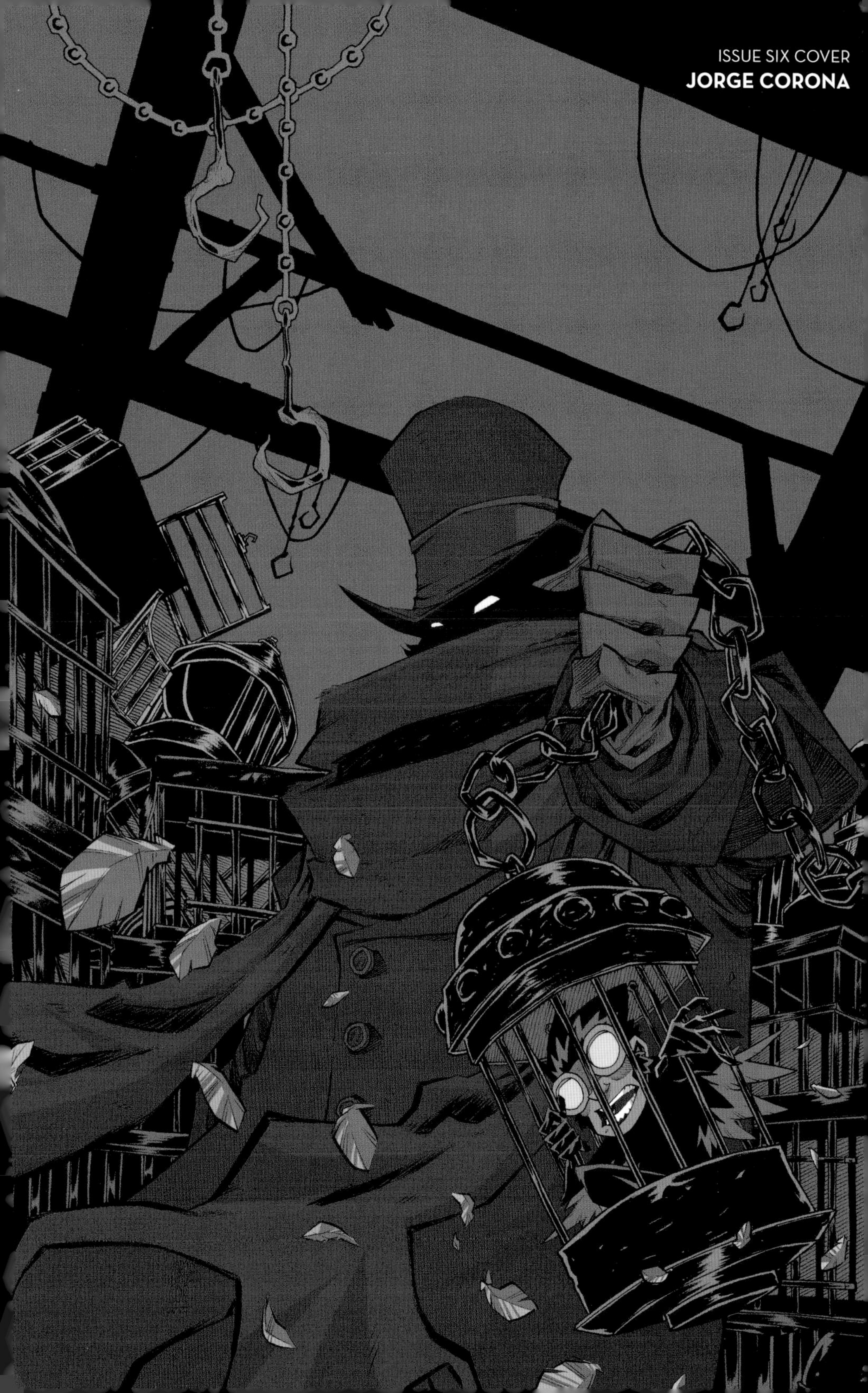

ISSUE SIX COVER

JORGE CORONA

CREATING FEATHERS™

WITH SKETCHES & COMMENTARY
BY **JORGE CORONA**

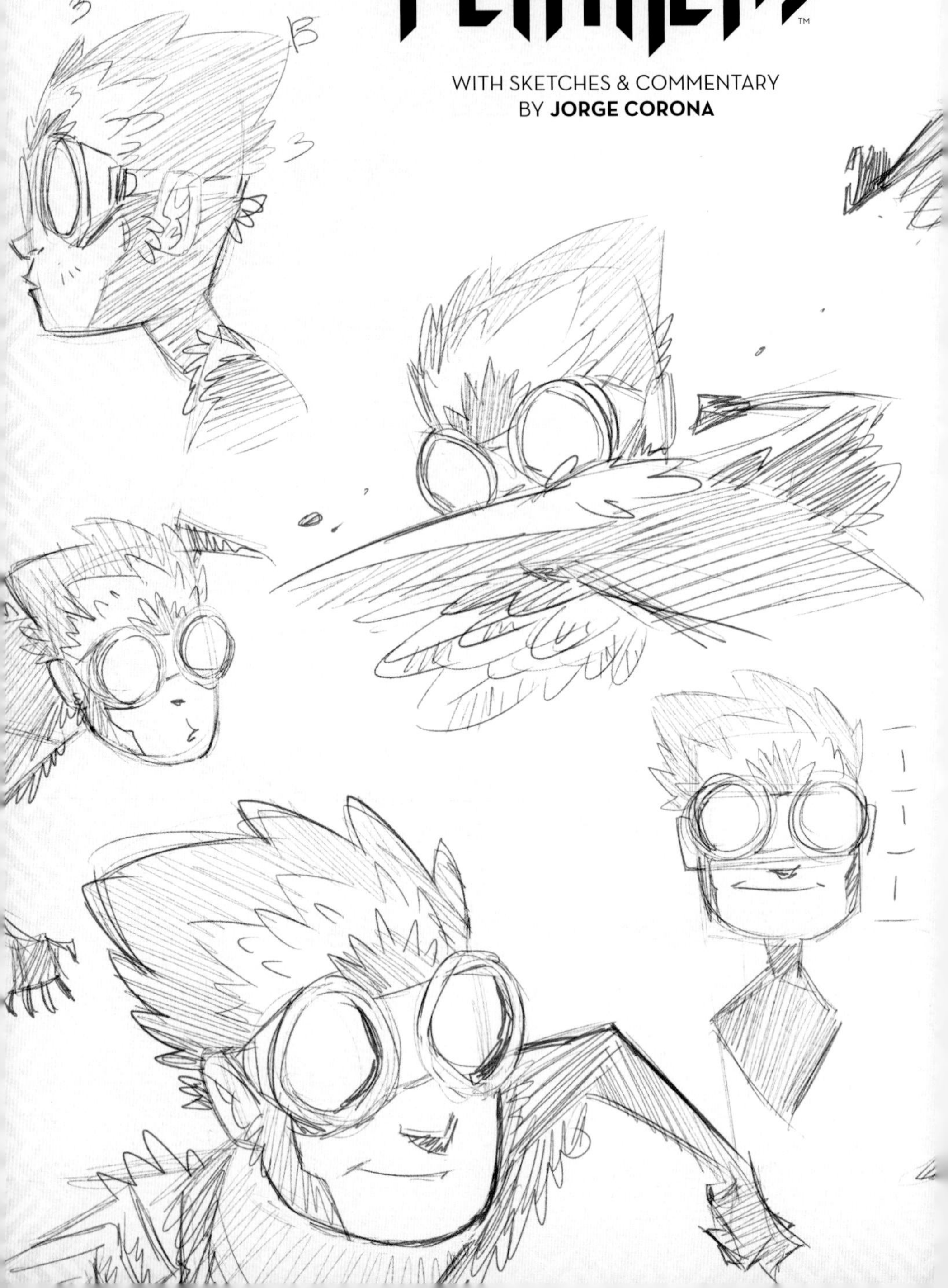

POE

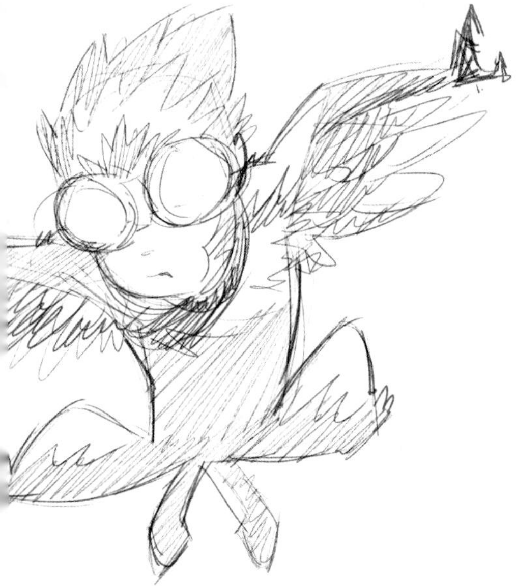

One of the hardest and most important things when first working on the idea for *Feathers* was finding the right voice and design for Poe. It was clear to me since the beginning that I wanted Poe to remain a shadow, a simple silhouette; coming up with it proved harder than expected.

"A boy covered in feathers." That was Poe's description from the get-go, but the first problem I encountered was to determine how different he would actually be from a "regular" boy. Was he a bird? Did he have a beak? Was it just a skin condition? The only thing I knew for sure was that I wanted something to break the silhouette, and that I really didn't like Poe's human face. The goggles were the solution to all that.

There was a lot of exploration into different aesthetics. Some rendered too cartoony, parting from what I wanted the mood of the book to be, other directions were more stylized, going for a more distinctive graphic approach. The thing about feathers (actual feathers, not the title of the book) is that they can be rendered very organically, but also very synthetic and finding that sweet spot in the middle took searching far in both directions.

At the end, it was almost taken down to a formula, one that I could play with so that the silhouette was constant but also allowed some room to bring an organic feel to it.

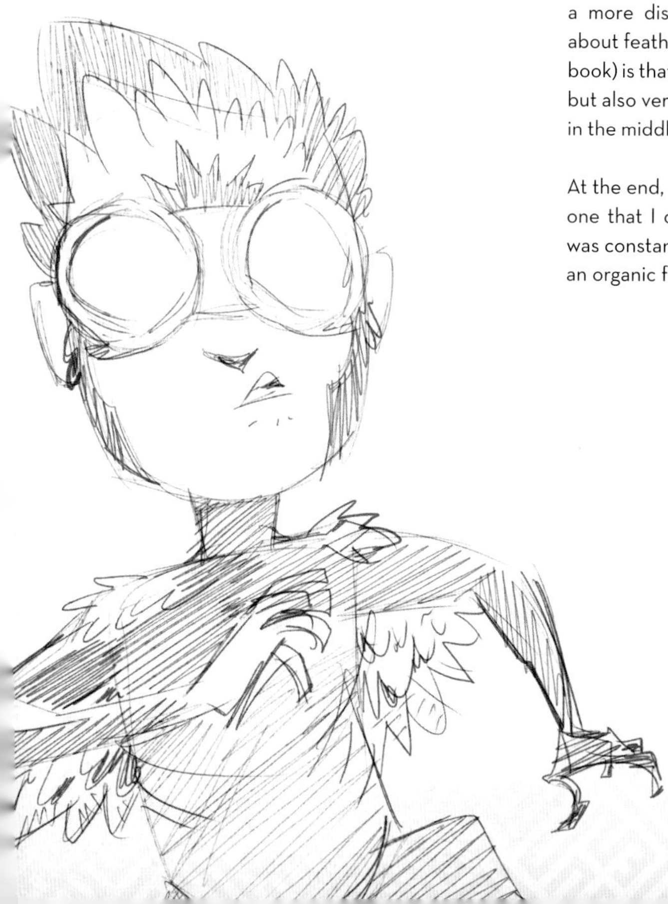

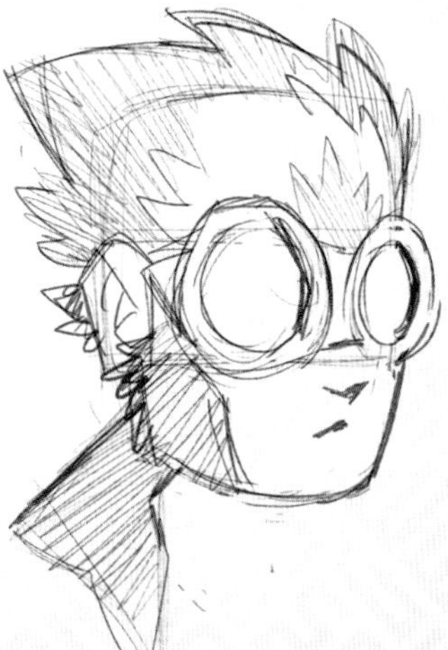

CHARACTER DESIGNS

Bianca's design had a wonderful challenge to it. The nature of the character was that of wealth and comfort on the outside, but a much more adventurous spirit on the inside. Bianca's strong personality had to come through, and that rebel strand of hair constantly getting in her face was the perfect balance to her otherwise princess-like appearance.

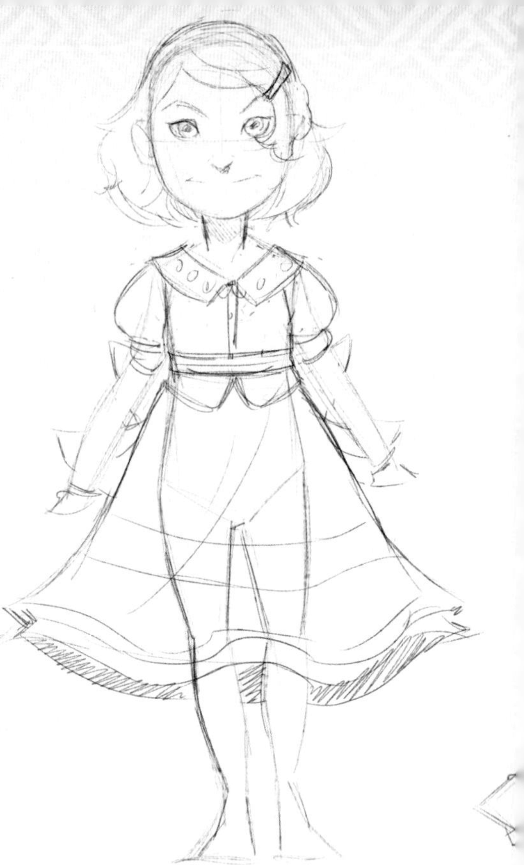

Another side of the character's journey that I wanted to reinforce was that, in contrast with some of the other characters, Bianca never compromises her nature. Her motivations and desires change throughout the story, but I never wanted her to feel like she needed to change in order to grow. When standing next to the rest of the cast, Bianca has her own voice. Next to Poe, she's a softer visual, a contrast to Poe's sharpness; ironically, the contrary is true when it comes to their personalities.

There was one particular character that I wanted Bianca to play against in terms of design. When it came to her family, Bianca was the black sheep in the eyes of her mother; **Eleanor** had to be a colder version of what Bianca could have been. After coming up with Bianca's design, it was just a matter of sharpening edges and we had Eleanor Chappelle.

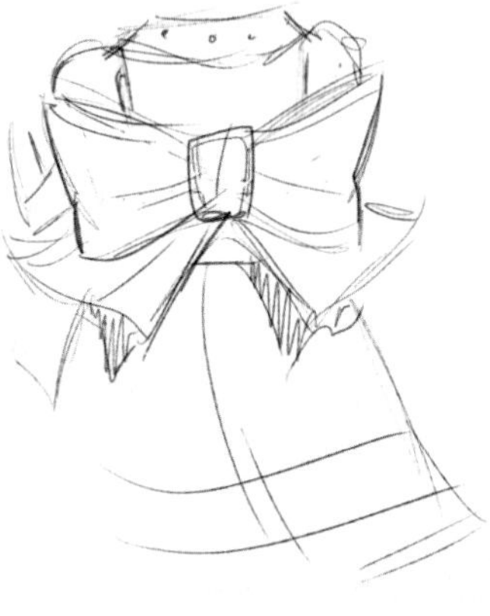

Two sides of the same coin, **Sebastian** and Eleanor are two different products of the City. Both accustomed to their way of life, they each have different views of their coexistence with the world beyond the Wall. Opulent in the way they dress, Sebastian had to project a bit of warmth that was definitely lacking in Eleanor's demeanor.

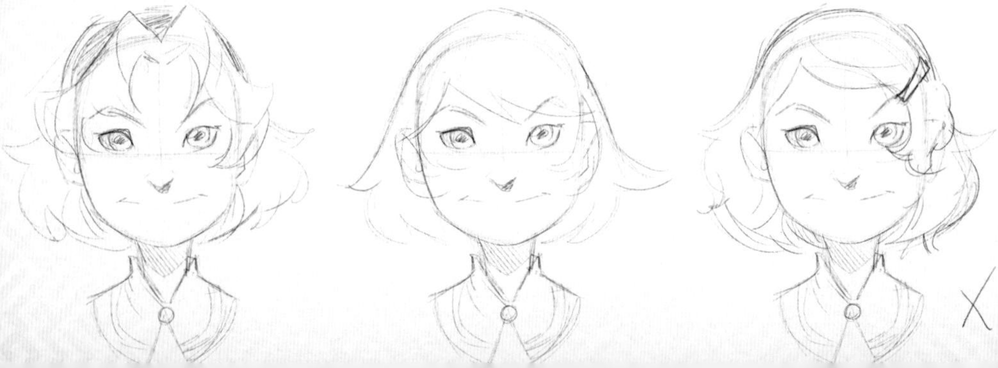

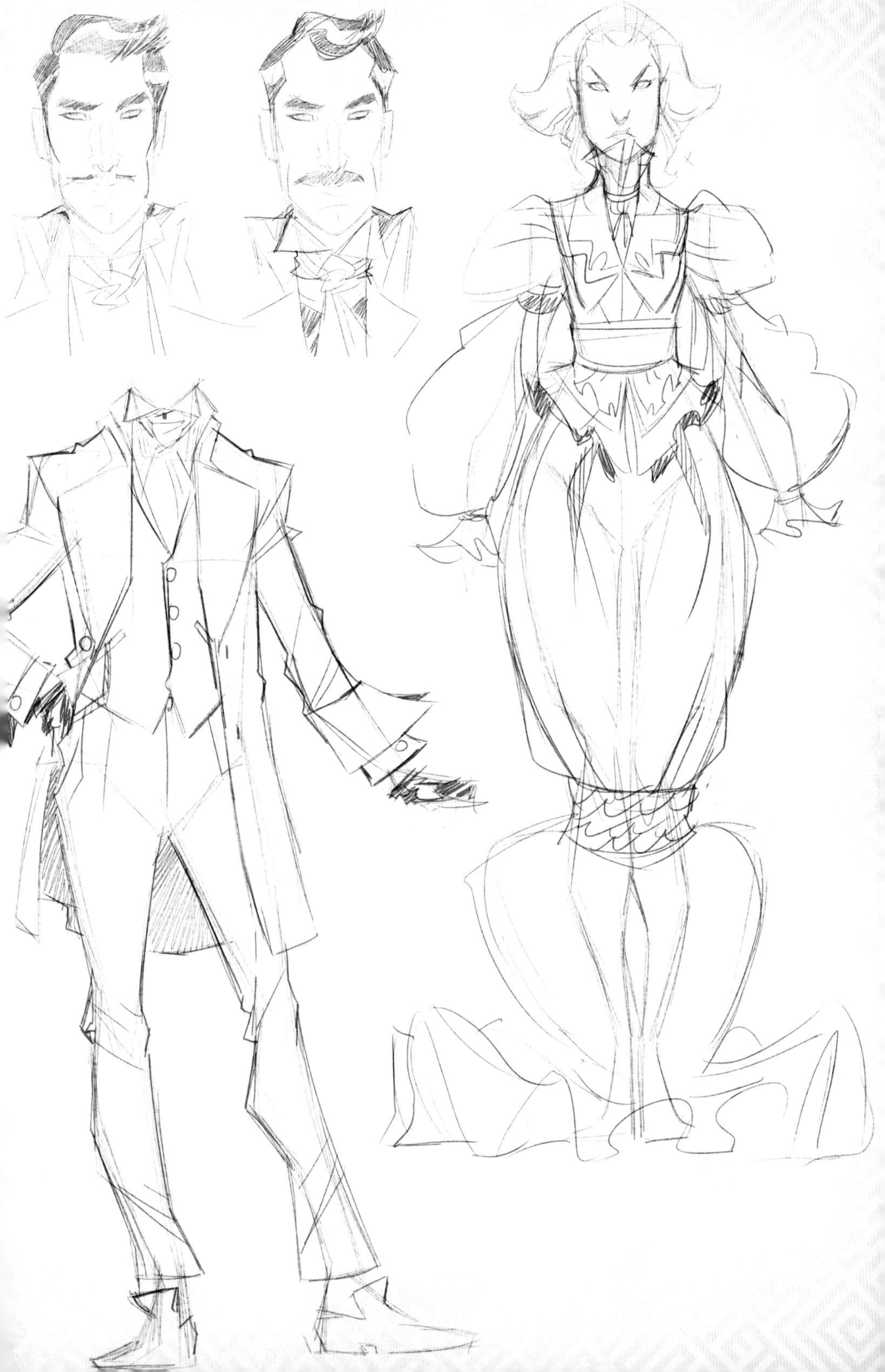

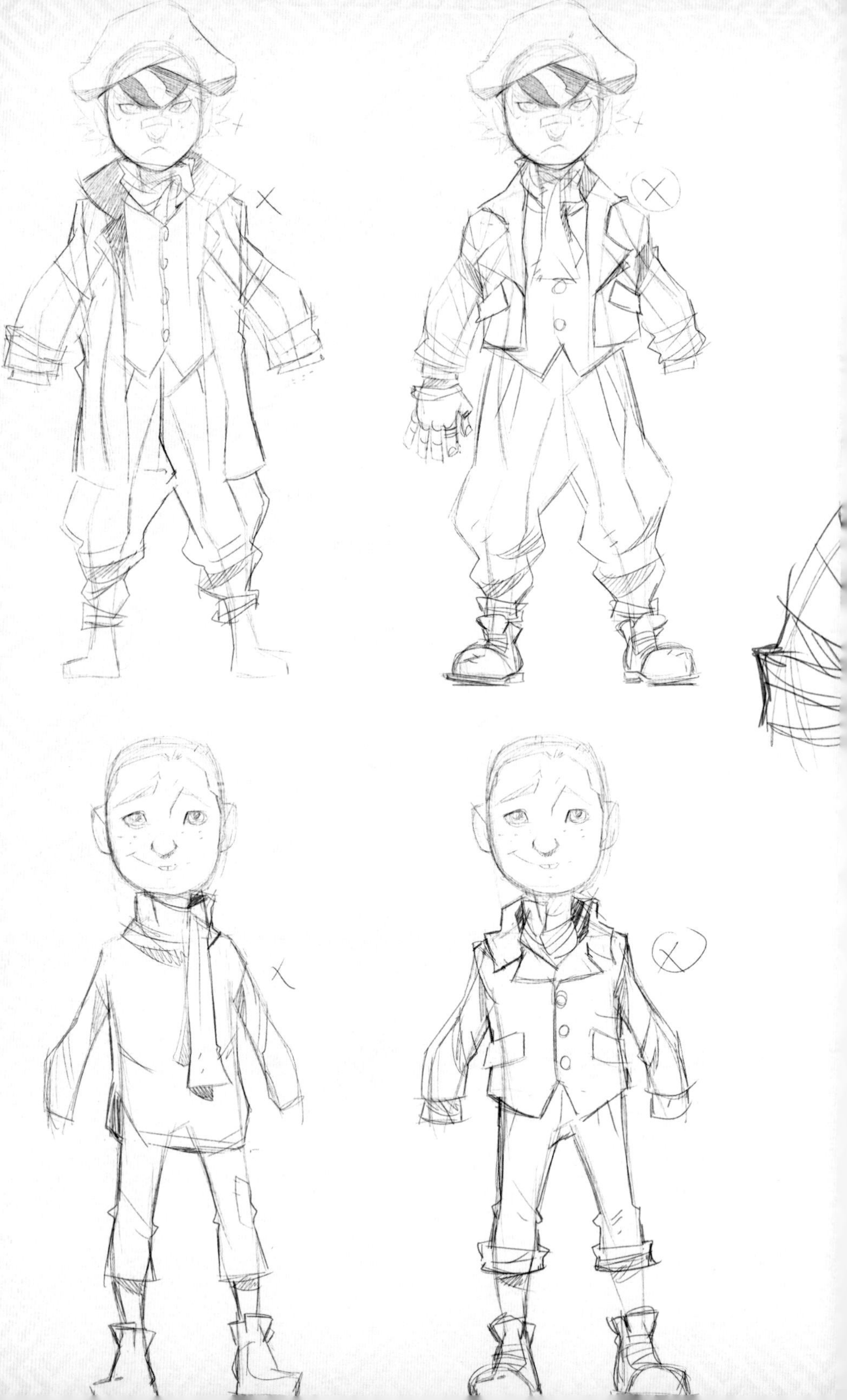

Z and **R** are the most prominent Mice within the story and, just like Eleanor and Sebastian, they are two outcomes of a similar environment. Z's harsh and tough personality had to be contrasted by R's more innocent nature. Z is the general, and the cap serves to embody that idea: everything in her outfit is meant to evoke the idea of militia. R, on the other hand, was straight out a Dickens story, the archetypal street boy. His silhouette, though, had to play against Poe's and Bianca's. As the third party in the main cast, he had to be the midpoint between Bianca's rounded features and Poe's spikier ones.

The **Guard**'s uniform was another one of the main challenges when designing the look of the book. I definitely wanted a bit of a Stormtrooper quality to them, a group mentality, with just enough room for individuality. The other main influence was the traditional tin soldier, and the only problem with that was referencing such a specific "real world" figure. The result was an amalgamation of different military uniforms from different ages. The **Captain** was an extension of that: streamlining the uniform and giving him a bulkier frame gave him enough presence to stand out as a figure of authority no matter the context.

Gabriel was one of the characters that I knew, from the very beginning, how I wanted him to look. A troubled soul with a painful past, Gabriel acts out of love, but sometimes that comes out in the worst possible way. One of the initial traits that I wanted for the character was that, since he's in a never-ending quest to find the perfect prescription for his sight, the frames of his spectacles were supposed to be wildly different from one another. This proved a bit too distracting, so I toned it down in the final pages.

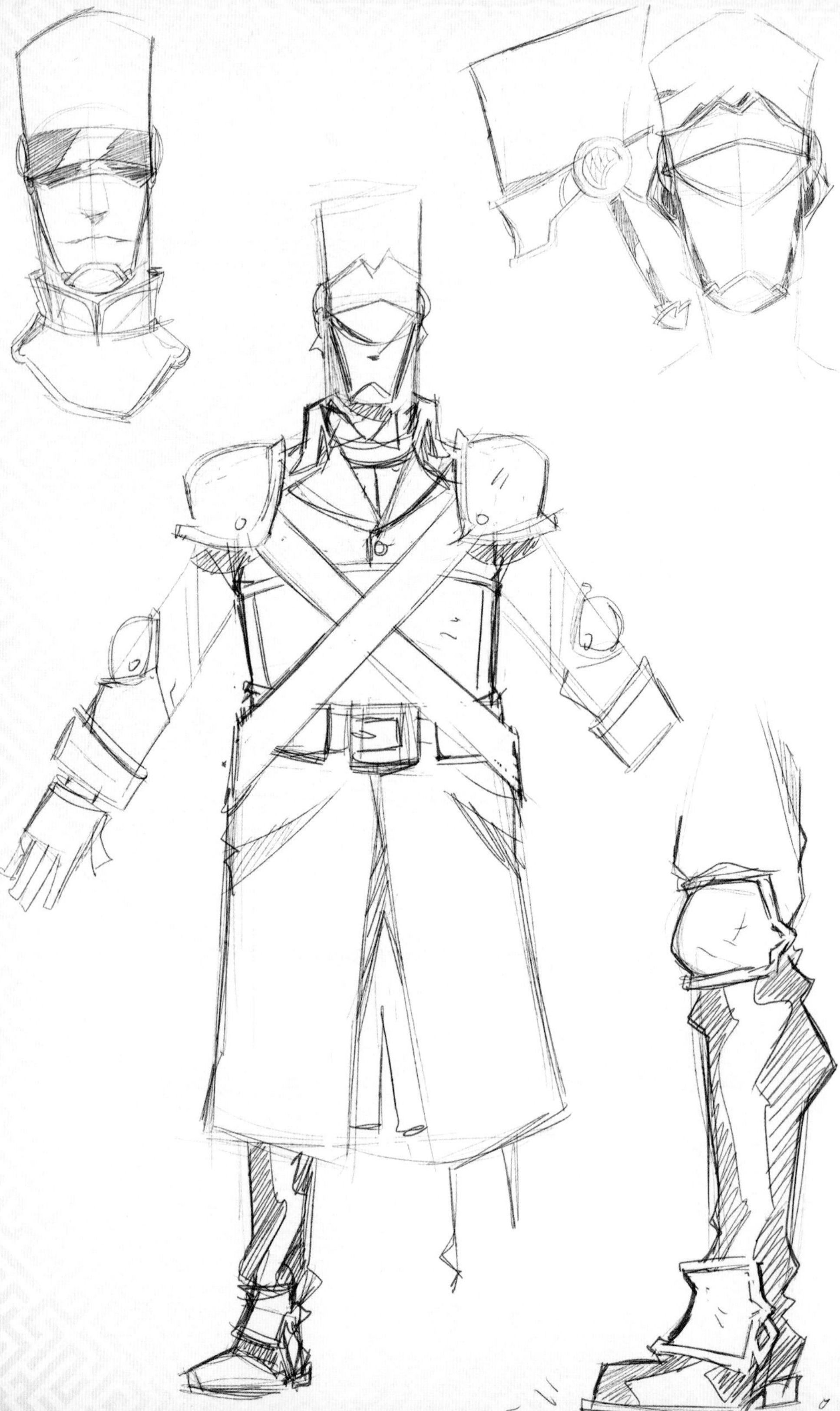

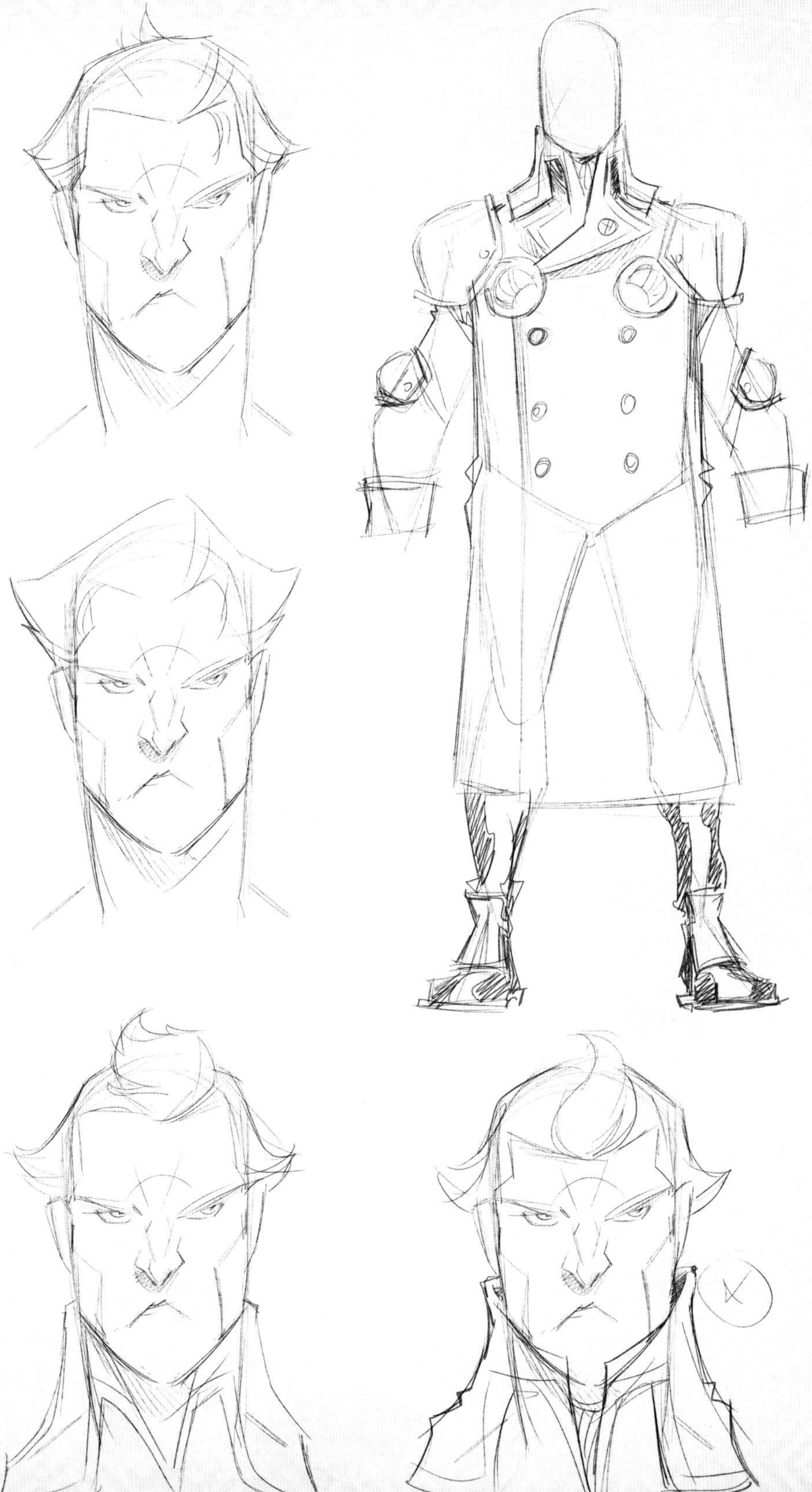

ORIGINAL PITCH

Back in 2013, after many years of only playing with the idea in my head and maybe drawing a handful of sketches, I decided it was time to try and get Poe's story out there. What follows is the original pitch I submitted to Rebecca Taylor and Archaia.

This was the first time I drew the characters in a comic format and, although these pages managed to stay very similar in the final book, the most important change came by the hand of Jen Hickman and the addition of her wonderful color palette, bringing new layers of life to the world of *Feathers*.

During the process of shaping the original idea for Poe and the world of *Feathers* all the way to the final product you now hold in your hands, some of its core elements evolved and changed. The wonderful malleability of a story, one that was now being worked on by a larger crew instead of a single mind, was truly enjoyable to experience. *Feathers* became this deceivingly complex world, and it wouldn't be here if it weren't for the extraordinary group of people I had the pleasure of working with.

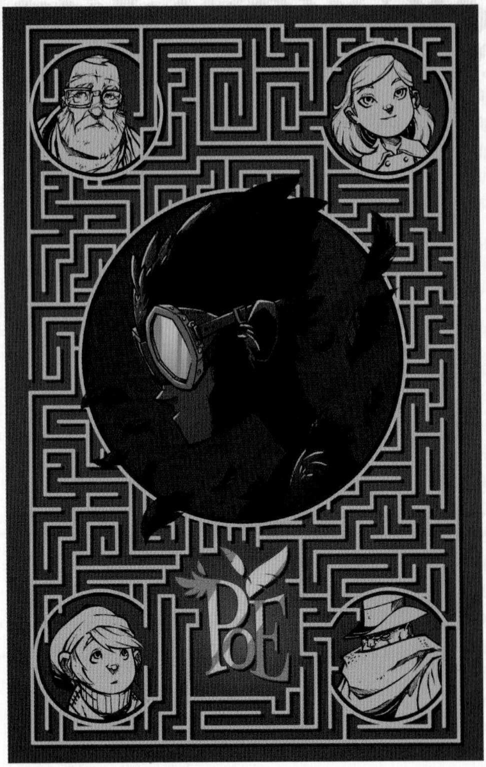
POE

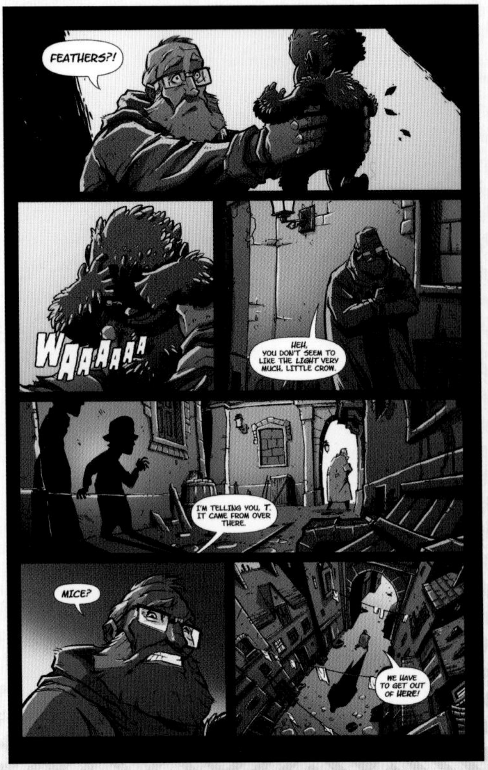
FEATHERS?!
WAAAAAA
HEH, YOU DON'T SEEM TO LIKE THE LIGHT VERY MUCH, LITTLE CROW.
I'M TELLING YOU, T. IT CAME FROM OVER THERE.
MICE?
WE HAVE TO GET OUT OF HERE!

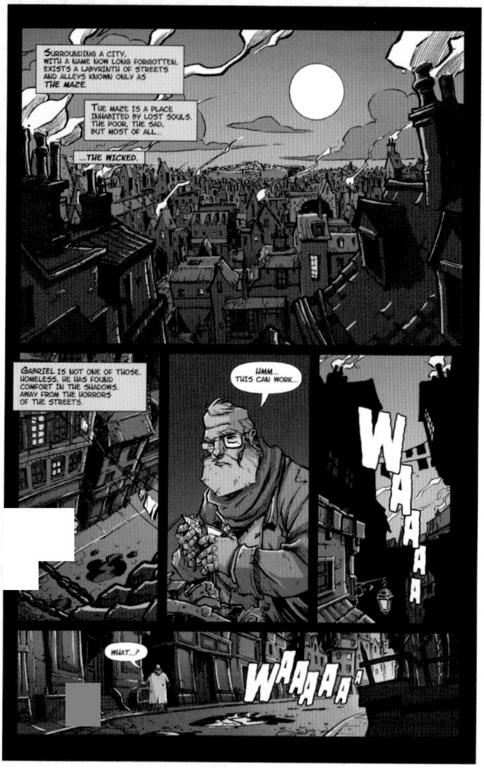
SURROUNDING A CITY, WITH A NAME NOW LONG FORGOTTEN, EXISTS A LABYRINTH OF STREETS AND ALLEYS KNOWN ONLY AS THE MAZE.
THE MAZE IS A PLACE INHABITED BY LOST SOULS. THE POOR, THE SAD, BUT MOST OF ALL...
...THE WICKED.
GABRIEL IS NOT ONE OF THOSE. HOMELESS, HE HAS FOUND COMFORT IN THE SHADOWS. AWAY FROM THE HORRORS OF THE STREETS.
HMM... THIS CAN WORK...
WAAAAA
WHAT...?
WAAAAAA

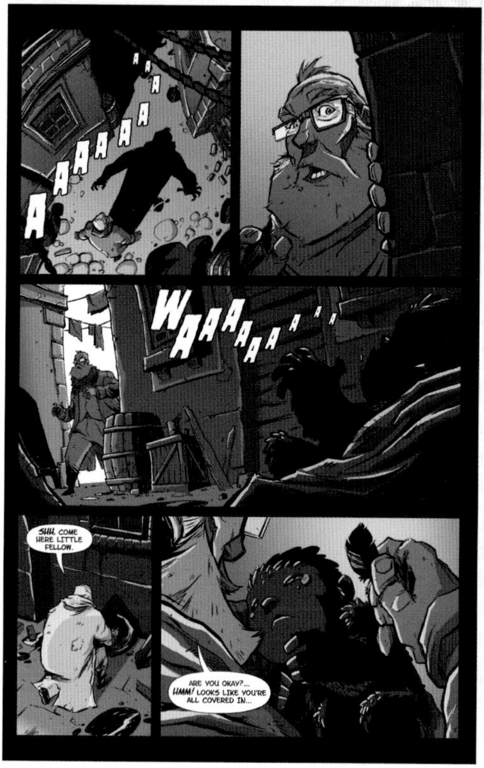
AAAAAAAAAA
WAAAAAAAA
SHH, COME HERE LITTLE FELLOW.
ARE YOU OKAY?... HMM! LOOKS LIKE YOU'RE ALL COVERED IN...

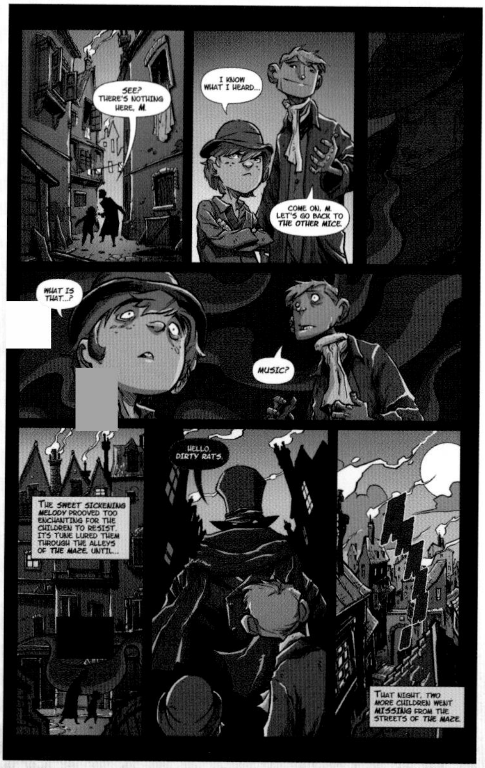
SEE? THERE'S NOTHING HERE, M.
I KNOW WHAT I HEARD...
COME ON, M. LET'S GO BACK TO THE OTHER MICE.
WHAT IS THAT...?
MUSIC?
HELLO, DIRTY RATS.
THE SWEET SICKENING MELODY PROOVED TOO ENCHANTING FOR THE CHILDREN TO RESIST. IT'S TUNE LURED THEM THROUGH THE ALLEYS OF THE MAZE. UNTIL...
THAT NIGHT, TWO MORE CHILDREN WENT MISSING FROM THE STREETS OF THE MAZE.

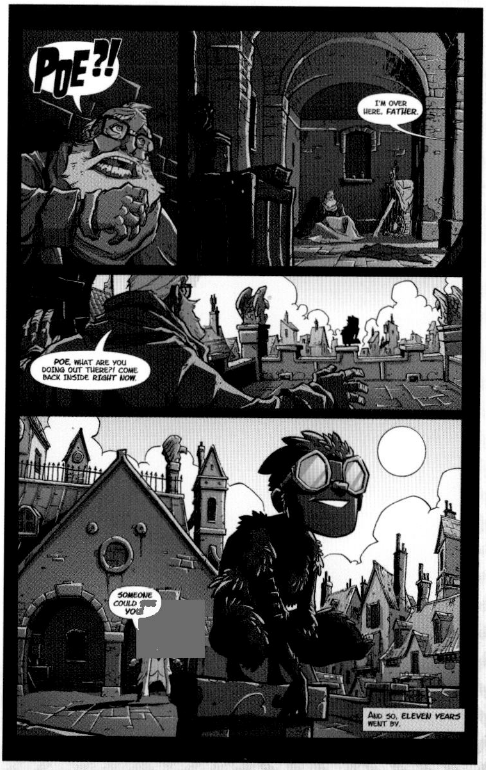
POE?!
I'M OVER HERE, FATHER.
POE, WHAT ARE YOU DOING OUT THERE?! COME BACK INSIDE RIGHT NOW.
SOMEONE COULD
YOU!
AND SO, ELEVEN YEARS WENT BY.

PROCESS GALLERY

From the get-go, I wanted to maintain a very classic structure for layouts within the pages of *Feathers*, but it was when we needed to expand (due to some changes in format) the scene of Poe and Bianca exploring the Maze that Rebecca asked me to break the mold with the panel layout. The result was one of the most iconic sequences in the book.

THUMBNAILS

After having a general plot breakdown, my first step, before even writing the script, is to tell the story visually. This is where the heavy lifting happens.

The thumbnails for this scene were a challenge for two reasons: first, the idea was to break the panel grid and try to convey the mess that the Maze really was while keeping track of readability and storytelling; and second, we had to deal with the fact that this was a scene where the reader (and the characters) are being shown two different realities at the same time.

On one hand, we had Poe leading Bianca across the Maze, showing her various sites that would speak of the nature of this place. Broken-down buildings, impossible structures, and dark corners would shape the Maze to the eyes of Bianca, but at the same time, she was leading Poe through another exploration. A big part of the world-building was done here in the form of Bianca's story about the first settlers and the White Guide. This, of course, was of great interest for Poe and, instead of just talking about it, the characters were sharing the space with actual imagery from the story being told, pulling them in as much as the actual world of the Maze was.

SCRIPT

After having a concrete idea of how the pages were going to look, the next step was to write the dialogue to go along with it. At this step, it is mostly the individual voice of each character that has to come through. The script also includes notations and descriptions of the panels for Jen and Deron to reference after the page is drawn.

PENCILS

Once I have the layout and the script, the pencil stage is where character acting and details in environments come together. For the most part, I use pencils to define composition and shape, making sure that everything has its place. That's the reason why lately I've been doing most of the penciling digitally. It allows me a faster exploration without losing time with too many redraws.

THUMBNAIL LAYOUTS

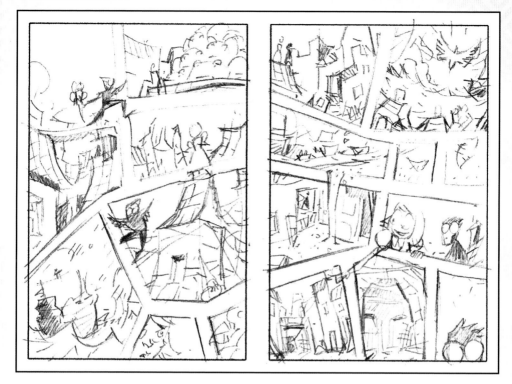

PENCILS

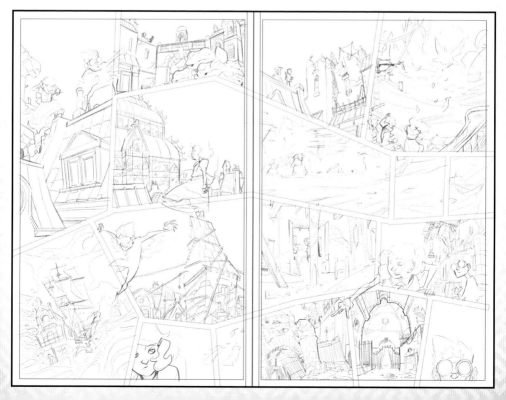

INKS

After having everything down on the page, it is time for inking. While I like to keep the pencils digital, I do prefer to ink traditionally. There is something about the feel of the ink on the paper that I can't seem to find when I ink digitally. It is at this point that I also look for the balance between black and white, making sure that everything is readable but also generating volume and depth where possible. Texture is also a priority when inking.

COLORS AND LETTERS

During the whole process of working on *Feathers*, this had to be my favorite part: waiting to see the pages come to life with Jen's colors and the voices from Deron's letters. And the best part of all? It was always a surprise to me! After spending weeks looking at the pages from thumbs to inks, it was here where I felt like a spectator and witnessed the world I wrote about take shape on its own. It was really a magnificent job these two did, and for which I will always be grateful.

For this specific sequence, the challenge came in keeping everything clear. Jen did a few versions of colors where the segments of backstory were treated differently in order to isolate them from the present time. It was a good trial-and-error approach that ended up defining the style we'd use for all sequences that parted from the "current" events.

Deron was the one who kept everything together, helping the reader to follow the dialogue in the right order. With a sequence where panels break the page in odd ways, and the traditional "left to right" way of reading can be compromised, he did an outstanding job making sure the eye followed each balloon, giving room for the reader to also experience the environments the kids were traveling through.

INKS

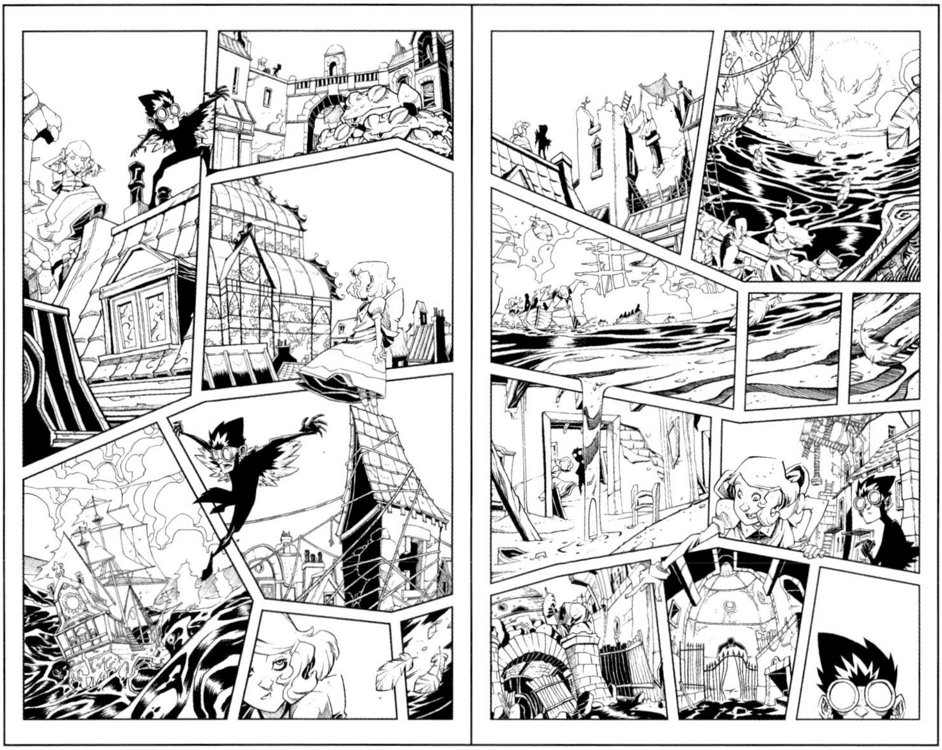

COLORS

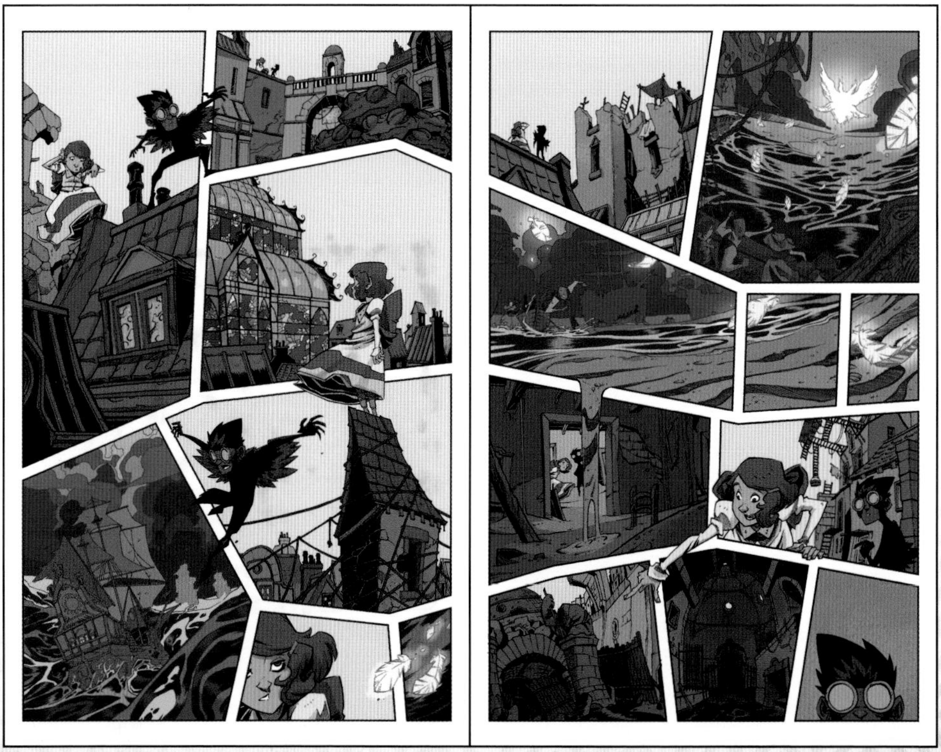

Jorge Corona is a Venezuelan sequential artist, winner of the 2015 Russ Manning Award. Writer and illustrator, his work includes *We are...Robin, Nightwing,* and *The Flash* for DC Comics; *Big Trouble in Little China, Adventure Time, Jim Henson's The Storyteller,* among others for BOOM! Studios; as well as co-creator of *Goners* and *Number One With a Bullet* (nominated for the 2018 Eisner Award for Best Cover Artist) alongside Jacob Semahn for Image Comics, and creator of *Feathers,* his all-ages dark fantasy, for Archaia.

Currently he's working as illustrator and co-creator of Image Comic's *Middlewest* with writer Skottie Young. Jorge now lives in Denver, CO with his wife and fellow artist Morgan Beem.

Jen Hickman is an illustrator and colorist based in California who drinks too much coffee and loves making comics more than most other things. Jen has worked on *Jem and the Holograms: Infinite,* the *Femme Magnifique Anthology, The Amazing World of Gumball Grab Bag,* and more.

Eisner and Harvey Award-nominated letterer, **Deron Bennett** knew early on that he wanted to work in comics. After receiving his B.F.A. from SCAD in 2002, Deron moved out to Los Angeles to pursue his career in sequential art. He quickly became a letterer and production artist with TOKYOPOP, but soon found himself returning to his hometown in New Jersey to raise a family. There, Deron founded his own lettering studio, AndWorld Design, and has been providing design and lettering services for a multitude comic book publishers ever since. His body of work includes the critically acclaimed *Jane, Hacktivist,* and *Jim Henson's Tale of Sand.* He has also written his own fantasy adventure in the form of *Quixote.* Check out his work at andworlddesign.com or on Twitter @andworlddesign.